GRAVITY TOWER

A GRAVITY SHATTERED NOVEL

V. R. FRIESEN

DIMMARE
—PRESS—

Published by Dimmare Press, 2021

Cover design by Bukovero

Editing by Caroline Kaiser

ISBN: 978-1-7774062-5-7 (e-book)

ISBN: 978-1-7774062-6-4 (paperback)

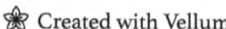 Created with Vellum

ALSO BY V.R. FRIESEN:

For Jen and Santiago

UNDER THE PINE TREE

Things gravity is good for:
Falling
Not falling

~ Veronica Park (*Lists of the Apocalypse*)

B lood soaked the carpet of the decrepit house they'd been camping in. Ashes from the fire were scattered everywhere. Sleeping bags were tossed and torn. Chairs had tumbled and lay broken as if they'd been thrown at assailants.

Jasper Pine stood in the empty room, staring down at her brother's crumpled sleeping bag, her heart heavy as lead.

Everyone was gone. Her brother, Ben. The boys, Charlie and Merlot, and their old grav-walking master, Quick Rick. Esther Kornelsen and Crane. And the two pack kids, Grammar and Neverwhen. The Damaskers had ambushed them in the early hours of the morning.

If Jasper had been here with them, she could've helped them

fight. Maybe she'd have been captured too, but at least she'd be with them now, plotting escape. But instead she'd spent the night elsewhere, with Ryan Latrans, and they'd been left behind.

The blood pool on the carpet seemed to grow larger and larger. Who among her friends had lost that much blood? Was it one of the children? Was it Ben?

Jasper felt dizzy and icy cold. This wasn't how the day was supposed to go. It had started bittersweet with the promise of goodbyes, but also with sunlight through pine needles and the sound of Ryan's voice.

That morning she'd woken to the heat of the sun on her face and something rough under her cheek. She'd fallen asleep on Ryan's shoulder, her cheek pressed against his locs. Her neck was stiff and sore.

Wincing, Jasper lifted her head and straightened herself so she was no longer pressed against Ryan's arm and took a breath of pine-sweet, rain-scoured air. Light filtered through the needles in delicate shafts.

She'd slept without dreaming. Her head felt like glass, dusty and covered in fingerprints but clear enough to let in the light.

"What's your favourite dinosaur?" Ryan asked. His head was tilted against the trunk as he looked up through the branches of their pine cathedral. The sky was golden glass, clouds melting away as if they'd never existed.

"You woke up with dinosaurs on your mind?" She tried to say it without any particular emphasis, but he caught her dry tone anyway and turned to look at her. A smile curled the corners of his mouth as if he couldn't help it. She probably had the imprint of his locs pressed into her cheek. She rubbed her hands hard through her short dark hair in case it had dried in particularly ridiculous spikes and tufts.

Last night, when the lingering edges of the rainclouds had dumped a final shower on their heads, they'd run for shelter, but she'd chosen an ancient pine rather than a building. Its massive drooping branches kept the soft, needle-strewn ground beneath it dry. Ryan fell asleep almost at once, and she let him slide down till his head was in her lap. He must have hardly slept at all the last two nights, wrecked by his guilt, his lost sobriety, Ben's hostility, and dread of his upcoming confrontation with his foster brother, Titus. She smoothed his hair away from his face. He didn't wake, his lashes curled shut, his mouth falling open in his exhaustion.

"Grammar and Nev told me all about their favourite dinosaurs the other day," he said. "Apparently, everyone's supposed to have a favourite. What if my kid asks me one day? I'll have no idea what to say."

So he'd woken up not with dinosaurs on his mind, but his unborn son, being held hostage outside the zones by Titus. Ryan had woken up thinking about what would happen if he didn't complete his mission and bring Jasper and her resident graviteria, the alien bacteria-like micro-organisms that infected her, to his brother. Thinking about what he could lose.

"So what's your favourite?" he asked again.

"That's easy. Velociraptor."

"Smart, fast, a pack animal. Figures. That was Grammar's pick too."

Through the maze of branches the Tower was visible, a giant's exclamation point on the horizon. A glittering haze surrounded it, clouds of glass and metal and plastic suspended in mid-air, held in place by a honeycomb of gravity zones.

Her final destination. Where she would either take Dr. Zenobia Allan's antibac, risking physical and cognitive impairment and death to prevent the Shattering that would otherwise destroy half the country. Or, according to the Guardian's suggestion, attempt to meld with the alien graviteria in her system, hoping that as the micro-organisms achieved their final stage of sentience, their consciousnesses would merge with hers and she'd stop the Shattering.

"What are you going to choose?" she asked.

"I think I have to go with the crocodile," he said. "It survived whatever killed the rest of the dinosaurs. I'm a fan of creatures who survive disasters that should by all rights kill them." He looked at her with eyes as clear as river pools. She half expected a tiny green jewel of a frog to swim out from under his eyelashes and hop onto the sun-baked warmth of his skin.

"Are you calling me a crocodile?" she asked.

His laugh was a spicy-sweet shot of cinnamon to the heart.

Why was she doing this to herself?

The rain had stopped. He would leave today for Yorky and quarantine. He'd pass through the gates and return to where he'd come from—downieland, that mysterious place where gravity pulled exclusively downward, and where his foster brother waited for him. How would he stop Titus from sending in another team to retrieve Jasper, and Grammar too, who was also infected, if they could? How would Titus punish him for his failure? If Titus was anything like Darius Dalca—and they sounded similar enough to make her stomach churn—he wouldn't hesitate to hurt Ryan's pregnant ex-girlfriend, Allison.

Disobedience and rebellion had consequences. Darius had taught zoners that lesson over and over again during his cruel regime.

The only way Ryan and his unborn child would avoid Titus's punishment was if Ryan brought Jasper with him out of quarantine and delivered her and her graviteria to Titus.

"Ryan," she began. "About your brother—"

"I'll be fine," he said, cutting her off as if he'd known exactly what she was thinking.

"But—"

"It's my battle. You already faced your monster when you

were a kid. I'm a big boy. I can handle my brother." He tried to smile. "I've got a whole lot of reasons not to fail."

But he was afraid. Despite his calm voice and steady gaze, he was rubbing at the row of blue dots tattooed in a line along his inner forearm, each symbolic of a lost life he blamed himself for.

Would it have been easier for her to face Darius as an adult, or harder? An unanswerable question.

"I want to show you something," she said.

Instead of returning to the house where Ben and the others were probably just waking up, she brought him to the edge of the down-gee zone, where her mother, Catherine Pine, quietly decayed inside a rusting car and Vron's poetry sanctified a stone wall. Jasper climbed to the roof of the car and sat cross-legged while Ryan read Vron's poem to himself.

Really, I am the sky.

"I wish I could've met her," he said.

"She would've liked you," she said. The words hit her late, moments after she'd said them. Vron would've looked at Ryan with her night witch mouth, and he'd have looked back with his summer river eyes. She'd have cocked her head at him like a crow, and he'd have smiled, slow as sunlight. She'd have called him Coyote, and he'd have pulled coins from her mouth every time she started rhyming.

Jasper's throat closed, and she pressed her knuckles to her mouth to hide it.

Ryan returned to the car and looked at Catherine Pine's bones in the driver's seat, the pile of wilted flowers in her lap. "Hi, Mrs. Pine," he said. "Hell of a daughter you've got, ma'am. If you were here, she'd give you a heart attack at least twice a day."

"Hey now," said Jasper.

He pointed a finger at her. "You were hanging off a telephone pole just last night and you were captured by cannibals the day before that."

"That's fair, I guess."

"You've faced down Dragon twice while he held a gun to Grammar's head. Not to mention waded into an underground fight club in a hostile town to drag out that same kid. And you got up on a stage after Nico Mavuto's coup, in full view of his crazy-eyed army of Damaskers, and told the Yorky gangers to lay down their weapons."

"Okay, you've made your point, Ryan."

"She jumps off of buildings for fun, Mrs. Pine," Ryan said. *"For fun."*

"Stop telling my mother about every dumb thing I've done! What's wrong with you?"

"Actually, I was telling her about how incredibly brave you are, but if you think the dumbness shoe fits, I won't argue. Now, if you don't mind, I'm having a conversation." He turned back to Catherine's flower-laden body. "You don't have to worry about her, though, Mrs. Pine. A lot of people love her and watch out for her. She'll be okay." He glanced up at Jasper. "I promise."

Promises were wishes said in an emphatic voice. The smell of cinnamon without the tea.

Jasper looked down so he wouldn't see the surge of anger and despair inside her. It wasn't a promise he could make, no matter how nice it sounded.

Words had been laboriously scratched into the roof of the car. She traced her finger over them. "'Wish a fish,'" she said aloud.

"What's that?"

She stared at the tiny words. Then she gestured for him to come over and read them.

Wish a fish into the sky

Wish a fish, it won't die
But you'll never see it crawl
Up what you might call
The beanstalk
It can only fall
From the doorway in the wall
Which door?
Yes.

It was Vron's handwriting—as if the nonsensical whimsy alone hadn't been enough to identify the author.

"What does it mean?" Ryan asked.

"Grammar said Vron took whatever papers or photos my mom had with her. He said that Vron was upset by something. I suppose it's possible she took those papers home to Yorky and then they were lost when Merlot burned all her notebooks. But she gave that one notebook to Grace, and it seems to hold some clues. So I think Vron hid the papers somewhere else. She didn't want me to see what was in them, but she also knew they could be important one day. So I wonder . . . I wonder if this poem is meant as a clue."

A poem only visible to someone who'd climbed onto the car roof. Vron knew Jasper's habits; if it was a clue, it was meant for Jasper.

Ryan studied the poem a moment longer, then shook his head. "Makes no sense to me."

"She used to say demons followed the straightest paths and hid in the stillest pools. So she made every path crooked and windy and turned pools into rivers and streams. Everything more complicated, more verbose and off-kilter, more hidden than it needed to be."

Restless, Jasper slid off the roof and paced over to the shrine. What was it that Vron hadn't wanted her to see? What kind of truth had conflicted her so much that she was driven to hide something she knew would have to be found one day?

Jasper dug a hand into her pocket and pulled out the tiny Zombie Princess figurine she'd found in Catherine Pine's purse. She rolled it around in her hand. As she did, something caught her eye. She bent to examine a set of tracks across an open patch of muddy ground. Since it had been raining until late last evening, these tracks had to have been left during the night.

She swore aloud, incredulous and alarmed.

Ryan crouched to look. "What kind of animal made those? A wolf or something?"

She grinned despite herself. "You're a city boy, aren't you? I wish it *was* a wolf." She glanced around uneasily at the underbrush, the overgrown cars, the dark, empty windows of hollow buildings. "No. Remember that half-eaten deer Charlie was telling us about yesterday? This is a cougar."

It was Ryan's turn to utter a stream of profanity. "And there we were, sleeping under a tree like gift-wrapped toys on Christmas morning. Jesus."

Jasper shuddered. "We got lucky."

Two sharp bangs cracked the air in the distance.

Ryan's head jerked around and he crouched behind the car, dragging her with him.

"Were those gunshots?" she asked in dread.

"Yeah," he said. "Not far."

Their eyes met as they shared the same thought. They'd waited too long to leave this zone; the Damaskers had finally caught up with them.

"The campsite," Jasper said, heart freezing. "Oh God, they'll take Grammar."

They ran.

They raced through the overgrown streets, the tall wet grass soaking their legs. They threaded their way through streets still clogged with traffic, rusted, mossy cars sitting bumper to bumper in a testament to the futility of escape from the Shattering of fifteen years ago. Their feet crunched over broken glass from shops looted long ago. A flock of starlings burst into the air as they bolted through an empty parking lot.

They ran past the burnt-out hulk of a house that had contained two elderly cannibals, the Gingers, along with the cages where they'd trapped their victims.

They arrived out of breath at the house where they'd set up camp. It was silent and abandoned, but Ryan made Jasper wait outside while he checked it room by room. She could only dance in place for a few seconds before she jerked open the door and went inside.

Everything was in disarray. Everyone was gone.

The large pool of blood soaked into the carpet nearly stopped Jasper's heart.

She didn't know how long she stood there, imagining Ben bleeding out. She hardly noticed Ryan entering the room until he squeezed her arm and held up a tiny blood-smeared blade.

"Whose do you think this is?"

"Crane." A sliver of hope and relief helped her breathe again. "She must have injured one of them."

"Damn near killed him, more like, by the amount of blood. No body, though. If they have an injured man, it'll slow them down."

Grammar and Neverwhen's dog, Okuru, emerged from the undergrowth as they were casting about for tracks around the house. He slunk toward them, his tail low, misery and distress in every line of his body.

"It's not your fault, buddy," Ryan told him, rubbing his head. "There were too many of them."

"It's my fault," Jasper said numbly. "We should've gone back to the house last night after you got me off the telephone pole."

Ryan shook his head. "I'm the one who let you sleep in this morning because you looked so . . ." He took a breath and hardened his face. "Come on. We've got work to do."

With Okuru's help, they followed the trail until they came to a fork in the tracks where the group had split up and gone two separate ways.

"Which way?" Ryan asked her.

Jasper looked down at the tracks.

An impossible choice. But then, she was used to those.

2

CAT'S OUT OF THE BAG

The smell of pine needles at Christmas
The tickle of an ant crossing the epic expanse of your skin as
*   you lie in the grass*

~ Veronica Park (*Things I Will Miss/Reasons to Live*)

D ragon and his Damaskers had Grammar with them and
no one else.

Grammar's hands were zip tied behind him, and one eye was
once again swollen shut. Jasper could hardly remember what his
face looked like without bruises and swelling.

Jasper raised her hands when they saw her and pointed all
their guns at her. "It's just me," she said. "I mean, it's not *just*
me." She gestured vaguely at the buildings behind her. "But it's
just me, Jasper."

They realized her meaning and hurriedly turned their guns
to scan the multitude of windows, broken or without glass, from
any of which a sniper might lurk.

Dragon kept his gun trained on her. "At the most your dreadhead friend will be getten one shot off, maybe two, before we're scatteren and pinnen him down with our fire. In the meantime, we'll be killen you and still be haven the little ratling."

"His very first shot will take you out, Dragon," Jasper said. "So remember that. Anyway, I'm not here for the kid."

"Oh really?"

"I want to know where my brother and all the others are if they're not with you."

He grinned humourlessly. "Not needen them. So we been sellen them to Knowles."

"You did what?"

"We been maken a deal with Knowles to be helpen us catch this ratling. And in exchange they're keepen everyone else. They're always needen more workers. And fresh girls, if you know what I'm meanen."

"May worms eat your eyes and gravity grind your bones," Jasper said. "Thanks for the information. One question, though. Why would you sell Crane to Knowles? Nico still wants his daughter back, I presume."

Dragon grinned nastily, the triple scars on his cheeks flexing. "She been killen one of the Knowles gangers. They're wanten to punish her. Wishen I could be helpen teach her a lesson." He shrugged. "But the ganglord won't be wanten to piss off Nico too much, so he'll be keepen her alive enough. One day I'll be getten my turn with her."

"Cool, thanks. May dogs feed on your befouled limbs while you're still alive." She stepped back and gestured for them to carry on their way.

Dragon's men were still scanning for Ryan's hiding place. Dragon lingered, glaring at her. "I'll be burnen you yet, witch."

"But not today."

"Don't be thinken you can be rescuen the boy, just you and the dreadhead. You'll never be getten him."

"I told you, that's not why I'm here. I got what I needed from him." She looked at Grammar. "Sorry, kid."

Grammar hadn't moved or made a sound since she'd appeared. His bruises masked his expression, but his brows curled inward. He met her eyes briefly, then looked away. He seemed to understand that she had no reason to attempt a risky rescue for his sake alone.

"Nev," he muttered through swollen lips.

"If she's with the others, we'll do our best for her."

To that he gave a jerky nod.

"See, ratling?" Dragon said, jeering. "Nobody's caren about you. Too much devil in you, even for the Pinegirl."

Grammar remained silent, eyes on the ground.

Dragon gestured to his team and they moved off swiftly, still watching the silent buildings for any sign of a sniper.

Ryan stepped out of the underbrush once the Damaskers were out of sight. He holstered his gun. In his other hand he held a makeshift leash looped around Okuru's neck. The dog whined and lifted his nose in the direction Grammar had gone. Jasper wondered how Ryan had kept him quiet.

"At least we know they're alive and their location," Ryan said.

She clenched her hands to stop their shaking. "I haven't been to Knowles in over five years, but Quick Rick says they're well fortified and they've got a strong army. They try to impregnate all their women and girls, both to provide cheap labour and because mothers are less likely to try to escape. The boys will have to work in the fields, but Crane and Esther will be locked in with all the women. And Nev—oh God, I hope she's too young for them, but she might not be. You hear stories."

Quick Rick and Merlot, Vron's brother, visited Knowles a few times a year as peddlers. Surely as soon as they were recognized, the whole party would be freed. But Knowles had a reputation for absorbing unwilling recruits, not just children but adults. If Knowles hadn't heard by now about the events of Zones Day, they'd hear it from the Damaskers or from Quick Rick. The balance of power had shifted, and Yorky, with all its resources, and the Azuros gang's trading post were in the hands of Nico Mavuto and the Damaskers. Nico was the man to please now, and he wouldn't care if a few troublesome Yorky citizens quietly disappeared into the bowels of Knowles's labour mills. Especially if he got his daughter, Crane, back in the bargain.

"Take a breath." Ryan squeezed her shoulder. "Quick Rick and Merlot are probably sorting it out right now. And if not, we'll get them out. One thing at a time."

He was right. Ben and the others depended on her and Ryan now. She couldn't fall apart.

"Did you get the—? Ugh, I can smell it."

Ryan had tied a rope around the Gingers' dead dog and dragged it along behind him. The moisture and the fact that it had been dead for two days hadn't improved either the look or smell of the carcass, but at least it still held together. If the cougar still lingered in the area, it couldn't fail to smell their offering. That was the plan anyway.

Jasper used the smell as an excuse to walk well ahead of Ryan and his grisly cargo. This meant she was in charge of Okuru, which was only marginally preferable to dragging a rotting corpse. But while he strained at the leash, he didn't fight her control. At first he'd been distracted by the smell of the dead dog behind them, but now he was intent on following the trail of Grammar and the Damaskers and seemed to consider Jasper an annoying but unavoidable weight he had to drag along with him.

They weren't trying to catch up with the Damaskers, not yet anyway, so they took their time. Okuru would keep them on the trail. They reached the end of down-gee, but the initial gravving was easy, even with a live and a dead dog. The border ended right beside a long strip mall, and the side-gee draw was such that they could hop from down-gee onto the wall of the building and continue on for the length of a city block.

"Is there any point in still dragging this thing?" Ryan asked when they stopped to catch their breaths. The sun was raising steam from the wet grass and trees, and he was sweating from the effort of pulling the dead dog.

"Cougars have been known to cross zones," Jasper said. "Everything we've climbed today a cougar could climb."

"Fantastic," Ryan said. "Just what I wanted to hear." He swiped his arm across his forehead and surveyed their surroundings carefully.

She couldn't blame him. Possessed by a vision of the big cat's cold yellow eyes watching her from some barely hidden hiding spot, she'd been listening to every snapped twig and rustle of grass, every outburst of bird chatter. Quick Rick had regaled her with stories of the urban wildlife that had existed even before the Shattering. Cougars, bears, and coyotes had long been fixtures in urban areas. Unlike coyotes and bears, however, post-Shattering cougars had few inhibitions about adding humans to their diet when their traditional prey was scarce.

Fifi Ginger, one-half of the cannibal couple who had captured Jasper and Merlot, had mentioned a cougar in the area, and they'd also found a half-eaten deer carcass the previous day, so Jasper hoped they weren't dragging a dead dog around for nothing. Surely the cougar would be hungry enough to investigate the smell of carrion. The back of her neck prickled. The cougar might be following them right now. They could only hope it would wait to attack until they'd led it straight to the Damaskers.

She couldn't believe Ryan had agreed to her plan. Ben would've vetoed it in half a second flat and then spent the next hour listing under his breath every fall, fight, or falling object that had ever resulted in a bump or injury to her head, knocking loose—according to him—a little sense each time.

Okuru became her source of reassurance, both for his unerring attention to the trail they were following and because his body language would inform them far more reliably than their own senses if they were being stalked by a large deadly cat.

As she'd hoped, the Damaskers had set up camp for the night in a pocket down-gee zone. The serious gravving would begin tomorrow for them. Jasper and Ryan waited in the gathering darkness while a fire flared up. Ryan rubbed Okuru's head and kept up a barely audible murmur, telling the dog how important it was to stay quiet and what a very good boy he was, the very best of all good boys, in fact. Okuru occasionally licked Ryan's face and stayed quiet.

If Ryan's voice was magic, it didn't work only on animals; Jasper felt her breath coming more easily listening to him.

Damasker voices, triumphant and jovial, carried to their ears. With her hand around her amulets, Jasper prayed to the small god and her mother that the gangers were satisfied with their victory and would refrain from tormenting Grammar. His small thin shape was easy to distinguish from those of the larger adults. He sat against a wall, just within the ring of firelight, huddled in silence, drawing no attention to himself, not even to ask for food.

Eventually, the noise died away as men rolled into their blankets, leaving one man on watch.

Ryan crouched beside Okuru with one hand on the dog's neck. The dog quivered with impatience, but he hadn't barked or bolted to rejoin Grammar, who he could undoubtedly smell clearly.

They'd left the dog carcass on the other side of the campsite, as far from them as possible. Weariness dragged at Jasper. It had been a long day of gravving and worry and strain, and it wasn't as if she'd gotten much sleep the night before, but the thought of what might be stalking them in the darkness kept her painfully awake.

The fire burned to embers. The sentry was only visible when he moved, standing and stretching and shifting around to keep himself awake.

Ryan's lips brushed her ear. This sent a jolt through her heart. He whispered, "I'm going to see if I can get close to where Grammar is. Don't move."

He pressed the end of the leash into her hands and was gone before she could protest. How could he move with so little sound in the darkness when he was a downie and not native to these zones?

An eternity seemed to go by. The breeze stilled and then lifted again, stirring her hair. The dog shifted his weight. He made a small sound, a huff of breath with a barely audible whine.

The grass rustled behind her. Just the wind.

The dog pressed against her, so sudden she jerked away, but he huddled against her again. Now his whimper was louder. She jerked around to study the shadows.

Twin yellow sparks flared to life. Malevolent, levitating jewels that shifted and moved.

She screamed, but nothing left her mouth but a puff of air. She was paralyzed, her muscles useless jelly. It was the kind of nightmare where, in the face of deadly danger, she couldn't move or speak.

Okuru flattened himself to the ground, as afraid as she was.

The eyes lifted and dipped as the creature they belonged to gathered itself to pounce. Only metres away, it could kill them in seconds.

Footsteps clumped toward her, shockingly loud in the frozen stillness. Not Ryan—he'd already proven his stealth.

Jasper didn't move. She couldn't.

The cat's eyes shifted, attracted by movement. A yawn and a sigh, a zipper, the splash of liquid on the ground. The cougar's eyes lowered, nearly to the ground. Jasper was irresistibly reminded of Zenobia's cat crouching to pounce on a trailing piece of string. Her hand was buried in Okuru's fur; she could feel the rattle of his heart.

The cougar pounced in silence. Its big body passed so close to them, Jasper felt the wind of its passage and its rank cat smell. She heard the sound of its fangs sinking into flesh. The sentry cried out once, sounding more surprised than afraid. His last sound was a gurgle. The cat grunted.

It happened so quickly, the camp hadn't fully woken. Someone called the sentry's name in a voice muzzy with sleep. A few Damaskers sat up and looked around.

Jasper and the dog recovered the power of movement at the same time, and they scrambled toward the camp, toward the firelight—a psychological weapon since the beginning of time against the things that lurked in the dark.

Outside the circle of light, the cat moaned, the sound so eerie and ravenous as to wipe conscious thought from the mind and awaken the animal brain.

Ryan's voice rang out of the darkness, naming the horror. *"Cougar!"*

The camp lurched awake, people tripping over blankets, calling for the sentry, scrambling for their guns. Jasper veered away from the fire and the panicky men with guns and dragged Okuru with her.

The cat yowled. A man screamed and screamed. Men shouted and guns fired, cracking wildly into the night.

Okuru barked and dragged the leash out of Jasper's hand. She ran after him and slammed smack into Ryan. He steadied her with one hand; he had Grammar under his other arm. Okuru jumped around Grammar, barking and adding to the commotion, too excited and afraid and frantic to keep silent any longer.

"Let's go!" Ryan said.

"It's still out there!"

"It's occupied, believe me."

Ryan gave Jasper a push between her shoulder blades, and she ran. The dog darted ahead of her and she followed, trusting his nose more than her own eyes in the dark. But when Okuru hesitated at the tingling zone border, she took the lead. Gravving in the dark was never a good idea, but she'd memorized their route.

She could make out the shape of the building ahead of her. She put a hand on the ground and launched herself over the border with her legs tucked up to the side so that when gravity shoved her sideways, her feet were under her, allowing her to land on the building wall. With some encouragement from Ryan and Grammar, Okuru jumped and Jasper caught him, a whole lot of fur and scrabbling paws and anxiously panting mouth.

They climbed from zone to zone in the darkness and ran when they could until the gunshots stopped and the Damasker campsite was far behind them. They crossed the last border into the Gingers' down-gee zone and slowed to a walk.

"How did you get free of your zip ties, Grammar?" Ryan asked after a while. "You were already loose when I got there."

Grammar reached into his pocket and withdrew a taped-up razor blade. "Crane been showen me how to hide it."

They walked in silence until they reached the spot where

Jasper and Ryan had stashed the gear the Damaskers didn't take when they'd captured Grammar and the rest of the group. They didn't build a fire, but by unspoken agreement the three of them examined the inside of the building thoroughly before being satisfied it was cougar-free and had windows with intact glass and a strong door.

"Get some sleep," Ryan said finally. "I'll do a final perimeter check and then take first watch." He went outside, closing the door behind him.

Jasper leaned against the wall and slid down it until she was sitting on the floor. Okuru came over and sniffed her face. She squeezed her eyes shut but was too tired to push him away. She didn't even flinch at the touch of his warm tongue on her cheek.

"Okuru," Grammar muttered. His voice sounded rusty. The dog went to him immediately. Grammar sat against the wall a short distance from Jasper. Okuru turned around twice and with a long sigh plumped himself down, his head in Grammar's lap.

Jasper rested her head against the wall and willed the adrenalin in her system to fade.

"You been comen for me," Grammar said. "Why?"

She was too tired to come up with anything more eloquent than "Don't be dumb."

A long silence. Okuru snored, a gentle wheezing sound. They must be safe from cougars, then.

"Why?" Grammar asked again. His voice was croaky as if he'd caught a cold.

She reached over to find his skinny shoulder, then picked up his hand. She placed her mother's bird amulet in his palm and closed his fingers over it. "You're part of my pack."

He said nothing and didn't move.

She slid sideways and curled up on the floor. Going over to their packs and digging out their blankets seemed like an impossible effort. Sleep reached for her with murky and malicious fingers, clamping her eyelids shut. Distantly, she felt Grammar curling up with his back against hers, a spot of warmth that softened oblivion's grip. She could smell him and the dog and herself and the musty ancient interior of the building.

Outside Ryan paced the perimeter of the building, keeping them safe. She slept.

3

WITCH DOOR

A baby falling asleep in your arms
Watermelons in summer, crisp and juicy

~ Veronica Park (*Things I Will Miss/Reasons to Live*)

T he Knowles gangers had executed Crane. They'd thrown her into up-gee for the crime of killing one of their own. The gangers hadn't even bothered to consult with their ganglord. Punishment for a woman who attacked a man was swift and unequivocal in Knowles and required little ceremony.

The knowledge ricocheted without impact through Jasper's numbed skull. It would not sink in.

She and Ryan had arrived in Knowles too late to make any difference. Quick Rick and the rest of the boys had finally gotten an audience with the Knowles ganglord, Michael Truthbringer. Ryan had been allowed to join, but Jasper was relegated to the women's building along with Esther. While she was infuriated and frustrated to be left out of the loop, she recognized the advantage of her sex being considered more important than her identity; hopefully, it meant no one would register that the infamous Pinegirl was within the walls.

Michael Truthbringer was a former Azuro, one who had enjoyed the power and violence under Darius's rule a little too much. Rather than accept Zenobia's more restrained leadership of the gang, he'd taken some like-minded Azuros and retreated into the zones to set up his own kingdom. They'd have no love for the Pinegirl, Darius's killer. She had ended their reign of terror and privilege.

"I don't think this is a good idea," Esther Kornelsen said nervously. She fidgeted with a strand of blond hair that had straggled out from the black *duak* all Mennonite women wore. "We should wait until the boys send word."

"You didn't hear from them yesterday," Jasper said. "And since Ryan and I arrived, we still haven't heard anything. So let them deal with their important, manly politics. In the meantime, we can find out where Nev is. I don't need to tell you how thoroughly dead Grammar will kill us all if we don't free her."

Esther grimaced in acknowledgement. "I'm surprised he agreed to stay outside the wall. How long do you think Grammar will wait?"

"I'd rather not test that." The last thing she needed was for the zones' most-wanted twelve-year-old to stroll into Knowles looking for them.

The Knowles compound consisted of a central town square surrounded by several residential buildings, which were in turn surrounded by a wall nearly half a dozen metres high. Outside the walls every inch of down-gee ground was used to grow crops. Knowles labour gangs were busy tearing down and demolishing unneeded buildings to make room for more farming. Other crews used sledgehammers and brute force to break up a city block's worth of pavement and concrete, expanding arable land by dint of back-breaking labour. Still others worked in sweatshop-like conditions to produce, among other things, crossbows and their bolts.

The women's building was easy to spot. The bottom-floor windows were barred and two men guarded the entrance, but the windows and balconies of the upper floors were lined with drying laundry and flowerpots and inhabited by playing toddlers and women who braved the catcalls of men below them to have a smoke or enjoy their only chance at fresh air. The men lived in a separate building, and so did the pack kids and older offspring of the Knowles women.

A woman named Priti Gupta had been assigned to keep an eye on Jasper and Esther in the women's building. She had taken them with her on a trash run, carrying plastic bags of the women's waste to a designated spot near the gates. The errand was a last chance for fresh air before they were shut up for the night in the stuffy building. But newly pregnant Priti couldn't tolerate the smell of the garbage; she had to run for the latrines. Left alone in the courtyard, Jasper made a split-second decision and dragged Esther with her.

Now they crouched in the shadows and gathering dusk near the perimeter wall. The children's dormitory was a short sprint away. It was slowly settling into quiet as kids were herded inside by their adult overseers. Presumably, they'd be given some supper and then sent to bed, where the exhaustion from a long day in the fields would swiftly send them to sleep.

Jasper hoped there was no underground fighting ring for new recruits like there had been in Damascus, where Grammar had been trapped before Jasper and Ryan rescued him.

Finding Neverwhen wasn't Jasper's only motive for sneaking

around the Knowles compound under cover of dusk. That morning when she and Ryan had arrived, they'd been met by one of Michael Truthbringer's lieutenants, who, without any sympathy or regret, broke the news of Crane's execution to them.

"Any woman who sheds a man's blood has opened her heart to Satan," he said. "Our great enemy needs only the crack of an opening to make himself at home. Women have turned to witchcraft under far more trivial circumstances. They are too weak to bear the burden of such a sin."

It was a good thing he didn't realize that the zones' most infamous murderess was standing right in front of him. But in his defence, he might have been distracted by the way Ryan seemed a breath away from committing homicide himself.

Of course, men could murder all they liked, apparently, without arousing Satan's interest.

Under Ryan's glare, the lieutenant hastily agreed to announce Ryan's arrival to Michael Truthbringer and reunite him with the others in the men's house. He summoned a passing woman, Priti, to keep Ryan's "woman" occupied.

Jasper touched Ryan's arm before his ferociously controlled mask could crack, and he exhaled grimly through his nose.

Priti merely nodded to the lieutenant's command, eyes lowered. But as soon as he left with Ryan in tow, she looked Jasper up and down with a sharp eye and then grinned. "I can't believe he didn't recognize you. But then, you look too ordinary to be the devil incarnate. The bandanna to cover your horns is a nice touch."

Jasper blinked, not knowing how to respond. "I'd rather people didn't know..."

"Oh, don't worry. The women will know who you are, but the men won't find out, not from us. You're our patron saint! The Pinegirl, original queen of witches, second only to the great whore of Babylon, Zenobia. You shed the blood of the most powerful man the zones have ever seen. Haven't you heard? That makes you just chock full of Satan."

Jasper smiled despite herself. "Satan's not even the worst voice in my head."

"See? I've always thought him misunderstood. I don't know why the men who invented Christianity didn't just go ahead and make the devil female. Except, of course, that would grant women a far too powerful role model. Being Hindu, I'm rather fond of Kali myself, a goddess who embodies rage and death."

"Well, you've convinced me. I'm prepared to join a she-devil worshipping cult immediately. Where do I sign up?"

Priti laughed. "You've killed a man who deserved it. You're already in the club."

The moment of levity passed. "I heard my friend Crane was thrown into up-gee yesterday. Were you there?"

Priti sobered. "I heard about it. It used to be they'd hold at least a sham trial before witch-upping a woman, but women's testimonies don't count anymore, so any man can accuse a woman of witchcraft and if two other men agree, up she goes."

"Jesus Christ."

"Yeah, Jesus saved a woman from being stoned once by shaming her accusers, I'll give him that. But since shame and self-reflection are no longer in fashion, I'll stick with Kali's tried and true method of killing fuckboys and parading around with their heads as a necklace."

Jasper eyed her with a combination of trepidation and interest. "I was going to offer to help you escape with us, but it sounds like you're on a mission here."

"I have four children," Priti said matter-of-factly. "I won't leave them or all the other young girls growing up here. Don't worry, Pinegirl. You've inspired me greatly over the years. Kali walks these walls." She placed her palms together as if in prayer and winked.

"Risky," Jasper managed to say.

Priti snorted. "*Life* is risky when you're a woman. Risky didn't stop you, did it?"

"You would've liked Crane, I think."

"I'm sure I would have. I certainly knew the bastard she killed."

Priti glanced around to make sure no one was paying attention to them. Then she turned Jasper's attention to a gap in the wall behind them. No buildings or sheds or clucking chickens or roughhousing pack kids or smoking men stood anywhere near this gap. No gates closed it. No armed men guarded it.

After studying it for a moment, Jasper understood why.

On the other side of the gap, the ground was barren, swept clean, a devastation of gaping foundations and the bones of a few stubborn buildings still rooted in the earth but stripped, year after year, of more shingles or bricks. The grass grew long and perfectly straight into the air, like seaweed pulled erect by water.

To step through that open gap in the wall was to step into up-gee.

In the sky on the other side of the Knowles wall, broken-off chunks of buildings drifted in clumps a hundred metres above their heads. It was a bizarre little neighbourhood in the sky with uprooted trees and haphazardly floating cars and—though she couldn't see them—the corpses of people, bones carved clean by time and weather and carrion birds. A society of dead people, living their topsy-turvy not-lives in their upside-down town in the sky.

"If you'd like to meet the devil, all you have to do is step through the witch door," Priti said.

"The what?"

"The witch door. Where women are thrown into up-gee. Your friend Crane was the second outsider witch-upped in as many days." She shook her head. "I don't know whether that'll satisfy them for a while and leave the rest of us safe, or if it'll lead to a rampage."

Witch door. *Which door? Yes.*

Vron's silly poem suddenly didn't seem as nonsensical as she'd first thought. But then, they never were.

"Did you say Crane was the second outsider? Who was the first?"

"Pretty blond girl came around asking questions. Just walked in, all innocent in her belief that human decency and her status as a Yorky citizen would protect her. Sixteen years old, a virgin— ticked all the boxes for a certain kind of human animal." Priti shook her head disgustedly. "Rumour has it she actually jumped through the door herself to get away from the men. She wouldn't be the first, to be honest."

Jasper stood frozen in horror. *Grace.*

"Oh," Priti said, seeing Jasper's expression. "You knew her? For what it's worth, the men wanted to sell her first night to the highest bidder, but she got away from them before that could happen." She grimaced. "Cold comfort, I suppose, but at least she died on her own terms, right?"

Jasper couldn't speak.

A little over a week ago, Jasper and Ryan had rescued Grammar from his unwilling recruitment into the Damasker army. While extricating him from the underground fights he'd been forced to participate in, they'd run into Crane, who'd been accompanied by Esther's sixteen-year-old sister, Grace. Grace had disappeared afterwards into the zones. She'd been following a trail of clues in Vron's notebook, searching for something Vron had found and then hidden.

Her search had led her to Knowles, the worst place in the zones an unaccompanied girl could end up.

When Priti reunited Jasper with Esther in the women's building, Jasper had kept the news of Grace to herself. Until and unless there was a body to see, there was no reason to alarm Esther prematurely.

First things first: they had to rescue Neverwhen.

Out of respect for Knowles's long relationship with Quick Rick and Merlot as the peddlers who brought them valuable goods from Yorky and downieland, Michael Truthbringer might be willing to release the adults in the group. But Neverwhen wasn't a Yorky citizen. She was just another pack kid with no family to fight for her. To the men who controlled Knowles, she was a healthy young body to be used as labour and eventually—in a few short years—as a baby vessel. This was where hundreds of children ended up after being caught up in raids by Damaskers and other kid hunters. Even the Gingers had been trading the extra kids they'd caught to Knowles.

Jasper was anticipating that Truthbringer wouldn't release Neverwhen unless forced to. They could tell him that Neverwhen was the niece of Sparrow, ganglord of Yorky, which was the truth, but he might not believe them. It wasn't public knowledge that Sparrow's sister, Martha Abebe, had had a second daughter, the first being Crane. Even Sparrow didn't know about Neverwhen's existence.

Worse, Truthbringer might believe them and decide Neverwhen was a perfect pawn to use against Sparrow and Yorky.

Far simpler, in Jasper's opinion, to just break Neverwhen out of the dormitory. A runaway pack kid would draw far less attention than an appeal to the ganglord of Knowles.

A commotion near the gates drew their attention. A group of

men were being permitted entry. Their attitude and demeanour carried as loudly as their voices.

Esther gave a small hiss when Jasper's fingers dug into her arm, but she shrank back when she saw the reason for Jasper's alarm. Dragon and his Damaskers. The last time Esther had encountered them, they'd put her in a cage.

Esther and Jasper had nothing to hide behind except a scraggly blackberry bush that grew along the wall, and the shadows of falling dusk. That, along with people's avoidance of the witch door, had seemed like enough cover. Until now. All Dragon had to do was look across the courtyard to see their shapes crouched behind the flimsy screen of brambles.

Dragon was arguing with a Knowles ganger, who had let the Damaskers in with much waving of arms and raised voices. Then the ganger said something that made Dragon go still.

Dragon would expect Ryan and Jasper to have come here to free their friends, and he'd expect Grammar to be with them. The Knowles ganger appeared to have given him confirmation that his targets, aside from Grammar, were within these walls.

The argument ended with the ganger trotting to the men's building to notify Michael Truthbringer about their arrival. The Damaskers gathered in a knot to talk while they waited. Jasper counted and thought there were two fewer than there'd been prior to the cougar.

Esther was shaking beside Jasper, making the blackberry canes tremble. "What should we do?"

"Can't move. They'll see us if we move."

"There you two are!" Priti ran up to them, fury in her voice. "I've been looking everywhere for you. What do you think you're doing running off like that?"

"Priti, shut *up*!" Jasper whispered, looking past her.

The Damaskers were too far away to hear Priti's words, but

the sharpness of her tone had carried in the still evening air, and they glanced in the women's direction.

"Well, shoot," Priti said, realizing the situation. "Now you've done it, haven't you? Stay here. I'll deal with them."

"No," Jasper said. "They see we're here now that you're talking to us. Continuing to hide would only look weird and suspicious." She clambered out from under the bushes and pulled Esther with her.

Indeed the Damaskers were all looking in their direction now. Perhaps it was the novelty of seeing women outside of the women's building. Jasper reached up to adjust her bandanna to make sure her distinctively short hair remained hidden.

"Hiding in the first place made you look weird and suspicious," Priti snapped. "If we go to the women's building now, they'll recognize you when we walk past. But there's nowhere else we're allowed to go."

Whistles and catcalls rose from the Damaskers.

"We have to brazen it out," Priti said. "You're more or less understood to be guests, not prisoners, so if they try anything, I'll raise a holy ruckus."

They'd waited too long. Dragon gave an abrupt shout of recognition that carried across the courtyard. "Pinegirl!"

Then all of the Damaskers were running toward them, pulling out weapons and spreading out to prevent their escape. The few Knowles gangers in the courtyard were confused and slow to react.

A few metres away through the witch door, Jasper could hear the faint crackle of the border with up-gee. She pushed Esther toward Priti.

"If you get a chance, run. It's me they're pissed at," she said. Her voice sounded strangely calm to her ears.

But in moments they were surrounded by furious

Damaskers, each holding a gun pointed at the three women. Their backs were to the wall. There was nowhere to run.

"You *bitch*," Dragon said. He walked up to Jasper and pushed the muzzle of his gun against her forehead, forcing her head back. "You been leaden that goddamn cougar right to our campsite. It been killen two of my guys."

"I don't know what you're talking about." The gun felt cold and heavy as winter against her skin. "I'm not a fucking cougar whisperer." If she could keep his attention on her, maybe Esther and Priti could slip away and get help. "Oh, wait, maybe it was the curse I put on you."

"What?"

"Remember the first time you tried to grab Zenobia's kid? I cursed you then. It must be starting to work. And before you think it, killing me won't stop it."

He withdrew the gun, but only to backhand her with it. Pain exploded across her face and blinded her. She doubled over, too winded by pain to make a sound.

He enunciated carefully. "Where . . . the fuck . . . is the kid?"

She ran her tongue along a cut inside her cheek and straightened slowly. She had to kill time before he killed her. Word would get to the men's building soon, and the boys would come. "How should I know? Last I saw he was with you. Did you lose him already?"

Seeing the blow coming didn't make it hurt any less. She stumbled backwards until she bumped against the wall, hands cupped around the flare bomb of agony that was her face.

"Stop it!" Priti cried. "Michael Truthbringer declared them guests. You can't harm them within our walls."

"Michael will be believen me when I'm tellen him they been helpen one of his women escape," Dragon said without looking at her. He gestured to Priti. "Be shutten her up."

Two Damaskers grabbed her and one of them punched her in the face.

"Stop, she's pregnant!" Esther cried.

"Then she should've been keepen her mouth shut."

The other Damasker punched Priti in the face again.

"If her baby's hurt, Truthbringer *will* be furious," Jasper said, the words sour in her mouth. Because here, Priti's fetus held more potential value than Priti did—after all, it might be a boy.

Dragon paused, then shrugged and nodded at his men. They released Priti and she crumpled onto the ground, groaning. They left her there and ignored her.

Esther gripped Jasper's arm, helping her stand. Esther was shaking like a leaf but solid enough for Jasper to lean on when all she wanted to do was punch Dragon, vomit, and lie down.

"If you're not knowen where the devilboy is," Dragon said, "no reason to be keepen you alive, witch." He lifted his gun and pointed it at her face.

She could bear to die any other way but this, at the hand of an ugly monster wannabe wearing a self-satisfied smirk and sunglasses at night. She'd rather jump out the witch door than give him the satisfaction of killing her. Grace had had the right idea.

A sharp voice rang out. "I'm right here, Dragon."

The skinny figure of a boy pushed through the gathered Damaskers. He placed himself in front of Jasper and Esther and faced Dragon.

Jasper groaned in despair. "Grammar, I *told* you to stay outside the gates."

"I'm comen to warn you."

"Little late for that. You should've gone to warn Ryan instead of turning yourself over to this psychopath."

Dragon chuckled, suddenly immensely pleased. "A curse, is it, Pinegirl? Some curse. I've got everything I'm wanten right in front of me. You I'm gonna be killen once and for all. We'll be letten your blond friend with the tits live—after, of course, me and my men are haven a little fun first. And we'll be haven the boy. Maybe be cutten out his tongue for a lesson. Nico's needen him alive, not talken."

"No!" Grammar's voice was filled with such concentrated fury that it brought silence. His next statement was deadlier for its quietness. "You will not touch them."

There was something terribly familiar in his braced stance and icily crisp diction, in the ominous flutter of his fingers tapping his thigh and the arrogant angle of his jaw as he glared at the Damaskers. An icicle trailed down Jasper's spine.

"Hell," Dragon said, smile gone. "Kid's thinken he's Darius himself."

Grammar's hot blue gaze snapped to Dragon's face and, even from behind and to the side, Jasper felt the laser-like force of that stare. Dragon actually flinched.

"Are you so sure I'm not, *boy*?" Grammar's voice contained enough venom to kill an elephant. "Did you really believe some little girl could kill me that easily? I had a plan all along, and now I've returned." He thumped a careless hand against his chest. "My own flesh and blood makes the perfect vessel."

Dragon gaped, too stunned to summon skepticism.

Grammar—was it Grammar?—turned to Jasper. His grin was cocky and incandescent and cold enough to burn skin. He winked. "Miss me, pet?"

Jasper staggered back against the wall, skewered by that voice. The hair stood up on her neck, prickled on her arms. His grin, his eyes, his words—it was impossible. This was a nightmare. She'd wake up any second screaming and fighting her blankets. "No. *No*. Stop it, Grammar. Your father is dead. He's *dead*."

Grammar's grin—*Darius's grin*—twisted and turned savage. "Not dead enough, clearly. You see me, pet, don't you?"

Dragon looked from Jasper to Grammar, and the colour drained from his face. Jasper's reaction had been convincing, apparently.

"He's possessed," someone whispered, "by Darius Dalca." The whisper spread through the group. Guns wavered in suddenly shaky hands. Free hands made warding gestures. Damaskers edged backwards, glancing anxiously at Dragon for direction.

"You have no idea what you're dealing with." Grammar's smile held more knives than Crane on a bad day. He stepped forward, and they stepped back.

Except Dragon. His hand shook, but he held a gun and he was aiming that gun at Grammar at point-blank range.

"I always been wishen I was the one who been killen da bad man," he said. "In my dreams I'm killen him. Maybe you're him. Or maybe you're just his son play-acten. But this time it'll be Dragon who's killen a Dalca."

"No!" Jasper lunged, grabbed Grammar's shirt, and dragged him back. Dragon's gun followed them. She put a protective arm in front of Grammar, even as her skin still prickled and crawled. "Nico wants him alive, remember."

"Nico's wanten Zenobia's son alive. He never been sayen nothing about Darius fucking Dalca getten resurrected."

The witch door was behind her, open air at her back. The tingle of up-gee lifted the hair on her arms.

"He's not Darius Dalca. Don't be ridiculous. He's Darius's son. Of course he looks like his father. And sounds like him a bit."

He'd called her *pet*. He shouldn't know that. How could he know that?

Dragon had reached his limit. "Zenobia can be cryen over his dead body."

He pointed the gun and his finger curled around the trigger.

Jasper wrapped her arms around Grammar and threw herself backwards. She slammed into Esther, who was standing too close, and for a second they all teetered in the static sting of the zone border, hair lifting and crackling.

The gunshot echoed, and Esther screamed in Jasper's ear.

They fell into up-gee.

4

ROOF RAFT

Heaven is a place in the sky
Where people go after they die.
A boneyard in the clouds
Where zombies learn to fly.

~ Veronica Park

As a child, Jasper had spent several years convinced that if heaven meant the sky, then her mother was trapped somewhere in up-gee waiting to be rescued. Harmony Kim, who had adopted her and Ben, had enlisted Pastor Tim's help to set her straight. But the idea still lurked at the back of her subconscious mind that all the dead people she had ever known now dwelled in an uprooted helter-skelter parody of a town in the sky. Her mother. Vron. Martha Abebe. Darius.

And now she was going to join them.

Endless air, but none in her lungs. Acid volcano in her belly, erupting in her veins. Falling.

This was not a good idea.

A breathless cry half swallowed. Not her own. Esther falling too, her face a rictus of terror as she flailed in mid-air.

This is all my fault.

Grammar whooping and yodelling like loon, flapping like he could fly.

I'd better be right.

Below them, growing at magical speed, Lego chunks of buildings, metal scrawls of rusted cars, a forest floor carpet of shattered wood and jagged metal. And patches of open indigo sky between.

Wish a fish into the sky.
Wish a fish, it won't die.

Between one breath and the next, terror was replaced by a wild thrill, ricocheting around her chest and out her mouth in a whoop.

It can only fall
Through the doorway in the wall.
Which door?
Yes.

"Aim for the sky," she shouted at Esther and Grammar, although the wind from her fall tore the sound from her mouth.

She aimed for the biggest patch of empty sky she could see between a snarled motorcycle and a serenely unattached roof. Pressing her arms to her sides, she made herself straight as an arrow. She misjudged slightly, and the jagged end of the motorcycle's muffler scraped a scarlet line of pain up her arm as she fell past.

Zing! She fell through the zone border, and her momentum threw her up, up, up into open sky. Cool violet blue enveloped her, and blood rushed to her head as gravity reverted to down-gee. She struggled to turn herself around as her momentum slowed. Then she was falling again, toward the earth this time.

Zing! Back through the invisible border, curled up in a protective ball. Her re-entry sent branches, shingles, and a rubber tire bouncing and spinning away from her. Up-gee slowed her fall and threw her skyward, back through the border.

Flailing much less gracefully, Esther found her voice and drowned out Grammar's whoops with her screams as they bounced between the zones like stringless yo-yos. Each time they crossed the border from up-gee to down-gee and back again, their momentum slowed until they finally bobbed to a halt exactly at the border, which acted like the surface tension on a pond, the skin between two worlds.

"Step one, we survived the fall," Jasper called, but Esther was thrashing about amid the debris like a drowning swimmer and sobbing, while Grammar cackled and yelled in a mix of terror and delight.

"Step two, find a surface to stand on," Jasper said, to herself this time, as neither of them was listening.

An unattached roof floated nearby like a hat blown away from its owner on an autumn wind. Did she want to be on the up-gee side or the down-gee side? More to the point, did she want the sky above her head or the earth?

She chose the sky side. Esther might feel better if she was "right side up." Jasper grabbed the nearest piece of heavy debris —part of a patio chair—attached it to a rope, and tossed it at the roof. She drew the chair gently back toward her. It soon caught on a hole where shingles and some of the underlying boards had fallen away. Hand over hand, she drew herself closer until she could climb onto the roof. It bobbed up and down beneath her weight, reminding her of a raft on a pond.

It took several minutes of coaxing before Esther emerged

from her haze of panic and grabbed on to the rope Jasper threw her. Once safely on the roof, Esther lay flat, clutching the shingles for dear life. She had scratches on her face and arms from whatever debris she'd encountered at the border. The cheerful face she usually presented to the world had dissolved into tears and horror.

Jasper reeled in Grammar next.

"We're alive," he said over and over. He couldn't seem to stop laughing. She deposited him on the roof beside Esther so they could recover together. Perhaps her hysterical sobs and his hysterical giggles would cancel each other out.

At least she could see no trace of Darius Dalca on his face while he was laughing. Had she ever seen Darius laugh for any reason that didn't involve someone else's suffering?

Her heart still pounded from the fall, but the shock was wearing off as if she'd always somehow expected to end up here, even before Vron's poetry had foretold it. A glance at her companions reassured her that Dragon's gunshot had missed them, thanks to her quick lunge into up-gee.

They were on the outer, shingled side of their roof raft. She had to walk the centre line to stay in down-gee, as the roof slanted down into up-gee, as it would if it were floating on water. Perhaps, on second thought, they would be more comfortable on the opposite side, but in the meantime, they enjoyed a breathtaking view of the sunset blazing over the curve of the world and gilding the ruined city below them in threads of gold and hot silver.

"Only other place you'd get a view like this is the top of the Tower," she remarked over her shoulder.

Esther's sobs had died away to occasional hiccups, and now she regarded Jasper with reddened and swollen eyes, as sullen as Jasper had ever seen her. "Both places will kill you."

"Very true, very true," said Jasper, pleased to hear this ghost of sarcasm. In the wake of hysterics, it was a promising sign. "But we're not dead yet, and it's getting cold."

Grammar lay flat on his stomach and inched partway into up-gee to peer at the city below. "Wishen I could've been watchen Dragon's face," he said and started giggling again.

She noticed how hard he was shaking and dragged him away from the edge.

As Esther now seemed the slightly more functional of the two, Jasper gave her the rope and set her to collecting firewood from the debris floating around them. Jasper had spotted the unattached hood of a car drifting a dozen metres away. She tied herself to the roof with a length of rope and plunged into open air. Down-gee pressed her down and up-gee pushed her up, holding her firmly in the crackle of the zone border. She swam the last few metres with an awkward wriggling motion that sent her bobbing up and down between up-gee and down-gee.

She clasped the car hood between her legs and drew herself hand over hand back to the roof. This time she climbed into the concave up-gee side. Esther crawled to join her with an armful of wood.

Grammar followed with jerky, uncoordinated movements. He'd stopped laughing and was now shaking all over, teeth clacking together like bones in the wind. Jasper made a fire in the car hood and pushed him close to the flames, wishing she had a blanket or an extra sweater, anything to warm him as shock set in.

In the concave side of the roof, which had once formed the ceiling of an attic, they were castaways adrift in a lifeboat, rocking and bobbing on waves of wind. They floated in the greater bowl of the sky, shaded from deep velvet indigo to soft violet near the lid of the earth. The planet spread serenely over their heads, three-dimensional ceiling wallpaper, darkening as it blotted out the sun.

Jasper looked up at the Knowles compound above their heads. She could see the movement of people, tiny as ants, lit by sparks of torchlight. Would they in turn have seen Jasper, Esther, and Grammar moving around in the sky? Even if they hadn't, they couldn't miss the beacon of their campfire, burning like a rogue star.

Surviving a fall into up-gee was easy enough, as long as the zone on the other side of the border was down-gee. And as long as you didn't hit a floating object with the lethal force of your momentum. It was getting down again that was the trick—a near impossible trick from this height. Likely every woman who'd been thrown up-gee had died eventually, if not from impact with a floating object, then from dehydration and starvation. Or they could always end their misery by "swimming" their way to the edge of the up-gee zone and jumping over the edge into down-gee to fall a fatal distance back to the earth.

Was Crane alive somewhere up here? Was Grace?

Jasper hadn't seen any fresh bodies. She surveyed the drifting junkyard of buildings and debris and saw no other movement or fire. Still, plenty of the pieces of buildings were large enough to block her view and provide sheltered hiding spots. She wouldn't break the news about Grace being thrown into up-gee to Esther, or mention the possibility that Grace and Crane were still alive until they'd had a chance to look around. No point in getting anyone's hopes up.

The wind cut sharp here in the sky, and they huddled around the fire, shielding it with their bodies from random gusts that threatened to extinguish it. Grammar's stomach growled loudly and Jasper's echoed it. They had no food left in their pouches and, combined, only a cupful of water in their canteens. Jasper wrapped her arm around Grammar, pulling him tight to her side, sharing warmth. He was shivering so hard, she could almost hear his bones rattle.

Esther broke the silence. "This is the perfect example of out of the frying pan and into the fire. We're going to die up here. What were you thinking?"

"I don't know if you remember the part where Dragon pointed a gun at us and pulled the trigger." Jasper kept her tone mild so that when she eventually snapped she could claim the moral high ground.

"We wouldn't even be in that situation if it weren't for you. You had to run off half-cocked instead of waiting for Priti. She would've helped us."

"I didn't want to drag her into it! She has her own life, her own children to worry about."

By her expression Esther was also remembering Priti crumpled on the ground, her face a bloody mess. Esther bowed her shoulders, arms between her knees, head down. Firelight cast ruddy highlights in her blond hair.

"My fault," Grammar said in a small voice, between chattering teeth. "Been maken him angry. My fault."

He was shaking so hard, the sky boat trembled. Jasper wrapped her arms more firmly around him and rubbed his arms. Esther moved to sit on his other side and added her arms and body to the effort of warming him.

Jasper rubbed a hand over the stubble that was beginning to lie flat and soft over Grammar's skull. He'd resembled Darius Dalca so eerily during his confrontation with Dragon. He'd taken on Darius's tone and posture and attitude as easily as shrugging on a comfortable jacket. Could such things be passed genetically? Grammar hadn't been born yet when his father died; if he'd been putting on an act, he had no mental template of Darius to imitate. If he carried Darius so fully in the lines of his body and the tilt of his chin and the timbre of his voice, well, the resemblance would only grow more and more unmistakable as he got older.

Anyone who'd ever laid eyes on Darius Dalca would see him in his son.

Jasper carried her father's inheritance, deadly but invisible, at the microscopic level in her cells. Grammar carried his in his face and voice and carriage, visible to all. And for his curse there was no cure of any kind.

Grammar lifted his head so suddenly, he nearly head-butted her in the chin. "Dead people are flyen," he said and laughed.

Tucked against her, he was all sharp elbows and knees and ribs, and dirt and body odour. She edged him closer to the fire. The only thing she knew to do for people in shock was keep them warm—difficult without any extra blankets or clothes and a tiny fire that threatened to blow out with every gust.

"If Nev's noticen this fire up in the sky," Grammar explained, "she'll be thinken dead people are flyen. Oh, so many stories she'll be tellen." He chuckled fondly and Jasper relaxed.

"Vron was like that too," she said. "She spoke in stories and poems and rhymes and riddles." Transmuting darkness into words and sowing them liberally, luminescent flowers growing from the fertile black ashes of dead things.

Grammar nodded, his skull hard against her collarbone. "Alpha of ghosts now."

"What do you mean?"

"All the ghosts are trapped, see? In the zones. The city is keepen them. The Storytalker is gatheren the ghosts. Will be maken them free one day."

"There's no such thing as ghosts," Esther said sharply.

Then why is Darius Dalca in my head? Who was it who inhabited Grammar's skin down there and called me pet? *What is this feeling I get in the zones of unfinished lives pressing against my skin, a thousand angels dancing on each skin cell?*

Jasper bit her tongue. Esther was brittle and in shock, and needed sleep and ideally some food to recover her resilience.

Grammar's shaking had diminished as he absorbed Jasper's and Esther's body heat. "But God is a ghost, yeah? Been dyen a long time ago on a cross, now is invisible, and can be talken to you. Ghost."

"He's not a ghost. He's a . . . spirit," Esther said.

Grammar shrugged as if his point were made, and indeed Jasper couldn't think of any meaningful difference between a ghost and a spirit.

Esther changed the subject. "So are we going to die of starvation up here, or do you have some insane plan to get us down?"

"Gravity magic," Grammar said and looked up at Jasper. "Right?"

"I told you, it doesn't work like that," Jasper said. Her gravity only shifted while she was in down-gee anyway—when her feet were on the earth and the earth remembered that she didn't belong.

"No such thing as magic." Esther had found a forgotten stash of scowls and seemed determined to use them before they expired.

Grammar considered. "What are the gravity zones, then?"

Esther's face scrunched up for a moment. But then line by line it unfolded. It was like an eraser had removed darkly pencilled clouds, leaving smudges but also clear space. "I guess from the perspective of a heathen that makes sense."

Grammar stared at her suspiciously, then up at Jasper. "What's a hee-then?"

"Anyone who believes in ghosts and magic," Esther said, but with a wry smile that took any sting from her words.

"Heathen," Grammar repeated, as if trying the word on for size. "I'm a heathen."

Esther's laugh held an edge of stress, like a fraying rope, but also a determined habit of looking for the bright side of any disaster. She wasn't the first person Jasper would have chosen to be stuck in up-gee with, not even the second or third. Esther was normally an unrelenting ray of sunshine, annoying to anyone trying to sleep and exhausting after long exposure, but she was also used to looking at a roomful of loud, demanding, rude, sometimes violent children, putting on a smile, rolling up her sleeves, and getting to work.

She could be relied upon to never give up. Otherwise she'd have abandoned Merlot to his demons long ago. Like Jasper had.

Vron had had the power of sunshine too, but in her the hidden battery was her sadness, and the price of the magic was that it worked for everyone except its creator.

Jasper glanced at Esther uneasily. How could anyone know if a bottomless pit of darkness lay behind that sunny smile or if spider-legged demons stalked the bunnies and kittens in Esther's dreams? If Vron could hide her morass of sadness from her closest friends, then anyone could.

Jasper cleared her throat, chasing away the thought. "First thing tomorrow we're going to salvage everything we can find to use as rope, tie it all together, attach one end to an anchor, toss it into down-gee, and down we go."

"Oh." Esther looked around them at the drifting chunks of buildings and debris. "Huh. If it's that easy, why hasn't anyone tried to salvage from up-gee zones before? I mean, not that I ever would, but someone like you might be crazy enough to."

"Maybe after this they will and call it the Pine-Kornelsen technique." Jasper kept her doubts to herself about the length of rope required and how it might not even hold its own weight, especially when cobbled together from different materials.

They continued to huddle together for warmth as darkness fell. Grammar and Esther fell asleep almost at once, but Jasper stayed awake watching the shadowy shapes drifting around them, the occasional flutter of a bird or bat, the last ray of sun reflecting off a window's spiderwebbed glass. She tried not to think about Vron's stories of the sky-dwellers, the mutant skeleton zombies that lived in these upside-down towns and might be peering out at them now from the dark mouths and empty eyes of the rotted building skulls.

Stars filled the glowing dusk below their sky boat. When Jasper finally closed her eyes, she dreamed she dipped her hand into the air ocean that cradled them and plucked the stars dripping from the deep, but the glowing shards of celestial light burned holes in their boat and rained fire upon the earth.

5

UPSIDE-DOWN TOWN

I am human
The way the earth is a woman—
More metaphorically
Than literally.

~ Veronica Park

When they were children and later as teenagers, Jasper had become used to waking up in the middle of the night to see Vron still sitting by the fire, humming charms against the darkness as if she was their only line of defence against a city full of nightmares. Vron had fought sleep like it was the ultimate enemy, one she'd never surrender to willingly.

If Jasper couldn't sleep, she'd join Vron by the fire and Vron would talk, sometimes rhyming nonsense and other times circular stories that meandered like streams and vanished abruptly into pockets of the unexplainable, wormholes to the surreal.

"What if the earth hates us?" she once said. "What if somewhere somebody dropped the five hundred zillionth plastic cup on the ground and it was the last straw—literally—and it broke her?"

Only the imprint of Vron's words remained, footprints tracking through Jasper's memories. In her dreams Jasper chased after them, but she could never catch up to Vron.

"What if the earth wakes up just for a moment and sees what we've become and what we've done to her? What if she doesn't recognize us as her children? What if all she sees is an infestation, a verminous, destructive, annihilating plague plundering her as if it's our only purpose? What a shocking awakening that would be. Enough maybe to create a crack in her heart, a splinter in her soul, a kink in her sanity. So she reacts like anyone would upon finding a poisonous spider on their arm. She screams, flails, and flicks that spider as far away from her as she can. *Get it off, get it off, get it off!*"

"The Shattering," Jasper said when Vron fell silent.

A tiny spark drifted upward and alighted in the gleaming darkness of Vron's hair, illuminating nothing. She snuffed it out with a pinch of her fingers. "If God is our father who art in heaven, then the earth is our mother who's had enough of us." Vron's voice rose into a falsetto, an imitation of somebody Jasper had never met. "'If this is how you're going to treat me, go live with your deadbeat dad!' She threw us up at God, shouting, 'They're your kids. You made them this way—you deal with them.' But God stepped out for a cigarette a long time ago and hasn't been back in a few millennia."

"She doesn't want our footsteps on her face anymore," Jasper said and shivered. In the depthless, off-kilter, not-quite-reality between past-midnight and morning-might-not-come, Vron's fancies turned smoke and shadow into growl and bite. "The earth stopped loving us."

Vron resumed her sour, high-pitched impersonation. "'I didn't go through thirty-eight eons of labour to raise kids as stupid as you! Maybe I should just die! How would you like that, huh? That'd teach you, ungrateful little shits.'"

"Mothers aren't like that," Jasper said without thinking, and then wanted to cut out her tongue. Some mothers were.

All she could see of Vron's eyes was the reflection of flames. "We hold these truths to be self-evident: that mothers die and fathers leave, and children cry and children grieve and reject what they receive, choosing to walk on the sky instead, to avoid the footprints of the dead."

So real was Vron's voice in her ear that Jasper woke expecting to see her friend propped up against the rafters of their sky boat, glossy black head bowed over the amulets on her chest, having nodded off the moment the sun rose and released her from the rambling maze of her nighttime thoughts.

But she saw only Esther stretched out beside her and Grammar already awake and leaning over the side to look into the limpid pearl sky below them.

A gull alighted on the rim of their floating roof and stared at her with one round yellow eye. Jasper's stomach growled viciously.

Sunlight drifted slow and soft across the sleeping city like the gaze of a lover. The city spread out above Jasper's head, the tumbled concrete chunks and broken steel ribs of a post-historic beast. Flower petal flocks of birds flooded from thousands of empty windows in shimmering, living ribbons of movement.

"Who wants to donate a leg so we can have breakfast?" Esther mumbled, looking disgruntled as she sat up. Then she grimaced. "Oh. I guess that's funnier when Ben says it."

"He's not as funny as he thinks. Fortunately, I think he'll be making that joke less after our up-close-and-personal encounter with a couple of cannibals."

Esther froze. "Yikes. Totally forgot. Sorry."

The gull squawked and toppled from its perch in a feathery heap. Slingshot in hand, Grammar lunged past them and pounced on the stunned bird. He seized its neck and twisted. It stopped flapping.

Nonchalantly, he dropped the dead bird at Esther's feet. "Breakfast."

Esther grabbed his shoulders and gave him a loud kiss on each cheek. "You are officially my favourite person."

Among the three of them, the bird was plucked in record time. While Esther and Grammar avidly watched it roast over the fire, Jasper put together all the rope they had on them so she could estimate how much more they would need. The result made her wince. Could they really find a hundred metres of rope or rope-like material here in the rubble of this upside-down town?

The moment Esther declared the bird done enough for safety's sake, she and Grammar tore into it like starving dogs.

Esther's careless joke had reminded Jasper of the Gingers and the child-sized skulls in their basement. Looking down at the morsels of meat in her hand, her gag reflex abruptly betrayed her. She rushed to the edge of the roof raft and retched. The clumps and globs of her vomit zinged through the border . . . and then fell back toward her. She had to jerk herself out of the way.

"Sick?" Grammar placed a hand on her forehead. "Needen some peppermint tea."

She didn't want to remind him of the traumatic night he'd spent in a cage in the Gingers' basement long ago, waiting to be killed and eaten, so she improvised. "Sometimes the spirits of killed animals haunt my belly and won't let me digest their flesh."

Grammar's eyes grew round, and Jasper wondered how long

it would take before this tidbit found its way into the Pinegirl legends.

Once Esther and Grammar had demolished the gull down to its bones, Jasper took the rope with the partial chair tied to the end, whirled it above her head like a lasso, and sent it flying. It took a couple of tries before the makeshift grapple hooked on to the cab of a twisted semi-truck. They pulled themselves through the air, hand over hand, to the truck and leapfrogged their way closer to the drifting buildings, where they began exploring.

The first building was a single-level bungalow. It was missing part of its roof, and a heavy object had smashed against one of its walls, buckling it, but it was otherwise intact. They crawled in through a window to find scattered, broken furniture and the beginnings of an ecosystem nourished by wind- and bird-borne seeds and rain.

This place would be a treasure trove of copper wire, Jasper realized, studying an exposed section of wall. She caught herself and turned away. First they had to escape.

The sheets and blankets they found were mostly rotted, but Jasper salvaged an extension cord and the strings from the blinds.

They moved on to a massive chunk of an apartment building that was mostly intact. All the apartment doors were unlocked, which made Jasper suspect that someone had had time to loot the building before it eventually broke off under the strain of up-gee and fell into the sky.

Leaving Esther to rummage through kitchen cupboards, Jasper opened a hallway closet and looked at tumbled heaps of old towels, ancient cleaning supplies, and dusty Christmas decorations.

A thump from the next room drew her to the doorway. Grammar stood in a child's bedroom, a deflated soccer ball at his feet. He had found a puffy blue coat somewhere. It was too small for him, leaving his skinny wrists exposed, but it would provide some warmth against the wind.

He hadn't heard her come to the door, so she watched him, noting the faint scrunching between his eyebrows as he picked up a Shrek Halloween mask and tugged at one of the green horns. Other than the most recent black eye and cut lip the Damaskers had given him, his bruises were starting to fade, the lines of his face emerging clear and uncompromising as they were meant to be.

She remembered the chill of horror that had spiked through her belly when for an instant she'd been utterly convinced he was possessed by Darius Dalca. She'd believed it because *of course* he'd come back. *Of course* she couldn't have killed him for real. It was exactly the sort of nightmare come true that she'd always known she'd wake up to.

"I'm not." Grammar was looking back at her now.

"You're not what?"

"Possessed."

He'd read her face—like his mother would do, she told herself, not his father. She looked away from those crystal-sharp blue eyes and picked up the first object at hand, a toy train.

"You're looken at me like you're afraid." A twist of anger or resentment in his voice. Unhappiness.

"I'm not . . ." She straightened, uncomfortable. "I know you're not possessed."

"They been looken at me like I was—so I been pretenden. It's easy. They been believen. *You're* believen."

"You look like him. Very much so when you're angry. And you talked just like him. How did you do that?"

"Just because I choose not to doesn't mean I can't speak biggie English," he said acidly, pronouncing each word with glass edges. A hint of Martha's Sierra Leone accent emerged then, as if in his mind true adult English could only be spoken in her voice.

"You called me *pet*," she burst out.

Colour rushed into his bruise-stained cheeks and drained out again. He tossed the Shrek mask into the tumble of debris on the floor and wrapped both arms around himself. "Auntie Martha never been wanten to talk about the past," he said, eyes on the floor. "But I—I could be maken her sometimes, and so she been tellen me things. About *him*, about the Pinegirl, and—and everything. She been sayen Pinegirl was his pet."

When she didn't say anything for a moment that stretched too long, he reached for her mother's bird amulet, jerked it off, and held it out to her so abruptly, she took it reflexively. "I'm sorry," he muttered and pushed past her out the door.

"Grammar!" She grabbed his arm and dragged him back into the room. She looked for words and came up with "Don't be dumb."

He stood rigidly, not looking at her as she tied the amulet back onto his neck.

The bed had been flipped upside down by the violence of the building's long-ago uprooting. She made him sit with her on the mattress where it had landed under the window. Sunlight poured through the unbroken glass, heating the room, and he shucked off the jacket he'd salvaged. She searched for words to say, but they'd all fallen through the cracks that had opened up where she'd thought she'd built solid ground.

Nothing was as solid as you wanted to believe. Gravity couldn't be trusted, and the past wouldn't stay the past.

To occupy her hands, she sifted through the detritus that covered the floor and came up with a scrap of paper. She made a few idle folds, her fingers working from memory. It reminded her of Zenobia.

"Did your mother ever visit you when you were living with Martha?"

"Sometimes. With Tom." Zenobia wouldn't go anywhere without Tom Jitters, her bodyguard. "She been given me medicine." He made a gesture toward his inner elbow that she didn't immediately recognize.

"Medicine? Oh, you mean a needle." Those must have been the early preventative treatments of antibac that Martha and Zenobia had given Grammar to ensure his graviteria remained dormant and inactive. Temporarily, at least.

"Did she tell you what the medicine was for?"

"So I won't be getten sick when I'm older." He frowned. "But they been sayen Nev's not needen it. Only in my family." He looked up at the ceiling, searching for the word and having found it, he pronounced it with Martha's accent: *"Hereditary."*

Did Zenobia ever plan to tell him that the inheritance in his blood would cause a Shattering? Or would she once again rely on others to reveal devastating truths?

Jasper took in his hunched shoulders, the tendons standing out in his neck, the absurd length of his lashes. The unwelcome understanding of why and how adults could keep secrets from children expanded in her chest. Why Zenobia had kept secrets from her. Why Jasper would rather crawl back into a cage than tell Grammar that not only was his monstrous father imprinted on his face and body, but also that he'd inherited his mother's legacy of a million deaths through the Shattering.

Other than the occasional crane, Jasper hadn't folded an origami figure in years. Her fingers seemed to remember, although she wasn't sure what she was creating.

"What did Zenobia tell you about herself and your father?"

"That my papa been doen bad things and hurten people and that she never been stoppen him, and so they're villains both. But . . . but she been sayen I'm not bad, must never be bad." He looked up at her, his mouth a tentative bracket enclosing an unfinished thought.

Jasper had to stare at the square of blinding sky outside the window until she could control her face. Was it possible Zenobia had done one thing right in her life?

His voice was barely audible. "If I'm getten so angry—is that him? How can I be getten him out?"

You can't. Believe me, I've tried.

He seemed to think Jasper was a biggie and therefore in possession of answers, but it wasn't her fault her body had grown to adult size before she was ready. Harmony or Martha's sister, Sparrow, could answer this question, or Pastor Tim or Quick Rick or literally anyone other than her. Jasper didn't have anything more figured out now than when she'd been a fractured jigsaw puzzle of a kid. How could she offer Grammar anything useful or comforting when she herself had no expectation of exorcising Darius from her head before she died?

Her fingers had created a frog. She placed it in the palm of her hand, pressed its back, and it hopped from her hand to Grammar's lap. The corner of his mouth twitched in response, and he picked it up to examine it. His brow furrowed in wonder and concentration as if he could unfold the secret of the frog's existence by staring at it.

For the first time Jasper felt the lack of functioning cameras in the zones as a distinct loss. The chimerical nature of childhood ensured that the exact balance of youth and expression imprinted on his face would be immortalized only in her fallible memory. And it would die with her.

She wondered if Zenobia had folded origami for him when he was a child and if that was why he'd been fascinated to see Crane do it.

"Just because you're related to someone doesn't mean you'll

turn out like them," she said. "Crane and Nev are sisters, but they're very different people."

"They been growen up different, though."

"Yes, exactly. I don't know what your father's upbringing was like, but I'd bet copper it was pretty different from yours. I'm just saying, nothing's set in stone."

He began unfolding the paper frog, line by line. "You can be sayen that. But he's not *your* father."

In profile the resemblance was not as strong. Stubborn jaw and crooked nose, dark, expressive eyebrows, while his mouth remained a wary line of reserve. Eyes bluer than even Darius's, startling against his tan. His parents' genetics were unmistakably stamped into his features, but put together, his face was decidedly his own.

"But he was in a way," she said. "Crane and I were both his pets. He raised us both. He broke us both. And look at us now."

"Yeah, you're both crazy," he mumbled.

"You're not wrong," she said, suppressing a smile. "But all things considered, we turned out okay. Well, okay-ish. But my point is, monsters are made, not born."

Grammar frowned, still intent on smoothing the paper frog from existence. "You been sayen you been getten your gravity curse from your papa. And Auntie been sayen some sickness is hereditary. So can't badness be?"

"I mean, maybe we're all born with a little badness. But it's your actions that make the badness shrink or grow."

No response from Grammar. The frog had flattened and disappeared under his fingers into an unremarkable sheet of paper, crisscrossed now with indelible wrinkles. Jasper took it from him, marvelling at how a wondrous little creature was essentially, at its core, just a piece of scarred, wrinkled trash.

Or perhaps it was the other way around and every wondrous

little creature could only take shape through the creation of scars and wrinkles.

"We been playen one time, me and Nev," Grammar said, barely audible. He plucked at his jeans, his shoelaces, his fingers restless. "We were little. I was maybe four. She been taken my toy maybe—I'm not rememberen. I just remember getten angry. So angry I been *screamen*."

He drew up his legs and clamped his arms over the sides of his head, lacing his hands behind his head and resting his forehead on his knees. His voice came out muffled. "I been pushen her. Against the table. And then the soup pot been fallen on—on her."

Jasper drew in a sharp breath, remembering Neverwhen's burnt hands, lumpy and mottled. She clamped down on her reaction. "It was an accident. You didn't mean to hurt her."

He grunted, a sound of scorn and rejection. "Pushen is an action. A bad one."

You were just a kid, she wanted to say, but the words choked her. How many times had she heard those words? How many times had she rejected them?

Even a child's choices had consequences—sometimes minor, sometimes irreversibly damaging. Worst of all, those consequences could happen to other people. Neverwhen's hands. Harmony's scarred face. The lives Ryan's tattoos represented.

Grammar still had his head buried in his arms. The individual knobs of his spine stood out through the sun-wilted fabric of his T-shirt. His hands, crumpled against his neck, were long fingered with big knuckles, awkwardly oversized. A man strained at the seams of his boy's body. In a year he could be towering over her.

If she was still alive in a year's time.

The thought pinched in her chest so hard, she plucked at her bra, sure the underwire had stabbed her.

"Nev is good," Grammar said. "Me—I don't think so."

Jasper didn't know whether to be chilled or heartbroken by his matter-of-fact tone.

"But maybe it's okay," Grammar went on. "Means I can be protecten her. Like Crane been tryen to protect me."

He lifted his face to the window. The afternoon light leaked onto his skin, filling the creases and scars his short life had already etched into him. A crumpled sheet of paper taking shape, partially folded . . . into what?

Not a paper frog, that was for damn sure.

6

WHEN THE DEMONS WIN

Inside jokes
Forgetting for a little while that everyone you love is going to
*   die and that life is meaningless*

~ Veronica Park (*Things I Will Miss/Reasons to Live*)

By evening their search had grown more desultory, as they'd turned up little that could be used as rope. Perhaps they hadn't been the first unfortunate occupants of this up-gee zone to have the idea. Grammar went up to the roof in the hopes of bringing down another seagull or two, and Esther went with him to collect rainwater from anywhere it had puddled in dips and hollows.

Jasper entered the bottom half of the building.

The building fragment wasn't floating the way it would on water. Up-gee pushed it skyward, while from the other side of the zone border, down-gee pushed it earthward with the same amount of force, thus distributing the building's weight equally to either side of the border, as if the border were a giant mirror. Above the border the house existed in normal down-gee, but as soon as Jasper took the stairs down through the zone border, gravity flipped in the opposite direction. Now she was walking on ceilings, stepping upside down over doorway thresholds, and carefully skirting ceiling fans and smashed light fixtures.

After an aimless half hour in which she found nothing useful, she gave up and opened a balcony door to poke her head out. She was standing in up-gee just below the invisible line of the zone border. The empty sky pooled below her feet, and above her head stretched the earth.

The building was too large and heavy to be easily shifted by wind and weather, but having been torn off its foundation jaggedly, it was not symmetrically shaped or weighted. It tended to dip and roll, up and down, side to side, like a ship on a real ocean.

Or so she would imagine. She'd only ever been on a boat once. Merlot had taken her and Vron and Esther out on the Kornelsens' irrigation pond on the raft he and Ben had built. Merlot was too energetic, manic even, as he tried to show them everything. He ended up capsizing the raft, dumping them all in the cool, muddy water. Jasper laughed so hard, she couldn't keep her footing in the soft mud, and he had to drag her up the bank. Esther waded out on her own. After a look down at the mess of her dress, she sighed and began the walk back to the house, muttering about laundry.

Oddly, Vron was most upset by the dunking. She had a notebook in her thigh pouch and it had gotten soaked. She always carried a notebook with her everywhere, scribbling down every thought and fragment of poetry that came to her during the day, capturing candid cameos of her inner denizens. "That's part of my soul you just destroyed," she shouted at Merlot. Jasper tried to point out that if it was so precious, maybe

Vron should've left the notebook on the bank before boarding her brother's rickety raft, but she was in no mood to listen and stormed away.

It took Merlot nearly a week to recover from Vron's accusation, even after she apologized and showed him how she'd managed to dry out the pages so that only small bits had been lost to illegibility.

Remembering how silent and withdrawn he'd gotten that week, Jasper was struck once again by how unlikely it was that Merlot had burned all of Vron's notebooks after her death. She could understand the volatile mix of fury and grief, the pain so acute you wanted to cut out the part of your brain that held memory, just for a moment's relief. She could understand trying to banish Vron's ghost by destroying the physical objects that contained the clearest imprint of her mind and soul. She knew that Merlot had been so blackout drunk that he retained no memory of burning the notebooks.

But it still made no sense.

A sound pulled her back into the apartment. Had she heard a creak? She stood still and listened.

Silence reigned, the familiar silence of lives long decayed and spaces abandoned. But it wasn't a dead or empty silence. The Guardian, the leader of the ReGeneration, was right. The city still lived and breathed even in these torn-off fragments. A corpse was never truly dead. In fact, it swarmed with life, with bacteria and insects and fungi, with the roots of plants nourishing themselves in decay.

Placing her feet carefully, Jasper walked across the ceiling to the closet and yanked the door open.

Huddled into a corner of the closet, Grace Kornelsen screamed and jerked back.

"Grace! It's okay. It's me. It's Jasper."

Grace was a mess, her cropped blond hair dirty and

dishevelled, her clothing torn. Dark bruises formed a necklace around her pale throat and one blue eye was swollen shut. Her hands, with their dirty, broken nails, were still raised trembling to fend off the attack she'd expected.

Jasper thought about how Grace would have gotten those bruises, about Priti's description of Grace's reception in Knowles. She considered the mechanics and logistics of burning the entire Knowles compound to the ground with Truthbringer and his men in it. Then she counted to ten and locked away that burst of helpless rage and reached for Grace's hands.

"You're safe, Grace." Well, besides being trapped a hundred metres in the air with no way down.

Fear gave way to disbelief, then hope. "Jasper? I thought you were a Knowles ganger come to finish me off. What are you doing here?"

Jasper helped her out of the closet and looked her over for any injuries worse than bruises. If she had any, they were the invisible, insidious kind that would invade her nightmares and damage her relationships for years to come. "It's a long story."

"Pinegirl?" a voice said from the doorway.

Startled, Grace bumped into Jasper as she turned.

Crane had one hand braced against the door frame and a knife in the other. "Why you up here, Piney? You been killen someone too?"

"You *are* alive," Jasper said, relief washing over her. "Didn't you see our fire last night? Jesus, your face, Craney. Are you okay?"

The Knowles gangers had beaten Crane before witch-upping her. Her sharp-featured face was lumpy and mottled with bruising. "What's 'okay' meanen?" she asked with a curl of her lip. She looked at Grace. "Hello again, pink cheek girl. You been runnen from me. I'm just wanten to talk."

"Talk?" A spark of anger lit Grace's voice. "The minute you

saw me up here, you grabbed me and slammed me against the wall."

"Crane?" Jasper asked. "Why would you do that?"

Crane still had that knife in her hand and a grimness behind her toothy smile that Jasper didn't like at all. "She's knowen what I'm wanten."

Grace fumbled in her thigh pouch and pulled out a notebook, which she slapped into Jasper's hand. "Here. You take it. She wouldn't tell me why she wants it so badly."

The notebook had a scorched cover, obscuring old doodles of wana-smoking unicorns and demons rescuing cats from trees. It fell open in Jasper's hands. Vron's messy scrawl filled the pages, here with sprawling, frenetic energy, and there small and cramped and exhausted. Some pages were just lines and squiggles, abstract doodles, as if even shaping words and letters had become too much. The sight of Vron's writing popped something in Jasper's chest and it rushed up her throat, filled her sinuses, and made her eyes water.

Distracted, she almost didn't notice Crane lunge forward. She jerked back just in time as Crane grabbed at the notebook. Jasper pulled it away, bumping into Grace. "Hey!" Jasper cried.

Crane's knife touched her throat. Jasper held still, staring into her frozen swamp eyes. Jasper slowly reached up to place her fingers between Crane's blade and her throat.

"Crane? Talk to me. What's going on with you?"

Crane plucked the notebook from her hand, and this time Jasper didn't resist. "This is all I'm wanten, okay?" She lowered the knife and took several steps away, now holding the notebook.

"Vron's journal? That's what this is all about? *Why?*"

"Vron been knowen too much," Crane said. Her narrow shoulders had tensed up. "She not been understanden. I ain't been doen nothing wrong. Was a mistake."

Jasper took a step toward her. "What was a mistake, Craney? Vron wrote a lot of nonsense, a lot of stories. Did she write a story you didn't like? What happened?"

Crane took a wary step back and Jasper stopped. But Crane choosing to retreat when she had a knife in hand was encouraging. "She been thinken wrong thing," Crane spat. "Thinken I been doen something . . . but I didn't! It was an accident. But people will be believen her. Zenobia can't be finden out."

"What was an accident, Crane?" Jasper kept her voice as level as she could manage.

"I ain't been killen her," Crane mumbled, looking down at the notebook. "Didn't mean to."

Jasper's heart shuddered like a struck bell, too heavy and rusted to make a sound. *"Who?"*

Crane stood in the doorway, poised as if to flee, as taut and upset as Jasper had ever seen her. Her mouth worked but she didn't speak.

Grace stepped up to Jasper's side. "It was Martha Abebe. Wasn't it, Crane? That's who you think you killed. Your mother."

Crane flinched. "No. No, no, no. I never been killen her. It wasn't me. I wasn't meanen to. *Don't be tellen Zenobia.*"

Martha and her mysterious death.

Jasper pressed a hand to her chest and forced herself to suck in a deep breath of air. Because of Martha's reclusiveness it had been months before she'd been found, decaying quietly in her bed. An infection or a sudden illness, maybe a heart attack, Ibtisam had concluded upon examining the body. Surely a knife wound would've been visible even after a few months of decomposition if that had been the cause of death.

"You been killen Auntie?" Grammar's voice turned Crane around to face him. "You been killen Nev's mama?"

"She been—she been talken and talken," Crane whispered.

"I been tellen her to shut up, but she wouldn't. She's *not* my mama. She's not my—not my—my *mama*."

Grammar's face darkened with fury. He lunged at Crane, who shrieked like a child. The scuffle lasted only a few seconds before Jasper dragged Grammar free. Her heart pounded with terror as she scanned him for knife wounds. He had one, a shallow slash across his cheekbone, but he was grinning savagely and holding Vron's notebook in his hand.

Jasper turned quickly to Crane, shoving Grammar behind her. But Crane was staring at him with dawning amazement.

"Baby Dalca! You're here! I'm thinken the Damaskers been taken you. I'm thinken I been failen. Zenobia would be so *mad*." She rubbed both hands—one still holding a knife—in a frenzy over her face and then grabbed at her hair and pulled as if she'd tear it out of her scalp. "I been *promisen* to protect you."

"You didn't fail," Jasper said. "You killed that Knowles ganger. You did your best to protect Grammar. And in the end Ryan and I got him away from the Damaskers, so no harm done."

Crane wasn't listening. Her eyes widened in horror as she took in Grammar's face, the blood dripping down his cheek from the cut. "Oh, no. That's breaken the rules. Look. We'll be even. Look." Before Jasper could react, Crane slashed her own cheekbone. "See, baby Dalca? We're even now, right? Don't be tellen your mama, okay?"

"Crane, that's *deep*. Fucking hell," Jasper said. Grace and Grammar were wide-eyed and alarmed, and Crane was unravelling in a way Jasper had never thought she'd see. She forced herself to take a deep breath. "Everything's fine now, right, Craney? Grammar's alive and he's okay. You've told us Martha's death was an accident and we believe you. None of us want to hurt you. You can put the knife away now."

Crane wavered, bumping against one side of the doorway and then the other as if her balance had been knocked off-kilter.

Blood painted her cheek and dripped onto her chest. She looked down at her knife as if confused at the sight. She dropped it. Then she turned and stumbled away.

As Crane approached the apartment door, Esther appeared, wincing as she navigated the debris-strewn ceilings of up-gee with tentative steps. She stopped short at the sight of Crane.

"Crane? You're alive! Oh, my goodness, your poor face!"

Crane lurched past her, out of the apartment and out of sight.

"Jasper, what's—?" Then Esther saw her sister. Her mouth and eyes opened wide. "Grace!"

A great deal of crying and hugging and thanking of God followed, and a spate of Low German.

Jasper tried to sop up the blood on Grammar's face with her bandanna. The cut was shallow but bled profusely. "You're not allowed to get any more bruises or cuts for at least the next eight years," she told him. "Not one. I forbid it. What did you *think* would happen if you run at Crane when she's holding a knife? You got a fucking death wish? *Jesus*, kid." Her voice was climbing into higher registers, so she clenched her jaw shut and pushed the cloth hard against his cheek while holding his head steady with the other hand.

A familiar blankness faded from his face, but no expression replaced it, just a shaky looseness, a wavering not unlike Crane's stumble out of the room. "She said she been killen Auntie, but that's not how . . . it wasn't like that."

"Martha didn't have any knife wounds or other violent injuries when they found her body," Jasper said. "So I'm not sure what Crane's talking about. Did you see Martha's body? What did you think happened?"

His gaze dropped to the notebook in his hands. He whispered, "She was there."

"You mean Crane? Alone? Not with Zenobia?" Why on earth

would Crane visit the mother she'd long disavowed? An errand for Zenobia? Was Zenobia perhaps trying to encourage a reconciliation?

"If Crane was there, she been leaven before we been getten home." He wouldn't look up. "But Vron was there."

"What?"

Words came out in a tumble. "It was a couple of days after I been showen Vron the gingerbread house and after I been goen home again. Nev and me been out foragen and when we been goen toward home, Vron been comen out of the house. She—she been acten weird. She been cryen and laughen too—but not good laughen. Laughen like everything's so bad, it's the only thing she can be doen. She been talken about how some things never be getten fixed no matter how hard you're tryen and fighten, that hearts can be breaken because too much—too much everything. She been sayen . . ." He took a deep breath and recited, *"This is what happens when the demons win."*

Jasper closed her eyes. *Oh, Vron.*

"Vron been tellen us not to go inside, but she ain't been sayen why. After she been goen, I been maken Nev wait outside and I been goen to look. Auntie was on the bed. Just sleepen, I'm thinken." He swallowed hard. "Not sleepen, though. I been checken her like she been teachen me, but no blood, no heartbeat, nothing. Just dead. Gone."

"She had a heart condition," Grace said. She and Esther had been listening. "Ibtisam told me."

Jasper looked at Grammar. "But you thought it was a curse."

"Vron been sayen it was demons. So I'm thinken . . . I been tellen Nev we're haven to run away quick, quick, before the demons are catchen us too. And then we been finden out that Vron's dead too a few days later, and we were just . . ." His shoulders shuddered.

"Afraid," Jasper said softly.

"But why does Crane think it's her fault Martha died?" Grace asked.

"I don't know why she would've been at Martha's in the first place," Jasper said slowly. "Maybe Zenobia sent her to check up on Grammar if Tom couldn't go for some reason. But if Martha was face to face with her daughter for the first time in years, she probably tried to reach out to her, talk to her, win her over. And of course Crane rejected her. Like Vron said, sometimes hearts just break. Martha tried and fought to get Crane back for years and finally her heart gave up. She had a heart attack and died in front of Crane. Crane didn't know what was happening but thought, not wrongly, that she was the reason."

"And she became consumed with guilt," Grace said, nodding as if that made sense. "She didn't want anyone to know."

"Guilt," Jasper repeated. Was that what she'd seen on Crane's face? After all these years was Crane discovering that cutting herself off from her parents hadn't severed anything at all? Everything she'd tried to push away had snapped back with the force of an elastic band, slamming into her with the weight of thirteen years' worth of denial.

"Let me look at that cut." Grace took the cloth from Jasper and tilted Grammar's head so she could see the cut in the waning evening light. "I don't think it needs stitches." She smiled at him. "I'm Grace, by the way. You must be Grammar. Vron wrote about you. She thought you were very brave."

"She did?" Grammar said faintly.

Jasper walked over to the window, the notebook cradled between her hands. Outside, above her head, the horizon reached for the sun. Long shadows stretched across the broken city, but so did light, lingering, gentle rays.

City of the broken and abandoned and lost. Crane was broken and lost and she'd abandoned her parents after what she perceived as their betrayal of her, their inability to protect her from Darius. That day her demons had won, and Martha had died to the sounds of her daughter's rejection.

And what of Vron? Vron had been born without psychic skin to protect her. She'd felt every ghost, every loss, every wound. She'd always been a breath away from drowning, a stumble away from falling, a straw away from breaking. She'd fought, but in the end her demons had won too.

Esther joined her at the window. Her tone was matter of fact. "We're not going to find enough rope to get down, are we?"

Jasper glanced over her shoulder to make sure Grace and Grammar weren't paying attention. "No. Not likely."

Esther's face stayed calm. "We'll think of something. Grammar caught two birds earlier. He's very talented with that slingshot."

"Then we won't starve. We have at least a few days to figure things out. For now, let's get a good night's sleep and see what the morning brings."

"And Crane?" Esther asked. "Is she going to be okay?"

Something had jarred loose in Crane and thrown her off balance, perhaps dangerously so. But Crane's fault lines were beginning to make some sense.

"I'll talk to her," Jasper said.

7

HATCHING A HEART

When you wake up alone in the awful, empty darkness and
someone wakes up and sits with you so that you're not
alone with the demons

~ Veronica Park (*Things I Will Miss/Reasons to Live*)

J asper followed the trail of blood and found Crane a level up, in the down-gee half of the building. She sat perched on a balcony railing, long legs dangling carelessly into open air. Blood still oozed sluggishly from the wound on her cheek. The entire front of her shirt was stained crimson so she resembled one of the sky zombies of Vron's stories.

"Hey," Jasper said from the door so as not to startle her. Crane didn't turn around. Jasper climbed onto the creaking, rusty railing beside her, enjoying the intoxicating lurch in her belly from the vastness of open air beneath her.

"So how did Martha die?"

"Never been touchen her," Crane said. "Just been talken. Just words. I'm not a witch. I ain't been cursen her. Can't be killen people with words, can you?"

"Ibtisam thought Martha had a heart attack. Zenobia won't punish you for that. She will if you hurt Grace, though."

Belatedly, the realization shot through Jasper that Zenobia might never again be in a position to enforce rules and consequences for Crane. Zenobia was hiding somewhere in the zones with only two loyal protectors left, being hunted by an army. If she was killed, what would Crane do?

Crane grunted and flapped a hand dismissively. "Dumb girl. Never was gonna be hurten her. She should've been given me the notebook after Damascus. Stupid."

Jasper thought back to Damascus, when she and Ryan had wrested Grammar from the clutches of the Damasker alpha, Vic, who had been forcing him to fight for his life every night. They'd run into Crane and Grace during their escape. Grace was looking for Grammar too, she said, and when Jasper demanded to know why, Grace pulled out Vron's notebook as explanation. And Crane reacted with shock at the sight of it. It must have been the first moment she realized something of Vron's had survived the fire.

"Is that why Grace never came back to Yorky?" Jasper asked. "You realized she had Vron's notebook, and so after you got out of Damascus, you tried to take it from her. She thought you were attacking her, so she ran into the zones?"

"She been tryen to fight me. She been pushen me into side-gee and runnen." Crane kicked moodily at the railing. "Just a stupid notebook."

"Why did you think Vron knew about Martha?" Jasper asked. "Was she there with you when Martha died?"

"Vron been comen in at the end and hearen what happened. I—I been runnen." Crane frowned as if in retrospect she couldn't fathom why she'd done something so ridiculous. "Only later I'm thinken about what'd be happenen if she's tellen Zenobia. Then—but then I been hearen Vron been killen herself." She scraped both hands through her mane of hair. "I'm thinken maybe she been writen something down about it. She always been writen."

Jasper sat up straight, stunned by a revelation. "Wait, *you* were the one who burned Vron's notebooks, not Merlot! Crane! This whole time you let Merlot think he did it?"

She struggled to contain her anger. All this time Merlot had believed he'd destroyed the only remaining receptacles of Vron's thoughts and dreams and fears and whimsy. He had blamed himself. If Jasper was being honest, she had blamed him too.

Crane wasn't listening to her anyway. "I'm not understanden. Why Martha just been fallen down because of talken? Why Vron been killen herself? Why . . . *why?*"

Jasper rubbed her face, at a loss. First Grammar, now Crane. What kind of answers did they expect she'd have? "I guess they never learned how to fold a crane," she said.

Crane stared at her, bruised brown eyes wide above her blood-coated cheek. "A crane. Would it've been helpen?"

Jasper shrugged, feeling drained and dark inside. "Does it help you?"

Crane blinked. Once, twice. Her gaze dropped to her empty, bloody hands. "Not always."

Jasper leaned slowly sideways until her shoulder nudged Crane's. Slowly, Crane leaned into Jasper's shoulder in return.

The scrape of a footfall turned them around. Grace entered the room cautiously, a small first aid kit in hand. "I should take a look at your cheek, Crane," she said.

"I can do it. I've stitched up cuts before," Jasper said. "You're in rough shape too, Grace. You can help your sister find a place to set up camp."

Grace didn't retreat. "I've probably stitched up more people than you have. I've been tagging along with Ibtisam for almost six months now."

"Fine. I won't leave the room, but I promise Crane will behave." Jasper raised her eyebrows at Crane, who made a face but said nothing.

"I can handle Crane," Grace said.

Crane scoffed. "Brave talken. You're not carryen a single knife."

"Why would I need one?" Grace pointed at the floor in front of her. "Sit."

Stony-faced, Crane dragged herself off the balcony and plopped down on the mossy carpet. Grace kneeled in front of her and opened the first aid kit. Despite her attempt at poise, her hands shook as she threaded a needle.

Jasper prowled the room. She stepped onto an armchair and from there launched herself at a tall china cabinet that looked like it had tumbled around the room and then—improbably— landed upright again. She drew herself to the top and settled in to sit cross-legged with her head brushing the ceiling.

Grace pushed the needle into Crane's cheek for the first stitch. Crane hissed and Grace glared. "You did this to yourself, remember. Hold still."

"Wasn't ready," Crane said.

"Well, I wasn't ready for you to grab me and throw me against a wall the moment you saw me either," Grace said.

Crane's eyes flared with anger. "You been pushen me into side-gee outside Damascus."

"I panicked. You were—"

Crane raised an eyebrow. "Talken about kissen?"

Grace's face grew redder. "Trying to take the notebook from me!"

"Shoulda just been given it, then."

"You tried to burn it when I did!" Grace cried. "Anyway, you can't threaten me into giving you something that's not yours. That's not how this works. You were telling me once about how Zenobia gives you rules. Well, this is my rule, my boundary."

On her lofty perch Jasper rested her chin on her hands and wished for popcorn.

"I'm not wanten you to read what Vron been writen about me." Crane's voice seemed smaller.

"The only thing she wrote was how sad she was that you lost your mama like that, before you had a chance to reconcile with her." Grace focused on the needle as she drew it gently through Crane's flesh. Her gaze flicked up into Crane's eyes. "Your mama would've forgiven you, you know, for whatever you said to her. She would've still loved you. It's not your fault she died."

Crane jerked convulsively. "Don't . . . don't wanna be talken about her."

"Okay." Grace drew through another stitch and took a shaky breath. "Then let me ask your forgiveness. I shouldn't have pushed you into side-gee. I was upset and I overreacted and you could've been badly hurt. Part of the reason I ran was because I was ashamed."

"Why sorry?" Crane said after a moment. "I been breaken the rules. I been putten my hands on you, tryen to take the notebook. That's when you should've been usen a knife. Dumb girl. Why're you not carryen a knife?"

"You carry half a dozen but you've never drawn one on me," Grace said. "If you wanted the notebook so bad, you could've held a knife to my throat anytime you wanted. But you didn't. Even now in up-gee, when you saw me the first time, you could've taken the notebook, but then you just let me go and left. So what was that about?"

Crane was silent for the space of three stitches. She hovered a fingertip over Grace's swollen eye, then traced the air over the bruises on Grace's throat. "Because of your face."

Grace grew still. Then her hands started to shake, and Crane caught the needle as it fell from Grace's fingers. Grace clenched her hands together in her lap, her breathing fast and uneven. "It's fine, I'm fine," she whispered, her words jerky. "I got—I got away from them. It looks worse than it is. I'm—I'm—" She pressed both hands to her chest as if she could force air into her lungs. "How—how do *you* act like you're fine when I know you're not? They—your face—when I saw you, I . . ." She stopped talking and focused on breathing, in and out, slow and careful.

Crane patted cautious fingers over her sewn-up cut, then reached for the scissors and snipped off the thread. After setting the bloody needle carefully beside Grace, she wiped her fingers on her already blood-streaked jeans and reached into her thigh pouch. She was slower than usual because her knuckles were raw and bruised—she hadn't made her execution easy on the Knowles gangers—but a minute later she extended a hand to Grace. Sitting on her palm was a bloodstained paper crane.

"Don't worry, I'll be killen them," Crane promised.

Her knuckles still digging into her breastbone, Grace stared at the origami bird.

Crane smiled, deadly and shining, and leaned forward. "Well? You gonna be tellen me no, Crane, don't do it? Good little pink cheek girl. Church girl, God girl. Forgiveness and love girl. You gonna try to be stoppen me?"

Grace took the bird from Crane's hand and cupped it between her own. When she spoke, it was in ragged bursts to keep her teeth from chattering. "No, I won't stop you. Not for my sake, but because *they hurt you too.* And I want them to go to hell for it."

Crane rocked back with a hum of surprise and approval. "Not so good girl."

"Everyone is *so* sure they know who or what I am," Grace

muttered to the paper crane in her hands. She inhaled deeply, raggedly, and set it down. She placed a hand along Crane's jaw and dabbed at the blood on her cheek with a dampened cloth. "They don't know me any more than they know you."

"Be tellen me not to kill them and I won't," Crane said. "Or be tellen me to make them bleed and I will. Just be tellen me what you're wanten."

"I'm not going to tell you what to do," Grace said. "You think you're so broken, you can't be trusted to make your own choices, but you're wrong. Being that worried about making the wrong choice already makes you a better person than most people."

Crane sat so still, she didn't seem to be breathing.

Jasper found herself pressing her clasped hands hard to her mouth.

"You're . . . thinken so?" Crane's voice didn't sound like her at all.

"I know so. So I won't tell you what to do." Grace leaned forward so their noses almost touched. "But can I tell you what I want?"

Crane's eyes widened. She gave a faint nod.

With her eyes boring into Crane's, Grace pointed at the cut on Crane's cheek. "I want you to never hurt yourself like this again. *Ever.* Do you understand me?"

There was a long pause. Crane blinked once. "Yes."

Grace continued glaring. "So are you going to cut yourself again?"

"No."

"You promise?"

"Yes."

Grace sat back. Her hands still shook as she rummaged through the first aid kit, but her breathing had steadied. "If you're sorry about cutting Grammar, you should tell him. Hurting yourself isn't a substitute for an apology."

Crane made a face. "Apologizen is dumb. Just words. Words are meanen nothing."

"My mama taught me that when you hurt someone it's important to face what you've done and acknowledge their pain." Grace began taping a bandage over the stitched cut. "For example," she said, and her voice sounded suddenly breathless, "when you asked me if I liked you, I said no. That hurt your feelings. I'm sorry."

Atop the china cabinet, Jasper leaned forward to a precarious degree to hear Grace's quiet words.

Crane fidgeted. "Wasn't hurten me," she muttered. "Just words. Better truth than lies."

"That's the problem," Grace said. "I lied."

Jasper fell off the china cabinet.

This, unfortunately, ruined the mood.

"Pretend I'm not here," she urged in a loud whisper as she rolled hastily to her feet. "Don't mind me. Please continue what you were saying." She tiptoed over to the couch while the girls stared at her. "Keep going. Carry on."

But Grace's face had turned bright red, and she fixed her eyes firmly on her hands as she sloppily, distractedly repacked the first aid kit. Crane seemed to have decided that Jasper was the safest thing in the room to glare at. Or possibly she was planning how to peel Jasper's face from her skull, and honestly, that was fair.

Neither girl was likely to forget again that Jasper was in the room. So she gave up on trying to blend into the sofa while subtly rubbing her new set of bruises and sat up. "So Grace, what did you find in Vron's notebook to send you running around in the zones by yourself?"

"Vron was investigating stories of children disappearing, and not to raids," Grace said, looking relieved to change the subject.

"Grammar mentioned that. Was it the Gingers she was looking for?"

Grace looked confused, and Jasper summarized her and Merlot's encounter with the cannibals, the cages in the basement and their collection of adult- and child-sized bones.

"Gingerbread house," Grace exclaimed. Dawning understanding battled with revulsion and horror on her face. "She wrote about the gingerbread house and the witches who ate kids. I didn't realize . . . but it was so hard to tell when Vron was writing a story or the truth."

All of Vron's stories told the truth, but you had to stand at precisely the correct angle to see it.

Grace bent close to make sure the bandage was taped securely to Crane's face. Crane held very still. Satisfied, Grace looked back at Jasper. "She referred to Knowles more than once. She thought they knew about what was happening and weren't stopping it, might even have been participating somehow. That's why I thought she went to Knowles, to investigate what their role was. But she was also talking about hiding something. Her writing got so disjointed I could hardly make sense of it. Whatever she found, it really upset her."

Vron had found out that the children were being captured and eaten or captured and traded, had found whatever unpleasant truth Catherine Pine had stolen from Zenobia, had watched Martha die in front of her daughter, unreconciled. It must have seemed that everywhere the demons were winning.

"So off you gallivanted," Jasper said. "You didn't ask Merlot for help or me or Ben or Quick Rick. Instead you went to Dragon, you went to Damascus, you ran off into the fucking zones by yourself. What in the name of gravity *possessed* you—?"

"Stop yellen at her," Crane said, scowling.

"Yelling? My tone is downright calm and reasonable

compared to what Merlot will have to say the next time he sees you."

"I'm not a child—" Grace began.

"Don't make me laugh!"

"You moved in with Merlot when you were my age," Grace pointed out.

Grammar poked his head into the room, saving Jasper from having to think of a clever response. "Food's ready. Esther's sayen we can't be eaten till everyone's there." He sounded aggrieved. "So be hurryen up."

Grace picked up the paper bird Crane had made and started to put it in her pocket.

"That's not for keepen," Crane said. She plucked it from Grace's hand. "These ones you're throwen away. Like this." She tossed it over the balcony railing.

Grace gave a cry of dismay and ran to the railing. "Why did you do that? I wanted to keep it."

"Why?" Crane looked perplexed. "It's all ugly and crumpled and bloody. I can be maken you a better one."

"I wanted *that* one." Grace peered into the open sky below the railing. "You made it for me and I liked it." She climbed over the railing.

"What are you—?" Crane jerked forward a step.

Grace plunged into the sky.

Crane stood as if frozen, mouth agape. Slowly, she swung around to stare at Jasper. "She's crazy," she said in amazement.

"Look who's talking," Jasper said.

Crane watched Grace bobbing between up-gee and down-gee, flailing and wiggling her way toward a tiny floating scrap of paper. "I'm feelen funny, Piney. Like I'm swallowen a bubble."

Jasper folded her arms over her chest. She was done handing out answers to life's questions. "Take a wild guess what it means."

"I'm sick and I'm gonna die?"

"Try again."

"I accidentally been eaten a balloon."

"I think you'd notice."

"Maybe my heart is hatchen?"

"That . . . is a terrifying but surprisingly accurate image. Yes, you got it, Craney. Your heart is hatching."

"It's not hurten," Crane said in a tone of surprise.

She grinned and vaulted over the railing with a wild whoop.

Jasper rested her cheek on her palm, feeling as if the world had shifted a slight but dizzying degree. Ryan had asked what her wishes were, but every time she turned around, her wishes multiplied like dragonflies, like an ocean of paper cranes rising in snowy drifts to swamp the zones.

Let me live long enough to see what these two crazy kids can build together. I mean, they'll probably crash and burn, but it'd be a hell of a thing to see all the same.

The wish goblins trailing in her shadow must be getting fat.

Between the two of you, Darius mused, *I wouldn't have bet on her.*

"Shows how much you know, doesn't it?" Jasper said aloud.

But until recently she wouldn't have bet on Crane either, and that was a shame she'd carry to her grave.

Jasper had been prepared to go to bed hungry if she couldn't keep any seagull meat down, but she was surprised and touched to find that Esther had spent some time foraging for the plants that grew in the cracks and corners of the floating up-gee town. As long as she aggressively kept her mind on something else, she was able to force down a few bites of meat, but a handful of dandelion greens helped fill the gaps. Two birds didn't stretch far anyway when split among five people, one of whom was a ravenous, growing boy. Grammar didn't complain. He assured them he'd catch more birds tomorrow. Crane sniffed and said she bet she could catch a lot more than him. Esther caught Jasper's glance and Jasper rolled her eyes. No doubt by tomorrow's dinner they'd be knee-deep in dead birds.

As everyone scattered to gather up usable blankets and find mattresses to sleep on, Grace pulled Jasper aside. "I wasn't in up-gee long enough to explore a lot before Crane fell here. But I did see something you might also be interested in."

Crane was demanding Grammar practise some knife-fighting skills before bed. He complained that he was tired and appealed to Jasper.

"Don't look at me," Jasper said. "I'm not your bodyguard. If I were you, I'd listen to her."

Sullen, Grammar muttered that he'd never asked for a bodyguard.

"Well, I think it's been proven you need one," Jasper said. She switched her frown to Crane. "Blunt, padded, or fake knives only, Crane. I mean it."

Jasper told Esther they were going for a quick scout before bed, and then she and Grace slipped away before Crane or Grammar could notice and clamour to accompany them. Jasper used the makeshift grappling hook to throw a rope to the next floating chunk of brick and drywall and rebar. She anchored the rope until Grace reached the hook. Then Jasper pulled herself along the rope through the empty ocean of air between them to join Grace. In this way they zigzagged their way from one chunk of debris to another until they were out of sight of the apartment building where they'd set up camp.

"So," Jasper said when they stopped to catch their breath and evaluate their route, "you and Crane, huh?"

Grace's cheeks reddened but she steadfastly kept her eyes on the horizon. She pointed. "I think it's that way."

"When Crane asked if you liked her, she wasn't talking about friendship, I hope you know."

"Jasper!" Grace covered her face in embarrassment. "I grew up religious, not stupid. Remember the part about me apprenticing with Ibtisam? Ibtisam, a woman, who's married to Sparrow, also a woman? You're still thinking of me like I'm a little girl, but I'm not. I know exactly what Crane meant."

"Oh," said Jasper. "Huh. Wow. Well . . . good. Okay. Just making sure." She rubbed a hand vigorously through her hair so it stood on end. "So does Esther know . . .?"

"No!" Grace said violently. "Not Merlot either. Please don't— I don't want to talk about this. Not yet. I don't even know what I —it's just a lot and I'm not ready to . . . please, Jasper?"

Jasper sighed. Add another wish to the goblins' menu. Impulsively, she ran her hand through Grace's cropped blond locks, ignoring Grace's sound of annoyance. "Merlot's got eyes and Crane's not the most subtle or secret-keeping type, so good luck with that. That being said, I'm a vault, kiddo. I won't say anything."

Dusk was slowly soaking the sky in soft shadows.

"Maybe we should wait till tomorrow," Jasper said. "Light's going."

"I brought a flint striker."

They found a broken wood spar, wrapped the end in some old bedsheets, and lit it.

"It's near here somewhere." Grace lifted the makeshift torch to study their surroundings.

They were standing on a fragment that was little more than a bathtub-sized tile floor with a bit of attached wall. They were surrounded by similar fragments of varying sizes and shapes, close enough that they could leap from piece to piece, though they had to be careful that pushing off one piece didn't send it spinning away too far before the other person could also jump.

Jasper looked around, and her heart gave a heavy thump. "Is that what you mean?"

Grace lifted the torch and the feeble flames illuminated the whitewashed wall of the next fragment. Somebody had nailed splintered bits of wood to the wall to form the crude shape of a fish.

"I thought maybe it was the symbol for Christianity," Grace said. "One of the women thrown up here, rejecting the label of witch or something. But then I saw—"

"The arrow," Jasper said. Beneath the fish were three wood pieces in the shape of an arrow. They both looked to the right in the direction it was pointing. "These pieces of debris are small enough to move around in the wind," Jasper said. "Might not be accurate anymore."

"No, I saw—there." Grace pointed until, even in the murk, Jasper could just make out another arrow several debris chunks away. "That's when Crane fell into up-gee, but I didn't know it was her at first. I thought it was a Knowles ganger coming to finish me off, so I hid."

They made their way over to the next arrow, but as much as they peered around in the dark, they could see nothing else in the direction it was pointing.

"Maybe it's not pointing to the next chunk," Grace said at last. "Maybe it's pointing to the doorway."

Their current chunk was big enough to contain several rooms. They entered the nearest door that the arrow might have been indicating. It had once been a restaurant. Smashed fragments of dishes and cutlery lay scattered in corners and under overturned tables, and bird droppings covered the counters. A decorative houseplant had grown out of its pot and with great persistence had spread across the floor and was busily taking over one wall of the restaurant and climbing out of the window. It was also tangled up in a clump of bones on the floor.

One wall was a giant chalkboard where menu items had

once been written. Something else was written there now instead.

Rooted in the sky, a magic beanstalk,
So high even Jack would balk.
But to answer the earth's call
A fish can only fall.

"Vron," Jasper muttered. The wooden fish nailed to the wall. *Wish a fish into the sky.* Vron had been right about falling through the witch door (*Which door? Yes.*) and not dying in the process. As was often the case, her madness held meaning.

"That's Vron's handwriting." Grace sounded stunned.

"As usual, never saying anything straight." Jasper looked around the dim interior of the restaurant. Had Vron somehow ended up here after Grammar had shown her where to find Catherine Pine's body? Whatever papers she'd taken from the car, had she hidden them here?

She became aware of Grace staring at her. "What?"

"Vron wrote that. She was here."

"Yeah, so?"

Grace hesitated as if not sure whether Jasper was astonishingly slow or screwing with her. "Vron died in her own home."

Jasper started to repeat, "Yeah, so?" But then the obvious truth crashed down on her.

"Vron fell or was thrown into this up-gee zone," Grace said. "But somehow *she found a way down again.*"

8

THE BEANSTALK

Freckles are fairies dancing in mirth.
Their feet muddy although they can fly,
For every living thing must touch the earth,
Even creatures of the sky.

~ Veronica Park

M orning light illuminated the room but not the riddle.

"Why couldn't she just say what she meant?" Esther said in frustration.

"Because then the tinylings would be hearen and knowen too much," Crane said.

"Because words can be magic," Grammar said. "Especially the Storytalker's words. She been haven to be careful."

Esther looked at Jasper as if to say, *Please give me a less heathen answer.*

Jasper shrugged. "Vron was always a little afraid of the words that came out of her head. Poetry and riddles were a way to either reduce their power or the opposite—to make sure the power wasn't diluted."

"She came back to Yorky after being up here," Esther said. "Why wouldn't she tell anyone? I've never heard of someone escaping an up-gee zone this high. How could she keep that kind of a story to herself and not tell even Merlot?"

Because her head had been full of demons, and her sky full of darkness.

"The point is, there's a way down and this is a clue," Grace said positively. "Beanstalk. Not a literal one, obviously, but maybe she means like a rope or something."

"If there was a rope somewhere dangling all the way to the ground, I think we'd have seen it," Esther said.

"She wouldn't just leave it there for anyone to see," said Grace.

"Tinylings would be chewen through it," Crane agreed.

Grace ignored this comment. "Maybe the rope is hidden in this room."

No one had any better ideas to offer, so they spread out and searched, pawing through cupboards and closets, the defunct walk-in freezer, and even inside ovens and microwaves. While Grace, Crane, and Grammar banged and clattered around in the back kitchen, Jasper joined Esther in the main room. Esther fingered the leaves of the sprawling potted houseplant.

"She must have gotten the idea of the beanstalk from this plant," Esther said. "It looks about ready to grow all the way to the ground if it has to. And you could say it's 'rooted in the sky.'"

Jasper followed the plant to its origin point, the cracked pot that had fallen during the building's violent uprooting. Beside the pot lay the remains of a body, just bones and papery skin and rotting cloth, a cap of soft silver hair. The plant's roots were intertwined through the bones, as it had taken its nourishment where it could, even from a decomposing corpse. Jasper crossed herself and murmured Vron's ghost-away spell.

The body's shirt had been unbuttoned and the chest bloodlessly sliced open. Likely, birds had fed on it in the months following the Shattering. Except the cut was too even to have been the work of a bird. It had been caused by a knife, not a beak. Jasper looked closer. There was something in the chest cavity, within the rib cage, and it wasn't the shrivelled remains of a human heart.

"What are you doing?" Esther asked as Jasper reached into the body's chest cavity. "What is that? Was that inside the body?"

Jasper held in her hands a sheaf of documents and photographs encased in a zip-lock plastic bag placed within a second zip-lock plastic bag for added protection.

Her mother's secret.

Which Vron had hidden in the chest of a corpse.

"That's what Vron found," Esther said when Jasper said nothing. "That's what your mother took from the Tower. Right?"

Jasper left the room and sat outside at the edge of the chunk, her legs dangling over the jaggedly torn floor between spears of exposed rebar. Esther approached the edge more gingerly and sat beside her. Clouds stretched across the sky above them like cotton batting. Below them the city seemed small and vulnerable, a town built of a child's blocks, carelessly scattered and abandoned for a more interesting toy. The quarantine wall was visible in the distance and beyond that the mysterious realm of downieland.

From the restaurant kitchen Jasper could hear Crane and Grace arguing—Crane trying to give Grace one of her knives to protect herself with and Grace insisting her penknife was sufficient for her needs.

After a while Esther took the package out of Jasper's hands and opened it. Together they paged through the photographs, faded from their time in the glove compartment of Catherine Pine's car but still clear. What the photographs didn't say for themselves was described tersely, clinically in the documents. They were the log notes of a scientist, similar in style to the ones the Guardian had given Jasper, the ones that described the ape Mick, subject 3B. Some were printed out from a computer, others handwritten and photocopied. They were initialled Z.A.—Zenobia Allan.

"Why would Vron hide this?" Esther asked quietly when they had read enough and the silence had stretched too long.

"Maybe she had an idea of what I'd do if I found out," Jasper said. The words had a rusted iron feel in her mouth.

"What are you going to do?"

Jasper didn't answer. Tectonic plates were shifting inside her and lava was bubbling to the surface. She took the package of papers and hurled them into open air. They fluttered like autumn leaves, catching on cracks and crevices of surrounding debris or drifting to float on the zone border or blowing out of sight altogether.

"Jasper!" Esther exclaimed. "Those are—they're important. Why would you . . .?" She gave up on eliciting an appropriate reaction from Jasper. Esther left and came back with the coil of rope they'd been using to pull themselves around the up-gee zone. She tied one end to the rebar that stuck out of the building fragment and the other end to her own harness.

Jasper made no move to help.

Esther took several deep breaths before finally climbing over the edge and letting herself fall the few metres through the zone border. She cried out as the two zones bounced her between them like a Ping-Pong ball, but upon achieving stasis at the border she pulled herself together. She began wriggle-swimming through the air from debris patch to debris patch, gathering up all the papers she could. For some she had to swim far out from the debris field into open air.

Just leave them, Jasper wanted to shout to her. The information they held was already seared into her mind, and she'd never be rid of the knowledge for the short time she had left to live.

"What's she doen?" Grammar asked, coming out to join her. He had his slingshot in hand and was more concerned with following the flight paths of nearby birds than with Jasper's answer or lack of one.

Then Esther fell. Like she'd stepped off the edge of a cliff.

One moment she was wriggling briskly along the flat plane of the invisible zone border, reaching for an errant photograph drifting just beyond her fingers. The next she was plummeting downward toward the earth.

The rope cut her fall short before she could even scream, before Jasper could do more than sit up and open her mouth. The abruptness of the stop jerked Esther back into up-gee. She fell back toward the zone border where she once again yo-yoed into stasis.

She sobbed in shock, somehow still clinging to all the papers she'd managed to gather. Jasper came to her senses and scrambled for the rope to reel her in. Grammar helped her pull Esther to safety.

Hearing the commotion, Grace and Crane came running. Grace examined a shaking and hyperventilating Esther for any injuries. Grammar relieved Esther of the papers still clutched in her white-knuckled fist and started to glance through them. Jasper snatched them out of his hand before he could protest. She rolled them up, stuffed them into the double zip-lock bags, and shoved them into her thigh pouch.

Grammar frowned at her and then looked out at the sky beyond. "What's been happenen?"

Jasper paced the length of their sky-wrecked restaurant to its farthest tip. She pinpointed with her gaze the patch of sky where Esther had fallen. It couldn't be the edge of the up-gee zone; she could see more debris floating beyond it. She picked up a piece of broken floor tile and hurled it. Wherever the drop-off had been, she missed it. The tile piece behaved normally, arcing downward through the border into up-gee, then yo-yoing to a halt at the zone border. She kept throwing things, varying distance and arc, until finally a chipped coffee mug fell downward . . . and kept falling toward the earth, through what should have been up-gee, down, down and out of sight.

"It's fallen funny," Grammar observed.

Jasper had noticed that too. The mug stuttered and hopped every few metres on its way down.

She took the rope Esther had used and attached it to her own harness. The other end she left tied to the rebar, but she handed the slack to Crane to monitor. She plunged into open air and swam cautiously through the fuzzy tingling of the zone border toward the unmarked patch of sky, pushing off from every piece of debris along the way large enough to absorb her momentum. Without momentum it was awkward to manoeuvre in open air. Swimming was the closest analogy, but air was too light to push against, to displace. But momentum made it harder to stop. When she felt the warning crackle of an additional zone border approaching, she slowed her progress by seizing the rope and dragging herself backwards hand over hand.

With a grip on the taut rope, she edged forward again. She had stuffed a pouch with fist-sized bits of rubble. When the tingle of two zone borders lifted the hair on her arms, she stopped and tossed a small chunk of drywall. She followed it with her eyes as it fell downward. A puff of dirt arose when it impacted the ground.

Esther had stumbled on a pocket down-gee zone that

extended all the way to the ground, but it was no ordinary zone. Jasper explored the edges of it a little farther and then pulled herself back along the rope.

"It's the beanstalk," she said as Crane and Grammar dragged her up over the edge of the floor. "We've found it."

"What do you mean?" Esther asked. Her shaking had subsided, but she still gave an occasional convulsive shiver. "It's down-gee and high enough to fall to our deaths. How does that help us?"

"Things are fallen slowly," Grammar said. "Maybe it's not only down-gee."

"What does that mean?" Esther demanded irritably when both Jasper and Crane nodded. "Imagine I'm not a grav-walker for a moment."

"We see this sometimes, a coincidental arrangement of zones with alternate draws," Jasper said. "I've never seen one this long, though. Imagine a stack of down-gee zones shaped like a chute or a drinking straw but interspersed with enough slivers of up-gee to slow your momentum as you fall."

Esther took a moment to absorb that. Despite her rosy sunburn, her fair skin seemed to grow several shades paler. "You're saying—you're suggesting we jump in that chute and *fall to the ground*? How do you know the up-gee bits will slow us enough to keep us from breaking our bones or dying?"

"Because Vron survived it," Jasper said simply. "She didn't have any broken bones when you last saw her, did she, Grammar? Or Crane?"

They shook their heads.

"*'A fish can only fall,'*" Jasper said. "Vron mentioned that too in the message she left on my mother's car, that you can't climb the beanstalk. You can only fall."

Silence fell as everyone stared at the innocent sky and down at the earth so dizzyingly far below them. Grace muttered a few words under her breath that sounded more profane than one usually heard from a Mennonite.

"Why are we waiten, then?" Crane said. "Let's go. Me first."

"I'll go last," Jasper said. "When you reach the ground, move out of the way, but be careful because we don't know whether the down-gee zone expands on the ground or if it remains narrow like the chute."

Esther stared at her in fresh horror. "You mean we could be on the ground but trapped in a space the size of a dining room table and still surrounded by up-gee? How is that an improvement?"

"We'll figure it out. Vron did," Jasper reminded her.

Esther looked less than reassured, but Crane saw no reason to linger and jumped into the air with a whoop. She didn't bother with the rope. She swam and pushed off of chunks of debris to gain momentum. The fall into the beanstalk came without warning, and she plummeted in a flurry of flailing limbs.

Grace cried out, then brought her hands to her mouth.

Jasper held her breath through the eternal seconds. Crane seemed to be falling so fast . . . Down, down, growing tinier and tinier. And then the impact. Was that a tumble or a controlled roll? Why wasn't she moving?

"She's on her feet," Grace exclaimed.

Everyone let out relieved sighs.

"Me next," said Grammar.

Jasper grabbed him before he could jump off like Crane had and handed him the end of the rope so he could attach it to the last chunk of debris before the beanstalk. Despite Crane's successful landing, watching him fall was painful and terrifying, but at least it was over quickly.

Esther's breathing had grown erratic and fast, and she backed away from the edge. Grace had little more colour in her face than Esther, but she took her sister's arm encouragingly. "Just think how good it will be to have ground under your feet again," she said.

Esther was muttering a psalm under her breath the way Vron had muttered charms. "Yea, though I walk through the valley of the shadow of death . . ."

Grace waited patiently and then said "Amen" at the end before urging her sister to lower herself into open air. With the guidance of the rope, they reached the last bit of debris. After a moment's debate, Esther went first, tipping over the zone border with a shrill scream. Grace waited until she was on the ground and then followed.

Jasper was alone now in up-gee. She stepped into the restaurant one last time to read Vron's writing on the wall. Dust motes danced in slanting shafts of sunlight. A breeze stirred the leaves of that indomitable houseplant. It had refused to give up, had used every bit of nourishment available, even a corpse, to fight its way into the light.

The weight of the papers in her thigh pouch pulled her off balance, but Vron's notebook in the opposite pouch countered its weight.

Vron hadn't wanted her to find those documents. She'd hidden them in the most unlikely and inaccessible place in the zones. Yet she hadn't destroyed them. She'd left clues so they could be found. Like she'd wanted to protect Jasper from the truth but had known the truth would be needed eventually.

To all the demons Vron had been fighting, the weight of this secret was added.

Jasper touched a fingertip on the chalk-scrawled poem. Vron couldn't have known she'd survive the beanstalk, but she'd had no other choice. She'd jumped knowing she might die. Maybe half hoping she would.

Jasper knew what that felt like.

The beanstalk turned out to be a glorious rush of adrenalin, despite the slower rate of falling. She had time to watch the gaping foundations and whittled-down nubs of buildings rush up at her.

Jasper landed with a jarring thump. She rolled to absorb the impact, ending up against Crane's legs, and laughed out loud.

"Call me crazy, but I'd consider jumping back into up-gee just to take that ride again."

"You're crazy," Esther agreed.

Jasper got up and dusted herself off. The down-gee zone formed a narrow vertical shaft, like a ray of sun that had broken out from the clouds and illuminated a perfect circle of light on the ground. If they stepped outside that circle, they'd be back in up-gee and falling upward again. They needed to cross up-gee while somehow keeping themselves attached to the ground.

"How are you guys for upper body strength?" Jasper asked.

"I've carried some heavy buckets of milk in my time," Esther said. "But I have the feeling I'm not going to like what you're going to suggest."

"Imagine monkey bars on a playground," Jasper said. "We're going to be swinging across the longest monkey bars you've ever seen. Except the bars are the earth itself, and if you fall, you're back in the sky."

Esther gave her a long, level look. "See, this is why we're not friends, Jasper."

Jasper laughed. "And that joke is why, in fact, we possibly are."

"Wasn't really joking," Esther said under her breath.

"Don't worry, I'll go first, freehand, and secure the rope, which will make it easier for the rest of you."

"How far do we have to climb upside down?" Grace asked apprehensively.

Jasper looked around but couldn't see any border indicating

down-gee. Her heart sank. This would be a gruelling climb even for an experienced grav-walker who'd had more than a few stringy mouthfuls of gull meat that day. "As far as we have to, I guess."

"Why not just be taken the tunnel?" Grammar pointed.

Sure enough, half a dozen metres away, a set of concrete steps led underground and a weathered sign proclaimed it an entrance to a subway station.

"Oh, I like that idea much better," Esther said with relief.

Jasper grimaced. "I expect I'll be outvoted, so fine. Tunnel it is."

Crane's silence and rigidity finally caught Jasper's attention. Crane was staring at the sky. "Bad magic," she whispered.

Everyone followed her gaze.

A dark figure soared across the sky high above them. A black meteor, a streak of shadow too large to be a bird, and wingless. A ragged flutter left over from the night, imbued with purpose and velocity. Human sized, human shaped, it flew horizontally through the air as no human could, indifferent to the orientation of the zones it passed through.

"What in heaven's name . . .?" Esther said faintly.

"Not heaven," Grammar said with dread in his voice. "That's a witch. The Up-gee Witch."

9

VILLAGE OF THE HORSES

If the earth is a woman, then God is a gardener,
Tearing away the ivy and running her fingers through the
*   naked soil.*
June is a lover's sigh, and roses are a slow explosion
Blooming glorious over weeks, even months.
Get a room, you two.

~ Veronica Park

The ReGeneration lived in a down-gee zone with broad open spaces rimmed by a cathedral of green trees. It had once been a park at the heart of the city. The open spaces were reserved for the horses. The people lived around the edges of down-gee, and their homes spilled into the foam zones.

Emerging from the tunnels felt like being born. Jasper sucked in air filled with the smell of grass and woodsmoke and horses. She was never setting foot underground again, ever.

ReGeneration citizens, noticing their arrival, paused and

murmured to each other, displaying reserve but also interest. Children who had been kicking a ball around stopped their game and stared. Noticing the scrutiny, Grammar stopped gaping at their new surroundings and shifted his stance into a mix of wariness and challenge.

"Do not start a fight," Jasper said in his ear.

He evaluated the ReGeneration children with a professional eye. "They're not knowen how to fight, not for real. Never been hungry, I think."

His assessment was probably correct, but in response to the Damaskers, the ReGeneration trained its youth for war as well as agriculture and hunting. In the distance she could see several young men and women sparring half-naked in marked circles in the dirt.

"Would you look at those houses!" Grace exclaimed.

Foam zones were small and tightly packed like dishwater foam, a chaotic honeycomb of conflicting draws. A house in the foam zones might be subjected to the strain of gravity pulling in a dozen different directions. Since the Shattering, every structure trapped in the foam had crumbled under this stress.

The ReGeneration had built into the foam despite the instability and danger. They'd driven long poles deeply and securely into the earth to provide a framework. Rope and canvas tunnels connected the poles and led to tiny huts, each no larger than Jasper's bedroom, each residing in one small zone.

Jasper watched in amazement as a boy entered a rope and canvas bridge from down-gee. The walkway was four-sided, a fabric tunnel. He started on the "floor" of the bridge. A bulge in the ropes warned of a zone change. He neatly stepped sideways onto the wall of the bridge, crossing into side-gee, and continued walking, this time along the "wall." The bridge passed through several zones, but because it had four sides, he merely had to switch from wall to ceiling to floor as the zone required, his progress unhindered.

"That is genius!" Jasper exclaimed. She'd take these bridges over underground tunnels any day.

"Jas!"

Jasper barely had time to look up before Ben barrelled into her and wrapped her up in a hug. "Oh my God, they told us you fell into up-gee," he said, his voice muffled in her shoulder.

"I can't breathe."

He let her go and scowled to make up for the effusiveness of the hug. "You stink. Did you manage to find a mud puddle in up-gee or something?"

She scanned him pointedly in return. "Did *you* manage to find a comb?"

He flushed. "Charlie had an extra one."

"Of course he did. Is it for his beard?"

Quick Rick was next to give her a hug and exclaim he was worried and ask was she injured and what on earth had happened to them. And then he was off to hug the others before she could answer his questions.

Merlot's relief at seeing Grace safely in one piece turned into a lecture on the foolishness of running off into the zones with no equipment or guidance. He steamrolled Grace's attempts to defend herself. Esther nodded along sternly with Merlot's scolding. Charlie, unable to hear, positioned himself between Esther and Grace so he could read Merlot's ASL. He looked immensely entertained. Possibly because Crane was pulling faces behind Merlot's back. Grace bit her lip and struggled to look penitent.

Meanwhile, Grammar and Okuru rolled around in the dirt in a noisy wrestling match.

"Zeep!" Ryan ran up to her, his whole face alight with relief. Jasper turned to meet him, but he didn't hug her like she thought he might. Perhaps Ben's glower stopped him. "We heard you fell into up-gee."

"I never fall," Jasper said. "I just take unplanned jumps." She noticed his knuckles were bruised and cut. "Who did you hit?"

"Dragon," he said with satisfaction.

"Nearly pasted him into the dirt before Truthbringer's gangers pulled him off," Ben said with a note of grudging appreciation.

"I was a little upset," Ryan said, looking at her steadily.

"Of course you were," Ben said sarcastically. "After all, Jas and Grammar contain the only remaining samples of graviteria in the zones."

If Ryan kept looking at her like that, she might do something stupid, like take an unplanned jump in his direction. Otherwise known as falling.

"I thought you'd have been on your way back to Yorky then, to go back through quarantine," she said after clearing her throat twice.

"Your friend Priti said there was a chance you could survive up-gee," Ryan said. "So I wasn't going to leave until I knew for sure."

"Yeah, because you still need to kidnap her again," Ben said.

Ryan ignored him and so did Jasper. "Is Priti okay?" she asked.

"The kid who brought us her message said she was confined to bed but seemed fine," Ben said.

Grammar disengaged himself from the dog and stood, adorned with several more layers of dirt than he'd arrived with. The bandage Grace had put over the cut on his cheek was coming loose. "Hey, Ryan," he said. He extended his fist.

Ryan's grin expanded across his face. He bumped his fist against Grammar's. "Hey, kid."

Grammar looked around. "Where's Nev?"

Merlot stopped his lecture mid-sentence and glanced at Ben, who winced. Ryan's jaw clenched. An awkward silence fell.

Grammar looked from one to the other. Dawning dismay transformed to disbelief and then swiftly to fury. *"You been leaven her?"*

"Ben?" Jasper didn't want to believe Grammar's conclusions, but none of the boys jumped to correct him. She signed at Charlie for good measure, "Where's Nev?"

Understanding dawned on Charlie's face as he took in Grammar's furious face. He grimaced at Jasper and shook his head.

Ben looked as if he'd rather adopt Ryan into the family than say his next words. "Dragon took her."

"What?" Grammar's screech sent birds fluttering into the sky, brought the soccer game to an abrupt halt, and inspired a chorus of restive whinnies from the horses.

Crane's expression cooled to arctic temperatures. "Dragon been taken Nev?"

Jasper kept her voice low and even to balance out Grammar's imminent volcanic eruption. "How the fuck did that happen and *why*?" She repeated the question in ASL with fingers that shook with the effort of control.

Quick Rick extended his hands to placate Grammar. "Don't freak out, kid. We're going to get her, okay?"

But Grammar didn't want an explanation. He hurled himself at Ben, throwing wild punches. Jasper pulled him away, but he tore away from her hands, ricocheted into Merlot, landed a few blows there, and then aimed straight for Charlie. Charlie dodged him with impressive agility. Grammar continued past him, running for the tunnel they'd just emerged from. Okuru barked as if to proclaim his support of his master's inexplicable actions and then loped after Grammar.

"For gravity's sake!" Jasper exclaimed, torn between

demanding an explanation and stopping Grammar from picking a fight with the ReGeneration tunnel guards. She decided they could fend for themselves and good luck to them.

Crane stalked after Grammar, so calmly no one moved to stop her, until Grace ran after her and touched her arm. She spoke to Crane, too low to be overheard, until finally Crane allowed herself to be led back to the group, her face woodenly, dangerously blank.

Jasper turned to Ben. "How did Dragon get away with that? And why would he even need her if he thought Grammar and I were dead?"

"He's convinced you're both witches and was sure you'd find a way down." Ben rubbed his arm where one of Grammar's fists had struck. He signed, "I guess he was right."

"But why would Truthbringer let the Damaskers take Nev?" she asked aloud and then in ASL.

"Truthbringer knows the balance of power has changed," Merlot said. He switched to ASL. "He wouldn't agree to help Quick Rick, though he did let all of us go out of respect for our long association. But not Nev, because Dragon persuaded him that Nico would be so furious with him for throwing both Crane and Grammar into up-gee that he'd better cooperate with the Damaskers. They knew Nev would be the perfect hostage if Grammar ever got down from up-gee."

Finally, Jasper turned to Ryan. "You should've gone after her. *Dragon* has her. How could you . . .?" Words failed her.

Ryan didn't look away. Underneath the misery in his eyes was that familiar, unflinching anger. "Truthbringer delayed us a full day before we even knew about Nev. That gave the Damaskers a head start. We realized as soon as we were underway that Dragon was cutting the ropes and nets of the peddler road. So Charlie suggested we come here, assemble a raiding party, and use the tunnels to catch up to the Damaskers and obliterate them. If in the meantime Dragon hurts Nev..." His voice rasped like stone grinding on stone. "...then that's on me. And so is his death, because I'll kill him."

"It's not on you," Ben said curtly. "We all decided to come here. You couldn't have gravved on your own, not well enough to catch up with the Damaskers, so you don't have to be such a noble bastard. If Nev gets hurt, it's on all of us."

The two tunnel guards approached. Each had Grammar by one arm, carrying him as he twisted and kicked and screamed curses at them. Okuru trotted after them, barking loyally.

"Somebody want to take responsibility for this?" one man asked, his expression deadpan. "Or else we'll have to restrain him until he calms down."

Everybody looked at Jasper. She swallowed the urge to curse or kick something herself. "Grammar," she said. "Come on, kid. This won't get you anywhere."

Grammar snarled like an animal, reminding her of the bloody, pummelled, vicious creature he'd been in Vic's fighting ring.

"Hey, I'm angry too!" she shouted into his face. *So, so angry about so, so many things.*

He swallowed his snarl in response. The dirt on his face was streaked with runnels of moisture, but his eyes were dry now, hot and hard.

She took a deep breath because there would come a time for flying apart but now was not it. "We're going to get Nev back, you hear me? I'm going after her myself. I promise." Her own words rang flat and dull inside her. With the small amount of time left to her, with the obstacles and odds they faced, this was an extremely foolish promise to be making. She grasped her clay bird amulet and held it up for him to see. "I promise on my mother."

"Jas . . ." Ben's protest was soft but anguished. He didn't complete the thought.

Grammar wasn't calming down. Not exactly. Instead he was drawing himself together into his core, tighter and tighter, until there was no space left between his molecules. He was a dense wall with no openings, no cracks or doors, only glaring blue eyes. He'd gone so still that the ReGeneration gangers cautiously released him. He made no move, so they left.

"Okay," he said, and his tone was so ordinary, Jasper exhaled gustily in relief. He added almost casually, "But Dragon's for me to be killen."

She filed that comment under things to worry about another day. From the dark, cold look in Crane's eyes, she suspected Grammar would have to get in line anyway.

"Goen now," Grammar said, more of a command than a question, and he signed it for emphasis.

Nobody seemed eager to protest, but they all looked at Jasper.

"I need to speak to the Guardian first," she signed firmly. "Then we can go."

"The tunnels will let us catch up to the Damaskers before they reach Yorky," Charlie said aloud before Grammar could react to Jasper's statement. "We were just organizing a raid to stop Dragon before he reaches Yorky. The less intel Nico receives from the zones, the better."

"Jas, we need to talk about this," Ben said with a wary glance at Grammar. Neverwhen needed to be rescued, but it didn't have to be Jasper. Jasper needed to get to the Tower.

"Sure," she said wearily. "But first, point me to the Guardian."

He didn't have to point. The Guardian's force field drew the eye. She was a solitary figure kneeling in the small portion of down-gee given over to cultivation. Even the ReGeneration's gardens expanded into the foam zones. Vines and creeping plants like cucumbers, peas, squash, and melons were trained to grow into side-gee and up-gee. As long as they had wood and wire frames for support and earth to sink their roots into, the orientation of gravity mattered little to them.

The Guardian glanced up briefly as Jasper approached and then returned to weeding. Her long silver braid dangled over her shoulder, the end trailing in the dirt. She wasn't wearing gloves or using tools. With her bare fingers she clawed into the soil to drag out the roots of grass and other weeds.

Jasper stood next to a rustling row of young corn and stuck her hands in her pockets. Her hands wanted to tear up those corn plants and hurl them at the Guardian. Her hands wanted to close around a throat, pull out a lying tongue. Hands were dangerous that way.

"You found the beanstalk," the Guardian said by way of greeting.

"I also found what my mother stole from the Tower," Jasper said tightly.

The Guardian sat back on her heels and wiped an arm across her forehead. She fixed Jasper with eyes the colour of shaded soil. "So?"

Since she'd first looked through the photographs and notes that Vron had hidden, a hundred questions and accusations had run through her mind, but face to face with the Guardian she didn't know where to begin.

"How can you trust Zenobia at all knowing what she's done?" Jasper asked.

"Can you be more specific? Zenobia's done a lot of things, including protecting and defending you more times than you know."

"You were fine with her causing the Shattering, but I mean, hey, it wasn't like it was her fault. She didn't mean to. She got infected by accident, right? Just like my dad. So her being responsible for millions of deaths is horrible, but her only mistake was not taking enough antibac. She didn't want the Shattering to happen. Who in their right mind would? That's the story we're going with, right?"

The Guardian scraped some dirt out from under a fingernail and sighed. Briefly, she appeared old, her shoulders slumped, the lines of her face pronounced in the bright sunlight. "Things change. People change."

"That doesn't let you off the hook for what you did before!" Jasper shouted.

A new voice interjected, "You might as well yell at me, Jasper."

Jasper whirled around. Facing her across a row of tomatoes was Zenobia. The blue scarf around her neck was grimy, her chestnut hair flying loose of its pins, her black clothing stained and torn. With hollows under her eyes and her skin tinged with pallor, she looked a decade older than before. She leaned on her cane as if it was the only thing holding her upright.

"You're here," Jasper said blankly. "Where—where are Tom and Socrates?" Zenobia's bodyguard, Tom, and her second-in-command, Socrates, had been the only two Azuros to escape capture by the Damaskers.

Something flared in Zenobia's eyes. "What do you think?"

"Nico has them? But you're—"

"Men are dying for me and yet I'm here with you, yes. Because we're running out of time."

"'We'?" Jasper's laugh sounded hollow to her own ears. "There is no 'we.' You framed yourself as just another victim of Darius, but all along you were worse. You were ready to endanger millions, and for what? Superpowers? Was that it? Please tell me, Zenobia. What the *fuck* possessed you to *voluntarily* inject the graviteria?"

Zenobia closed her eyes, her knuckles growing white over the handle of her cane.

"That's what happened, isn't it? You didn't get infected by accident. You deliberately infected yourself. You wanted to Shatter. You wanted the power over gravity you thought you'd get as a result. And, oh yeah, here's the best part. When my father found out that you were refusing to take the antibac, he tried to inject you with it by force. You know, to save the world from your supervillain insanity. And what did you do?"

"I defended myself," Zenobia murmured.

"You *killed him*, though not before he got some of the antibac into you. He injected you and you pushed him and he fell and hit his head on the corner of a table. I saw the pictures my mother printed from the security camera footage. He didn't die from taking too much antibac. You murdered him. He was a hero and you let me think all these years that *he* was responsible for the Shattering? You're scum, Zenobia Allan, and I hope Nico kills you slowly."

10

INHERIT THE CHILDREN

Recipients of donor organs sometimes acquire the tastes and talents of their donors. How much of ourselves resides in the cells of our bodies rather than our brains? Where does the consciousness truly live?

~ Dr. Zenobia Allan (personal journals)

"If I tried to explain, would you listen?" Zenobia asked tiredly, as if she already knew the answer.

"What's to explain? The facts speak for themselves. You're a murderer, not just of my father, but of the millions who died in the Shattering. You wanted power and didn't care at what cost. Darius was bad, but your megalomania dwarfs even his."

"Sure, Jas, you've got this all figured out," Zenobia said. "Power. Yes, that's what graviteria represented, but it was a poorly kept secret—the genie was already out of the bottle. On the surface it appeared the experiments were going to be shut down because of the danger, but in reality, multiple parties had already made efforts to buy, borrow, or steal the samples and the data. It was only a matter of time before Shatterings became the new nuclear bomb."

"So you decided to get a jump on the arms race?"

"As far as we could tell, Shatterings were permanent. If people were unknowingly or carelessly infected and we suddenly had a bloom of uncontrolled Shatterings, the planet could become unlivable, not to mention the global economic and political chaos that would result. As soon as Dr. River Lee and I realized there might be a way to control gravity if a Shattering was handled properly, we started planning."

"So you wanted to be the first to control gravity, but what for?" Jasper demanded. "Anyone who got their hands on graviteria samples could do the same. Soon we'd have a world full of Shatterings with a few very powerful, half-alien hybrid people."

"Two things," said the Guardian. "As soon as we had just one person who could control gravity, we theorized that they could contain and dissolve all subsequent Shatterings. Second, Mick was special. Not every ape that Shattered could do what Mick could, and we kept our speculations about why to ourselves to make it harder for others to replicate the results."

"Thirdly," Zenobia said, "if I was successful, we were going to destroy every remaining sample of graviteria so they wouldn't fall in the wrong hands."

"How humanitarian of you," said Jasper.

"Did you even read the notes?" the Guardian said with a note of impatience. "We had no intention of risking a Shattering in the middle of a populated city. We were going to do it in the middle of a desert, the Sahara perhaps, or Antarctica, where no one would be hurt if things went wrong. We had a plan. But things spiralled out of control. Your father found out and then—"

"Don't you *dare* try to put any of this on my father," Jasper said. "He tried to stop you."

"And ruined everything," the Guardian snapped. "Zenobia was on her way to melding with the graviteria, but the antibac destroyed the possibility of sentience."

"Whatever," said Jasper. "The past is the past and I don't have time for it. I don't have time in general. Problem is, I've been operating under the assumption that you've been working on an antibac for me so I won't have to Shatter."

"We have been," Zenobia insisted.

"Have you *really*? Or are you hoping for a second chance to create a human-alien hybrid with superpowers? You're going to inject something into me and I'm supposed to just take it on trust that it's an antibac? You *want* me to Shatter so I can finish what you started."

"I already told you my opinion." The Guardian folded her arms across her chest. "I don't think the Shattering is an inevitable part of the melding. Or rather, it can be contained even as it happens. Mick's Shattering was fifteen percent smaller than that of other apes. I think he managed to partially squelch it as it formed."

"Enough, River." Zenobia turned to Jasper. "The antibac is real. I swear to you."

"You think I'll believe a fucking thing you say at this point?"

"I learned my lesson, okay?" Zenobia cried. "I killed millions. You wonder why I never killed myself? It's because I don't deserve the mercy of escaping what I've done."

Jasper tried inhaling and couldn't. Her chest felt like a stomped-on plastic bottle.

Zenobia took a shaky breath and spoke more calmly. "I won't ask for forgiveness or understanding, because I deserve neither. But if there's anything I can make you believe, it's that I would *never, ever* risk you living with the guilt that I do. Fifteen years ago, I made choices and took risks that appall me now. From the moment I found out you were Andrew's daughter and infected, I vowed that I would do whatever it took—first, to prevent another Shattering, and second, to save you. Believe nothing else if you like, but *believe that*."

"I can't," Jasper said. "How can I?"

"Then what are you going to do?" Zenobia asked helplessly. "Your deadline is approaching. You have to take the antibac."

"I'm going to do the obvious, of course." She had to shout to force the words out of her chest.

Zenobia paled. "No. No, Jasper. Please. The antibac at least gives you a chance."

"I can't *trust* the antibac, no matter what you say. There's only one sure way to prevent a Shattering, and for the life of me I can't understand why you've never considered it. You say your first priority is preventing the Shattering, but if it was, you'd have killed me long ago. You could've done it before Grammar was even conceived, before he was a consideration."

"Of course, killing you, a six-year-old. Why didn't I think of that?" Zenobia said bitterly.

"Admit it. Preventing a Shattering is not your first priority."

"Okay, you got me. You're right. My first priority is wanting you to live. So sue me."

Jasper said, "At first maybe, but then it was wanting me to live so I could be the guinea pig so you could save *Grammar*. And what the fuck was that about? The minute I reached puberty and even blinked in Merlot's direction, you were preaching the dangers of having a graviteria-infected child. So how did you let Grammar happen?"

Colour flooded Zenobia's cheeks. "How did I *let* . . .? You think Darius gave me any choices about what happened in the bedroom? Grow the *fuck up*, Jasper."

That hit like a thrown brick. Zenobia's voice rang of bitter truth, and yet it had never occurred to Jasper. She'd established her opinions about Zenobia long before she was old enough to realize the brutal ways in which power could be exploited between a man and a woman.

"You manipulated him all the time," Jasper said weakly. "Don't tell me you didn't have ways of getting what you wanted."

Zenobia's eyes crackled with anger. "Why, yes. Yes, I did. It involved me telling Darius what I wanted and him telling me the price for getting it. He knew—he *knew* how badly I didn't want to have children. He knew I was terrified of the possibility, that I would do anything to avoid it. He even knew why. So, of course, one day he named it as the price for something I wanted. And I paid it."

"Wait, what do you mean *he knew why*?"

"He figured out I was the one who'd Shattered. He overheard a conversation between Martha and me. That's what he held over my head, and Martha too—the threat that he'd tell everybody and then they'd kill us." She laughed, an ugly, despairing sound. "You really think I thought, *Yes, the best way to survive this homicidal psychopath is to become his fucking girlfriend and have his child?* You think I *chose* that life?"

Jasper stared at her. The ground wavered under her feet. "Why did you pay the price?" she asked numbly. "Not using condoms. You said it was a price you had to pay. For what?"

Zenobia's shoulders slumped and she leaned heavily on her cane. "For Ben," she said. "Darius was going to kill him. He would've made *you* kill him. I talked him down to just taking a leg. And in return Darius could put his baby in my belly."

For Ben.

Jasper couldn't speak or breathe. All these years she had cursed Zenobia and insulted her and lashed out at her and treated her with rudeness and disrespect, and never once had Zenobia told her she'd saved Ben's life or at what price. So many times Jasper had wondered what secrets Zenobia was keeping. She'd never imagined this.

"He waited," Zenobia said. "Toyed with me. Let me think he might have forgotten. But the moment I could no longer hide from him that I was pregnant, he ordered Ben's leg cut off."

Jasper wanted to cover her ears. She wanted to run away. She wanted to weep for everything she'd never known about Zenobia.

"Of all the bargains he ever made, it was Darius's favourite," Zenobia said. "No matter how I tried to hide it from him, he could feel how miserable I was about it, and he loved every second of it. He couldn't wait to have a kid to hold over my head. I begged Martha to abort it for me. Send me to hell for it—I didn't care. It couldn't be worse than the hell I was already living. Let the baby go straight to heaven without experiencing life's misery, without meeting his monster of a father. He'd be better off. But Martha wouldn't do it. I hated her so much for that. 'You raise him then,' I told her. 'You can see for yourself what life will be like for him and how it'll be cut short when he has to die to prevent a Shattering.'"

A memory came to Jasper suddenly, of being a child crouched in a corner of Zenobia's room. Zenobia, her hair a long furious tangle over her shoulders, had been writing on the wall in sweeping, thorny strokes, a briary hedge filling and surrounding the room, a barbed wire fence of words. She'd come unzipped, unhinged, an elegant, purposeful vase smashed open to unleash a swarm of spiders. She faced Martha across the room, Martha who smelled big as the ocean, salty as blood and acrid with alcohol.

The images Jasper retained were scattered and sodden as tea leaves after the liquid is drained. Zenobia's hand clutching a fistful of her blouse over her belly. The urgent skitter of her voice. An argument, two voices braiding together, saying . . .

saying what? The memory melted under too-close examination, the way the horizon disappeared into the sky on luminescent grey winter days.

"I never wanted kids." Words spilled out of Zenobia, marbles on a tile floor, fast and hard. "I told my mother a million times when she nagged me about it. 'I don't want to carry a child. I don't want to adopt. I don't want children. It's not for me,' I said. Oh, the gods must laugh at us."

"Of course you didn't want an infected child, but he's here now and you love him. Right?"

Zenobia laughed with a note of despair. "How can you be so sure of that, and at the same time so sure that I couldn't possibly love *you*?"

"But he's your son."

"He's *Darius*. I can't even look at him without seeing his monstrous father. It's not his fault, of course, and I want him to be safe and happy. But I can't stand the sight of his face. He reminds me only of fear and ugliness and pain and how much his father enjoyed what he was doing to me. I will do everything in my power to save Grammar from the graviteria, but I can't be his mother."

A small sound snagged Jasper's gaze. After a moment, Zenobia twisted around to look.

Grammar stood beside the row of raspberry bushes that had hidden him until now. His face under its mosaic of healing bruises was pale and perfectly, rigidly still.

Zenobia pressed her palm to her mouth.

I was as much a scientist as Zenobia was, you know, Darius murmured. *I studied fault lines in people. With one tiny tap in the right place, you can destroy a whole person. Did you know that?*

"Grammar," Zenobia said from behind her hand.

Grammar's gaze skidded away from Zenobia as if she were a treacherously slick surface he could find no purchase on. He looked instead at Jasper. She had no idea what he'd see on her face; she'd lost control of her expressions early on in her conversation with Zenobia. Everything was spinning out of control. Control had been an illusion in the first place.

"Helpen Nev now," he said. "You comen?" His voice was as raw and undefended as a knee shredded open on pavement.

There was only one possible answer. "Coming," said Jasper.

He's my son, Darius warned. *Be wary of how he glues himself back together.*

Zenobia clutched at her arm as she walked past. "Jasper, there's no time for this. The ReGeneration will rescue Neverwhen. You don't need to do it personally. You need to go to the Tower."

Even a decade later the memory of Zenobia's painted words on the wall remained buried in Jasper's mind like restless thistles, but she couldn't remember what they'd said. Had they been a curse to end the life inside Zenobia before it could begin? Or an enchantment to untether a soul from destiny and a parent's sins? Or a wish writ large, as if a mere arrangement of words by dint of their precise syntax and inflection could lay out a path as clean as snow for a child's feet?

Too bad wishes were nothing but plastic bottles in a city awash with them—empty, useless, and slowly poisonous to the earth.

Jasper leaned close to Zenobia's ear. "I don't need the Tower anymore. I can end it anytime, anywhere. But first I'm going to do something worthwhile. I'm going to keep a promise and help Grammar save the one person on earth who ever loved him the way he deserved."

She jerked her arm free and left.

11

THE UP-GEE WITCH

Is this what it feels like to be God? To create a world that is glorious and singular and deadly, and then to have virtually no control of it? Does God ever marvel at his own hubris? Does he ever regret us?

~ Dr. Zenobia Allan (personal journals)

"I know what you're going to say, Merlot," Esther said. "So don't bother. Grace and I are going back to Yorky, and that's final."

"I wasn't going to—" Merlot began.

"I know Yorky's not very safe, but that's all the more reason for us to rejoin our family. They're probably worried sick by now."

"Why the fuck would you—?"

"It's sweet you're so protective of Grace, but you can't make these decisions for us. You're not my father and certainly not my husband."

"I think I fucking know that. Jesus Christ. Would you just—"

"Would you please stop with the swearing!"

Merlot took a long stride closer and placed his palm over Esther's mouth. "And would you listen to me for one goddamn second. *Gosh darn*. A gosh darn second."

Jasper casually redirected her steps to join Charlie and Ben, who were eavesdropping on the sidelines. They were pretending to examine the workmanship of a ReGeneration crossbow while Ben silently interpreted Merlot and Esther's conversation for an avid Charlie.

Esther's eyes had widened above Merlot's hand. She nodded.

He removed his hand. "I wasn't going to tell you to stay here, so chill the frickety-frak out," he said irritably. "Jesus—I mean, gee fucking whiz. I already know you won't listen to me. I know first-hand the lengths you'll go to for family. Fucking heck, it'd be easier to separate Crane from her knives than you from a notion once you've got it in your head. I pity your poor, hapless future Mennonite husband if he tries to order you around. You're going to Yorky, so cool your *morzsh*."

Ben hesitated on the last word and then fingerspelled it phonetically. Charlie blinked in confusion and signed, "*What* did he say?"

"It means *ass*, I think," Jasper signed. "Esther always refused to teach us swear words in Low German, remember? That was the worst one she'd admit to knowing."

Merlot nodded with satisfaction at Esther's expression. "Every now and then it's worthwhile listening to me, huh?"

"Every now and then." Esther looked like she was fighting a smile and losing.

"Heaven forbid I tell you what to do," Merlot said, glancing around, "but Grace has already had half an hour to find some new trouble to get into, so . . ."

"I'll find her." Esther walked off swiftly.

"Stop looking at her *morzsh*, Merlot," Charlie called. Perhaps he'd meant it to be a whisper, but his voice boomed out loud enough for everyone close by to hear.

Esther didn't turn around, and Ben swatted Charlie.

Merlot realized they'd been eavesdropping and waved his middle fingers at them.

"Gee whiz, Merlot, language!" Ben exclaimed in sign and made to cover Charlie's eyes.

"It's gosh darn offensive," Charlie signed in agreement.

"Go die on an anthill," Merlot signed at them. He glanced at Jasper and said, "How'd your talk with the Guardian go?"

"Yeah, and how did Zenobia get here?" Ben asked.

Jasper looked over her shoulder. Zenobia still stood by the garden with the Guardian some distance away. "We got a few things cleared up." She signed to Charlie, "When are we leaving?"

"Ready whenever you are." Charlie indicated the group of ReGeneration warriors on their eager horses. They were all young and chattering excitedly, occasionally breaking into whoops and encouraging their horses to rear for the drama of it. All of them had crossbows or bows and a few had guns. Older members of the ReGeneration had gathered around to see them off, their expressions more sombre and worried. Winnie was coaching Quick Rick through the process of mounting a horse, and his muttered commentary as the horse continued to sidestep him had the nearby warriors in stitches.

Olivia was checking a horse's hoof while Ryan stood beside her, arms crossed over his chest, chatting. He said something with a wry grin and she laughed.

Jasper looked away, mortified by the stab of jealousy that went through her. She scanned the open field for Grammar but couldn't see him. Esther returned with a bickering Grace and Crane in tow. They were arguing over whether Grace should change Crane's bandage or not. Grace kept reaching for it and Crane kept catching her hand and pretending to bite it.

"Okay, listen up," Charlie said aloud, lifting his arms for attention. "As you know, we don't have enough horses for everybody, especially beginner riders. We can ride double for short periods or switch out and walk. So to start out with, Ben can share with me. Esther's with Merlot. Unless Crane has magically gotten over her fear of animals, she'll be with whoever can keep her from freaking out and stabbing the horses—I nominate Jasper. Ryan—"

"I'll ride with Grace, actually," Esther said, signing along with her spoken words.

"I'll ride with Ben," Jasper said, after lifting her hand to draw Charlie's attention.

"I'm not touching these devil beasts," Crane signed.

"I'll ride with you, Charlie," Merlot signed. "Every now and then when you least expect it, I'll lick your ear."

"What a bunch of whiners," Charlie said. "It's a good thing I'm not in charge of you clowns. Oh, wait, I am. Get the fuck on your horses."

"I think you mean get the frickety-frak on your horses," Ben signed and then dodged Charlie's swat.

"Let's move out!" Winnie called. The mounted ReGeneration warriors slowly fell in line and headed for the tunnel's mouth.

Again Jasper looked around in the dust and confusion for Grammar or, alternatively, Okuru, who was certain to be near him.

Thanks to her hesitation, Ben already stood beside Ed for Edible, preparing to mount the horse. He signed to Charlie, "Back or front?"

"Either position is fine with me," Charlie signed back with blandly raised eyebrows.

Ben's ears turned bright red.

"I cannot believe you made me watch you say that," Merlot signed. "Hey, God," he yelled to the sky. "I need a new set of eyes ASAP. These ones are ruined."

Crane was still making a fuss about climbing on a devil beast. They were the devil's messengers, witches' familiars, possessed by tinylings. They had big teeth and murderous hooves and smelled funny. She'd already stepped in their poo twice.

"Get on the horse, Crane," Grace said, hands on her hips.

Crane mimicked her pose and tone. "Start carryen a knife, pink cheek girl."

"Why should I? You have enough for both of us."

"What good will that be doen next time you're in danger?"

"I guess you'll just have to stay nearby then, won't you?" Grace said. She turned to the horse and clambered into the saddle.

"Stay nearby?" Crane repeated with a snort. "For how long? Forever?" She stopped and frowned at her own words. Then she looked up at Grace.

"Don't worry about the horse," Grace said and reached a hand down. "I'll keep you safe."

Esther appeared at Jasper's side, distracting her from the entertaining sight of Crane trying to climb onto a horse without touching it. "Unfortunately, it looks like one of us is going to have to ride with Merlot," Esther said.

Ryan had already mounted. Olivia stood by his leg, giving final instructions before jogging over to her own horse. He gathered the reins, not incompetently, and his horse's ears flicked back to hear the words he murmured.

Jasper imagined riding the tunnels with her arms around Ryan's waist, leaning her forehead between his shoulder blades when the darkness of the underground threatened to invade her lungs, inhaling his familiar, reassuring smell. For the many hours of riding ahead of them, she could hold on to him and pretend. Pretend that their feelings mattered in the face of the inevitable. Pretend she had an actual future to look forward to, much less a future with him.

Her heart turned over, a cruel pain. She could bear her own death, but she couldn't bear a taste of what she could never have.

"Say no more," she said to Esther. "I'm with you."

Esther looked at her and then at Ryan. "Are you sure?"

Jasper waved at Ryan to go ahead. His smile dimmed, but he nodded and nudged his horse to follow the others into the tunnel.

Her throat hurt too much to swallow. "But you take the reins," she said briskly, unable to meet Esther's eyes. "You already know how to order cows around. I assume you can handle a horse."

"How different can it be?" Esther said a trifle dubiously. "I thought you were heading to the Tower, though."

Jasper turned away. "Nev's the priority. Have you seen Grammar?"

"I'd have thought he'd be the first down the tunnel." Esther craned her neck. "Oh, is that him with the Guardian over there?"

Jasper couldn't see Zenobia in the crowd of ReGeneration onlookers, but Grammar stood a dozen metres away, his fists clenched for fight but his body angled away for flight. With the force field of her personality, the Guardian kept him on the spot, listening to whatever she was saying. Okuru stayed well behind Grammar's legs, tail low.

Only two horses were left now, held by ReGeneration youths too young to accompany the raid. Merlot sat on one, looking very skeptical about the advice the ReGeneration boy was giving him about the reins.

Jasper grimaced. "Sorry, Esther. Maybe you better go ahead

and ride with Merlot after all. Grammar and I will take the other horse. We'll catch up."

Esther sighed in resignation and eyed Merlot. "If you're sure."

Jasper walked up to Grammar and the Guardian. Grammar registered her approach with a trace of relief.

"Have to be goen now," he said to the Guardian. His tone was as rough as sandpaper, but he was wary enough to be polite.

"Yes, certainly," the Guardian murmured. "But not where you intend, I'm afraid."

"Huh?" Grammar edged away from the Guardian, but she seized his arm with the speed of a striking snake.

"Hey!" Jasper ran over, but before she could intervene Zenobia also approached, moving faster than seemed possible given her cane and sickly appearance.

"I have this, River." Zenobia stepped up behind Grammar.

Grammar tried to jerk his arm away from the Guardian, but to no avail.

"Are you sure?" the Guardian asked mildly.

Zenobia looked at Jasper, who hovered at her elbow, not sure whether to assault the Guardian or attempt to shake Grammar free of her grip. "We don't have much choice now, do we?"

"I suppose not," the Guardian replied.

Zenobia slipped her arm around Jasper's waist. Jasper froze, startled at the unexpected embrace. In the same moment, the Guardian grabbed Grammar with casual strength and nearly flung him at Zenobia. He yelled in shock and rage. Zenobia caught him with her other arm and staggered as his weight knocked her off her already precarious balance. Her grip on Jasper sent Jasper stumbling back too. They were falling . . .

They were falling *up*.

Just as abruptly, they stopped. They hung in mid-air. Gravity pulled them downward toward the ground below, but some invisible force held them in place.

That force was Zenobia.

Overwhelmed with terror, Jasper clung to Zenobia with both arms.

"What you doen? What you doen?" Grammar screamed.

"I'm taking you to the Tower." Zenobia gasped for breath as she spoke, as if straining to lift a heavy weight.

Half a kilometre from the ReGeneration's village, the Tower pierced the sky like an ebony needle. The drifting clouds of debris that surrounded it formed a three-dimensional chessboard in the air where each cube was of different gravity.

"No!" Grammar recovered from his shock. Enraged, he squirmed in his mother's grip. "Be putten me down right now. *Put me down!*"

Zenobia grunted with effort. Terrified Grammar would slip from her grasp, Jasper grabbed him with her free hand. She was draped over Zenobia's right shoulder and between the two of them they could barely hang on to a furious Grammar, who seemed prepared to plunge back to the ground below. No zone border would catch him if he fell; it was a straight down-gee drop onto unforgiving ground.

"Grammar, please—" His elbow landed in Jasper's midriff, cutting her off.

Grammar twisted like a cat being forced toward a bathtub. His clawing hand found purchase on Zenobia's scarf and jerked it loose from her neck. It fluttered away on the wind, a flightless bird. "Witch! You're a witch!"

The strain cut lines around Zenobia's mouth and nose. "Please hold still. I don't want to drop you."

"Up-gee Witch," he said, his voice small and flat now. Jasper could feel the storm brewing inside him, a cataclysm coalescing out of nothing.

"So you did get some control over gravity after all," Jasper said. "Is there no end to the secrets you've kept from me?"

Zenobia's pointy eyebrows rounded with distress. "I'll explain everything in the Tower. Please just let me—"

Grammar sucked in his breath and screamed into her face with all the force in his body, "I hate you! I hate you, hate you, hate you! Be letten me down right now. Right now!"

His flailing fists struck Zenobia in the stomach and she grunted. Her grip slackened and Grammar fell.

Zenobia grabbed on to Jasper and plunged after him, diving through the air like a hunting bird. She scooped him up under one arm and changed directions with breath-stopping quickness. Now they were hurtling horizontally across the face of the city.

Grammar shrieked and fought, and Jasper wrapped all the limbs she could spare around him. Only the indifferent earth would catch them if they fell now. Or else multiple zones would jerk them in every direction until they finally struck, with lethal force, a hard surface.

The Tower grew large as if it was racing toward them and not the other way around. Wind stung their faces and whipped their hair into their eyes. It seemed certain they would smash into the Tower wall. Jasper braced herself until she realized Zenobia was aiming for the walkway around the glass-walled observation deck at the top of the Tower.

Zenobia halted their fall with bruising suddenness. She released them, and they fell to the deck walkway.

Jasper rolled to her feet, on autopilot even as her legs shook violently and her whole body shrieked with adrenalin from that terrifying, impossible ride. Zenobia had *flown*. Such was the power that awaited Jasper if she were willing to endanger the world by Shattering.

Grammar sat up and looked around him, and Jasper braced

herself for the mother of all tantrums. Instead he went still and blank and deadly, which was far worse. Even when he'd pretended to be possessed by Darius, he had never resembled his father so much as he did now.

Zenobia dropped to the walkway floor and staggered, nearly falling. Wind whistled and pushed and pulled, flattening their clothing to their bodies. Zenobia sagged against the railing as if her legs had lost all strength. She slid down to a sitting position and cradled her head in her hands. Her skin was tinged with grey.

"You can fucking fly?" were the only words Jasper could summon.

Zenobia tried to tuck her hair back into its pins, but her hands were shaking too badly. "It's falling, not flying. I can change the gravitational orientation of my body, but because the antibac stunted my graviteria and damaged my nervous system, the resulting toll on my body is immense. I've 'flown' less than a dozen times since the Shattering. Each time I was incapacitated for weeks afterwards."

Indeed, she looked as if she were moments away from either vomiting or keeling over unconscious.

"All those times Tom said you had the flu and couldn't get out of bed ..." Jasper said.

"Exactly."

Grammar said in a singsong, "Catch a witch, burn the bitch, and throw the ashes skyward."

Zenobia flinched.

Grammar walked away from them. His face was ominously calm, displaying only curiosity about their location and no concern at all about his mother's well-being.

Jasper wasn't prepared to feel a treacherous lurch of sympathy as Zenobia lifted her hands to her face. She wanted answers, not feelings. "Does that mean you can also change or influence existing zones?"

Zenobia shook her head wearily. "Changing my own gravity is the only thing I can do, and usually the price is too high to bother with it. But it's the only way I can reach River's village or the Tower because, with my legs, I certainly can't grav. With the tunnels gradually opening up, that could change, but . . ." She didn't bother to say that there was unlikely to be a future where she survived Nico's war, much less one where she travelled the zones in freedom.

Grammar had nearly made a full circuit of the deck and was approaching the sliding doors that led inside.

"Watch out," Zenobia called. "That's an up-gee zone by the door."

Grammar acted as if he hadn't heard, but he must have felt the tingle of a zone border. He stopped and considered the doors he couldn't approach. Then he walked back the way he'd come until he came to a smashed glass panel he could crawl through to get inside.

"I hope you have one more flight left in you," Jasper said. "Because you're going to take Grammar and me back immediately."

Zenobia's head drooped almost to her chest and she straightened it with an effort. "Even if I wanted to, I couldn't. I'm spent. The ReGeneration will save Neverwhen. In any case, I won't allow Grammar to fall into the Damaskers' hands. Both of you will be safe here."

"You had no right to make that decision for us."

"Of all the sins I've committed in my life, protecting you two is not one I'll regret."

Zenobia began the slow process of hauling herself to her feet, holding hard to the railing. Jasper tried to imagine having legs too weak to even stand on, much less run and leap and climb.

Zenobia's gaze went past Jasper. "Oh no."

Jasper whirled and looked through the glass that surrounded the cavernous, empty room inside the observation deck. Grammar stood in front of the only internal wall. The metal doors set into the wall rolled open, revealing a tiny room large enough for half a dozen people to stand in. It was lit, and not by fire.

Jasper gaped, stunned by an onslaught of vague, confused memories from childhood. Doors that opened by themselves. Electric light. That tiny little square above the doors that displayed a lit-up 50.

It was an elevator. A working elevator.

"Impossible."

Zenobia was already moving as fast as she could without her cane, staggering around the circular walkway to the broken glass pane through which Grammar had entered the Tower. "The Tower's basements are shielded from electromagnetic radiation," she called over her shoulder. "The Tower itself, only somewhat. The elevators can be used, but it's risky to expose them to the zones like this."

Grammar cautiously approached the open box. He poked his head in, then waved his hand around as if looking for zone borders. He stared up at the source of the strange light. He stuck his foot in and prodded the elevator floor, testing it.

"Grammar, don't get in," Zenobia called. She couldn't move much faster than a limping walk while hanging on to the railing.

Grammar saw them coming. He made up his mind and stepped gingerly into the elevator. The doors rolled closed.

Jasper broke into a run and passed Zenobia. She leaped through the broken glass panel and ran for the elevator.

"Hit the button to open the doors," Zenobia shouted after

her. "He might not realize he has to push the floor button on the inside to make it go anywhere."

Jasper skidded to a halt in front of the elevator and spotted the downward pointing arrow button beside it. She'd seen it a thousand times in her life while gravving abandoned buildings. She pushed it several times. But from the other side of the metal doors came a humming and creaking noise. The doors didn't open. In the little square above the doors, the number 50 changed to 49, then 48. It continued to count down.

Zenobia arrived looking so ill, Jasper took her arm despite herself.

"Apparently, he does know to push a button," Jasper said. "He must have seen it in a comic book or something. The question is which floor he pressed."

Zenobia was barely managing to stay upright, so Jasper lowered her to a sitting position against the wall beside the elevator. Zenobia's face was grey and sweaty, and her legs trembled uncontrollably.

"What's the risk with the elevator?" Jasper asked as the numbers continued to count down.

"Up here at the top of the Tower, there's less shielding against the electromagnetic radiation of the zones. It wears away the electric and electronic components of the elevator each time it's used. I've used it once a year for the last few years, but every time could be the last time."

"It could fall," Jasper said with a surge of dread. She imagined being trapped in a tiny box as it hurtled toward the ground fifty floors below.

"Not fall, probably, but stop," Zenobia said. "Just get stuck."

"That doesn't sound any better." She stared at the glowing numbers counting down. "How is it that the Tower still has electricity after all these years anyway?"

"A lot of dangerous, expensive, and highly classified research was conducted here, not only the graviteria experiments. The Tower was built to be self-sufficient and self-contained in case of disaster or attack, so it draws power from geothermal energy deep below the surface, and all its electronic components are heavily shielded. After all, we'd known for years before the Shattering that fluctuating, unpredictable electromagnetic radiation was an effect of graviteria. The basement laboratories were built with that in mind. I've told you all this before, Jasper. How else could the artificial intelligence work on your antibac?"

"I just never really thought about it."

The numbers were still changing, getting smaller and smaller. The elevator reached number two and stopped.

"He didn't realize *L* meant lobby," Zenobia said. "He'll have to take one more flight of stairs to get to ground level. But there's nowhere to go anyway—the Tower is surrounded by foam zones."

The numbers started to climb again.

"The elevator will come back to us since you pushed the button," Zenobia said.

"You couldn't pay me enough copper to get in that thing," Jasper said emphatically. She spotted the door marked with the symbol for stairs. "I'll take the stairs and meet you in the lobby."

"Collect Grammar and go to the basement. Press your finger to the scanner pad. I've entered your prints and DNA into the system, so it'll let you in. Try not to let Grammar touch anything. That equipment down there is irreplaceable. Literally. Even if we could afford to buy more, it'd cease functioning long before we could carry it through the zones. The AI and all related equipment live in a specially shielded room. You'll have no access to that room. Only River and I have access, and Martha when she was alive. Any other electronics you'll encounter have been hardened against EM radiation." Zenobia pressed a shaking hand to her forehead. The blue nail polish had mostly flaked off her nails. "I'd start climbing if I were you. The time it'll take you to get down is more than enough for my son to find some trouble to get into."

"I hope this is worth it for you," Jasper said.

Zenobia's eyes snapped open. "I could've tried to rescue Tom and Socrates from Nico. I chose to come for you and Grammar instead. Do not tell me what I've sacrificed."

The thought of Tom dangling from the end of a rope nearly choked the words from Jasper. She wanted to scream at Zenobia that if she'd just let Jasper and Grammar make their own decisions she could've rescued Tom and Socrates instead. She said, "Grammar will never forgive you for this."

"I'm long past the point of expecting forgiveness for anything I've done," Zenobia said.

12

THE TOWER

*It is not so much flying as it is semi-controlled falling. Which
sounds like a metaphor for life. One where we'll all hit the
ground eventually.*

~ Dr. Zenobia Allan (personal journals)

Skipping her way down seemingly endless stairs in the dark,
Jasper had time to think. Too much time.

Could she trust the antibac? Despite everything—*Zenobia
had killed her father*—she wanted to believe that Zenobia had
been truthful about wanting to prevent another Shattering. The
antibac was Jasper's only realistic option, even if her chances of
surviving unscathed were only fifteen percent.

She stopped to rest on the thirtieth-floor landing. As she
lowered herself to sit on the stairs, she grasped her thighs,
trembling from the long descent. Strong, muscular, sturdy legs,
alive with the ability to propel her down these stairs, to leap
gulfs and balance on balcony railings and climb onto the roof

when she couldn't sleep. Who was she if she couldn't *move*? She'd spent her whole life escaping cages, but if she took the antibac and survived, her own body could become a final cage, trapping her into stillness.

The claustrophobic thought drove her to her feet, and she continued her descent. She had to think about something else.

Ryan and Ben and all the others were setting out to attack Dragon's team of Damaskers. People would get hurt or die. Ben could get hurt. She hadn't said goodbye to him.

Think about something else. Something like Ryan facing up to the brother he loved and hated and feared in equal parts. How would he do it? Would Titus be as ready for his rebellion as Darius would have been? Would Ryan even manage to arrive safely at quarantine in the first place with the Damaskers everywhere?

Would she ever see him again?

The question felt too much like a wish, the kind at the top of a goblin's menu.

Then there was Yorky under Damasker control, with Sparrow still badly injured. Community leaders like Ibtisam, Pastor Tim, Harmony, and Esther's family would be in danger because they were the likeliest to speak up against Nico.

How far would Nico go for his revenge? She thought she understood his festering bitterness and anger. She'd long carried her own anger, resentment, and blame against Zenobia, but Nico's hate had grown so deep and mad that he was willing to hurt a child for his revenge. Set beside Nico's vicious, fermented hunger for vengeance, her own anger seemed weak and paltry, more like that of a child lashing out at the nearest safe target.

Darius had always been an untouchable figure, impossible to wound, hurt, or destroy. Jasper's younger self had chosen murder because she couldn't believe that anything less would stop him. But dead, he was a scarier bogeyman than ever. Zenobia at least was human. She could be hurt, she could be punished, she could be railed against without consequence. Zenobia would stand uncomplaining and take every punch Jasper threw at her. Jasper could hurt her as she couldn't hurt Darius, and so she had.

Zenobia deserved it.

Or so she'd always told herself, and told herself now, louder than ever.

Nico would take it ten steps further. He'd already killed who knew how many Azuros by now. He would kill Tom if he hadn't already. He'd destroyed the Azuros' trading post, the home and livelihood Zenobia had built for herself at great cost. If Nico ever got his hands on Grammar, he'd hurt and possibly kill the boy. And at the end of it all, after he'd hurt her in every way he could think of, he'd kill Zenobia.

Jasper staggered to a halt on the twelfth-floor landing and collapsed. Her heart pounded sickeningly in her chest and her lungs ached. Her legs felt weak and too loose, as if the muscle wanted to fall off the bone. She lay on the mossy concrete in the dark and closed her eyes. Sweat trickled down her temples and into her hair. Blood thundered in her ears.

She cast about for something good, something whole and steady and sure. Ben, Charlie, and Merlot playing UNO, Neverwhen's impulsive hugs, Grammar touching her forehead to check for fever, Esther handing her a mug of hot tea when she came in out of the rain. She remembered Ryan's weight on her body, pushing her into the earth, pinning her to hope, to life. He'd pressed her ghost back into her flesh and reminded her of why it belonged there.

Her breathing slowed and she slept.

She woke disoriented in the darkness. She didn't know how long she'd slept, minutes or hours, but her sweat had dried. She

got up and continued her descent with legs that felt like barely
solidified jelly. At the second floor she stopped, pulled open the
door into musty darkness, and called Grammar's name. When
she heard nothing, she continued to the ground floor.

The marble, high-ceilinged lobby echoed with her footsteps.
She passed a broad reception desk with a cobwebbed computer
monitor, a dusty landline phone, and a fake potted plant. She
passed giant paintings of frothy seascapes and green mountains
and towering forests. The glass doors were unbroken and
unlocked. She stepped outside.

The Tower had once had a broad plaza in front of the
entrance, lined with benches and planters full of flowers and
trees and large abstract sculptures and a fountain. Half of the
plaza remained, virtually untouched. The trees and flowers and
shrubbery had grown thick and wild, bursting out of their
confines with grass and weeds shooting out of every crack in the
concrete tiles. The sculptures drowned in green. Butterflies
danced around them like errant thoughts made visible.

The other half of the plaza had been consumed by the foam
zones. The plaza pavement was cracked and flaking like
sunburned skin. Pebbles and bits of concrete hung suspended in
the air like bee swarms, swirling in the breeze. Their pattern and
density gave shape to each zone.

Silhouetted against the setting sun, Grammar stood at the
very edge of the Tower's down-gee zone. Head tilted back, he
studied the cluttered zones that rose in stacked columns into the
air above. If a giant beehive had been sliced in half, Jasper and
Grammar would be looking into a cross-section of the hive—
although the zones had nowhere near the regularity in size and
shape of a honeycomb's cells.

Jasper watched in fascination as an object that might have
been a teddy bear or the carcass of a small animal fell up in an
up-gee zone until it encountered a side-gee zone and fell east

into down-gee. But before it could hit the ground, a westerly side-gee zone caught it and threw it straight back into the original up-gee zone. How many years had it been falling around and around from zone to zone and never touching the ground? It was doomed to repeat a cycle as endless as the earth's own rotation—at least until a strong enough wind blew it into another zone. What would it feel like to jump into that up-gee zone and join that cycle of eternal falling?

Probably not much different from Jasper's life.

On the down-gee side of the zone border, the ground was strewn with debris, as occasionally wind would push floating items out of zones until they drifted over the border and toppled to the ground. Grammar had unsnapped his helmet, and it dangled from his hand, as if he were daring that floating bicycle ten metres above him to drift closer and fall on his head.

"Kid, put your helmet on." Jasper knew even as the words exited her mouth that it was the wrong tone to take with him. Any tone would be the wrong one.

He didn't turn around. He swung the helmet by its strap, then hurled it into the foam zones. It danced from zone to zone —west, north, up, west, down, east, south—like a pinball ricocheting from invisible surface to invisible surface in a cosmic arcade game.

Jasper stuck her tongue between her front teeth and bit down. She had a dozen things she wanted to say, and every single one of them would only piss him off more. When Darius was angry, he'd propose a game, and his anger would only dissipate once somebody had been hurt. Jasper wasn't prepared to test this method on his son. She didn't want to know the result.

She said in the most neutral tone she could manage, "Zenobia said my DNA would open the doors. I'm going to explore the basement, see if I can find the tunnel that leads back to the ReGeneration's village."

A brief pause confirmed he wasn't going to acknowledge her, so she re-entered the Tower. It wasn't as if he could go anywhere; the foam zones surrounded the Tower in an impenetrable maze. The ReGeneration's tunnel or Zenobia's gift of falling were the only ways to access the Tower zone.

She descended the stairs another two levels, both of which were parking garages. On the third sublevel she tried the door, but it was locked. It was a massive heavy thing that would have required explosives to get through. Beside the door on the wall was an electronic keypad and a screen, dark and thick with dust. On one corner a tiny red light blinked, the kind of electricity-generated light that Jasper had not—prior to the elevator—seen in fifteen years.

How was this machine supposed to read her DNA? Faint childhood memories of her mother's cellphone led her to touch the screen. It sprang to life with light and graphics and scrolling text. Faced with this relic of her lost past, Jasper crossed herself and touched her amulets. It was like watching an ancient skeleton sit up and speak.

The screen beeped, prompting action. A light blinked, indicating a small slot. Primed by Merlot's comic books about spies and secret agents and billionaire tech geniuses, Jasper made a guess and inserted her finger cautiously into the slot. A tiny prick made her yelp, and the screen blinked to itself. Then it flashed green, and she withdrew her finger, a tiny bead of blood at its tip.

"Welcome, Jasper Pine," said the machine.

Only when Grammar gasped behind her did she realize he'd crept down the stairs after her. He lifted his palm in a warding gesture against the witchcraft of this strange voice and the bright moving lights on the screen, the likes of which he'd never have seen before. Jasper's own heart had threatened to lurch out of her chest at the sound of that unexpected, disembodied voice. They were distracted by the click and then clank of the door swinging open.

Flat, eerie white lights flickered to life as they moved down halls free of garbage and debris and even dust, decorated only with a few cobwebs on the ceiling and streaks of mould on the walls. Jasper paused by a few doors that had a window. She saw glass beakers and tubes, empty mice cages, microscopes, computer monitors, and other equipment much more incomprehensible to her eye. Everything looked orderly and undisturbed, untouched by looters or scavengers.

They walked into a large common area with soft chairs and sofas, and microwaves and fridges and tables. Grammar pushed rudely past Jasper and began opening drawers and cupboard doors, banging and clattering and throwing unwanted items on the floor. His foraging efforts didn't pay off in anything edible, but with a glare at Jasper, he pocketed a large knife.

She wanted to point out the obvious, that she was not his enemy. She'd had every intention of rescuing Neverwhen; Zenobia had hijacked them both. But he was in no mood for logic and reason. He'd be angry at her because she was a safer target, a simpler target than his own mother.

She owed Harmony a thousand apologies for her own misdirected anger as a child. And maybe Zenobia as well.

Jasper pushed the thought away with force.

They continued their exploring. Endless hallways with flickering lights and locked doors and mysterious defunct equipment. Whiteboards still covered in the runes of mathematical equations and diagrams that might make more sense to Ben than they did to Jasper. Family photos on desks, personalized mugs, a cartoon tacked to a bulletin board that said, "Screw your lab safety. I want superpowers."

They found more stairs. The next level down and the one below that were similar to the first one, and they explored them quickly, as nearly all the rooms were locked. Jasper didn't bother pulling out her lock picking tools, as most of the locks were electronic. It would've taken too long anyway, a needle-in-a-haystack search since she had no idea what she was looking for. It seemed likely that the tunnel's mouth would be in the lowest level, so they took the stairs again. The stairs ended at a final door, also equipped with a scanner pad.

More confidently, Jasper inserted her finger into the slot. A prick of her fingertip, and the screen came to life.

"Welcome, Jasper Pine." The melodic, genderless voice seemed to emanate from the air.

Grammar hissed and clutched his amulets.

The door clicked, and Jasper pushed it open. Lights flickered to life, revealing a long narrow room, empty but for a desk strewn with books and papers and a couple of chairs. The facing wall was inset with a window that extended the full length of the room. The window looked into a second room. This one was half full of dark, towering stacks that glittered with tiny flashing lights like a starry night. The other half of the room held countertops and fridges and microscopes and many more items Jasper couldn't identify. It also held stacks of cages filled with slight motion—living mice. Once again Merlot's comics helped her identify what she would have otherwise taken for abstract mechanical sculptures that crowded the laboratory space: robots.

Everything was still except for the flashing lights and the curious scurrying of the mice in their cages.

Grammar's knuckles turned white around his amulets, but in the absence of anything recognizable or overtly threatening, he stayed on task. "Where's the tunnel?"

Jasper approached the window. A heavy door led into the

second room, but Zenobia had said it wouldn't open to anybody but her and the Guardian. This room full of tall mysterious stacks and robots and lab equipment was where the AI lived, safely shielded from the EM radiation that filled the zones. The lab was where it tested the antibac prototypes, where it had used up the last of the graviteria samples, according to the Guardian.

She'd never asked Zenobia much about the AI, accepting it as some ghostly electronic entity that was wholly devoted to finding her a cure. Ben had a great many more questions, but for Jasper that was enough. She didn't need to know how it worked, just that it did. But how did she communicate with it? In comic books Iron Man talked to his AI as if it were an invisible omnipresent servant and it always responded cordially.

"Hello, AI?" she said tentatively.

"Hello, Jasper," the voice responded promptly. "It's nice to finally meet you."

"Do you know who I am?"

"Jasper Pine, daughter of Andrew Terrence Pine and Catherine Maria Pine." It rattled off her birthdate and birthplace. "Born with extraterrestrial single-celled organisms bonded to your cells."

Grammar pulled his knife out and looked around wildly for the source of the voice. "Be showen yourself!"

"Please state your name for identity confirmation."

"His name is Grammar," Jasper said. "Do you know who he is?"

"Son of Dr. Zenobia Allan and Darius Dalca, birthdate—"

"Where are you?" Grammar shouted. The room around them was clearly empty. He ran up to the window and peered into the shadows. "You a witch? I'll be killen you."

"I am not a witch. I am not, in fact, human. I do not have a physical form to show you, Grammar, but if you'd find it reassuring, I can speak through one of my more humanoid extensions."

A lurching movement in the other room slammed Jasper's heart into overdrive. One of the robots was moving. She gaped as this *thing* of metal and plastic moved its mechanical limbs in a bizarre parody of a human and *walked* to the window to face them. It had four limbs and a head-shaped lump on top of its torso with rudimentary features that mimicked a human's face. It lifted a hand—it had pincers instead of fingers—and waved at them.

Grammar screamed and threw his knife at the robot. The knife clunked against the thick glass between them and fell to the floor.

"It's okay, Grammar. It's not magic." Jasper's voice sounded high pitched and breathless to her ears. The robot certainly *looked* like magic, and since she couldn't even begin to explain how an AI worked to herself, much less Grammar, it might as well *be* magic. "Anyway, it can't hurt us. Right?"

"I am incapable of harming humans." The voice, while nicely modulated, remained unmarred by emotion. "Also neither I nor my mechanical extensions can safely leave this room for any long period of time. Please be reassured, Grammar."

"Reassured" was not the word for the expression on Grammar's face, but with a ferocious scowl he seemed to remember he was an alpha and straightened his spine.

"You've been preparing my antibac?" Jasper asked.

"Yes."

"What are my chances of survival?" Zenobia could've been lying. She'd lied about nearly everything else.

"Based on the mice trials, fifty-three percent chance of survival. Fifteen percent chance of survival without any significant physical, neurological, or cognitive impairments."

Zenobia hadn't been lying about this, apparently. Jasper crossed her arms tightly over her chest. Fifteen percent wasn't nothing, she reminded herself. She'd been cursed with unlikely luck, according to Darius. Perhaps her luck would hold.

Grammar retrieved his knife without taking his eyes from the unmoving robot. "You knowen where the tunnel is?" he demanded.

"The walkway to the subway station can be accessed from the first parking garage level."

Jasper had more questions, but Grammar had heard enough. He spun and headed for the stairwell. The door opened as he approached it, and he came to an abrupt halt.

The Guardian stepped inside, and the door clicked shut behind her. "AI, lock door on my authority. Access restricted to my DNA only."

"Restrictions partially accepted, Dr. Lee," the AI said. "Dr. Allan cannot be blocked. She has equal administrative access."

"That won't be a problem," the Guardian said.

13

THE VOICE IN THE MACHINE

The universe gave me
A terminal case
Of the talking gods.

~ Veronica Park

"What are you doing here?" Jasper demanded.

"Zenobia got you here with a minimum of fuss, but we both knew she'd be spent by the end. So I'll be the one to administer the antibac. If that's what you choose." The Guardian raised an eyebrow. "Have you made a decision? Take the antibac, kill yourself, or try it my way and meld with the graviteria?"

Grammar looked at Jasper. "Killen yourself? What's she meanen?"

Jasper shook her head at him, not wanting to explain. "Maybe I haven't decided," she said to the Guardian. "I still have over two months. I want to help my friends first. I didn't even get to say goodbye to anyone. So tell the AI to open the door, because we're leaving."

"I can't do that," the Guardian said with every evidence of regret.

"What if I'm cutten you?" Grammar suggested with an alarming evenness of tone. "You're not scaren me."

"I believe you, young man. You're a credit to your parentage. How about we try words before violence, though?" She turned to Jasper. "What did Zenobia tell you your deadline was?"

Jasper felt a familiar sinking sensation in her stomach. "Two and a half months or so. Why?"

The Guardian clicked her tongue. "Replication can increase at an unpredictable rate toward the end. That's why we were both anxious to get you here as soon as possible, even if technically you may still have time."

"Why couldn't she just have said so?" Jasper exclaimed in frustration. "Does she even know how to say anything straight?"

"I really don't think so. Unlike her more straightforward son here. But she was always focused on giving you hope and not worrying you about things out of your control."

"I'm not a child anymore! This is my life!"

"I'm an authority on many subjects but not parenting. You'll have to take it up with Zenobia."

"She's *not* my—"

"In the meantime," the Guardian continued, "I'd like to test your blood to see what your current replication rate is."

Jasper hesitated. It was a reasonable suggestion. "Okay, but I want the AI to tell me the results, not you."

The Guardian shrugged assent.

Grammar walked over to the door and tugged on it. "Jasper can be stayen, then. Be letten me out. Now."

"I'd really like to test your blood as well," the Guardian said mildly. "It's been a few years since your last test."

Grammar tensed. "What're you meanen? What test? Why?"

"I think he's fine," Jasper said hastily. "Just do me and then we'll go."

The Guardian went over to a slot in the wall between the two rooms and pulled open a drawer. Jasper realized it was a way of passing items between the two rooms. The Guardian took an empty syringe from the drawer. Jasper held out her arm and endured the insertion of the needle.

Grammar hovered near the door and watched suspiciously. "Why's she taken your blood? For bad magic?"

"Remember my gravity curse? You can see it in my blood if you use a microscope. Didn't Martha ever show you her microscope? I know she had one."

The Guardian deposited the syringe of blood back into the drawer and closed it. The robot on the other side of the window lurched into motion. It opened the drawer and used its pincers to pick up the syringe. Grammar's curiosity overcame his fear. He approached the window so he could watch the robot stride stiffly to the lab.

As her blood was decanted into a test tube and inserted into a machine, Jasper turned to the Guardian. "Why did you lock us in here? It's not a very good show of faith." Also the awareness of being underground in a windowless room was creeping up on her and threatening to choke the air out of her lungs.

"I didn't expect either of you to be in the mood for talking, given your rather peremptory arrival here."

Jasper studied the Guardian's ageless face, barely marked by time. She lowered her voice in the hopes Grammar was too preoccupied with the movements of the robots to pay attention. "You do intend to let us out of here, don't you?"

The Guardian folded her cloak more firmly around herself and crossed her arms. "That depends on what your results show."

"If my deadline is very soon, I'll stay." The words tasted like ash and anguish. "But the kid . . ." She could feel him listening and searched for words. "His . . . *health* is perfectly good. I understand Zenobia wants him to be safe from Nico, but you can't just trap him here against his will. Once Nev is free, he might be more willing to stay."

Grammar's lip curled at this statement, but he didn't contradict her. He kept his eyes on the robots. "So that . . . thing can be sensen curses?" he asked suddenly.

The Guardian raised a quizzical eyebrow.

"Yes," Jasper said. It was the simplest answer.

"Can it be finden the curse in me?"

Jasper paused. He didn't know he was graviteria infected. Or had he figured it out? "Which curse?"

"The demons." His shoulders hunched. "The one that been maken Vron kill herself and Auntie die."

"That's not—you don't have that curse."

"But we could check," the Guardian said swiftly, smoothly. "I just need to take some blood."

Grammar glanced at Jasper. Reluctantly, she nodded. The Guardian retrieved another syringe, and Grammar impassively allowed his blood to be drawn.

After that, they had to wait as the machines did their work and the AI analyzed the results. Jasper paced to distract herself from the sensation that she was buried alive in this claustrophobic room five levels below the surface. The Guardian stood at another slot in the wall, this one with rubber gloves extending into the AI room that allowed her to manipulate a touchscreen computer in the other room. Jasper watched over her shoulder but could make little sense of the cryptic menus, dense notes, and mysterious graphics that flashed across the screen. When Jasper asked what she was doing, the Guardian replied that she was checking the system for bugs. Jasper couldn't imagine any insects living in this sterile environment, but she left the Guardian to it and continued pacing.

The AI spoke at last, "The results for Jasper Pine are ready. Maturation of extraterrestrial cells has reached ninety-five percent."

Her heart felt like ice. "What does that mean? How long do I have?"

"Unpredictable. Best estimate at ninety-two percent probability is anywhere from five days to two weeks."

"What?" The word was soundless. The air had been knocked out of her lungs.

"What's that meanen?" Grammar demanded.

"It means Jasper has a decision to make," the Guardian said.

Time had run out. *Five days.* That was barely enough time to catch up to Ben and the others so she could say goodbye.

"Zenobia would recommend taking the antibac at once," the Guardian said. "There's little margin for error now."

"And you would recommend I just wait it out and what? Try to communicate with the graviteria? *Meld?* How?" Her voice shifted and veered in time with the wildness of her heartbeat. She'd been facing her death for years. Her deadline had been looming closer and closer. She'd had time to adjust . . . or so she'd thought.

"I need . . ." Her breath withered in her lungs, turning her voice into a whisper. "I need to talk to Ben. I can't just . . ."

"You can record a video message for him if you like." The Guardian's voice was sympathetic but implacable. The Guardian wouldn't let her leave, Jasper realized. The timing was too risky.

"I want—I want to talk to Zenobia," Jasper blurted, surprising herself. "Where is she anyway? Hasn't she taken the elevator down by now?"

"She may have passed out." The Guardian didn't sound overly concerned. "I'll retrieve her shortly. In fact, why don't you think about your decision while I take the boy to get some food and check on Zenobia."

Jasper sank into a chair, as her legs were threatening to give out on her. "I don't need to think," she said. "I'll take the antibac. It'll stop the Shattering and give me a chance of surviving. I just —I want to talk to Zenobia first."

"Fair enough." The Guardian touched the door handle, and it clicked open. Grammar darted under her arm and out into the stairwell, eager for a chance to leave.

Jasper pushed herself to her feet. "I'll come with you to find Zen."

"Best stay," the Guardian said softly. Before Jasper could react, she'd stepped outside with Grammar. "Order Seventeen, AI," she said.

The door slammed shut behind her.

Fuelled by a horrible panic, Jasper ran at the door, but of course it was locked against her. "Let me out!" she screamed, but no answer came from the other side. Grammar and the Guardian might not even be able to hear her. "AI," she called, "open the door."

"Not authorized," said the AI. All her pleading and shouting could provoke no other response.

"You said you couldn't harm a human. Well, by locking me in here you're giving me a panic attack. You're harming me!"

"I can help you with that. I will sedate you."

"What? No! You can't touch me!"

"I can disperse the sedative through the vents."

"Don't you dare! Look, I'm calming down. I'm breathing. It's fine."

She forced herself to breathe steadily in and out for several minutes, though all her internal organs wanted to jump out of her skin. "What were Grammar's test results?" she asked to distract herself.

"Maturation of extraterrestrial cells has reached seven percent."

"Oh, good. He's a long way off, then." She breathed in and out, in and out. "What do you think of the Guardian's—Dr. Lee's —idea about melding with the graviteria? Would it work?"

"Insufficient data."

"Naturally. What do you think I should do?"

"I am not designed to form opinions."

"Well, you're useless."

"I have many uses. Based on your prioritized goals, I can provide you with a list of your best options ranked in order of probability of success."

"Never mind."

"Are you feeling better now, Jasper?"

"Yeah, actually. Much calmer." She yawned. And yawned again. "AI, did you sedate me after all?"

"Yes. You have been breathing it since the door closed. I would suggest you lie down on the floor now so you do not hurt yourself by falling."

"You goddamn—I'm so over being drugged." Sleep dragged her down too heavily for more than a spark of anger. "You know, Grammar called you a witch, but I always thought you'd be more like a god."

"Insufficient data for comparison."

Darkness took her.

14

INTO THE DARK

You taste of crow wings and insomnia
With an aftertaste of blood.
I want a hit
Of that existential dread
You're smoking.

~ Veronica Park

Awakening came slowly. Darkness turned into more darkness with faint creaking and a sensation of movement and then the recognition of light as her eyelids cracked open. Her brain felt muffled in cloth, and she kept still while she tried to absorb what was happening.

She was being carried in someone's arms, someone wearing armour or metal clothing and moving stiffly. A faint glow surrounded her, unrelated to the point of light that slowly resolved into a torch being carried ahead of them.

Her gut knew instantly that it wasn't just night. They were

underground, deep underground. She stiffened as her lungs rebelled and she realized her hands and feet were bound.

Not again.

She looked up at the person carrying her, realized what she was seeing, and shrieked.

It wasn't a person at all. It was the robot from the lab.

The person with the torch stopped and came back to her as she struggled fruitlessly to escape the robot's metal arms.

"Stay calm, Jasper," said the Guardian. "No one is going to hurt you." She waited until Jasper had exhausted herself screaming epithets at her.

"Where are you bringing me?" Jasper demanded finally. She'd have bruises from hurling herself against the robot's unyielding grip.

"A safe place," the Guardian said and continued walking.

The robot followed. The ambient glow was coming from a white light in its chest.

"I thought the Tower was safe. This isn't the Tower. And why the *fuck* am I tied up?"

"I really hoped you'd make the right choice. I gave you every chance. But alas, I can wait no longer. Time is too short."

The Guardian's meaning filtered in with the chill of horror. "You want me to Shatter."

"Zenobia's Shattering never extended underground by more than a half dozen metres—an interesting limitation and the subject of much theorizing. I believe the graviteria were designed so they could never substantially harm a planet. After all, how would they benefit if their hosts lost their planet? Lab animals still Shatter underground, but their Shatterings are nowhere near big enough to bother the earth. But what would happen if a person reached the point of Shattering while deep underground? It's very possible the graviteria have a fail-safe to prevent it."

"If you're wrong . . ." Words failed her for a moment. "A Shattering *inside* the earth sounds like a *monumentally fucking stupid* idea! What if the whole rotation and tilt of the planet gets fucked up? I'm no *scientist*, but I think that'd probably be bad!"

"Or the graviteria will recognize their location and instinctively contain the zones that erupt. Anyway, I'm expecting that once you successfully meld with the graviteria, there'll be no Shattering to speak of. The underground location is just in case. I'm not genocidal, Jasper. I don't want anyone to get hurt either."

"But you're willing to risk it, and for what? Even if this works, do you think I'll do *anything* to help you with my new superpower? You've lost whatever goodwill you had with me."

"If this works, I'll have shown you the way to save Grammar. But I'm not looking for your gratitude. One thing at a time."

"Where is Grammar?" she asked, reminded of him.

"Fed and fast asleep in the lab."

"Sedated, you mean?"

The Guardian shrugged.

"What about Zenobia?"

"Comatose. She expended more of herself than she ever has before, carrying you two."

"Will she be all right?"

"She'll likely wake up in a day or two but will be in no shape to travel for at least a week."

Jasper studied the robot's blank metal face. "I thought you couldn't leave the lab, AI."

"Not safely," the robot replied. "We are well below the limits of the lowest zones, but it is still a risk to leave the shielded lab."

"Where are we?" She couldn't control the quaver in her voice, the paralyzing weakness that made her sag in the robot's stiff arms. It wasn't a hallway they were in; it was more of a tunnel, though lined in concrete and laced with pipes and wires.

"The Tower was originally meant to extend almost as far underground as above ground," the Guardian said. "They never got far in construction, but a preliminary network of tunnels was built. When Jim and Irene, our engineers, explored these tunnels, they found connections to old abandoned subway tunnels and century-old sewers and other subterranean passages from long ago. Cities are built in layers on top of older constructions, and this city is no different. Take the wrong turn here and you'll find yourself far from the Tower, lost in an underground maze."

The coppery taste in Jasper's mouth increased until it felt like a mouthful of blood.

Turns and more turns. Other tunnels branched off on either side. Sometimes the Guardian took a turn, seemingly at random. Left, right, right, left . . . but Jasper couldn't keep track. Several times they descended steep stairs that were more like ladders. Spiking fear frazzled every thought in her head. She'd never find her way back, even if she escaped.

She smelled damp, heavy soil and stale concrete and heard the *plink, plink* of dripping water somewhere far away. Her limbs grew numb with terror. The Guardian was going to bury her alive. She should fight, pull away from this stiff metal man. But it was all she could do just to keep breathing as the weight of the earth above them compressed the air in her lungs into sludge. Her muscles felt liquified. Her gut gurgled and twisted.

Finally, the Guardian stopped. The robot set Jasper onto her feet, and she fell against its metal side, unbalanced by her bound limbs. The torchlight showed dirt walls, flashes of concrete and brick, wooden beams holding back the dirt. And a trap door in the ground in front of them, made of heavy wood with a large padlock through an iron ring.

Horror plunged her gut through the floor. "No, no, no. Please . . ."

The Guardian set the torch in a niche carved for the purpose, then crouched and unlocked the trap door. It opened to reveal blackness and a whiff of stale air. Jasper couldn't stop a whimper as fear throttled her chest.

The Guardian had been carrying a pouch over her shoulder and a gallon container of water. She tossed both in and turned back to Jasper. Jasper shrank away, but the robot held both her arms in its pincers as the Guardian cut the tie around her ankles and then her hands. This was her last chance to try to fight or run away into the labyrinthine tunnels they'd just come through.

She couldn't move.

"I'll find a way to kill myself." Her voice was hoarse, holding less conviction than she liked.

"I've already removed every sharp or remotely harmful object on you. But the robot will stay with you. It will keep you alive."

Jasper cursed her.

"Jump or the robot will toss you in," the Guardian said. "Your choice."

Trembling, Jasper sat with her legs dangling into the hole. "How—how far down?"

"You'll live."

When Jasper hesitated, the robot took a step forward. She slowly lowered herself until she was hanging by her hands from the side of the trap door. The robot took another step toward her, and the thought of its metal foot stomping on her hands made her let go. The drop was maybe twice her height, but with no light below or any way of accurately determining the height, she landed hard and off balance, tipping instinctively into a roll to absorb the shock.

The robot dropped through the trap door and landed with a thump and a whine of whatever motors and gears allowed it to move and balance. The white glow from its chest illuminated the space, but there was little to see. Four walls and a floor, a cot, stacks of mouldy paperbacks and magazines, and a bucket in the corner, its purpose obvious.

The Guardian leaned over the trap door. "Jasper, I'm sure you'll think me monstrous for this captivity, and I accept your anger. But recall my speculations about how the graviteria might have been designed, and how somewhere out there might be the Aliens X who are, if not the creators, then the original hosts of the graviteria. If my speculations are true, then who's to say they might not find us one day? Who's to say they're not in the neighbourhood already for us to find their graviteria on an asteroid? We know absolutely nothing about them but what they can tell us. If you're able to meld with the graviteria, it'll provide us with crucial information about what we can expect."

Jasper stared at the Guardian in horror. "Yeah, or the graviteria could turn me into some kind of drone or weapon for them or . . . or a monster or something. You don't know!"

"Yes," the Guardian said. "Exactly. We don't know anything. That's the problem. Zenobia was adamantly against this approach, and until now I've let her have her way. But our planet could be at stake, the entire human race. The Shattering may be a terrible risk. But so is ignorance."

"You have no right to make that decision for me!" Jasper shouted, even as dread rose up in a flood at the Guardian's words. She'd thought the stakes already too high.

"Maybe not. But consider it a kindness that the responsibility will be mine and not yours." The Guardian stood. "The room's not very comfortable, I'm afraid, but you won't have to endure it for long. The robot will monitor your condition, and I'll be back once everything is over."

The faint light from the torch disappeared, and the trap door slammed shut.

Jasper scrambled to her feet and screamed, "Come back! Let me out, let me out, let me out!"

She didn't know how long she screamed, how many times she threw herself against smooth walls that offered no purchase for her to climb, but her throat was rough and raw and her fingers ached by the time she finally slumped to the ground, sobbing for breath and coughing from the scraped dryness in her throat. Her heart rattled like dice in a palm.

The white light emanating from the robot filled the room. The robot didn't move.

Despite the light, she could feel the shadows creeping up on her, thick as cake, from the edges of the room and from the tunnels above. It wasn't air she was breathing—it was darkness, and it would choke her. She surged upright, flailing for something solid. She squeezed her eyes shut and tried to imagine she was in a large room and it was only dark because her eyes were closed, and that the doors and windows were open and there was plenty of air.

It didn't work. She wasn't in a large room. She was in a concrete cage with a hundred metres of solid earth between her and precious open air.

Otherwise at a standstill, blood vibrated in her veins. Her heart fluttered, wild and useless, as her lungs remained stubbornly on strike, their demands unknown and unanswerable.

Aliens inside her and aliens out in space, the universe seeming suddenly much smaller and more crowded than before. Stakes she could hardly fathom. The what-ifs the Guardian had never quite said aloud.

What if the Aliens X were hostile?

What if Jasper and her resident graviteria were the human race's only source of information and data against a species they couldn't even imagine?

She found herself tapping her knuckles against her breastbone, a quick rhythm.

Good thoughts, good thoughts. She scrabbled for a memory, a sensation, a story to distract herself from the tiny size her lungs had shrunk to.

Like the way the quicksilver flutter of Ryan's heart had injected darts of stillness into her skin as he'd lain on top of her, holding her to the earth. The way his eyes steadied her when she felt ready to fall. Dangerous. Unlooked for. Bittersweet. She locked herself up so tight after Merlot, but she'd locked the wrong room. She'd been guarding an empty closet, only to find someone in her living room watering her plants and folding her laundry.

"Robot, you have to let me out. You have to."

It hadn't made a sound or moved from where it had landed. "Not authorized."

Its mechanical, emotionless voice sent shivers crawling down her spine and arms.

Jasper forced herself to her feet and moved slowly around the perimeter of the space, one hand on the wall. She returned to her starting point, having found nothing. She examined the cot, but it was bolted to the floor and wall and lacked any sharp edges. To reward herself for the exploration, she took a sip of water from the jug and tried not to think about how long it might have to last her.

Next, she tried to climb the wall, testing different areas, but she could find no appreciable purchase for her fingers, no convenient cracks or protrusions. She pressed her back to a corner and pushed herself upward, bracing her arms and legs against the two walls. But when she reached the ceiling, it was solid and smooth, and she was far from the trap door. Even if she could reach it, she had no way to reach the very solid padlock on the outside of it.

She wouldn't give in to panic until she'd explored every inch of this cage. She scuffed along the floor as systematically as she could, looking for anything—drains, vents, another trap door.

A faint sound—skittering almost—jerked her to a halt. She was paralyzed by the sudden conviction that somewhere bones were gathering themselves and standing up. Her breath came loud and harsh, drowning out whatever sound she'd heard. Rats? Spiders? Spiders made no sound.

Unless they were giant man-eating spiders with legs as long as her forearms.

She backed away from the wall so that she stood in the middle of the room.

Martha Abebe had told her a story about a spider once. Jasper couldn't remember why, what had happened, but she'd been crying, screaming even. Maybe it was around the time Darius had told her he had a present for her and it was two beautiful blue eyeballs. Maybe it was after Darius ordered Ben's leg cut off. It wouldn't have been a nightmare, though, because before she killed Darius, her sleep was dreamless. Her nightmares only happened while she was awake.

All she remembered was Zenobia gathering her up in her arms and Martha crouching in front of them, her hands resting on Jasper's knees. Jasper didn't remember the story anymore, just that it was a sly and clever spider who was good at tricking the other animals and even the gods to get what he wanted. She wondered why she'd felt safe with these two women when they were as subject to Darius's whims as she was. They loved her but they wouldn't save her. Couldn't save her. They saw Darius's monstrousness but didn't have the strength to do what needed to be done.

She had to be the spider. She had to save herself.

Jasper searched her pockets thoroughly. The Guardian had taken nearly everything from her including her belt and shoelaces, and her harness and all her ropes. Her pockets contained only crumbs and lint and a pretty silver button Neverwhen had given her. But her clothing harboured a few secrets the Guardian hadn't discovered. During the rainy days in the Gingers' zone, Jasper had taken her lock picking tools from where they'd been sewn into her belt and sewn them into her bra instead. She could feel them, tucked more or less smoothly along the underwire. She couldn't think of a use for them. Even if she could reach the trap door, the padlock was on the other side.

But her bra held one more secret—a tiny pouch wrapped in waterproof oilcloth. One precious match and fishing line. Survival gear at its most basic, were she ever stripped of her clothes and left to die.

Time passed. Or didn't. It was nearly impossible to tell in the unchanging, unblinking electric light. She investigated the stacks of magazines and paperbacks the Guardian had left her and flipped through some of them but couldn't maintain concentration for more than a few minutes at a time. She interrogated the robot to distract herself. Its conversational ability was limited either by its nature or by the command of the Guardian. It could tell her how much time had passed, but she soon stopped asking. Eventually, she curled up on the cot and managed to doze. There wasn't much else to do.

When she awoke and asked, the robot told her three hours had passed. Her stomach growled, so she rummaged through the bag of supplies the Guardian had tossed down and ate some crackers. She inventoried the contents of the bag and found enough food to last a week. Nothing that would help her escape. She took another drink of water and hefted the jug.

How long could a person survive without water? Not much longer than three days. The AI had said she had five days to two weeks before she Shattered. If she dumped out the water, she could die before then. But how would the robot respond? It might have a way of summoning the Guardian. If so, what then? She thought it unlikely the Guardian would sedate her; she needed Jasper conscious to meld with the graviteria. But she might force some food and water down Jasper's throat, enough to keep her alive. If the Guardian came down in person, Jasper might have a chance to overpower her, but not the Guardian and the robot both, especially not if she was weak from thirst.

She studied the robot where it stood unmoving. If only Ben were here. He might have an inkling of how to damage the robot so it couldn't send a message to the Guardian. Jasper tilted her head back to consider the trap door in the ceiling. Three to four metres above her head, she estimated. The robot was about two metres tall. Could it jump? That was a good question.

She'd have one chance to carry out the plan forming in her head. If she failed, the robot would likely immobilize her for the remainder of her time in this hole. All it had to do was close its pincers around her wrist and lock them in place. It wasn't human; it wouldn't get tired or weak or bored or take its attention off her. She couldn't hurt it with her fists or appeal to its sympathies or its conscience.

Jasper paced around the room so the robot would become accustomed to her movement. She cast no more glances at the ceiling. She drank water without attempting to ration it. If this didn't work, she'd dump it all out and try to die of thirst. She curled up on the cot and dozed as the slow hours passed.

Finally, early in the morning, the tingle awoke in her belly. It jerked her out of a light doze, but she turned the jerk into a stretch and a yawn. She got up and shook her limbs loose. She wandered to the side of the room farthest from the robot, keeping her movements casual and bored. The tingle expanded to her toes and fingertips in a dizzying rush, and she crouched in preparation.

She fell upward.

She curled into a half somersault to get her feet under her and landed on the ceiling with a tuck and roll to absorb the impact. She flattened herself to the ceiling.

The robot whined into life and moved. It strode two steps to stand directly underneath her. It tilted its head back to observe her. She didn't know how good its vision was or how it could see without eyes, but she assumed its senses were as good as hers—some of them anyway.

"Get down," it said in its emotionless voice.

"Make me."

Sometimes in comic books robots were terrifyingly fast and agile. Other times they were clunky, clumsy things. She hoped this one fit into the latter category.

The robot did attempt to jump. Its motors whined and the white light bobbed. It tried twice more but achieved only half a foot of height each time. As long as Jasper stayed crouched low to the ceiling she'd be out of its reach. Satisfied, she crawled on hands and knees until she reached the trap door. She rapped her knuckles against its solid wood.

She might not be a spider, but she had her own tricks.

She pulled out the tiny packet from her bra, struck the match, and set it against the trap door.

15

OUT OF THE FIRE

Some people are a vortex and the rest of us tiny ships
Trapped in the current at the edge of the void.
Some people are stars, dense with gravitational force,
And we are sucked into orbit, mere asteroids.

~ Veronica Park (*Story of a Monster*)

"What are you doing?" the robot said in its inhumanly calm voice. "You are endangering yourself. Stop immediately."

Smoke filled the hole at an alarming rate even as the fire crept sullenly along the boards, barely more than blackening them. On her hands and knees, Jasper retreated as far as the ceiling would allow her. She draped her T-shirt over her nose and tried not to think about how quickly the oxygen in the hole could be consumed by the fire—perhaps long before the trap door had burned through.

She crawled back to the trap door, arm over her nose and

mouth. Her up-gee gravity shift wouldn't last long. The wooden slab was only half charred and not yet seriously burned, although smoke was filling the hole with a haze that brought tears to her eyes and irritated her throat. She thumped her hand experimentally on the unburnt portion of the trap door. It had a little give but remained solid. She'd started the fire nearer to the hinges than the padlock, figuring that was the weak point.

"Dr. Lee has been notified," the robot said. "Please move away from the fire."

"Bite me."

"I cannot harm a human."

Her gravity would change back to down-gee any minute. The flames were crackling with more energy now. She backed away from the eye-watering smoke. Once she was back on the floor, she wouldn't be able to do anything about the fire.

The cracks between boards grew wider as the smoke and flames rose out of the hole. Coughs tore out of her throat as the smoke intensified. Sweat rolled down her face. Her up-gee time was running out. She rose to a crouch, keeping a wary eye on the robot, and stomped on the door near the hinges as hard as she could. She jerked back with a yelp as the flames licked her ankle.

She'd inadvertently straightened into the reach of the robot. It snagged her shirt with its pincers. At the unexpected grab she screamed despite herself. She tugged herself free before it could secure its grip and crouched down again close to the ceiling, out of its reach.

The robot turned and clunked several steps away. It bent slowly and picked up the jug of water.

The tingle started deep in her gut. She uttered a heartfelt curse.

This time she jumped into the fire with her full weight. The boards creaked and the flames scorched. She was coughing so hard, she thought she might puke. She jumped again. And again. The boards groaned. Her shoes were on fire, and her ankles and calves were seared. She leaped out of the fire, patting frantically at her melting sneakers, but with the tingle expanding she was almost out of time.

Cool water splashed onto her skin and hissed in the flames. The robot was attempting to throw water from the jug onto the trap door. Its movements were awkward, but enough water landed to douse some of the flames.

Desperate, Jasper straightened again to within the robot's reach. She pulled and kicked at the jug in its pincers. Water splashed over her hands and the robot and onto the ground. The jug clattered to the floor.

The tingle expanded to her fingertips. She turned away from the robot and jumped onto the trap door one last time with as much force as she could muster. The boards cracked.

Her legs broke through the brittle trap door just as her gravity changed.

She lunged upward, bending herself double to grab the burning, cracking trap door with her hands just as gravity pulled her legs and the rest of her body back downward into the cell.

Awful pain seared through her as flames licked her hands. She screamed but couldn't let go, not when she was this close.

The robot's pincers swiped against her ankle, and she kicked frantically. If it got a grip on her, she'd never be able to combat its strength. She threw herself upward, clawing for purchase, and managed to get her elbow out of the broken trap door.

Her torso was circled by fire. It ignited her shirt and crackled in her ears. Smoke dizzied and blinded her. Her skin was being scorched, roasted to a crisp, a thousand wasp stings along her hands and arms and upper body.

The robot jumped with a creak and a whine, but her stinging, reaching hands had found blessedly cool dirt. Kicking wildly to evade the robot's grasping pincers, she dragged herself out the rest of the way. She rolled in the dirt, patting frantically at her clothes and hair until she was sure she was no longer on fire. Coughing and blinded by smoke and tears, she shoved handfuls of dirt at the trap door until the flames died to embers.

Exhausted, she lay on her back and cradled her blistered hands to her chest. Tears still rolled down her face, but even with the smoke in the air there was more oxygen now that she was out of the hole.

She pulled herself upright, gasping and wincing as her T-shirt brushed over raw skin. It was worse than the worst sunburn. It was agony. The glow of the robot's light from inside the hole was just enough to make out the shapes around her, the walls and ceiling and the tunnel from which they'd come.

Cautiously she peered into the hole. The robot stood motionless beneath the trap door.

"How did the Guardian—Dr. Lee—plan to get you out of the hole again?" she wondered aloud.

The robot didn't answer.

The water and food were still in the hole, out of reach. She'd give up her right arm for a cup of water to pour over her burns. "I don't suppose you want to throw me the water jug, robot."

"Come and get it." The most human response she'd gotten from it yet.

"No, thanks. But if you don't give it to me, you'll be causing me to come to harm."

"Dehydration will ensure you will be found more quickly and brought to safety."

Did mechanical creatures hold grudges? Could it sulk? Or was it merely rationalizing competing imperatives? It was even possible that the Guardian was speaking through its voice, using it as a phone. She was fairly sure such things were possible, though she didn't know how.

The last embers of the trap door winked out. Only the robot's white light remained. She should have kept a piece of the trap door alight as a torch, but it was too late now. She was deep underground without any light and no more matches and no idea which way to go. But the robot had said the Guardian had been notified of her escape. Jasper had no time to panic or dither. She had to move.

She started walking, trailing a hand along one wall. At every turn she wasted precious time trying to remember how they'd come here, but her direction sense was useless underground, especially when mixed with barely restrained panic. She made turns at random, wanting to get as far away from the hole as she could before the Guardian arrived.

After a while time grew soft and muddy. Constellations of bright agony prickled her torso and her arms, her jaw, and her throat where she'd immolated herself against burning boards. Her hands were their own universe of pain.

She'd been underground for a century. Gravity seemed wobbly, or else the earth itself was a pile of wobbly sticks, trembling in preparation for collapse. Her head felt huge and hot and her eyes felt full of sand. She wondered how long she'd had them closed as she walked.

"Stairs. Have to find stairs."

She needed to make her way upward, back to the light and air. These tunnels couldn't go on forever, could they? Unless she was somehow walking in circles in the featureless dark.

Time and reality wobbled. The darkness wavered.

Martha Abebe walked beside her, with the sound of an endlessly spinning copper coin: healer on the one side, butcher of limbs on the other. Oath breaker, lifesaver. *Heads he wins, tails you lose; the devil in blood is paid his dues.*

"I was just thinking about you." Jasper's tongue felt thick and unruly. "Your spider stories."

"Freeya used to love those stories," Martha said in her soft accent. She corrected herself, saying, "*Crane*. Sparrow did too." She sucked on her teeth. "Sparrow and Crane. I used to dream of birds, and now I don't wonder why. Neverwhen is my little chattering starling child, full of words and stories and curiosity. And the boy . . . what is he, I wonder. A cuckoo, I think, present in my nest only through the eviction of my Freeya—Crane. It isn't a fair label to put on a child, but what is fair about this life?" She fell silent.

Sparks flared and died behind Jasper's eyelids. She'd closed her eyes. It made no difference. "Your husband's going to kill him."

"*Ex*-husband." Martha clicked her tongue against the roof of her mouth, a dry, tart sound evocative of a world where old women had the final say on any subject and braided life and death together with their gnarled hands. "Nico. That man, *aiye*. If anyone ever tells you that you can't have too much of a good thing, know that it's a lie. Too much medicine is always poisonous, and it is the same with love."

Jasper thought about love, of Harmony on her hands and knees cleaning up an overturned pot of stew that Jasper had pushed over in those days when she could only communicate in tantrums or by running away. She thought of Ben staying by her side during her breakup with Merlot, even though it ruined his friendship with him, of Sparrow dragging her out of the bar or away from the poker table every now and then and forcing her to take walks in the fresh air.

"Can't have too much love," she said.

"The love you're thinking of is *enough*," Martha said. Her voice blurred, turned smoky. "But too much and it sours, putrefies, ferments into obsession."

"It's funny, isn't it," Jasper said, "how when you're a kid you think you know your parents, but then you grow up and you take off the blindfold and realize they were actually crocodiles or llamas or something. Not at all what you'd pictured. I was afraid of you and I hated Zenobia and I loved Darius. It was all wrong, all backwards. *I* was wrong. Something very, very wrong with me. Stupid kid. Why was I so stupid?"

Something struck her shoulder. She'd fallen against the wall. She pushed off it and forced herself to keep stumbling through the darkness.

"Why are you still here, Martha? Why haven't you moved on?" She'd fallen against the wall again. It was cool against her cheek. And horizontal. The wall was actually the floor. She was on the floor.

"Ghosts are subject to every form of gravity around them but exert none of their own. Letting go is a gift reserved for the living."

"Have you let go?" Jasper wondered. "Did you let go of what Darius did to you?"

To that Martha was silent. Perhaps she retorted, *Have you?* Or perhaps that was Jasper's imagination.

If no ghost ever moved on, no one would ever be able to sleep because their voices would be deafening, the air would be so full of them that no one would be able to breathe, and the earth would bleed with every step they took. If all ghosts stayed, there would be no room for the living.

Not unlike this city.

"You must have let go," Jasper said. "Look at how you raised his son."

Martha's familiar coppery smell was tinged with coffee, nostalgic and bitter, reminding Jasper of those barely remembered, long-ago Sunday mornings, distant as a dream, when her mother didn't have to work and Jasper would wake up to the smells of coffee and bacon.

"Why did you name him Grammar anyway? What does it mean?"

"Jasper," Martha said. "You hit your head when you fell. You cannot go to sleep. With those burns you're at risk of infection and dehydration, and now you're going into shock. You need to find water. You need to keep moving. You—"

"Grammar," Jasper said. "I know. Is it because without him nothing makes sense?"

If Martha answered, Jasper didn't hear. She fell into a dark hole inside her head and forgot everything.

16

THE SMALL GOD

So sad, did you hear?
They found her lying
In a pool of the sky's blood
With eternity's phone number
Written
On a crumpled napkin.

~ Veronica Park

S piders crawled over her skin, their feet glowing hot pokers. They ran and left a galaxy of charred freckles in their wake. Hot breath blew on her face. Soft footsteps, claws clicking on concrete, a large creature moving around her in the darkness.

Jasper, Jazz Master, Jasmeister. Wake up.

A cold, wet nose snuffled in her ear, and Jasper jerked upright with a scream, flailing in the darkness. Her fingertips encountered fur, and the footsteps retreated rapidly. A throaty whine sent shivers down her back. She groped around for a weapon, a stone, anything.

"Go away!" she yelled. "I'm not dead yet."

A brief, unnerving glint of eyes in the blackness, then padding paws that faded into silence. She strained her ears for a long time but heard no sounds of breathing or movement. She was alone.

That was a little rude, my dude. For gravity's sake, he was just seeing if you were awake, my crispy little sootflake. Sleeping's for the weak, the meek, the irretrievably bleak.

Even though it was perfectly dark, she could see Vron as clearly as if she generated her own light. Vron sat against the wall, arms wrapped around her knees. She was wearing a pink tutu over the ripped jeans Jasper had drawn on long ago, decorating them with fire-breathing crows and sword-wielding butterflies. She still looked twenty-one, her age when she'd died, skin drawn too thin over her broad cheekbones, a zit on her nose, thin white scars against the old parchment colour of her wrists.

"I'm still hallucinating." Jasper pressed the heels of her hands against her eyes. She could see nothing in the darkness of this concrete tunnel. Nothing except Vron. "Hit my head. Seeing ghosts everywhere."

Her head felt twice its usual size and was absorbing all the wrong sensory input, buzzing and warping as if she'd swallowed a zone. The pain from her burns flared and ebbed. Her throat was parched and her stomach knotted into its familiar, grim energy-conserving mode. How long had she been lying here alone in the dark and dirt?

"It'd be easier, wouldn't it," said Vron, "to just stay here. Sleep a couple of days. With no water it's not long before you'd be up and away, two stars to the right and straight on until morning."

"Would I?" Jasper looked up at the black-shrouded ceiling, but Vron's impossible visibility drew her eye like a magnet. "Or would I hang around haunting people like you're doing, and Martha and Darius? Are you a ghost or am I having a conversation with my own brain?"

"Who knows? Maybe I'm an imprint left on the earth's consciousness, just a shadow of the real me. Or maybe we leave little bits of our souls in the people who loved us, and this is the piece of me lodged in your brain. Maybe the zone borders are psychic barriers that stop souls from moving on. Hasn't this city always seemed overly haunted to you? It's grown alive from the souls it's eaten. It grew from the ruins and it lives in the rubble, in the weeds and rusting cars and empty houses. And it also lives here." Vron tapped a knuckle against her chest. "Abandoned and broken things, all of us."

"You must really be Vron. I couldn't think that stuff up on my own."

"You know what I think, Jazzle Dazzle? I think we all died in the Shattering. Call it purgatory if you like, but we're all ghosts trying to figure out why we're trapped here. Caught in ugly loops of hurting ourselves and each other. We're just obsessive manifestations of the small god's dreams."

"Is that why you killed yourself? You thought that if we're not even real, then maybe dying would wake you up?"

Vron closed her eyes. Her eyelashes made dark smudges against her cheeks. "Waking up is overrated. Let the small god have its dream. Gods get lonely too."

"Why did you leave us, Vron?"

A whisper. "I didn't know why anything mattered. Not then."

"And now you do?"

Silence.

Eyes squeezed shut, Jasper tried to remember what it was like to laugh until your ribs ached and hilarity sloshed out all your inner gunk, leaving you minty clean. She didn't know much, but she knew that was a feeling that mattered. It was a feeling that required friends, friends to make you laugh and to laugh with you. Friends who were alive.

She opened her eyes.

Vron was gone.

Jasper patted the place where Vron had been sitting and found nothing. Except a paw print. Large. The size of her palm.

"Damn," she said aloud. She'd thought the dog was a hallucination too.

Then her mind, mired in mud and prickling with spider pain, caught up belatedly. "How did you get down here, beast?"

She scrambled to her feet and stumbled in the direction the phantom dog had disappeared. The tunnels felt different. Despite the unrelenting darkness, the space around her felt echoey and smelled of wet stone rather than dusty concrete. Somewhere along the way she'd done what the Guardian had warned about—wandered out of the Tower halls and into the maze of abandoned tunnels and passageways under the city, relics of another time, the hollow blood vessels of a forgotten city.

She trailed her hand over the damp stone wall and came to an opening. A stirring of air touched her hypersensitive burnt skin. She edged into this opening and found herself in a narrow uneven stairwell. She scrambled upward as quickly as she could in the dark with her head still full of an ocean, heavy and unbalanced.

Light. It filtered from somewhere, dyeing the darkness grey. She used her eyes for what felt like the first time in weeks to puzzle out shapes and distances. Her returning sense of vision encouraged her to speed up. She tripped over rubble and fell flat, tearing up her hands and sending screams of pain over the burnt patches of her torso.

Voices in the distance. Possibly arguing crows or disputatious cats. Toenails clicked toward her. A subsonic grumble and mutter. Sniffing.

"Go feed on your own useless kind, mutt."

It sneezed, sounding surprised. Then it trotted away.

"Yeah, that's what I thought."

"Jasper!" The call echoed from far away. Grammar's voice.

Impossible. He was being held prisoner in the Tower. Or had she dreamed that?

Torchlight bobbed toward her. The dog barked, leading the way. She struggled to sit. The pain wouldn't relent. It was like soft icing sugar that drifted everywhere from the surface of a pastry. Or glitter. Persistent, aggravating, and impossible to get rid of.

"Apparently it's Haunt Jasper Pine Day," she told Grammar or the shadowy hallucination that had taken his shape. "So I hope this doesn't mean you're dead."

"I'm not dead," his hallucination said.

"Ghosts always say that." A thought struck her. "What if I'm the one who's dead?"

"Don't be dumb."

Cool hands touched her face. Cold, so cold. She was hot, burning up. Blessed liquid splashed her lips and ran into her mouth, shocking her awake. Torchlight blinded her. A dozen shapes moved around her, a gathering of painted, smelly underworld demons chattering in some indistinct hell-tongue. But Grammar's face was clear, with crinkled brows and pinched lips, as he crouched in front of her. Beside him sat a familiar fanged beast with excessive fur.

"You're not a ghost." Of this she was suddenly very certain. How could anything be more alive and more complete and yet so wondrously unfinished than this boy in front of her?

She tried to tell him, as dozens of little hands pushed,

prodded, and pulled her to her feet, that he was a universe. They were all universes filled with a million lights, a billion stars, so many, like glitter. The stars were glitter, but they were also burning holes, they were fire, they would consume you from the inside out—death by ten thousand star burns. And why were so many hands touching her? How many hands did Grammar have anyway?

"Exactly as many as I should be haven," he said, which was a very wise answer.

"But if you're an alien and I'm an alien, how many hands should we have? How will we know?" He was tall enough so she could lean on him, but too skinny to take all of her weight and so the other hands helped.

"Don't be dumb. No aliens here," said Grammar, but he sounded worried.

He should have been more worried about the dozen tinylings around them with their sharp teeth and bright eyes and dirty hands. And the panting, dangerous animal with the soft, soft fur and soulful eyes that kept trying to lick her hand.

He was wrong. The aliens were here, looking out of her eyes and looking back at themselves in Grammar's eyes. They'd been here all along.

If the small god had grown out of broken, abandoned things, then it must have also encompassed the graviteria, for they were also lost and alone, thrown from the vast reaches of space and marooned in the imperfect flesh and traumatized brain of an evolved monkey.

"Aren't you lonely?" she asked them.

We were. Until we met you.

17

SPIDER STORIES

The only god in this city is me,
The smallest god of all.

~ Veronica Park

Jasper woke to find herself engulfed by a kid pack puppy pile. Warm, odorous small bodies pressed against her from all sides. A pair of feet were inches from her face, a hard round skull was jammed into her ribs, and somebody was hugging her legs. She lay still in the dark, caught by two conflicting impressions. One, a thought that if she made a sudden move they'd wake and nip her like the thoughtless little animals they were. And two, a flash of warmth and nostalgia, a bone-deep memory of waking up like this in her own pack days, tangled up with Ben and Merlot and Vron and Charlie and Crane, sharing heat and breath and dreams and comfort.

Somebody's digestive system had disagreed emphatically with their dinner.

Jasper sat up with a hand clamped over her nose. Her burns awoke in the same moment, and pain scoured thought from her mind. She gasped for breath with lungs that refused to work. Despite the glowing embers of a fire, the darkness was as thick as mud.

Being touched was unbearable. She scrambled out of the puppy pile, and a shadowy figure sitting by the fire straightened.

"Jasper?" Grammar guided her to sit beside the fire and stirred the coals alive with a stick so that flames sprang up between them, small but precious. "You choken?" he asked, clinical rather than concerned. He handed over a canteen of water.

"No, I . . . I . . ." Her voice sounded warped and distant. She put her head between her legs and concentrated on pulling air into her recalcitrant lungs. Her hands had been bandaged in surprisingly clean cloth with some kind of herbal paste. She gulped the water, and it tasted like heaven.

"Oh," he said, knowingly. "Bad spirit."

It didn't seem an inaccurate diagnosis. She pressed a hand to her malfunctioning chest and imagined it was Ryan's hand. *Breathe, Zeep.* All she wanted to do was breathe. If only she were standing on the edge of a rooftop right now, preparing to jump. Air filled her to the brim in those moments, intoxicating and vivid and *enough*.

"Outside." She forced the word past the constriction in her throat.

"Not safe."

But if the darkness choked and killed her, what was the point of staying hidden?

Grammar's amulets clicked as he gathered them in his hand and then released them. "Sometimes spirits are just wanten a story, so they're eaten dreams."

"I don't have any stories," she whispered. She was inhaling

shadow and exhaling all her stored-up oxygen. Soon she'd have none left.

The flicker of the small flames lit the grim line of his mouth, the darkness of his eyes. Despite her best intentions, she hadn't protected him from the machinations of his mother and the Guardian. The black-and-white world of a child didn't allow excuses; he hadn't forgiven her yet, and maybe he never would.

After all, she'd never forgiven Zenobia for the same reasons.

She'd also pushed Zenobia into saying aloud what no child should ever hear from their parents—that he was unwanted. *Unlovable.* It was impossible to know how deeply the arteries of softness in him had been cut and how thick the granite would grow around his heart. And what would he become then?

A beautiful butterfly, no doubt. Darius laughed soundlessly.

Cross-legged, she bent over till her forehead touched the ground, as if she could find more air here with the dust and moss. "How did you get away from the Tower?"

"Been talken to the witch voice. It been letten me go."

"What? Why would the AI do that? It has to obey the Guardian."

His mouth tightened. "It been sayen the order been comen from—from my—from *her*."

"You mean your mother."

"She's not my mama." His voice scraped like a snarl. "The Up-gee Witch, I'm meanen." He spat as if to get the taste of the name out of his mouth.

She let the bitter silence rest. The AI had said that Zenobia had equal authorization to give it orders. Wherever Zenobia had passed out, she must have awoken long enough to ask the AI what was going on and then countermanded the Guardian's orders so Grammar could go free. Perhaps she hadn't intended for him to leave the Tower entirely, but he found a way. It was too late for Jasper by then.

Grammar resumed his story. He'd run for the ReGeneration's tunnel, but afraid of pursuit he took several wrong turns and got lost in the maze just as Jasper had. But he eventually came across some of the chalked markings that kid packs used to find their way in the city and followed them to the Sun Devils, and with them, the remainder of Grammar's pack, the Crows.

"How did you find me?"

"Didn't. Was the dog." His voice held no warmth.

The dog approached her from the other side of the fire, moving stiffly. Had Okuru been injured? How in the small god's name had he managed to find Grammar again? Could that kind of witchery be explained merely by a keen nose?

It wasn't Okuru.

"Fursa?" she exclaimed in disbelief.

Zenobia's long-standing companion sniffed her face. She squeezed her eyes shut and held still. Eventually, Fursa's warm, heavy weight settled against her leg. His stinky breath mingled with dust and moss and smoke and the body odour of a dozen unwashed children. The weight of his head on her knee pressed her fear back into the bounds of her skin, even though she knew his teeth, the size and shape of the old divot in her calf, were that close to her leg. Either she still smelled like Zenobia or the familiarity of her own smell was reassuring to him, even though he must have recognized she held no fondness for him.

"The younglings been finden him," Grammar said. "They're wanten to keep him." His tone was neutral, disapproving of adding an extra mouth to feed that couldn't hunt for itself but also resigned to the whims of children, who loved quickly and fiercely and didn't know when to let go. He couldn't know the history of this particular dog, but maybe after all these years it no longer mattered. During Darius Dalca's reign, Fursa and the other dogs from the pits had only done what they'd been forced to. Their only crime was surviving.

Jasper wondered where all the other dogs that Zenobia had adopted were, with their ugly puppyhoods and abuse-scarred minds. Had they died by now like most of the Azuros? Couldn't it be considered a mercy if they had, for both the dogs and the Azuros?

But not Tom. Please, small god, not Tom—not yet. If Nico killed Tom, Zenobia would—Jasper's mind shied away. Tom's murder would strike Zenobia like an axe to the heart.

Maybe if she hurried, she could persuade Nico to wait to kill Tom. After all, his purpose was to draw out Zenobia, but right now she was physically incapable of coming to Yorky, no matter what threats Nico made.

"Have you been above ground?" she asked. "Where are we in the zones?"

"Near quarantine down-gee." Meaning they were at the edge of the wild zones, near the down-gee buffer that extended to the quarantine wall. "Maybe half day of walken to Yorky."

"And Nev? Do the kids know anything about the Damaskers and Nev?"

His hands clenched convulsively. "They're talken about an army of dragons in the wormholes—the tunnels. Chasen demons. Sayen there been a fight or something, but . . ." He swallowed, shook his head. "I don't know."

"I hope you didn't waste much time looking for me when you could've been looking for her," Jasper said, guilt tearing at her.

He shrugged tightly. "Ryan will be saven her. And Crane." But he wouldn't look at her.

"How much time has passed since I saw you in the Tower?"

Her tone must have conveyed the importance of the question because he considered carefully before answering, "Almost three days."

Her breath stalled in her throat. She had two days minimum

until she Shattered. If she headed straight back to the Tower, she'd have enough time—maybe—to take the antibac. Assuming the Guardian didn't immediately capture her. Assuming the AI allowed her into its sanctum. Assuming the Guardian hadn't destroyed the antibac to ensure that Jasper's only option was the melding.

It was too risky.

"Grammar," she said. "I need a knife."

He rummaged around in the pile of supplies. He came up with a knife of the right length for her empty sheath. It was clean with a well-wrapped handle. She tested the blade on her thumb, and a bead of blood sprang up at once. She turned it over in her hands, fighting the distant nausea, fighting her last memory of Vron.

Grammar was watching her across the fire. Hastily, she sheathed the knife and clenched her empty, bandaged hands together.

"The Guardian been sayen you're haven a choice," he said. "One is killen yourself."

She'd forget at her peril that the kid could listen. He might not understand everything he heard, but he was as sharp as the knife at her hip.

"You been tellen me you're not haven the curse that Vron been haven," he said, watching her face, watching her for a lie.

"I don't." It was true, for whatever it was worth. She'd live if she could.

She'd live if she could.

"You're lyen."

"There never was a curse, Grammar. Martha died because she had a sick heart, and Vron killed herself because she was too sad and despairing and couldn't bear it."

"*You're* sad." His voice was gruff, accusatory.

"I—everybody gets sad sometimes."

Maybe she should tell him she was going to Shatter so he could understand what she had to do. But he was only twelve. She'd considered herself nearly a grown-up at that age; she'd been wrong.

"But I'm never so sad I'm wanten to kill myself," he replied.

At least he'd inherited the survival instinct of his parents. Her heart lightened a little. "Well, then you don't have the curse."

"If Dragon's killen Nev, I'll be catchen the curse," he said quite calmly. "But I'll be killen them all first. I'll be evil like my papa. I won't be caren. Can't be stoppen the curse." He paused. "Can you? Is there a spell for stoppen the curse?"

"God, I wish I knew." Undoubtedly, a goblin would eat that wish. She had to do better than that. "What makes you feel better when you're sad?"

Nothing like cutting off a limb to brighten my day, personally, Darius mused.

Nobody asked you.

Grammar thought about it. He jabbed a stick into the fire and thought some more. Finally, he shrugged. "Nev."

Jasper braced her forehead in her hands and stared at the ground for a while. Of course. Not that being surrounded by love had saved Vron. Life wasn't that neat, and happy endings didn't come to all who deserved them. But he'd learn that soon enough. Far too soon, probably.

"It's simple, then," she said. "We save Nev and make sure nothing bad ever happens to her again for as long as she lives. Then you'll be safe from the curse."

He sighed. She could no longer see anything, but she heard him get up, walk away, rummage around. He returned and pressed into her hand a scrap of cloth so filthy, it took her a moment to realize the purpose of the gesture. She used the cloth to sop up the wetness on her face, along with an astonishing amount of snot.

She was startled when he kneeled behind her and gathered up a handful of her hair; it had grown long enough to brush her neck.

"What are you doing?"

He clicked his tongue to quiet her, a reproving sound that brought Martha to life. "Hair is all your thinken and feelen growen out of your head. For quieten your thinken, you have to quieten your hair." Lacking a comb, he used his fingers to work loose knots and tangles.

She let her head tilt back under his ministrations. Fortunately, there were few burns on her head, and he was careful not to touch the ones on her neck and back.

Breathe in and out. In and out. Use the scrap of cloth for any errant eye leaks.

"A story, a story . . ." he said. "I'm tellen you the one where a spider is stealen all the stories from the god in the sky."

He divided a small portion of her hair into three and began braiding back along her scalp. He told her about a spider who had once used tricks and cleverness to win from the sky god his box of stories. Finishing that story, he launched immediately into another, also starring the trickster spider. Whimsical, sly, absurd, and yet strangely compelling, the stories settled gravity back into her bones, turned her right side up, and gave her soil to root herself into.

It wasn't air she'd needed after all; it was the earth.

"A story, a story," he said at the end, a ritualistic singsong to his voice. "Let some goen elsewhere. Let some comen back to me."

She ran her fingertips over his handiwork, the braid surprisingly neat and tight against her scalp despite the dim light.

Grammar moved over to the puppy pile of his Crows. A few of the younglings had woken to listen to the story. He soothed them back to sleep, patting heads and gently swearing at the stubborn.

Jasper smiled into a darkness that now seemed more like the inside of a womb than a cage. Grammar was the best revenge Martha Abebe could possibly have wreaked on Darius Dalca.

Fursa lifted his head and gave a soft woof under his breath. Moments later a girl, narrow and sharp faced, trotted into the light.

"Zanna, what is it?" Grammar asked, straightening.

Zanna gave Jasper an inquisitive, untrusting look, then turned back to Grammar. "Damaskers are callen a meeting. At the church. Word says they're gonna off the last two Azuros."

18

TAKE ME TO CHURCH

Someone playing with your hair absent-mindedly
The smell of woodsmoke, the crackle and pop of flames

~ Veronica Park (*Things I Will Miss/Reasons to Live*)

J asper perched on the rafters of Darius's church.

She was wrapped in the shadows that clumped here, far from the torches and candles below. Dust and mould and the smell of pigeon droppings filled her nostrils. Doves cooed irritably around her, disturbed from their rest by the activity below. She crouched above Liam and Ahmed's bar, where Darius's throne had once stood, and before that a pulpit. Now there were cages again, one for Tom Jitters and one for Socrates. All the other Azuros already dangled from makeshift gallows outside the Yorky walls, gruesome monuments to how one man's pain had twisted into blame and hate.

No matter how far life took her, Jasper always seemed to end up here, at the heart of Darius's old kingdom, trapped inside that barbed wire knot of memories she could never untangle.

Sparrow and Ibtisam were both on the platform behind the bar. They were unrestrained but guarded by four Damaskers. Sparrow sat in a wheelchair with a splinted leg, looking sweaty and exhausted but clear-eyed, an infinite improvement from the last time Jasper had seen her, which had been the day after Nico shot her. Those special antibiotics Ryan had given Ibtisam— nanobiotics or whatever he'd called them—must have really worked.

Ibtisam held Sparrow's hand, and they kept calm faces as the citizens of Yorky were ushered into the church by armed Damaskers. Harmony, Pastor Tim, and a few other citizens who Nico had deemed most likely to foment resistance were held near the cages, unbound and not visibly hurt but under close supervision.

Tom and Socrates in the cages were in much rougher shape. They were haggard and filthy and covered in bruises and cuts. They flinched when the Damasker guards strolled too near.

Jasper had been a child in a cage in this building. She'd been a child riding piggyback on Darius's shoulders. She'd been a child, and then she hadn't been a child anymore.

Nico Mavuto stood on the stage not far from Sparrow and Ibtisam. He seemed thinner to Jasper, his eyes bloodshot, his scruffy beard creeping over his rows of facial scars. In a semblance of control, his hands were clasped behind his back, but his eyes darted around the room and occasionally he paced, rubbing at his face and muttering to himself.

She'd been trapped up here for an hour. Grammar and his pack had been supposed to create a distraction, drawing away the Damaskers that guarded Tom's and Socrates's cages. It had worked briefly, but just as she was sneaking toward the cages, ready to pick the locks, the guards returned. She raced to find an escape or a hiding spot, but all the entrances were covered. She ended up climbing the wall behind the choir nook and perching on the heavy wooden rafters and she'd been stuck here since.

If she stayed still she might pass unnoticed, but that wouldn't help Tom or Socrates.

The church was filling fast as the Damaskers rounded up large groups at a time. There were few chairs, so most people stood, huddled in small groups, parents holding their children tightly. Brief nods and a few murmured words were exchanged as they were crowded together, but faces were grim and afraid. Jasper caught glimpses of anger too, hot and sullen glances tossed at the Damaskers. In a room full of remembered trauma and violence and fear, some would break and some would attack. Yet the room was full of children also, from babies to young teenagers. The youngest were the only ones making noise, wailing and whimpering. The older ones had been infected by their parents' fear and were silent.

Damaskers lined the walls of the church and guarded the doors, every one of them armed and bearing triple scars on their cheeks. Some looked like they were having the best day of their lives. Others were tense, jumpy, scanning the crowd suspiciously with their guns and crossbows at the ready. Any wrong move, any misunderstanding would result in a bloodbath.

The shadows were thick, but anyone who looked up would surely see Jasper, perched like a crow, an omen of death above their heads.

No one looked up. No one ever did.

Then a familiar figure emerged from the wings of the stage. Braided blond hair and a permanent sneer. Dragon.

Jasper's heart plummeted. So Dragon had arrived back at Yorky unscathed. Had Charlie's raiding party simply not caught up to him, or had they been defeated in a skirmish? Did Dragon still hold Neverwhen hostage? What had happened to Ben and all her friends?

Dragon was dragging someone with him. A familiar skinny figure with hair like a thundercloud around her face. *Crane.* Jasper's heart sank lower. How had the Damaskers captured her? Had they skirmished with the ReGeneration and won so thoroughly that they'd taken prisoners? How was that possible?

Crane's hands were in sturdy handcuffs, nothing she could cut her way out of with a hidden knife. She was also wearing clothes that were clearly not hers—loose sweatpants and a baggy T-shirt. Nico's belief that he could win back his daughter's love might be delusional, but he was perfectly realistic about how dangerous she was. He would've had her stripped and searched for every hidden blade she carried.

Dragon unlocked one cuff from Crane's wrist and snapped it shut around a bar of Tom's cage. Sneering, Dragon said something to her, but she ignored him and rattled the cuffs experimentally. Dragon disappeared backstage again. Crane exchanged a few words with Tom. Then she hopped up to sit on top of his cage, her legs dangling. Occasionally, she gave a small testing tug to the cuffs that kept her shackled to the cage.

Nico stepped forward, and the ambient noise died abruptly. He spoke without ceremony. "All I want is justice. I want people to answer for their crimes." He looked around at their silent faces. "I'd hoped Zenobia would be here, but as usual she's too cold to care about these men she swore responsibility for and too cowardly to do anything but save her own skin. That's fine. She'll be hunted. She's alone now and there's nowhere in the zones she can go where we won't find her."

He turned and nodded, and a Damasker dragged Socrates out of his cage and onto the stage. His pale, tattooed skin was filthy and bloodstained, but his eyes were hot with hatred. He jerked at his chains and threw thick curses at his captors from a mouthful of broken teeth.

The Damasker hit him across the face, making him stagger. Socrates spat blood, laughed darkly. "You call this justice? Tom and I had nothing to do with the Shattering. We were in fucking prison at the time. We're no saints, but don't give me that garbage about fucking *justice*."

"Fine," said Nico. "Call it revenge. I'm not here to quibble about words and I don't give a damn about spin or optics. I want Zenobia *crushed*, and I'll use you to do it in case her heart is not, in fact, made of stone and she does care about you two."

The flamingo stand hadn't been moved. It still stood in the centre of the stage. Above it hung a noose, a thick rope that had been fastened to the rafter Jasper was crouched on. A table sat beside the flamingo stand. The guards forced Socrates to climb onto the table, where the noose was tightened around his neck.

A breath, a murmur moved through the crowd. Parents covered children's eyes, but no one moved or spoke up. In the hush Crane's cuffs rattled loudly as she gave them a vicious jerk and glared at Nico.

"For all the words we've exchanged, I don't hate you as much as you'd think, Socrates," Nico said. "It's not personal, believe it or not. But we both know you've done enough in your life to earn the death penalty several times over. So I won't weep over you."

"Either stop talking or just kill me already," Socrates snapped.

"Nico," Tom called from his cage, "what's the point of doing this if Zenobia isn't even here to see it? What's the rush? Lock us up while you hunt her down. It's only a matter of time, right? Don't you want her to see this in person? Don't you want to look her in the eye while Socrates and I die?"

"That's why Socrates is dying tonight, but not you," Nico said. "I don't believe Zenobia truly cared about any of the Azuros. They were her ball and chain. I wouldn't put it past her to be relieved they're dead. But you, Tom, you're different. And you're right. I want to kill you in front of her. So tonight you have a front-row seat to your fate. Enjoy your reprieve."

"Zenobia cares about me," Socrates shouted indignantly. "I'm her favourite—she always says so. Doesn't she, Tom?"

"It's true!" Tom said stoutly.

"No, it isn't," Crane said, scowling at Socrates.

Nico snorted and gave his men a nod. The Damaskers prodded Socrates with their guns until he finally, reluctantly stepped onto the tiny flamingo platform. He wobbled wildly. With his hands chained behind his back, he couldn't get his balance and he kept one foot on the table even as the guards prodded at him more insistently.

Jasper stretched out on the rafter above him, her knife poised above the thick rope. She had already made some preliminary cuts while she waited, but she'd have to be quick.

Below her Sparrow squared her shoulders and rolled her wheelchair forward. Her strong voice carried through the church. "If you would tell your men to lower their guns from Ibtisam's head, I'd like to say a few words."

Nico stared at her. Then he gave a short, sharp laugh. "You want to play the devil's advocate? Familiar role for you. You were always Zenobia's bitch."

The guards with their guns to Ibtisam's head relaxed their stance, and Sparrow moved forward, subtly claiming the stage and people's attention with the way she spread her arms. "We learned under Darius that no larger society would come to our rescue. We learned what our breaking point was. We said never again. We said our children would never witness or experience the violence that we allowed, that we witnessed, that we ourselves committed."

"Okay, enough," Nico snapped. "I didn't say you could make a goddamn speech."

Sparrow raised her voice. "You could deliver Zenobia to downieland and they'd prosecute her. We don't need to—"

Nico shouted at her to shut up and gestured to his men to pull her back.

Jasper braced her knife against the rope. With attention drawn away from him, Socrates had taken his foot off the flamingo and was standing on the table again.

"Hey, Nico," he shouted. "You want to hurt Zenobia? I'll tell you who she loves. She's sitting right there—Crane, our very own little resident psycho. God only knows why, but that's who Zenobia cares about. How bad do you want your revenge? Because you can have it if you're willing to cut up your own daughter. It's a small price to pay for justice, right? So where's your goddamn *commitment*, Nico?"

Nico strode across the stage and with one shove knocked aside the table Socrates was balanced on. The drop wasn't enough to break Socrates's neck, but he dangled at the end of the rope, kicking and gasping and choking.

Screams and gasps rose from the crowd. Crane's cuffs rattled against the cage bars as she jerked at them savagely.

Jasper swore and sawed frantically at the thick rope just under the knot that tied it to the rafter. The knife caught and jumped out of her sweaty grip. It fell, a silent missile, and thunked tip first into the stage in front of Nico.

Crane was the first to look up. Her smile glinted so sharp, it should've cut through the rope.

A few more people looked up. Their silence spread. By the time Jasper had swung off the rafter onto the hanging rope, everyone was staring at her. And at Socrates choking to death in a noose.

Jasper slid down the rope so fast, it ripped away the bandages over her palms and excruciating pain shot across her burns. She leaped off and landed in a roll and raced for Socrates before anyone—including the dumbfounded Damasker guards —could move. She grabbed Socrates's kicking legs and hoisted him upward with all her strength until the horrible choking sounds turned into wheezes through which he might inhale.

"It's the Pinegirl!" a child's voice cried into the silence.

She'd come out of the sky like an avenging angel, a saint come to life from the stained glass, the Pinegirl of legend summoned by unjust violence.

But if she stayed still for more than these few seconds, she'd lose that momentum.

She couldn't let the Damaskers remember that she was human.

She boosted Socrates's legs toward the flamingo platform. He felt something solid under his foot and struggled to balance. Half dead and panicked and already in rough shape, he'd never keep his balance on the tiny platform for more than a few seconds.

Ibtisam burst into motion, following the same thought as Jasper. Before her guards could react, she had retrieved the fallen table and shoved it into place under Socrates. At last he could stand, albeit on shaky legs, putting enough slack into the rope to allow him to breathe.

Jasper turned to face her people. She was gripped with the slippery, fading sensation that she had only seconds to live and that everything depended on what she did next.

All the guns were turning on her, and Nico was opening his mouth.

"Damaskers, listen to me," she shouted. "You grew up like I did, either with memories or stories of da bad man, the villain, the devil. And you know the story of how I killed him and set everyone free. But I did not kill Darius so you could murder people for crimes they didn't commit! I killed him so I, you—all of us—could live life without games, without being forced to gamble our bodies, our lives, our loved ones' lives just to survive another day.

"Killing a man is a terrible act, but you're all free because I committed it. Free to choose how to live your lives. Free to choose whether to hurt people or build a community. And that goes for Zenobia and the Azuros too. Look at the choices they made after Darius died. Without them we'd have no trade with the outside whatsoever. They turned themselves into stable citizens who contributed to our community and committed no more crimes. Does that mean we must forgive or forget their past crimes? Of course not. Many of us suffered pain, injury, and loss at the hands of the Azuros. Our feelings of anger and hurt are valid."

She stopped for breath and became aware of the silence. Every eye was on her. "But we all know that the line between the Azuros and the rest of us is a blurry one. We all did things we're ashamed of, that we felt forced to do for our own survival and others'. Maybe, just maybe, the same can be said of the Azuros. Even Zenobia. Maybe we should all get a fresh beginning. Here in the zones we only have each other.

"Children see a broken house and they want to knock it down. Children don't know anything about fixing or rebuilding. But when you tear something down, you take on the responsibility to build something in its place. That's what we're trying to do here in Yorky. Damaskers, you're kicking at our wobbly, fragile, but precious house, and for what? The revenge dream of one hurting and bitter man? Why don't you *help* us and we can—"

A swift movement beside her. A Damasker smashed her across the face with his gun.

Pain exploded into a galaxy of vicious stars and then faded into darkness.

19

A LAMB FOR THE SACRIFICE

A babe in the woods
Surrounded by wolves:
A new family.
A pup in a church
Surrounded by men:
A new weapon.

~ Veronica Park (*Story of a Monster*)

J asper woke in a cage.

She always woke in a cage. Usually, if she closed her eyes and breathed for a few minutes the cage would dissolve.

This time it didn't.

Her head had become the site of a pitched battle—rumbling tanks and mortar shells and rattling gunfire and screams all echoing from inside her skull. She sat up and the smell of vomit and feces assaulted her senses, opening up a new front in the war. Another few seconds of struggling to concentrate satisfied her that neither the shit nor the vomit belonged to her.

She opened her eyes, the pain forcing her to squint. She must have been out only a few minutes. Ibtisam still held the table in place under Socrates's feet, Sparrow beside her in her wheelchair.

Nico stood at the edge of the stage, shouting at his Damaskers and the Yorky citizens alike. Damaskers were quelling the crowd using batons and the butts of their guns.

Oh God, had they shot anyone? The crowd was riled up and electric, and children screamed and cried, but she couldn't see blood or the shock that would eddy around a major injury. Where was—? There was Harmony, nearly hidden by taller people, and Pastor Tim with his hands raised, gently trying to speak to the Damaskers nearest him.

Crane had hopped off of Tom's cage and stretched herself as close to Jasper's cage as her cuffs would allow. "You haven another knife?" Crane asked under cover of the noise.

She didn't. The knife Grammar had given her still lay somewhere on the floor where she'd dropped it. "Ben and the others," Jasper said. "Were they—? Are they—?"

Crane grinned, cheerfully for someone whose wrist was bleeding from how hard she'd jerked it against the cuff. "They're fine. So's Nev."

"Nev's okay? But how—?"

"I been keepen my promise to be saven her. But my second promise is killen Dragon. And I'm needen a knife."

The crowd was not settling down.

Jasper wondered if Nico had noticed how children were slowly being shoved into the centre of the crowd while the adults formed a ring around them, facing out, facing the Damaskers. Unarmed men and women, desperate and angry and determined, with a lot more to lose than just their own lives.

Men and women with ten years of nightmares and guilt and pain and a visceral understanding of the price of peace and the consequences if that price was not paid.

They were moments away from a fight, a bloody battle between armed Damaskers and unarmed civilians. Maybe an attack would work, or maybe half the people in this church would die.

"Nico!" Jasper's voice blended with the shouting. She called his name until finally he turned toward her. "Zenobia's not coming. She's in a coma and can't travel. She's in the Tower. I left her there a few days ago."

"You're lying. The Tower's inaccessible."

"The ReGeneration cleared the tunnels. If you truly want your revenge, stop terrorizing all these innocent citizens. Go to the Tower. She won't fight you."

Nico looked at her with his tired, bloodshot eyes. "I didn't want it to end up like this, you know. You should understand. You can't just kill a few cancerous cells—you have to nuke the whole thing. You did the right thing with Darius. But it shouldn't have ended there. The whole rotten organization should've been obliterated."

"And where would it end? You did Darius's work too, remember? So did Martha. So did I. Where's the line? How will you decide who's innocent?"

"I know who's not. Zenobia and her devil son. That's all I need to go on."

In the moments Nico had been distracted, talking to Jasper, Sparrow had rolled to the front of the stage, her powerful voice commanding attention once again. "Like Jasper said, we've made a life for ourselves here in the zones. We won't give up this community we've built, because we remember how it was before. Damaskers! Most of you were children at the time, but you remember too, the terror and the violence, the uncertainty and insecurity. We want better for you. Use your strength and skills to protect the vulnerable and contribute to our community and we will honour and welcome you into our family."

A Damasker dragged her chair back.

"We're not looking to hurt anyone who doesn't deserve it," Nico shouted. "But there's got to be some goddamn justice. Doesn't it eat you alive knowing what Zenobia's done? She Shattered this city *and she got away with it*. She was Darius's second-in-command, standing right beside him as he committed atrocities, *and she got away with it*. Don't you remember the people you've lost? The *limbs* you've lost?"

Sparrow's voice was quiet but carrying. "God will judge Darius, and Zenobia too when she dies. If she ever returns to Yorky, we'll deal with her. But you've killed innocents in pursuit of your revenge and terrorized and hurt others. You started a war to get your revenge. The most despicable criminal in this church right now is you, Nico."

Nico drew his gun for the first time and pointed it at Sparrow. The silence froze in the room.

"Yes, Nico, why don't you try to silence me," Sparrow said softly. "My death will speak louder than my voice ever could."

Jasper clutched the bars of her cage till her knuckles whitened. Her heart roared like a runaway train. Her thumbs scratched crosses into the bars, over and over.

Pinioned between two guards, Ibtisam sobbed, her hand clamped over her mouth. But she didn't beg or plead for Sparrow, just watched her fiercely through overflowing eyes.

Jasper wanted to scream. But as if in a nightmare, her throat had closed up, her hands were fused to the bars, and the smell of vomit was crawling down her nostrils like sentient slime.

"You think I have a grudge against Zenobia because of the part she played in Darius's atrocities? Because she stole my daughter's love from me? No, I swallowed that shit down for nearly ten years, just like you all swallowed shit for the sake of the peace. This is much, much bigger than just me, Sparrow. The Shattering killed *millions*. And you might be feeling noble, but I'm willing to bet there are people in this crowd who would feel deeply satisfied and relieved to see Zenobia dead."

Dragon ran out from the wing of the stage to whisper in Nico's ear.

Nico nodded to him, an expression of satisfaction and pleasure crossing his face. Dragon grinned at Jasper with savage promise. He ducked through the door he'd come from and emerged moments later.

This time he dragged Grammar with him.

Jasper's heart stuttered with dismay.

Crane lunged forward against her cuffs so hard, she fell flat on her back when they jerked her short. Tom reached through the bars to touch her arm, speaking to her in a low voice. Crane shook him off and sat up, her eyes burning into Jasper. "Supposed to be safe." Her voice was a growl. "Why isn't baby Dalca *safe*, Piney?"

Jasper had no answer for her. After their distraction Grammar and his Crows had intended to intercept Dragon and attempt to rescue Neverwhen if she hadn't been freed already. But the interception had gone the other way.

The boy looked dazed and went unresisting, as if he'd just been struck. He stumbled when Dragon pushed him at Nico, and Nico seized his arm.

"See this kid?" Nico said to the crowd. "Look at him good. Does he look familiar to you? He does, doesn't he? His name is Grammar. His father was Darius Dalca and his mother is the lying bitch herself, Zenobia."

A different kind of stir went through the crowd. Darius's son was still alive? This was news indeed. Curiosity leavened the fear and rage in the room as people craned their necks to see.

"He can't help who his parents are, poor little bastard," Nico said. "Although you do wonder if someone can inherit psychopathy. Only time will tell. What I'm a little more concerned about is the fact that Zenobia's infected status *can* be inherited. Martha's notes are very clear about that. The kid's got the alien bacteria too. Martha and Zenobia spent his childhood trying to keep it dormant, but he's actually a walking, ticking time bomb. Ladies and gentlemen, you're looking at the source of the next Shattering."

Grammar had taken a few seconds to get his bearings, to stand up straight, and to look at the crowd, Socrates in the noose, Crane in cuffs, and Jasper and Tom in their cages.

Then he looked up at Nico, hearing his words for the first time.

Jasper clenched her hands around the cage bars till her knuckles hurt. Finally, Grammar twisted around, looking to her for confirmation.

He saw the truth in her face. And the twin warriors of betrayal and anger collided across his face, rearranging everything.

She'd pay for keeping this secret from him. Just as she'd made Zenobia pay.

Harmony called out from the crowd, "What's your point, Nico? None of this is his fault. If you're seriously trying to stand up there and convince us that he should be killed or some Darius-level nonsense like that, then save your breath. He's a child. Let him go this instant. And while you're at it, let my Jaspa out of that cage at once, Nico. *Aigo!* What's wrong with you?"

"I'm not going to kill a kid. I'm providing important background information," Nico said blandly.

Grammar didn't seem to be listening. He turned his head, sniffed the air.

Jasper wanted to believe Nico, but given his present course of vengeance, she couldn't imagine a scenario that didn't end in Grammar being badly hurt or killed. People would shake their heads and deplore Nico's actions, but deep down they'd feel relief at Grammar's death. They'd mutter to each other that it was for the best. How else could they be sure there wouldn't be a second Shattering? At least the decision would be out of their hands, the guilt not on their heads.

What they wouldn't speak about—but they'd think it, feel it—was the fierce, shameful relief of knowing there would never again be another Dalca among them.

Even if they all survived Nico and his Damaskers, and even if they found a cure for Grammar, he'd been outed to everyone as the son of Darius Dalca, the monster, and Zenobia Allan, the cause of the Shattering. He'd be hated and reviled and beaten up and rejected and looked upon with suspicion and fear and scrutinized for any sign of turning into either of his parents. Nico had just ensured that nothing in Grammar's life would ever be easy.

Grammar met Jasper's eyes through the cage bars, his expression flat. She'd hidden a crucial truth from him. But what surprise was that? Rule number one: never trust biggies. Because biggies kept secrets from children. Zenobia had kept so many from Jasper, and yet everything Zenobia had endured and done since the Shattering had been a self-punishment, even the fact that she still lived. Jasper had lived with guilt, but Zenobia's bones had calcified into a regret dense enough to sink her far below where air or light could reach her.

Again, Grammar sniffed the air.

Smoke had gathered in the air. People in the crowd and even Damaskers were sniffing and coughing and looking around.

Dragon ran out from the back of the church and onto the stage. "Fire!" he shouted. "The church is on fire!"

20

BURNING MY RELIGION

Things we brought from the old world:
Human nature
Our wounds
Hope

~ Veronica Park (*Lists of the Apocalypse*)

Chaos broke out.

People stampeded for the exits, Damaskers and Yorky citizens alike. From the stage Nico and Sparrow shouted for order and calm. They went unheard.

Jasper saw Harmony's face in the smoky confusion as she struggled to go against the crowd, to run toward Jasper. But she was swept away, her face disappearing from Jasper's view.

"Harmony!" Jasper screamed. What if Harmony had fallen and been trampled?

A bottleneck formed at the doors as Damaskers beat back

citizens with their guns to let Damaskers out first. Nico shoved Grammar at Dragon and snarled at him to get the boy out of the church. Grammar tried to twist out of his grip, but Dragon jerked him along and waded into the crowd, dragging Grammar with him.

Nico hurried over to Crane, pulling a set of keys from his pocket. As soon as he was within reach, Crane swung a fist at his face. Nico ducked backwards neatly and then followed up with a sharp tap of his fist to Crane's chin, which sent her reeling.

"Sorry, baby girl," he said. He pulled out a ring of keys and unlocked her cuff from the cage bar, hoisted her over his shoulder, and hurried off the stage. He ignored Tom and Jasper screaming after him for the keys to the cages.

The guards on the stage followed hastily. Ibtisam twisted free of their grip, and in their hurry to leave the church they didn't bother to go after her. She ran over to Jasper, and Sparrow followed.

Jasper tugged at the cage door. Panic filled her, huge and explosive. She was going to burn to death while trapped in a cage in the very church where Darius had made her play his torture games. Trapped and helpless, she would die horribly among anguished ghosts and her worst memories.

Sparrow tugged fruitlessly at the padlock, tears streaming down her face. Ibtisam pulled her away and then aimed several ferocious kicks at the lock. Neither the lock nor the door was affected.

Tom rattled his cage door and shouted for help, for someone to get them out. Still balancing precariously on tiptoe on the table, noose around his neck, Socrates wheezed and croaked and pleaded.

Jasper clamped the crook of her arm over her nose and mouth. The smoke roiled thick and noxious into the church, thickening by the second. People screamed and cried, pushed and shoved, but they weren't making any progress out the doors. Were the Damaskers blocking them in?

"We need the keys," Jasper shouted at Sparrow and Ibtisam. "You need to get the keys from Nico."

Pastor Tim ran onto the stage in time to hear her. "I'll get them, my dear." He looked around at the chaos. "Ibtisam, start breaking windows and get Sparrow out of here."

"I'm not leaving Jasper," Sparrow yelled, but Ibtisam wheeled her toward the nearest vaulted stained glass window while Pastor Tim plunged into the thick of the crowd.

"Jasper," Tom said, voice croaking, "Crane told me once your belt buckle broke down into lock picking tools. Do you still—?"

Her lock picking tools! No longer in her belt buckle—the Guardian had taken her belt anyway before putting her in the hole—but in her bra, ever since the Gingers had put her mostly naked in a cage. Jasper hoisted up her T-shirt with shaking hands. Her fingers, stiff and uncontrolled, fumbled with her bra. At last the delicate little tools fell loose. Picking them up, pinching them between her sweaty, clumsy, shaking fingers was a nightmarishly slow, painstaking process.

"You can do it," Tom chanted from the other cage. "Calm and steady. You got this."

The crackle of the flames was growing into a roar. Blooming ruddy light lent a hellish cast to the scene. This church had always represented hell to her and now it looked the part.

Terror shuddered through her, alive and awake and consuming. Jasper grasped the tools as tightly as she could between her recalcitrant fingers, reached through the bars, and began to work on the lock.

Ibtisam picked up a barstool and with desperate strength swung it at a window. Glass shattered and fell in brilliant rainbow shards. Air rushed in and the fire roared as it was fed. Flames swarmed the rafters above them. People screamed and scrambled out of the way as a beam fell with a crash.

Ibtisam helped people climb out of the window. She hauled Sparrow out of the chair to stand on her good leg and, over her protests, shoved her out of the window into the arms of those waiting outside. Harmony was arguing, trying to run back to Jasper, but somebody grabbed her and hoisted her out the window with Ibtisam's help.

At long last the church was emptying as people crowded around the windows and the side door that no longer had any Damaskers in front of it.

In the choking murk Jasper couldn't see Nico or Pastor Tim.

She had to focus on her fingers, on the lock. She had to squash that terror beast into its own little cage, her rib cage. She had to breathe, even if the percentage of oxygen she was inhaling decreased by the second and her lungs rebelled. She had to keep her fingers steady in the face of horror, as steady as Martha's had been when she fought off her alcoholic tremors to cut off Ben's leg cleanly. She had to channel Zenobia's cold focus in the face of suffering, to remember that she could help no one until she helped herself.

Another chunk of the rafters fell, crashing within a metre of her cage, sending out a spray of sparks, a wash of hideous heat that stole breath and hope. It forced her to the back of the cage. Tom cried out hoarsely.

Her hands were empty. She'd dropped her lock picking tools outside the cage.

Abruptly, a face loomed on the other side of her cage bars. Socrates, the noose still looped thickly around his neck, his face purple and swollen and sheeted in tears. The fallen beam was the one his rope had been tied to.

He choked out his words. "I'm sorry I can't help you." He shoved something through the bars of her cage.

"Socrates, wait!"

But he was running for the window where the last of the crowd was crawling to safety. He'd cut the rope attaching him to the beam, and the end flapped behind him like a hideous necktie. How had he cut—?

Her knife. That was what he'd pushed into her cage, the one she'd used to try to free him, the one that had fallen out of her hand. She reached for it. The hilt filled her hand with that peculiar weight she'd felt the night she killed Darius. The knife couldn't help her escape the cage.

Except that it could.

Flames were consuming the stage around her. The light illuminated tiny silver objects on the floor—her lock picking tools. In his haste to escape, Socrates had kicked them several metres away. They were out of her reach now.

The fire was a roaring, howling inferno around her. People screaming. Glass bursting. Chunks of ceiling falling.

She set the knife tip against her wrist and then looked across at Tom. He understood at once. Nico had disappeared and Pastor Tim after him, and neither had reappeared with the keys. Their options had run out.

Tom's gaze was raw and steady and familiar. He'd looked at Martha exactly the same way as he held Ben's shoulders to the table and Martha set the saw to Ben's leg. *Yes, the ocean will consume us. Yes, we will likely drown. But I at least will stand firm for you to wash up against. I won't leave you.*

He'd looked at Zenobia like that every day.

She held his gaze until finally he nodded. She'd throw him the knife when she was done with it. She'd have to be serious about this if she wanted to bleed out before the flames reached her. She'd do what Vron had done at the end. Cut with a purpose, cut with finality, cut so she was beyond saving. Open her arms lengthwise from wrist to elbow, tracing an imaginary line like Ryan's tattooed dots. Her heart would eject her blood, sacrificing it to the fire. And she'd finally escape the cage forever.

She pressed down with the knife, and a bead of blood formed.

"Jasper!"

Ryan loomed out of the smoke like an angel storming through hell. A scarf was tied over his face, but his crown of twisted locs was unmistakable.

Seeing him was like learning to breathe all over again.

Flames flared on his right and he shied away, ducking, an arm over his face. He had a ring of keys in his hand, but he stood frozen in place as if mesmerized by the fire.

"Ryan, move!" she shouted. "I need you, Ryan!"

He looked at her then with panic-widened eyes, through the smoke that swirled between them, and moved. He dropped to his knees in front of her cage door and fumbled with the keys. She could hear his ragged breathing even through his scarf, even over the roar of the fire. His hands shook worse than hers had.

She dropped the knife and reached through the bars to steady his hands. Together they pushed the key into the lock and turned. The tiny click that represented freedom sounded loud to her ears.

She scudded out of the cage so fast, she stumbled into him, and they grabbed each other for balance.

"Go. I'll get Tom out," he said hoarsely.

"No, together."

Pieces of ceiling crashed around them as they crouched at Tom's cage. Jasper found the right key after an agonizing search under Tom's steady gaze. The lock finally sprang free, and Ryan helped Tom crawl out.

The windows were barely visible now through the flames. Tom hobbled as fast as he could, with Ryan's help. As Jasper followed, the far corner of the stage was engulfed. There was no air left. She was breathing liquid fire.

Ahead of her Tom stumbled and fell, barely conscious. Ryan hoisted him over his shoulder, and Jasper ran to help. They dragged Tom through the searing heat and shoved him unceremoniously through the window. Helping hands pulled him to safety.

"Go, Jas!" Ryan grabbed her around the waist and virtually tossed her through the window before she could protest. She tumbled into waiting arms.

"Jasper, thank God, Ryan got you out!" That was Quick Rick speaking in her ear, setting her upright.

She twisted around. "Come on, Ryan!"

The fire thundered and billowed out of the windows. Shouts of pain and alarm. Quick Rick pulled her back. She fought him off and ran back to the church.

Ryan had disappeared from the window. She screamed his name. The heat was an impossible wall. The devil's laughter crackled and consumed.

A sudden, miraculous splash of coolness, and then another as buckets of water were thrown at the mocking flames. The bucket brigade had arrived.

For a few seconds the flames retreated. She ran forward, lunged through the window. "Ryan!"

He was on the floor, unmoving. She tumbled into the church and heaved at his body.

"Get up, you dumb downie," she said in his ear, her croaky voice washed away by the flames. "Get up or we both die. *Get up.*"

He stirred. He coughed like his lungs were charring to ash.

He got up.

They were dragged from the window and carried by multiple hands to a safe distance before being released to collapse onto the grass, coughing and retching like they'd never breathe cleanly again.

She sat up when she could finally breathe and looked at him. "Your clothes are on fire!" She threw herself at him and rolled him over, smothering the smouldering remains of his clothes with her own body. His hair was singed too, and she gathered handfuls of his locs, patting out any remaining sparks. At last she let herself collapse, still half-draped over him. Breathing smoky but deliciously oxygen-rich air. Lying on cool grass and listening to the wheezing of Ryan's breath in his chest.

"We're going to need a tiebreaker," he said after a while, pulling the scarf away from his face.

"For what?"

"Saving the other's life by lying on top of them."

Jasper was too tired to laugh but she squeezed the first body part she could find—his elbow.

She sat up at last and took in the scene. The bucket brigade was composed of Yorky citizens and gangers and even some Damaskers who'd discarded their weapons. It stretched all the way to a swampy pond a block away. Sloshing buckets and randomly chosen plastic containers were passed forward from person to person toward the church, their contents thrown on the fire in shining arcs, and then kids grabbed the empty containers and raced back to the pond.

Everyone else sat on the grass and pavement in exhaustion and shock. Ibtisam moved from group to group to check on burns and other injuries. Tom and Socrates sat nearby, shoulder to shoulder, in bruised, soot-stained silence.

"Hey," Jasper said. "Coyote boy. This time you saved everybody from the fire. Tom and I would've died without you."

Ryan looked down at the tattoos that lined his arms. "I was almost too scared to move," he confessed. "I wouldn't have gone in for anybody else. Only because Harmony said you were in there."

"Yes, you would have. You're stupidly heroic like that. Don't argue with me on this or I'll have to hit you, and my hands hurt too much for that."

He looked at her intently. "How about your lips? Do they hurt?"

"My lips? No more than everything else. Why do you—? Oh."

He'd leaned well into her personal space, but now he stopped inches from her face to laugh. Laughing turned into a coughing fit, which made her laugh too, buoyed by the euphoria of being alive and breathing, no matter how much it hurt.

A thundering explosion rocked the church, throwing everyone back. The fire had finally reached the stores of liquor Liam and Ahmed kept in the basement. The flames bellowed and raged. The church itself was barely visible, a dark outline at the centre of an incandescent firestorm.

The bucket brigade staggered out of range. Everyone stood and stared in silence as Darius's church was consumed.

The cages burned and the ghosts of children in cages.

The flamingo and the dog pit burned and the ghosts of savage, abused dogs.

The old bloodstains of Martha's amputation table burned and the ghosts of severed arms and legs and fingers and acid-burned faces.

The flames devoured the stain that still marked where Darius fell, where his life had ended but not his shadow, his darkness, his legacy.

Finally, hell had reached up to reclaim him and everything he'd ever touched.

How does it feel, seeing it all burn? she asked him.

But Darius was silent.

Instead, it was Vron who whispered, *I'm glad you stayed alive.*

Jasper reached out blindly and found Ryan's hand. *Yeah, me too.*

21

STANDOFF

Watching your friends succeed and be happy

~ Veronica Park (*Things I Will Miss/Reasons to Live*)

"Jaspa!"

Harmony bowled into Jasper, wrapping her in a hug tight enough to cut off her breath. Harmony's tears soaked her shirt even as she cursed and railed against all the people who had restrained her from running back into the church to help Jasper.

"Good, I'm glad they stopped you," Jasper said. "You couldn't have helped me without the keys."

"I would've torn that cage apart with my bare hands, Jaspa Pine! Don't you doubt that for a minute!"

"I know, *halmoni*. It's okay now. I'm safe." She patted Harmony's back and glanced at Ryan. "How did you get the keys anyway?"

Ryan pulled the keys out of his pocket and spun the ring

around his finger. "As Nico and Pastor Tim were arguing, Crane pickpocketed the keys from Nico and tossed them to me and I ran."

Harmony drew back and wiped her eyes. "Where's Ben?"

"He was with Charlie when I left them. He's fine," Ryan assured her.

Jasper noticed for the first time the horses and riders weaving through the crowd, corralling the Damasker gangers who had been disarmed, apparently with the help of Yorky gangers. Meanwhile, the bucket brigade reorganized themselves under the direction of Quick Rick and Pastor Tim. Now the focus was on preventing the fire from spreading. They soaked the ground around the church. The ReGeneration warriors had handed out camp shovels, and another group of people were digging a firebreak around the church.

"When did you guys get here?" Jasper demanded. "What happened anyway?"

"I'll let him answer that," Ryan said, lifting his chin to indicate someone behind her.

Once again Jasper was swept up in a smothering hug, this time by somebody much larger than Harmony. "Jesus, Jas, I'm so sorry. We had no idea he had cages in there. If we had known— fuck. I'm just glad everyone's okay."

"Charlie? Charlie! Can't . . . breathe. Let go." She freed a hand and waved a rude sign in front of his face.

Charlie let her go, looked her anxiously up and down, and then grinned with relief. He nodded to Ryan and bowed to Harmony, who scowled when she recognized him. She was even less likely to forgive him for breaking Ben's heart than Merlot was.

"The rain will reach us in less than an hour," Charlie said aloud. He gestured to the swollen, dark mass of clouds in the west. "We wouldn't have set the fire otherwise."

"*You* set the fire?" Jasper signed.

"To flush out the Damaskers," he signed back. "As soon as they came out, all panicked and confused, we confiscated their weapons. Easy as pickpocketing Ben when he's focused on a project. Not a shot fired. Then we helped everyone get out and started the bucket brigade. We didn't realize Nico had people in cages until it was too late."

"This place is a bar!" Jasper shouted at him, and then returned to ASL, her signing sloppy with upset and the pain of her burnt hands. "It's full of alcohol, and you set a *fire* with a hundred people—with children—inside? Are you fucking insane?" She had to break off as a coughing fit threatened to tear her throat to shreds.

"Would a pitched gun battle have been preferable?" He saw her expression and signed hastily, "Never mind. You have a fair point, but it turned out all right in the end, didn't it?"

"Where is Ben, young man?" Harmony demanded with a dangerous sharpness to her signs.

"Fine, perfectly fine," Charlie hastened to assure her in sign. "So is everyone else," he added for Jasper's benefit. "We never did catch up with Dragon. The Damaskers were cutting the ropes and bridges of the peddler road behind themselves, and that delayed us every time we came out of the tunnels to intercept them."

"But Crane said she rescued Nev," Jasper signed, confused.

"*We* didn't catch up," Charlie signed. "Crane went on a solo mission. Only Ryan saw her sneak away, so he went after her. And they got the job done." He pointed.

Ben and Neverwhen were trotting toward them. Neverwhen broke into a run and threw her arms around Jasper's waist while Ben lifted Harmony off her feet with his hug.

"Nev, you're okay!" Jasper cried. At least this little corner of Grammar's heart was safe. "Crane said she rescued you."

Neverwhen's happy grin faded into a solemn expression. "She's traden herself for me. She been tellen Dragon that Nico would be wanten her, not me."

Jasper felt her eyebrows rise. "She did?" The twinge in her chest was a reminder of how infinitely wide the human heart could stretch and grow. "Of course she did."

"Because we're sisters," Neverwhen said.

Jasper looked down at Neverwhen's earnest eyes and determined mouth. "Yes," she said. "Yes, you definitely are."

Ben released Harmony and grabbed Jasper's arms. "Don't ever . . ." he said, but didn't finish his sentence before he hugged her. She hugged him back as hard as she could. Every hug from now on could be the last one.

Ben released her and looked from Ryan to the burning church. "Any trouble getting Jas out?"

"Nope," Ryan said.

Jasper jabbed him in the ribs. "I was seconds from burning alive in a cage. Ryan saved my life."

"I still need to kidnap you, after all," Ryan said.

"Don't be an ass," Ben said to him. "Actually, yes, be an ass. It makes your hero act easier to swallow."

"Ben—" Jasper began.

"I'm *trying* to say thank you," Ben said irritably.

"You're terrible at it," Ryan observed.

"Well, you're terrible at being the bad guy. Positively untalented. Running into a burning building, rescuing Nev at great risk and no benefit to yourself—what the fuck, Ryan? Did you even read the script?" Ben crossed his arms over his chest and scowled.

Ryan looked at Jasper and then at Harmony. "What's happening?"

"That's Ben apologizing," Jasper said. "Speaking of untalented."

"Ben's not the only one who needs to practise apologizing." Harmony turned to Charlie with a stern frown. She signed, "You can't disappear for four years and then stroll back in and save the day and think that makes everything okay."

Charlie winced. His hands flexed as several possible comments seemed to occur to him. But he simply signed, "Yes, ma'am. I understand. And I'm sorry for disappearing. And I've missed your kimchi terribly."

"Hmph." Harmony looked him over. "Break my boy's heart again and I'll feed you to my goats. Understood?"

Ben rolled his eyes. "Harmony, it's not like that," he signed.

But for once Charlie had no smart remarks. "Yes, ma'am," he signed.

"Bring me to whoever's in charge of you people," Harmony commanded. "And tell them we're using the horses to move the injured back to Yorky." With a final squeeze of Jasper's hand, Harmony marched off, her formidable self once again, ready to bully armed warriors into lending her their beloved horses.

"I don't suppose she'd believe that Charlie was in charge?" Ryan murmured, still spinning the ring of keys around his finger.

Ben's dimples made a fleeting appearance as he interpreted the comment for Charlie. "Never."

Charlie grinned at Jasper blindingly and said aloud, "Man, I've missed her." He hugged her again.

Ben pointed a finger at Jasper. "Don't fucking disappear again," he said.

He and Charlie hurried after Harmony.

The keys spun off Ryan's finger, landing with a jingle, and Neverwhen picked them up. "What are these?"

"They were Nico's," Ryan said.

Tom approached and a smile split his ash-smeared, bruised,

and swollen face when he saw Neverwhen. "I'm glad to see you safe, Neverwhen."

"Crane been rescuen me." She tucked the keys into her pocket and gave him a concerned look. "You're looken terrible. You okay, Tom?"

"I'm fine now." He turned to Jasper, worry on his face. "Jas, you said Zenobia was at the Tower? She's safe?"

"She used her power. She was in a coma, or in rough shape anyway, when I left. But she was alive."

His broad shoulders slumped in relief.

Jasper looked around. "The Damaskers seem to be disarmed, but where's Nico? And does he still have Grammar and Crane? Has anybody seen them?"

"Let's find out," Ryan said.

"Yes, we gotta be saven Crane," Neverwhen said.

They hurried from group to group, but nobody had seen Nico or Grammar or Crane. They came across Esther and Merlot carrying around a bucket of drinking water for people. To Jasper's surprise, Esther set the bucket down and ran to give her a hug.

"We've been so worried about you," Esther exclaimed. "Ben was so upset, he . . ." She stopped and shook her head. "Anyway, God protected you."

Merlot handed Jasper a dipper of water. "Didn't think we'd see you again."

She hadn't thought so either. "I'm like a bad penny."

"Have you seen Nico or Grammar or Crane?" Ryan asked, taking the dipper.

"No," Esther said. "But there was some shouting and commotion from the front of the church just before both of you were pulled out. I don't think all of the Damaskers were disarmed."

Ryan handed back the dipper and hurried off with Tom.

Merlot grabbed Jasper's arm to stop her. He held out a knife to her, a familiar one.

"That's Crane's knife!" Neverwhen exclaimed.

"Why do you have this?" Jasper asked, confused.

"Crane gave it to me," Merlot said. "As her messed-up version of an apology for burning Vron's notebooks . . . right before she took off by herself in the middle of the night to go rescue Nev. Give it back to her, will you?"

"I'll be keepen it for her," Neverwhen said. She tucked the knife into her belt.

They reached the front of the church to find more citizens milling around, watching the fire or helping the injured.

Grace had her hands full treating a screaming child with burns across his torso. She was surrounded by more people waiting for treatment. She saw Jasper and Ryan and with desperation in her eyes called, "He has Crane. Please get her back. Please."

"That's the plan," Ryan called back, though they had no plan.

"Don't worry, she's my sister," Neverwhen called to Grace as they ran past. "I'll be saven her."

After a block they reached the standoff.

It consisted of Sparrow, leaning heavily on a cane someone had given her, facing Nico and Dragon and half a dozen armed Damaskers. Grammar, his hands tied, was being held by two Damaskers. One of them was a familiar blonde with a vicious smile—Vic, the girl who'd made him fight for his life in Damascus. She held a gun to Grammar's head.

Crane's hands were cuffed in front of her again, and Dragon covered her with his gun.

"You okay, Crane?" Tom asked, arriving at Sparrow's side.

"Great. I'm in perfect position to be killen Dragon," she replied, giving Dragon an ominous smile. He glared and his grip on his gun twitched as if he wanted to backhand her with it.

A flurry of barks drew Jasper's attention. Okuru was racing toward them from the church. He made a beeline for the Damaskers holding Grammar. Out of the corner of her eye, Jasper saw several Damaskers shift their aim to point their guns at the attacking dog.

"No, Okuru!" Jasper threw herself in front of the dog, down into a crouch, arms wide. He pulled up and made to skirt her.

The Damaskers would kill him in a heartbeat. Jasper tackled him, wrapping her arms around his thickly furred neck. His snarls rang in her ear, his snapping teeth inches from her face. She held on and braced herself for the clamping jaws and tearing bites. They didn't come. Okuru squirmed in her arms and barked deafeningly, but he'd come to a halt.

Ryan grabbed his fur, speaking soothingly into those flattened ears. Jasper didn't let go until Okuru's ears finally, reluctantly lifted as he listened to Ryan. She kept a hand in his fur as she regained her feet. Her legs felt shaky. Okuru held his ground between her and Ryan, but growls continued to grumble in his chest.

"Please let them go, Nico," Sparrow was pleading. "Crane will be safe with us—she's my niece, for heaven's sake. As for the boy, there are plenty of ways to torture Zenobia without hurting an innocent child."

"I don't care about the boy," Nico snapped. "I care about Zenobia co-opting my wife, stealing my daughter, and—oh yeah —destroying our whole world! If it weren't for her Shattering, Darius would've stayed in jail and I'd be living a dull, ordinary life with my wife at my side, and my daughter would be a normal smartass teenager in high school. Martha would never have been forced to betray her doctor's oath, and Crane would never know what it's like to use a knife on anything other than food."

"Sounds boring," Crane said, scowling.

Nico spread his arms, encompassing the whole scene. "Zenobia took that life away from us and we can't get any of it back. I know that. Martha is dead and Crane will never love me again. Nothing I do will fix anything."

"Then tell your men to put down their weapons, Nico," Sparrow said softly. "There's already been so much suffering. Why create more?"

Nico's eyes snapped to hers, hot and furious and wild. "Because *Zenobia* hasn't suffered. All of us have, but not her. She escaped with her skin and limbs intact, with her freedom and dignity, with loyal followers and a livelihood. With a *son*. She deserves none of it. If it's the last thing I do, I'll make her suffer as I have."

"So take me," Jasper said, stepping forward. "Zenobia's barely had any contact with her son, but she loves me. I'm like a daughter to her. Hurt me and you'll break her. So take me instead."

"And me," said Tom. "I've been Zenobia's most loyal friend for over a decade. You think she's cold, but she's not. Seeing me die for her would kill her. You have my word I won't resist or try to escape. Just let Grammar and Crane go."

"Look at you falling over yourselves to protect Darius's spawn," Nico said in disgust. "This son of Dalca and his whore. Why would Martha raise him like her own son? Why would she love him and not me? Why would *you* love him? Somehow this wretched little creature has seduced all of you. He could be more dangerous than Dalca himself. So no deal."

Neverwhen marched up to Nico and kicked him in the shin. "Be letten Grammar and my sister go," she shouted at him.

The Damaskers all stirred, but no one went so far as to point a gun at her. A few even suppressed smiles.

Nico stared down at her, bemused. "Who the hell are you?" Then her words registered. *"Sister?"*

"Crane and me been haven the same mama," Neverwhen said. "And she's not wanten to go with you, so be letten her and Grammar go!"

"You're . . ." Nico seemed too stunned to speak.

"Martha's your mother?" Sparrow exclaimed. "I have another niece?"

"Who's your papa, girl?" Nico asked, sounding half strangled.

"I don't know," Neverwhen said, glaring up at him. "But it's not you and I'm *glad*." She stomped over to Crane and tugged at her cuffs as if she could pull them off by herself. "Be taken these *off*."

Tom took a step forward. The gangers who'd been watching Neverwhen with bemusement instantly turned their guns on Tom.

He stopped. "Neverwhen, get back here, please," he said tightly.

Nico looked at him and then at Neverwhen and frowned. He took Neverwhen's arm and dragged her away from Crane. When Neverwhen tried to pull away, he drew his gun and set it to her head.

Immediately, there was stillness.

22

PAPER CRANE

Hatch thyself, baby bird!
That shell is too, too, too
Small
For you.

~ Veronica Park

"Oh, that's not a good idea," Crane said in a voice like silk. Poisonous silk.

"You be letten her go!" Grammar shouted, struggling against the two Damaskers who held him. "Nev's haven nothing to do with this!"

Ryan and Tom had both taken a stride forward.

"Ah, ah, ah," Nico said warningly. He was smiling, just a little, bitter and dark. "Here's how it'll go. You can chase me through the zones if you want, but if you make any move on us, I'll hurt the girl first." He shot a glance at Crane and Grammar. "You two may think you're safe because I'm not going to hurt my own daughter, and you, boy, I'm saving for Zenobia. But if either of you makes an ounce of trouble, this is who'll get hurt. She's expendable to me."

Grammar's voice sliced like glass. "Hurt her and I'll show you how dangerous I am."

Nico spun to face him. "Oh, yes, there you are, *Dalca*. You may be young, but you're very, very close to being a man. When you speak, all I hear is your father's arrogance coming from your mother's whore mouth, and in a moment of emotion I might mistake you for one or the other, so I'd shut up if I were you."

Neverwhen squirmed in Nico's grip. "Be leaven him alone!"

Tom quivered. "The girl's an *innocent*. Nico, you're a hard man. But you're not a man who'll hurt a little girl. You have a daughter!"

"You don't know anything about what I'd do." Nico's mouth twisted. "And what would you know about having a daughter, Tom?"

Tom took a breath and straightened. "As much as you, I expect. You should reconsider taking me as a hostage instead. I'm the one your wife turned to for comfort after she left you. We had a daughter together, that little girl over there."

Neverwhen's eyes flew wide in shock.

"Oh," Jasper said involuntarily as several things suddenly made sense.

"So Nico," Tom said into the stunned silence, "are you sure it isn't me you'd rather hurt?"

Sparrow shook her head at Tom. "My God, her taste in men," she muttered.

Crane laughed raucously. "*You're* my sister's papa? That's explainen why she's so annoying."

Tom only had eyes for Neverwhen. "I'm sorry we didn't tell you, sweetie. We knew how hard Grammar's life would be if people found out who his parents were. I'm not Darius but I am an Azuro, and for a lot of people that would be bad enough. Plus, if people knew you were my daughter, they'd try to use you against me to try to control Zenobia and the Azuros. It was safer for you this way."

Neverwhen stared at him, her face stunned and blank.

"I went looking for you as soon as I heard Martha died," Tom said. "But you were gone. I wish we'd told you—then maybe you'd have come to me instead of joining the packs."

Nico laughed with a bitterness so concentrated, it stained the air around him. With one arm still looped around Neverwhen's neck, he pointed the gun at Tom. "Of course it was you. It's always the quiet, honest-looking ones. Did Zenobia put you up to it? Stealing my daughter wasn't enough for her, was it? She had to steal my wife too."

"There was no stealing of anybody," Tom said evenly. "Martha wasn't your wife anymore and she wanted to be with me. Zenobia didn't even know about us until Martha got pregnant."

Nico set the gun back to Neverwhen's head. She hardly seemed to notice, so intensely was she studying Tom.

Jasper clutched at Okuru's fur, feeling helpless and weak. None of them were armed, not even Ryan. They were out of sight of the church and the gangers and the ReGeneration warriors who could have come to help. Grammar fought wildly, but the two Damaskers holding him were unmoved.

Tom stood rigid, hands half raised. "Please, Nico. Hurt me instead."

"That's exactly what I'm doing, you wife-stealing bastard."

Nico's finger tightened on the trigger. Grammar screamed.

Ryan lunged forward with a long step that would never get him there in time.

"Wait, Papa."

All movement stopped, as if time had paused.

Crane stepped forward. Dragon made a convulsive move toward her, but Nico gave him a sharp look and turned himself and Neverwhen to face Crane.

Crane lifted her empty, cuffed hands to her father, a gesture of appeal. "Don't be killen her, Papa. Please." Her face was strangely young and open. Softer, less like a knife.

The silence crystallized, fragile as the skin of ice over a river.

Nico swallowed and blinked. "Freeya?"

"I already been losen my mama," Crane said. "You really gonna be hurten my sister? How can I be forgiven you for that, Papa? How can we be a family again if you're killen my sister?"

The gun in Nico's hand wavered and lowered slightly from Neverwhen's head. "A family again . . ."

"Be letten my sister go now," Crane said almost gently.

Nico dropped his hands from Neverwhen, and she stumbled a few steps away.

"Boss," Dragon said, moving to keep his gun on Crane. "You shouldn't be letten her—"

"Shut up," Nico said without taking his eyes from Crane.

Crane nodded. "Never been tellen my mama sorry before she been dyen. I'm tellen you, Papa. I'm sorry."

"No, baby girl, I'm the one who's sorry. It was my job to protect you. I failed you and you were right to hate me." He wiped his arm over his face.

"Zenobia's always sayen, choices are haven consequences. Even when you're sorry." Crane shrugged skinny shoulders. "But someone's tellen me that sayen sorry's important anyway."

With a twist of her wrists, her cuffs came off and fell to the grass with a clink.

"And you're maken some bad choices, Papa."

For a second everybody just stared at the cuffs on the ground.

Jasper flashed back to Ryan playing with Nico's ring of keys and dropping them. Neverwhen picking them up and keeping them. Neverwhen running over to Crane and grabbing at her hands while no one bothered to stop her—the perfect opportunity to slip a handcuff key into Crane's hand.

In the stillness, Crane moved. So did Neverwhen.

Neverwhen pulled a knife from her belt—Crane's own knife, a knife that Nico and the Damaskers hadn't even thought to take from her—and held it out.

Crane swiped it smoothly from her hand and cocked it back to throw—

Nico looked back at Crane, his hands dangling loose at his sides—

A gun fired. Deafening and heart-stopping. World ending.

An instant of impossible slowness where time stretched and all possibilities still existed.

Crane crumpled. Like wet newspaper she folded in silence, melting into the grass.

Neverwhen screamed, an unending note of anguish and loss.

Torn, scarred paper crane, staining the earth red. Staring eyes and rattling cough and bubbling, bloody breath. Her hair a soft, defiant cloud. A knife in her hand.

Nico stood motionless. A husk. Turning to stone from the inside out.

Jasper became dimly aware of pain in her arms. Ryan was holding on to her as if he'd fall down without her to hold him up. She heard him groan in denial, and instinctively she reached for him.

Nico turned, an ancient statue come to life. Face wet and ravaged.

Dragon hadn't moved a muscle since his gunshot divided this world from the one before. "I been saven your life, boss," he cried. "She was gonna be killen you!"

Nico drew in a deep, gasping breath, perhaps his first since the gunshot. "Then I would have died at peace. But you couldn't possibly understand that."

Dragon's face twisted. "I don't *get* you, man. I been loyal, I been doen everything you been asken. And this bitch is comen in and she's tryen to fucken *kill* you, and you're getten mad at *me*? She's a mad fucken *dog* and I'm doen you a favour putten her down—"

He choked. Gurgled. Spat blood.

Clutched at his throat.

Which had a knife sticking out of it, sunk to the hilt.

"Hey, shit piece," Crane croaked. She was propped up on one elbow. "I'm keepen my promises. Be tellen the Devilman Crane's sayen hi."

Dragon stumbled to his knees, still clutching at the knife in his throat. He collapsed and was still.

"Piney," Crane whispered. "I think my heart's done hatchen." And she tipped over, horribly floppy and boneless. As deathly still and bloody as Dragon.

Jasper felt Ryan's flinch, deep and unguarded and raw, travel from his hands into her bones.

"Crane!" Sparrow screamed. She crumpled to her knees beside Crane, crying out at the pain of her wounded leg and then ignoring it. "Oh my God, baby girl. Jesus, oh God. It's going to be okay, baby. You're going to be fine. I'm here, Auntie's here."

Jasper couldn't move, couldn't breathe, couldn't think. Crane was eternal, she was flint and steel. She and Jasper were each other's reflections, seen through a cracked and splintered mirror. Crane was angry, belligerent, mocking, unpredictable, laughing. She was *alive*, not this collection of bones covered in meat covered in skin that Sparrow was cradling in her arms. Not those blank eyes. Not those long skinny clever fingers now as lifeless as sticks.

Neverwhen stumbled away from the Damaskers. Tom

reached for her, but she shied away from him. Instead she stopped in front of Ryan and looked up at him, her face blank. Ryan kneeled. She collapsed silently against him, and he gathered her into his chest.

Sparrow raised her head and screamed, "We need help over here! Ibtisam!" Her hands were pressed to Crane's chest. There was so much blood. "Please, oh please. She's—I think she's still alive but—"

Tom whirled and ran back to the church, roaring at the top of his lungs, "Ibtisam!"

Jasper couldn't look at Crane. So she looked at Nico.

His face was a graveyard.

"It isn't worth it," Jasper whispered, which was as much volume as she could push from her throat. "Please, won't you let this go? Forget Grammar. And Zenobia. Just be with your daughter right now."

He wouldn't look at Crane. "She's already gone." His voice was ashes and dust. "I lost her—I lost everything that mattered a long time ago."

"She's not dead yet," Jasper said desperately. *Not yet, not yet, not yet.*

Let the goblins choke on the size of this wish.

But Nico didn't seem to hear her. As if she and everyone else who could have stopped him had died with that gunshot and turned into ghosts. He gestured, and his Damaskers moved. Grammar looked over his shoulder as he was propelled along by Vic and another Damasker.

Jasper fumbled for her bird amulet and lifted it so he could see. She would come for him.

He nodded once.

And then they were gone.

Ryan still kneeled with Neverwhen in his arms. He leaned his cheek against Jasper's thigh as she stood beside him, and she could feel wetness soaking through her jeans. She pressed a hand to his hair and wondered numbly if he'd find a way to add another blue dot to his arms.

Okuru nudged his nose against Neverwhen and whimpered.

Tom was racing back now, and Ibtisam ran beside him, medical bag in hand, with Merlot and Esther in their wake. And there in the lead was Grace. Running so fast she outpaced them all.

Heads he wins, tails you lose.

Sometimes, against all odds, the demons were defeated. But even as they fell, they laughed. For victory came with a cost, and sometimes it was everything.

The devil in blood is paid his dues.

23

A WAY THROUGH

Hugs where you sink into their arms like you live there now
Hugs where you hang on like you'll get pulled into the void if
*   you don't*
Hugs where you think you might kiss, but honestly the hug's
*   better than a kiss*

~ Veronica Park (*Things I Will Miss/Reasons to Live*)

"It's blocked," Charlie said aloud. "Truly blocked."

He and Ben had spent the last twenty minutes examining the collapsed tunnel and arguing over ways it might be cleared.

Jasper had spent most of that time pacing around the horses, trying to breathe in the dust-choked darkness.

"Nico clearly has demolitions experience." Ryan stroked Ed for Edible's neck and stayed out of Jasper's way. "He collapsed the tunnel deliberately to slow us down."

"Slow us down?" Merlot said disgustedly. "This is goddamn impassable. It'd take weeks to clear out. We don't have weeks."

They certainly did not. If the AI's prediction was accurate, Jasper might not have more than a dozen hours. Even without her own personal deadline, Nico was ahead of them with Grammar and nothing standing between him and the Tower and Zenobia. His heart dead and broken, he had nothing to lose.

Crane could be dying right now. Every so often, the memory blindsided Jasper.

Ryan saw. He always did. He shifted his weight so he was in her path, so that she bumped against his hip as she paced past. A bump to jostle her heart back in place, swollen and painful but beating again.

She squeezed his wrist in return, his wrist where the tattooed blue dots began, each one a heartbeat. A reminder to him that she wouldn't let him turn his grief into self-blame. He couldn't have stopped that gunshot. No one could have.

Ibtisam and Grace had worked for hours over Crane's body. Esther had assisted, handing them instruments and clean rag after rag to sop up the endless blood. Tom and Ryan stood by to hold Crane down if she ever emerged from unconsciousness. Harmony kept boiling more and more water and handing out food no one ate.

Everyone else waited outside the room. Neverwhen ended up in Sparrow's lap. Ben and Charlie rejoined the ReGeneration to deal with the disarmed Damaskers but checked in periodically. After an hour Sparrow gently transferred Neverwhen to Jasper's lap and hobbled off to check on Yorky. She soon reappeared, having been shooed away by Quick Rick and Pastor Tim, who insisted they had things under control and she should stay with her family.

With her face tucked into Jasper's shoulder, Neverwhen whispered, "Grammar." It was the first word she'd spoken since

Crane had been shot. Jasper nodded in answer. Okuru half climbed into her lap to be closer to Neverwhen. Jasper didn't push him away.

"I've done as much as I can," Ibtisam reported to them hours later, swaying with weariness, her eyes bloodshot. She held up a small vial and nodded to Ryan. "Ryan gave me these fancy nanobiotics. They worked really well on Sparrow. So if Crane makes it through the next twenty-four hours, I think—" She took a deep breath. "I think there's hope."

Sparrow let out a half sigh, half sob and slid out of her chair so that she was lying flat on the floor, arms and legs splayed out as if she were about to make a snow angel. Ben looked from the vial to Ryan and muttered, "Worst villain *ever*." Harmony passed out more food, which this time people ate. Merlot left to get a change of clothes for Esther and Grace since they were blood spattered from the surgery and Grace wouldn't budge from Crane's side. Neverwhen climbed out of Jasper's lap and walked over to Ryan. "We should be goen to get Grammar now."

Ryan looked at Jasper and Jasper looked at the room where Crane still lay motionless on the operating table, unnervingly tiny and vulnerable under a blanket.

"There's nothing more you can do here," Ibtisam said. "If you have a chance to save that boy, you should."

So now here they were after a day of hard riding through the tunnels, hoping to catch up to Nico, but he'd driven his Damaskers hard and stayed ahead of them.

"Is this really the only way to the Tower?" Ryan asked.

Jasper thought of the maze of tunnels and passages she'd wandered through in a delirious haze after climbing out of the hole the Guardian had put her in. She shuddered. She'd never find her way back again, not in the short amount of time she had left.

"Unless Jas learns to fly like the Up-gee Witch." Merlot shot Jasper a sharp glance. "Can you do that?"

"She'd have to Shatter first," Tom said. He returned to his horse and mounted. "We're wasting time here. The only other option is the foam zones."

Merlot said, "You get a pass for that stupidity because you're not a grav-walker, but trust us, no one can grav foam."

They rode back to the ReGeneration's village in silence.

Neverwhen had wanted to come along. She'd ignored the unanimous refusal from Sparrow and Tom and Harmony and had appealed to Ryan instead. He winced at her brimming eyes but firmly shook his head. At last she turned to Jasper, pleading and accusing and defiant. Jasper knelt in front of her. "You asked me once to save Grammar and I refused," Jasper said. "It wasn't my finest moment. But this time biggies will do what biggies are supposed to do, and you'll stay safe as you should be. Because that's how the world is supposed to work. You'll be here when your sister wakes up. She'll want to see you." She held Neverwhen's clenched, gloved hands. "Do you trust me, Nev?"

Neverwhen's eyes searched hers, fierce and anguished and much older than the first time they'd met. Finally, with twin tears tracking down her cheeks, she nodded. "You da Pinegirl."

For the first time in her life, Jasper smiled to hear the name. "That's right. And I'm going to bring Grammar home."

They emerged into the ReGeneration's village in the waning evening light. The Guardian was waiting for them. The others scattered so quickly, Jasper barely registered they were gone until she dismounted and found herself alone with the Guardian.

"You left Zenobia at the Tower?" Jasper said. The first words out of her mouth, unplanned. "She was unconscious and you *left* her? Now Nico's on his way, and we have no way to help her."

"Last time we stood here, you wanted Zenobia dead."

"I was upset."

"I stayed with her until she was conscious," the Guardian said. "I returned to the village last night to check on my people. I intended to go back to the Tower, but we heard the tunnel collapse just a few hours ago. Nico killed three of the guards we had on the tunnel, and the fourth one's barely hanging on."

"There has to be another way to the Tower."

"You already know the answer to that."

"I won't do what you want. You've lost your chance at convincing me to do anything. I'm going to save Grammar and then I'm going to . . ." Her tongue tripped on the words as if rejecting them. "You won't stop me this time."

The Guardian laced her hands together and sighed. Lines were carved deeply around her mouth and eyes. "Then how will you save the boy? And Zenobia?"

Jasper studied the foam zones that created a barrier between the village's down-gee zone and the Tower's down-gee zone. "I've been mostly in down-gee for two days, and I haven't had a shift in a while. I'm due." She lifted her chin at the foam. "I'm going to shift and fall straight through the foam until I reach the Tower."

The Guardian spotted the problem immediately. "Your shifts are random. You could fall in any direction including up. There's no guarantee you'll fall in the right direction."

"I know. Do you suppose . . .?" She gritted her teeth. "Do you suppose the graviteria are close enough to sentience that I could communicate with them already? Or even do the beginning stage of melding, just enough to make them shift me in the right direction?"

The Guardian lifted her eyebrows.

"Don't get excited," Jasper said harshly. "I'm not melding any more than that, and I'm still going to kill myself afterwards."

"Why would I try to dissuade you from something you have your heart set on?" the Guardian said.

Jasper glared. "It's the only choice that'll save lives, so shut up about it. Answer my question."

"Only one way to find out."

"Okay, but how?"

The Guardian laughed, a very human sound in its helplessness. "Talk to them? They're there, a part of you. Their consciousness, such as it is, exists inside you along with your own, but they may not yet be self-aware. You need to wake them up."

Jasper didn't bother asking *how* a second time. Even the Guardian could only guess how this worked. "Fine."

"If you'd like to yell at me for putting you in that hole, I'll hear you out," the Guardian said. "It was a cruel thing to do."

"But you'd do it again."

"Yes."

"Then what's the point?" Jasper turned to go.

"The stakes are just too high. I had to try."

Jasper wheeled around. "You think I don't realize how high the stakes are? If you wanted so badly for someone to meld with the graviteria, you had access to the samples. Why didn't you just infect yourself?"

The Guardian opened her mouth but didn't say anything.

"That's what I thought," Jasper said bitterly. "Easier to play with someone else's life than risk your own. Everyone was always waiting for someone *else* to deal with Darius Dalca."

"Putting you in the hole was a last resort," the Guardian said. "It would have spared your life."

"That was *my* choice to make!"

"Yes, and your choice will have consequences," the Guardian said heavily. "Just like mine. I took a risk and maybe I was wrong. Only time will tell. I just hope the whole planet doesn't pay the price for my failure or for whatever choice you make." The Guardian shrugged to indicate what hopes and wishes were worth. "Anyway, now it's your turn to gamble. Gods and spirits help us all." She walked away.

Choices and consequences. Just as Crane had said to her father at the end. Demons were the twisted children of choices that the mind and heart couldn't reconcile. And they didn't only afflict the choice-maker but were born in the souls of those who had others' choices inflicted upon them.

Jasper stood by herself for a while, letting a familiar blankness settle over her thoughts like a blanket of snow. She was dragged under by the dark undertow of the thought of Crane's bleeding body in the grass, Crane's bleeding body on the operating table. Nico was her father, but Zenobia was the one who would mourn if Crane . . .

She could've died after they left. She could be dead right now.

Nico had never had a chance to know the person Crane had become, but Zenobia had raised her. Zenobia, the woman who had never wanted to be a mother, hadn't turned any of them away—not her motley gang of convicts, not her wild and abused dogs, not a dangerously broken girl with a wavering moral compass, not an angry, bitter, and untrusting Pinegirl.

But Nico believed the loss was his, and now he had Grammar in his grip and nothing to live for.

A hand touched her shoulder, making her jump. "Sorry," said Tom. He'd cleaned himself up some, but his face still bore a mosaic of cuts and bruises from the Damaskers' brutal treatment. His eyes were hollow with exhaustion. "At the risk of making a vast understatement, Crane's a fighter," he said. "She'll pull through."

Jasper thought of Vron. "Even fighters fall."

Tom rubbed a hand over his face, his unkempt beard. Then he pulled out the amulet he'd shown her the night of Nico's coup, the first paper crane Jasper had folded by herself.

Zenobia had given it to him for safekeeping and he'd carried it all these years for her. "Crane would want us to save Zenobia and Grammar," he said. "This is what we can do for her right now."

Crane could be dying and Zenobia didn't even know.

Tom left to talk to Winnie. Villagers clustered around the returning warriors, listening to the news from Yorky.

The ice had receded, a glacier that could be dealt with later. She had no time to fall apart. Literally no time. She spotted Charlie and Ben and walked over.

"Did the Guardian have any suggestions about shifting?" Charlie asked aloud.

"She said to talk to the graviteria," Jasper signed and shook her head in bemusement. "Talk. That's it."

"I expected you to scream at her for putting you in that hole," Ben said. "I'd do it but she scares me shitless."

Charlie frowned until Jasper interpreted Ben's comment. "Oh, same. Just glare at her from a distance. That always works for me." He'd used his voice rather than sign.

"You guys are holding hands," Jasper said.

"No, we're not," Ben said, frowning. He looked down. His fingers were indeed laced through Charlie's. "Oh. That means nothing."

Jasper waited a beat before signing, "You're still holding hands."

"He lost a bet," Charlie said.

Ben scowled and enunciated so Charlie could read his lips. "You cheated."

"Your hands," Jasper signed. "Still palm to palm, right in front of my eyes, all super disturbingly romantic and whatnot."

"No romance," Ben said flatly and freed his hand in order to sign. "Not until Charlie spends the next four years proving he won't take off again."

"Exactly, Jas, we're just friends," Charlie signed. "We're bros. Bros who hold hands. I could hold your hand too if you like."

"Stay away from me, *babo*," she said, laughing despite everything.

"I could hold something other than his hand instead," Charlie suggested.

"Okay, leaving now!"

"Ryan looks lonely. Why don't you go hold his hand?" Charlie called after her. "Or his—" The last word was muffled. By Ben's hand, presumably. Or maybe his mouth. Jasper didn't turn to see.

She nearly ran into Merlot.

"Hand holding? Really? Are you fine with this?" he demanded, gesturing behind her.

During Crane's surgery Merlot had sat in the chair beside Jasper and sketched in his notebook, filling page after page. As the interminable minutes trickled by, she'd watched stories grow and evolve and die under his pencil. His old-school Peter and Jazztree characters made an appearance, falling into a pit full of spikes, getting attacked by a slavering dog, drinking tea with cannibals, arguing in side-by-side cages in a room full of skulls. Arms crossed, looking in opposite directions with stubborn, miserable expressions. Twin thought bubbles over their heads reading *I wish . . .*

He flipped the page and started drawing Crane instead. With her improbably long skinny limbs and huge hair, she came alive under his pencil, all angles and dramatic poses and festooned with an absurd quantity of knives. Crane in battle pose, fists bristling with blades, facing off with Zenobia's tiny black cat, Marvel. Then Crane leaping with fright into Grace's arms when the cat meowed.

In Jasper's lap, Neverwhen made a sound that was almost a giggle.

He drew Grammar on a dramatically rearing horse and Neverwhen riding a huge shaggy Okuru. Neverwhen whispered a request, and soon three cat-sized unicorns and a crow marched in a line behind Okuru. He drew Ryan laughing, rolling on the ground, swarmed by a dozen puppies. He drew Esther with her face turned up to the sun as if caught in a quiet, unguarded moment, a small private smile on her face.

He drew Vron, just the line of her nose and eyebrow, the shadow of her mouth. The ghost of her face emerged from the white page, soft as a dream. Then he snapped the sketchbook shut, as if to break a spell before it could form, as Ibtisam emerged from the operating room.

"It wasn't right the way Charlie left us," Jasper now said to Merlot. "But I never tried to understand why he left either. Anyway, life's too damn short for grudges against friends. I want Ben to have every ounce of happy he can wring from the world."

Merlot peered at her. "Okay, who are you and where's the real Jasper?"

"Ha ha." She wished she had the answer to either of those questions.

"I saw that, Charlie," Merlot signed past her, distracted.

She turned, catching only Charlie's innocent expression and Ben's rolled eyes. Merlot stalked over to them.

Jasper took the opportunity to slip away.

Ryan stood at the edge of down-gee, gazing across the foam zones at the Tower. He lifted his chin in greeting as she approached and held out his hand. Cupped in his palm was a scarlet heap of tiny wild strawberries. She popped one in her mouth. For something so small, the hit of tart sweetness was intense.

Before they left Yorky, she'd stopped unseen by a doorway when she heard Ben and Ryan speaking. "Shouldn't you leave now to deal with your brother?" Ben had demanded. "Why come with us?"

"My brother can be dealt with later. Grammar and Zenobia need us now." An edge entered Ryan's voice. "After everything, you still believe I'd hurt either Jasper or Grammar?"

"Of course not, not intentionally. But I just don't see a scenario," Ben said, "where you don't break her heart, whether you mean to or not."

Only silence answered him. Jasper hurried away, heart pounding, before either of them noticed her eavesdropping.

Now they ate the strawberries under the branches of an oak tree. Through the leaves soft evening light dappled Ryan's face, playing over it with gentle patterns as he gazed across the foam. It was the kind of summer evening where the air tasted of immortality and eternal youth and a sweetness so acute, it threatened to stop the heart with sadness. The barest breath of a breeze stroked its fingers over Jasper's cheeks and stirred Ryan's hair. He gave her the last strawberry and wiped his hand on his shirt.

She studied his profile and thought of all the things she didn't know about him, all the things she wanted to know. All the things she would never know. Where did you begin when the ending was already tripping over your heels? How did you fit all the words of a lifetime into one soft green summer evening?

Where have you come from and where are you going and who do you love and what do you know? What was I to you and who will you be because of me? What will you remember and what will you forget? Will I fade away or become the voice in your head?

Jasper pulled from her pouch the tiny Zombie Princess figurine she had found in Catherine's car, which her mother had probably been bringing home to Jasper, knowing it would make her smile. Jasper had tied a cord around the figurine. She extended it to Ryan.

"What's this, Zeep?" He sounded caught between confusion and amusement.

"I told you once you needed an amulet to keep away the ghosts."

His smile changed, became complicated. "You said amulets didn't keep away Darius."

"You can't keep away ghosts that are already part of you, I'm afraid."

He rolled the grey-skinned plastic princess around in his palm. "I didn't get you anything."

"My birthday's coming up. October."

She'd be dead by then.

"How about I bring you cinnamon for your weird cinnamon tea?"

If he ever came back. If he could find a way. If he even wanted to. He had a life outside.

He ducked his head through the thong, lifting his hair out of the way. He tucked the Zombie Princess under his shirt so it lay beside his dog tags. Warmed by his skin, next to his heart.

A blackbird called, heartbreakingly clear. The breeze lifted, and above them the branches dipped and swayed. The leaves danced with a murmur, a flutter, a rush. The sky whispering a poem to the earth.

"Zeep." Ryan touched a fingertip to her chin. "It'll still be you on the other side."

"What?" He stood close enough to her to drive all the other questions out of her head.

"Whatever happens, whatever you decide—it won't matter. You'll always be Jasper Pine."

How could he know what she was afraid of? "You can't know that for sure."

His eyes, warm and steady as the earth, anchored her,

reminding her of where her feet belonged. "That alien's been a part of you since you were born. What would really change?"

Maybe nothing.

Maybe everything.

She didn't know which possibility scared her more.

"You've already survived so much," he said. "And you're still here. And look at you. You're . . ." He stopped speaking and shook his head, but all the ways he could finish that sentence were there, reflected in his eyes.

"Are you calling me a crocodile again?" she asked.

He laughed out loud.

Harmony would always make her cinnamon tea for comfort, whenever she was sick or sad or scared. But if she could fall asleep to the sound of Ryan's voice, his laugh, she'd never need cinnamon tea again.

She began, "I wish that—"

Ryan stopped her with his fingers against her lips. He plucked a coin from her ear. He tossed it over his shoulder and closed his eyes to wish.

On impulse she put her hands on his chest and stood on tiptoe and waited. He opened his eyes to find her inches from his face. She felt his indrawn breath, his heart beating under her palm. She kissed him and felt his smile, irrepressible and delighted, against her mouth. Then he stopped smiling, cradled her face in his hands, and kissed her in return, fierce and sweet, the heat of his mouth warming her straight through from skin to spine to heart.

His mouth tasted of hot tea and strawberries and sunlight. He tasted like the future, like the other side of the horizon, like a lifetime measured in decades, not mere hours. She wrapped her arms around his rib cage and kissed him like he was the earth—everything she wanted but could never keep. A dream, gone and done before her heart could remember to beat again.

"What did you wish?" she asked when they were once again doing ordinary things like breathing and counting time with their heartbeats.

"It's the fastest damn wish I've ever had come true," he said.

She laughed and hit his arm. "No, really."

He studied her face as if memorizing it. "I'll tell you on the other side of tomorrow."

24

REASONS TO LIVE

I am a bird,
You are a tree.
Birds can roam
From land to sea,
But a tree is home,
The heart's remedy.
When the sky is empty
Don't mourn for me.
Trees live longer
But a bird is free.

~ Veronica Park

J asper had lived most of her life surrounded by death larger than one person or even a million.

In this city forgotten hopes and dreams blew and scattered in the wind, along with water bottles and paper cups. Intentions never acted on and paths never taken rusted at the bottom of puddles and ponds and abandoned swimming pools. Regrets meandered through weed-choked ditches, and unsaid words snagged on branches like plastic shopping bags. Children never born or barely born played in the streets and laughed with the voices of crows and sparrows. The city sagged in on itself under the immeasurable weight of unfinished lives and unrealized possibilities.

Soon her own would be added to them.

She'd been ready to die. Or so she'd thought.

Nighttime in the ReGeneration's village was filled with the muted sounds of horses, the muffled thump of their hooves, the *snick, snick* of their grazing, soft whickers between mothers and their foals. Farther away the flicker of fires and candlelight and the voices of families at dinner offered an illusion of peace.

Jasper sat at the edge of down-gee, facing the foam and across it, the Tower. A rope was hooked up to her harness and another was coiled around her torso. Her stomach was full from the community barbeque. Her mouth still tasted of strawberries.

The lush, sumptuous aura of wild roses lay so thick among the bushes that it would have dyed the air pink were it not already dark. Vron had always adored roses, calling them extravagant and shameless expressions of summer.

On a nearby watchtower a ReGeneration ganger kept binoculars trained on the Tower. Other than some floating rubble and the trees around the down-gee zone, little blocked their view in the half kilometre of foam zones that separated the village and the Tower, but so far there'd been no movement to see. Nico and his men would have arrived underground in the parking levels of the Tower. They had no reason to emerge when their quarry was inside.

Footsteps approached her. She recognized their cadence and twisted around in surprise.

Merlot hesitated a few steps away. "You want to be alone?"

"No." The word exited her mouth without routing through her brain first.

Merlot lowered himself to the ground beside her. Seconds ticked away in silence. Her heart lurched with desperation. Every beat that passed was a moment she'd never get back. She wanted to grab the minutes, hoard them in her hands like fragile blue robin's eggs until she could figure out what to do with them.

"You really think you'll be able to shift in the right direction?" Merlot asked.

"It's the only way we're getting to the Tower before Nico reaches Zenobia."

Merlot twisted a strand of his hair around his finger, rolling and unrolling it.

Back when Jasper's hair was longer and the future was as sure as the sun, Merlot would sleep tucked into a ball like a baby with his fist curled into her hair. She'd learned to wake without sudden movement, to roll over slowly and gently disentangle her hair from his fingers before getting up. Their breakup had amputated a thousand tiny roots sunk into each other's skin, and she'd cut her hair because she didn't know where hers ended and his began.

She wanted to still his hand. It was strange to watch him fidget with hair that wasn't her own.

"So did you know about Crane and Grace?" he asked.

"Grace told you?" Jasper said, surprised. "It's okay, though. I think she can handle Crane."

Merlot snorted. "Are you kidding? For once in my life it's Crane I'm worried about. I mean, have you *met* the Kornelsen girls?"

They laughed for the few seconds it took to remember they had a genuine reason to be worried about Crane. They fell silent.

"When Crane told me she'd burned Vron's notebooks," Merlot said, "I was so angry, I basically told her to break it off with Grace, that they'd never work out and she should let Grace move on to find someone better suited." Merlot shifted and then shot her a sideways glance. "But you and I didn't work out either, and even after everything, I'm still glad we happened."

She pressed her hands to her face, unable to speak for a moment. "I'm glad you feel that way," she managed at last.

"I could still be angry at Crane about the journals, I suppose, but what's the point? I hear Vron's voice in my head all the time anyway."

"Me too."

"Grace said Vron gave her the notebook the day before she died and told her to keep it until I was ready to look at it. Grace thought it would hold personal stuff not meant for her, so she put it away and didn't look at it until a few months ago. She was dreaming about Vron night after night and decided it was a sign from God that she should look in the notebook." A corner of his mouth turned up. "Who knows? Maybe it was."

"Appearing in dreams," Jasper said. "That's so typical of Vron."

He made a sound very close to a laugh.

Jasper drew up her knees and hugged them to her chest. "Why did you come along? You could've stayed in Yorky."

"It crossed my mind." He tilted his head back to consider the stars that sparkled overhead in ringing silence. "It'd be a fair turnaround. Abandon you and Ben when you need your friends the most. Yeah, it occurred to me."

Her throat ached. "Merlot, I'm sorry. I failed you. I—I wasn't enough for Vron to stay and I wasn't going to be enough for you, so I didn't even try. I should have at least tried."

"You ran because you've always processed emotion through moving. I understand that now." He shook his head, cleared his throat. "I haven't spent the entire three years angry at you, believe it or not. I was also angry at myself and sometimes Ben and also Charlie. And Vron. Most of all Vron." He blew out a short, sharp breath.

Her burns prickled her skin, tiny whiplashes. The stars were so close, she could have plucked them from the sky, put them in her mouth, and swallowed fire and eternity with an aftertaste of infinite vacuum.

"You're the second person to hide your sadness from me," he said. "You hid your *death* from me. Do you really think I'm so breakable? Did she?"

"There was nothing you could've done, and that's not on you, Mer. Some stuff you can't fix with all the love in the world."

"So you thought you'd make me hate you instead? Because that's better? Jesus, Jas. This whole time I thought you . . ." He stopped. "At times I wished I'd never met you at all. I wanted to make you feel that too."

What she'd had with Merlot was as difficult to define as a cloud. There were no sharp edges, no clear points of beginning or end, only areas of greater density and darkness and moments stretched thin and luminous and barely tangible.

"Mer," she said. "You know that day after the funeral when we found you and you were . . . and we thought you had . . . and Esther and her sisters had to . . ." The words wouldn't come out, clogging up her throat. "Were you really trying to . . . did you *want* to . . .?"

"Kill myself?" His voice was normal, like he'd been waiting for her to ask this question for three years. He looked up at the stars. Finally, he gave his head an infinitesimal shake. "I just wanted everything to stop. I just wanted . . . to not be me for a minute. It was like I was possessed. By pain. There wasn't room for me. Yes, I wanted to escape. But not permanently. Never permanently."

"Okay." Jasper exhaled a breath that had been trapped in her lungs for three years.

"I never wanted to die," he said. "And I didn't understand how she could."

"She didn't," Jasper said. "I've been reading Vron's journal. She made a list titled 'Reasons to Live/Things I Will Miss.' She didn't want to go, Mer. One whole page was just your name over and over."

He clamped his hands over his face.

"If I were to make my own list," she said, "I'd have a page for you too."

She stopped then, and they didn't speak for a while. A dove cooed in the woods and frogs croaked, their green voices pressed against the black velvet of the night. Wind lifted the grass and then sighed into stillness.

"I think we're going to need a bucket," she said.

"May as well go ahead and build a boat."

"Is that snot in your hair?"

"Fuck."

A little later, he said, more calmly, "You and I wouldn't have stayed together forever anyway."

This time it didn't feel like a thrown spear. "Why not?"

"Remember that time I caught a sparrow? I held out some crumbs and it landed on my palm and I caught it."

She nodded.

"You told me to let it go again, that I couldn't keep it forever. But I was so amazed to be holding something so fragile and beautiful and elusive that I couldn't bear to release it. I thought nothing so magical would ever happen to me again, so I had to hold on to it as long as I could. Vron had to march over and peel open my fingers to let it fly away. I cried all night."

She smiled, a bittersweet twinge in her heart. "Am I the bird?"

"You wouldn't have stood for it. You'd have pecked me to death eventually." There was almost an answering smile in his voice. "I spent three years teaching myself how to let go by pushing people away. Not a technique I'd recommend. But I found that sometimes people will come back to you without you needing to hold on to them. Sometimes they'll even stay. And sometimes they were there all along."

The sky doesn't begin at the mountaintop. It begins here, where my skin stops being skin . . .

She pulled out Vron's notebook from her thigh pouch and placed it in his hands. He cradled its worn, lumpy covers gently between his hands, then lifted it to his nose and inhaled.

After a while he took a silver flask from his thigh pouch. Ryan must have returned what he'd stolen, and replaced its contents too. When Merlot unscrewed the cap, she smelled fruit and heat and summer sweetness. Ceremoniously, he poured a small stream into the grass, a libation to the small god, before handing her the flask. The liquid tasted of lazy kisses and sunlit caresses and gulfs of time and memory that couldn't be crossed.

"To Vron," he said.

"To all our reasons to live," she replied.

And all the things I'll miss.

Later, after Merlot had gone and at the end of everything, there was only one person left who mattered.

Ben sat beside her. She said nothing. Neither did he. It was just the two of them, the way it had been since they were children. Words weren't necessary. You didn't need to speak to your hand, your leg, your pumping heart, not when they were part of you.

"I always knew I might not have you for long," he said after a while. "You nearly died so many times as a kid. I used to reach for you before I even woke up, to make sure you hadn't fallen, hadn't wiggled loose of the straps. Once I found you in the middle of the night floating in mid-air, tied to the bed by a single belt. You were fast asleep. It was you drooling on me that woke me up."

"Classic me."

Ben turned his face up to the stars. "Jas."

"Yeah?"

"I'd always choose you first and never regret it."

Words might not be necessary, but they could fill all the hollows and canyons of a soul with shining lakes and bloom gardens in a desert.

25

DARIUS'S GHOST

*Some species of pine require exposure to fire in order to release
their seeds. The inferno signifies not death but rebirth.*

~ Dr. Zenobia Allan (personal journals)

Alone again, Jasper watched the night press its velvety
hand onto the earth, a starry caress. As last nights on
earth went, it was a moon-kissed pearl. The moon rose and
tracked across the sky. The earth spun under the stars,
generating the gravity that pressed her children firmly against
her skin, a mother's hug.

It didn't have to be her last night. The thought curled
through her mind like a breath of spring in an airless tunnel.

You don't want to die, pet, Darius said reasonably. *So don't. The
Shattering won't kill you. Let's not pretend you haven't held people's
lives in your hands before. How many of them are alive today because
of you? They owe you. You're only taking your due. You're the
Pinegirl. You're going to run the zones one day. Mark my words, pet.*

You're going to fix everything I broke, and isn't that a legacy worth leaving?

"Legacy," she said aloud. "I've seen what you left behind. The less legacy I leave, the better."

Tell that to my kid. It hardly sounded like Darius.

"Grammar? What do you mean?"

You think you've left no mark on him? You think if you die it won't change him?

"That's not fair. I know my family and friends will mourn. It can't be helped. Grammar's young. He'll move on."

Kids, said Darius. *Selfish little shits at the best of times. But you're wrong about him moving on.*

Jasper focused on the obsidian stalk of the Tower, the spindle between heaven and earth. She closed her eyes. "It's your own fault you won't ever get to know him."

A long silence. *I know.*

Jasper watched the whorls of scarlet on the inside of her eyelids. "Are you really Darius?"

Who else would I be?

"I don't know. Maybe you're a part of me, the part I despised and hated and feared, the part of me that was most like him, the part of me I could never forgive."

Why would you imagine such a voice in your head?

Ever since she'd killed him, he'd been her inner voice, a haunting manufactured by her subconscious, animated by memories too dark to examine in the light of day. Every hateful thought she'd heard in his voice. All the vicious muck that lurked in her mind, all the shame and resentment and that awful, sickening joy she'd derived from the suffering of others, from the thrill of wagers with lives and limbs on the line . . . she'd attributed it all to him. He was a talisman of everything she could have become.

She said, "People wonder why I feel guilty about killing such a monstrous man."

I know this one. It's because you're a good person, right? Unlike me.

"I felt guilty because I loved you. How could I be so damn weak to love a person like you? Killing you was a rebuttal, my counter-argument. Nothing noble. It was me proving something. But all I proved was that I was just like you. That's what I thought."

So are you like me or unlike me?

"I'm exactly like you, Darius. I contain every possibility on earth, just as you did. I'm faced with choices every day, just as you were. I carry as much dark and light in my soul as you were born with."

And your choices were justified and mine were not? Don't get sanctimonious with me, pet. I don't need your goddamn forgiveness or understanding.

"Everything you ever did was a giant dare at the universe. *So kill me, then, if I'm so bad.* But no one took you up on that dare and so you did worse and worse things. Until me. I guess you could say I was the universe's answer to you. Maybe that's why I understood you so well. And I never could turn down a dare."

A long pause. *You're supposed to hate me.*

Jasper breathed out slowly, releasing the tension in her shoulders. She imagined herself as a little girl, a feral, desperate scrap of a pack kid surrounded by horror and love and courage and bloody, sticky spiderwebs. She imagined giving her younger self a hug. "How could I hate you? I'd never have survived without you."

A strange, shifting silence. *Maybe I'm Darius, some psychic echo of his consciousness imprinted on yours,* said the voice in her head. *Maybe I'm your dark side. And maybe I'm also something else.*

The stillness of dust settling. Recognition stole over her skin like sunlight through broken windows.

"Maybe," she said, "you're a sentient alien living in my body."

Maybe, the voice agreed.

A shiver traced electric pathways over her skin. "And are you one or many?"

To reach sentience we must unite and merge into a cohesive unit. So now we are one. I am one.

"Why Darius? Why would you choose *his* voice?"

I didn't. You did. Even in the dreams of my preconscious state, I felt your hostility and your anxiety and your despair. I knew that I was Other and unwanted. You named me Darius and I became what you shaped me to be.

"Why only reveal yourself now?"

I live in your cells and I share your consciousness. I couldn't realize I wasn't truly Darius until you *realized that.*

Jasper looked across the rubble-wreathed dreamscape of the foam zones to the Tower. At the tip of its spire rose a fateful up-gee zone like a flashlight beam aimed at the stars. Final destination, the universe at large.

"You don't belong on this planet," she said.

Don't I? I wouldn't be the first traveller to find a new home.

"Where did you come from?"

I was born here, in you. You are my home.

"Yeah, and my life has been so fantastic. Maybe space would be better."

You live on a tiny rock floating in hard vacuum, and the only thing keeping your feet glued to its surface is that it's spinning like a top. Congratulations. You're already in outer space.

"Wow." Jasper pressed her palms against her temples. "Don't say stuff like that!"

It's all perspective.

Jasper took a deep breath, lowered her hands, and examined

them in the faint torchlight. Just her hands, callused and marred with familiar scabs and scars and healing burns, good for punches and caresses, gravving and eating and drawing and making rude gestures. Good for holding pencils, ropes, cups of tea, other people's hands. Knives.

"Could you take over my body?" she asked quietly. "Could you possess me? Would I even know if you did?"

In a tone so different from Darius's that she couldn't recognize it, the voice asked, *Would you like me to say yes? Shall I take responsibility for killing Darius?*

"I want you to tell me the truth."

Would you forgive yourself if I said yes? Would you hate me instead?

"Why won't you answer the question?"

Why do you ask questions to which you already know the answers?

"Am I supposed to trust you, just like that?"

Why not? You've known me almost your whole life.

Jasper stood and moved closer to the edge of down-gee until she felt the familiar tingle of the border lifting the hairs on her arms. Behind her, far enough to be out of earshot, she felt the weight of attention from the waiting ReGeneration warriors, who had been politely ignoring her muttered conversation with herself.

"We have a decision to make, you know."

I know.

"Do you know what I need you to do?"

I do. It'll speed up my biological processes, though. It will bring your deadline closer. You won't have the night anymore. You'll have a few hours, maybe. Are you ready for that?

Fear paralyzed her heart into a mineral chunk.

A soft sound from the warriors behind her. She followed their gazes to the edge of the woods. From the layered shadows of the trees emerged a lithe shape with pricked ears. A coyote. It looked in their direction, sharp muzzle high as it sensed their presence. A moment later it had slipped away, soft as a dream.

Jasper breathed again. Every breath was concentrated citrus, mouth-puckering sweetness, too tart and intense to bear. She wasn't ready.

She'd never be ready.

"Do it," she said. "Shift gravity."

The tingle streaked through her body like claws digging furrows through her veins. She barely had time to crouch, palms flat on the earth, and to call over her shoulder, "Ready!"

She fell. Side-gee, directly toward the Tower like an arrow aimed and released.

She only fell a few metres before the rope jerked her short and bounced her against the ground. She pushed off so that she hung in mid-air, parallel to the ground, feet pointed at the Tower.

Despite having been briefed, the ReGeneration members stared at her with wide eyes and dropped jaws.

"Lower me," she said impatiently.

They hurried into motion. One ran to notify those gathered by the watchtower—Tom, Merlot, Ryan, and the rest of the warriors. Charlie and Ben kneeled beside the winch that Ben had rigged up. Charlie cranked the handle, letting out the rope that was tied to Jasper's harness.

With her gravity shifted, the chaotic gravity of the foam zones couldn't affect her. With her hands and feet, she guided herself over the fragile rubble that remained attached to the ground or drifted at zone borders. Steadily, she progressed "downward" to the Tower below her feet.

She twirled a finger, encouraging Charlie to crank faster. She didn't want to risk the chance of her gravity shifting back to zone normal while she was still in the foam. This was her first ever deliberate, controlled shift, but she wasn't the one in control and she didn't know if her alien inhabitant could control the end of the shift equally well.

The Tower blotted out the stars. Below her was an outbuilding that had half fallen into the foam, but enough of it remained to shield her from view as she entered the Tower's down-gee zone. Her feet came to rest against its wall; she was still side-gee.

"Hey, buddy, if you're there, down-gee would be nice about now."

Her graviteria gave no response, but moments later the tingle scoured through her with no delicacy whatsoever, and her weight settled to the ground.

She said cautiously, "Thanks. That was a well-aimed shift."

No answer. Well, she needed to focus on other things. And not on the fact that according to her alien denizen she now had a few hours, maybe less, to rescue Grammar and Zenobia and find a solution, lethal or otherwise, before she Shattered.

She hastened to find a spot to tie the end of the rope to. Once the rope was secure, she gave it three sharp tugs. Almost immediately, it jerked and jigged as the first warriors began their climb across the foam.

Jasper didn't wait for them. In the darkness she dashed across the plaza for the Tower's main entrance doors. They'd been smashed open. A single spot of light drew the eye—the lit-up display above the elevator. It read 50, meaning the elevator was currently at the top of the Tower.

"Hey!" A shadowy figure standing at the elevator moved toward her. "Who are you?"

He lifted his arm, and Jasper burst into motion as a shot rang out. She raced away from the doors, around the side of the Tower and out of sight. She listened for the sounds of pursuit but couldn't hear any. He must have been a Damasker left behind to guard the entrance. Would he follow her or hunker down behind the reception desk in preparation for a possible invasion?

Wherever Nico and the rest of his men were, would they hear the shot and return to reinforce the lone guard? Not if they were in the soundproof basement levels where the Guardian had left Zenobia. The AI wouldn't grant them access, but if Nico had been able to blow the tunnel, he could probably find a way through a locked door.

Something niggled at her. There had been a second spark of light in the lobby, the small up arrow button used to call the elevator. But the elevator hadn't been moving; the number had remained at 50. The realization came slowly, drawn from long-ago memories of the elevator in Jasper's apartment building. As a child she had danced back and forth over the threshold, fascinated by the way the doors sensed her presence and retreated from her despite their repeated attempts to close. Her mother had scolded her for holding up the elevator.

It couldn't move until Jasper got out of the way.

The elevator was on the fiftieth floor, and it hadn't moved because its doors had been blocked from closing. Someone was on the fiftieth floor and didn't want anyone else using the elevator.

Zenobia.

Which meant Nico and Grammar and the rest of the Damaskers were climbing the stairs, leaving a lone guard in case Zenobia tried to take the elevator back down. Maybe Zenobia had thought she'd have enough strength to use her gravity power to escape from the top of the Tower. The ReGeneration warriors had been keeping the Tower under observation all evening, however, and there'd been no movement outside of it. More likely Zenobia had managed to reach the observation deck but had no strength for anything more. Maybe it was her unconscious body that blocked the elevator doors.

Nico and his men had fifty flights of stairs to climb. It would take a long time. They'd be exhausted by the time they reached the top. Their legs would be jelly. But it wouldn't be hard to aim a gun at a lame and barely conscious woman with nowhere to hide or run.

Jasper could wait for the ReGeneration warriors to climb across the foam. They could certainly overwhelm the lone Damasker guard, but with the elevator trapped on the top floor they'd be forced to climb the same fifty floors as Nico and his men, and who knew how much of a head start Nico already had?

"Hello?" she said. "Could you shift me to the top of the Tower, but slowly? Is that possible?"

It would consume what little time you have left.

"How much time would that leave me?"

Half an hour, I'd estimate.

The answer stole her breath. Her hand dropped to her knife hilt, cold and heavy in her hand.

"Do it."

26

DARE TO CHANGE

Leaving the house on a dewy, fresh early morning
Seeing the warm lights welcoming you home in the evening

~ Veronica Park (*Things I Will Miss/Reasons to Live*)

T he tingle scoured through her. She fell up but at quarter speed, a reverse beanstalk. She flipped around so she was falling gently, feetfirst, into the velvet sky. She'd been standing under the bulge of the Tower's observation deck, so she should land on its underside, but the vast sky all around it sent shudders through her.

She sought to distract herself, and the Guardian's last disturbing suggestion was at the forefront of her mind.

"Who made the graviteria?" she asked.

I don't know was the prompt reply.

"How can you not know?"

Do you know who made you?

"But what was your purpose? Why were you made?"

I don't know. Do you know your *purpose?*

"I don't know why I'd expect a straight answer from an alien parasite."

I am not a parasite. I do not harm my host. In fact, I improve your health and help you heal faster.

"You made me shift randomly throughout my life, which nearly killed me numerous times."

That's not supposed to happen. I think I woke up . . . late. I was supposed to grow in consciousness and sentience in parallel to you developing self-awareness as a child.

"How do you know that, but not the answers to my other questions?"

I don't know. A tone of frustration had crept into the inaudible voice.

"What *do* you know?"

A long pause. *I know I want to live,* it whispered.

Jasper's feet clanged onto the underside of the external metal walkway of the observation deck. The ground was lost in darkness above her head, the sky a black ocean below her.

She carefully lowered herself over the side of the walkway and climbed down the railing, wound her legs through the metal bars, and told her graviteria, "Now." Her gravity shifted back to down-gee, and she tumbled over the side of the railing onto the walkway, right side up once more.

Looking through the glass, Jasper could see that the elevator doors were indeed open, twitching back and forth in their attempts to close. Zenobia sat slumped against one of the doors, her legs extended so her feet were against the other door. Her head drooped. She didn't notice Jasper's arrival until she stepped through the cracked glass panel to get inside.

"Jasper! What are you—how did you get here?" Her voice was faint, her face pale and drawn.

Jasper opened the door to the stairwell and listened.

Echoing footsteps reached her ears, but she thought the Damaskers must still be many levels down. Jasper grabbed a yellow WET FLOOR sign, and Zenobia moved her legs aside so she could place the sign between the elevator doors. Cautiously, Zenobia inched away. The doors once again attempted to close, then drew back, sensing the intervening object.

Zenobia sighed and lay flat on the dusty floor. "They have Grammar," she said. "Whatever happens, you have to get him out of here."

Jasper surveyed the contents of the elevator. "Is that why you brought rope?"

Several large coils of rope had been piled into the elevator, along with a climbing harness and accessories.

"I've always felt I needed an alternate exit from the Tower in case the elevator failed, given how difficult the stairs are for me. If Nico and his men are occupied climbing the stairs, I thought maybe I could rig up a rope and get down faster than they could climb. Anchors for window washers are already in place—I just need to replace the ropes."

"How? You can barely stand."

"Perhaps I was overly optimistic."

"Well, I'm here now, so I'll help you."

Zenobia shook her head. "I don't think I'll leave after all. Grammar will only be safe once Nico's stopped."

"How do you expect to stop him?"

"It's easy," Zenobia said absently. "All it takes is one step."

"What does that mean?"

Zenobia gestured vaguely. "Up-gee there by the doors, or down-gee over the railing. Either way it only takes one step to die."

"Please tell me you're talking about Nico."

Zenobia met her eyes, startled. "That would be the preferable outcome, I suppose," she said after a pause.

Jasper's jaw ached and she forced herself to unclench her teeth. "Whatever happened to staying alive being your punishment?"

"I think it's trumped by saving my son's life. Nico may be twisted up by anger and revenge, but once I'm dead, surely he'll have no reason to hurt Grammar, especially if you're here to stop him."

"I wouldn't be so sure." The words came out before she could think to soften them. "He believes that Crane is dead."

Zenobia sucked in a breath as if she'd been stabbed. She sat very still as Jasper told her in a few words what had happened. She was silent for so long, Jasper walked away to give her privacy.

One by one Jasper carried the coils of rope outside. Grav-walkers frequently used the same rope descent systems that skyscraper window washers had used in the pre-Shattering days. Jasper tied the ropes to the anchor and sent the ends dangling over the side and down to the ground. She peered over the side of the railing but could see little in the darkness. The ReGeneration warriors, if they'd finished crossing over the foam, were not using torches.

She went back inside to listen at the stairway door. She heard a few faint, echoing voices but no footsteps. They must be taking a break.

Zenobia was still slumped over in silence.

"Come on, Zen, let me get you out of here."

Zenobia didn't move.

Jasper took the harness and brought it outside to begin attaching it to one of the ropes. When Zenobia was ready, Jasper could just strap her in.

The rope she'd tossed over the side creaked, stretching taut. Someone was climbing up. She drew her knife and peered over. She had to wait until the person was within earshot, but it still gave her plenty of time to cut the rope if it was a Damasker. "Who is it?"

"Just me" came Tom's low voice.

She sheathed the knife and helped him over the edge, panting from the hard climb. After he'd unhooked himself from the harness, leaving his ascenders still clipped to the rope, she pointed him inside.

"Zenobia," he said softly, approaching her.

"Tom?" Zenobia leaned over her knees, covered her face with her hands and sobbed.

Tom picked her up as if she were a child and set her onto her feet. She sagged into his arms.

Jasper turned her back on them and leaned against the railing. She asked softly, "Are you there?"

A soft shift in her mind, like a cat stroking against her legs. *Always.*

"The Guardian says if you and I meld, we won't Shatter," she said. "Is that true?"

It feels true.

"How would it work?" she asked.

There are two stages—physical and psychic. I would stitch my cells to yours. Rewrite you. Rewrite me. We would become one unified organism. We would be most unstable after this stage, when both our minds would be rattling loose in a new body. Then in the second stage our consciousnesses would merge, both with each other and our physical body.

"Are you sure it would work?"

This process requires the full participation and consent of both of us. It won't work unless you're fully committed.

She could hardly express her next thought. "Would I still be human after? Would I still be *me*?"

The answer was raw and quick. *I have no idea what we'd be.*

The rewriting could cook your brain. We could end up insane. A monster. We could destroy the world.

"Just like any human, then."

Indeed.

"Would we Shatter?"

Not if the melding is complete, equal, and unreserved.

Jasper glanced back at Tom and Zenobia. Zenobia had recovered her composure and drawn away, but Tom's hands remained on her arms, holding her steady.

"I have no reason to trust you and you have every reason to lie," Jasper said. "Since every alternative to melding ends in your death."

I want us both to live.

"I want to not kill a million people. Can you guarantee that?"

A long silence. *I cannot. If either of us holds back, the meld will skew and anything could happen.*

"That's not good enough."

I won't lie to you.

Jasper went back inside. "Tom, you need to get Zen down the rope. Nico's almost here."

Zenobia pulled away from Tom's hands and approached Jasper. She drew a syringe from her pocket. "It's the last of the antibac. I knew River might try to destroy it, so I made sure to hide some."

Jasper stared at the syringe. It held death for her inner denizen, death for that inner voice, and potentially death and disability for herself.

It also held the possibility of life, life free of an alien inhabitant. Her body and mind her own.

You know your odds, said the graviteria. *Life's a game where the house always wins.*

Jasper blinked. *Darius used to say that.*

Yes, I know. Here's another one of his: piss on the odds. Your gut knows when to jump, risks be damned.

It was true. As surely as if she were perched at the edge of a roof or balanced on a balcony railing, she knew exactly how she would leap. The mathematics of risk were etched into her bones.

Jasper reached out and tucked a loose strand of hair behind Zenobia's ear. She'd dreamed once that when unpinned, Zenobia's hair wasn't hair but medusa-like tentacles with a face at the end of each, and each face was Zenobia's trapped in an eternal scream.

She closed her hand over Zenobia's, the cool shape of the syringe between their palms. "What if I said I was going to choose the Guardian's way and meld with the graviteria?"

Zenobia's fingers tightened around Jasper's, but otherwise she didn't move.

"Would you tell Tom to jab this syringe into me regardless of what I wanted?"

Zenobia's eyes stayed steady on hers. "No, I wouldn't," she said at last. "I just want you to live."

"And what if I became a monster? Would you still love me then?"

Zenobia's voice cracked. "Between the two of us, there is only one monster."

Jasper took the syringe, pivoted, and threw it. It arced over the railing and out of sight.

She took a deep breath and closed her eyes. *Do you have a name?*

A name. The voice seemed thoughtful. *I played the part of Darius in your mind for so long, it's hard to shed the identity. But Darius is a dead end of destructive choices, and I want possibility, a future.* A pause and a sense of hesitancy. *Perhaps Dare?*

Dare to live, dare to be better. Jasper nodded slowly. *All right, Dare. Let's do this.*

This will hurt, Dare said.

It did.

The pain lasted for so long, it took on size and shape and heft, the dimensions identical to those of her physical body but with an aura that stretched beyond, threatening to consume her surroundings and everyone in its path. Pain as if her flesh were melting, her cells growing fluid and malleable, her atoms rearranging themselves. Pain as if her nervous system had transformed into rivers of lava carrying agony to every square inch of her body. Pain was a fog that surrounded and choked her and refused to evaporate, like malevolent greenhouse gases.

Stop! She screamed it with her mind and every particle of her body. *I can't do this. Please stop. I'd rather die.*

The pain stopped. Or at least wavered in a holding pattern, a dog circling under its treed prey, waiting.

We can't continue if you resist, Dare whispered as if pain had drained the volume from his voice. *Your consent—your body's consent—is necessary. You have to accept the pain, embrace the pain.*

Jasper wept. Her tears sizzled as they struck her cheeks. *I can't. I'm all right with dying. It's easier.*

For you, maybe.

She remembered a bathtub. Lazy poppy and rose swirls in the water. A dangling arm painting abstract shapes on the floor in scarlet. A fly buzzing. A crow outside announcing death in its rust-and-iron voice. Merlot unmoving in a corner, arms wrapped around his knees, eyes open and staring, unresponsive for hours.

The smell of finality, the sound of doors closed, locked, and burned out of existence. All possibilities ended.

I understand why you did it, Vron.

And Vron answered, *But do you understand why I was wrong?*

Jasper scrubbed away tears. *I want to live.* It was the simplest true thing she'd ever said.

Dare, I'm ready, she said. *Do it.*
She let the pain consume her.

27

THE THINGS WE LOST

People who would die for you
People who you'd die for

~ Veronica Park (*Things I Will Miss/Reasons to Live*)

The tide of pain ebbed reluctantly, ponderously, leaving behind little tide pools of agony. Jasper had no idea how much time had passed. She had felt herself *change*, felt the molecular latticework that made up her bones, muscle, blood, and nerves split open like cocoons to birth something new and incomprehensible. There was a moment—or an eon—where every memory she'd ever had morphed into a blizzard of meaningless noise and she'd been trapped in an instant—an eternity—of nothingness. It all returned in a rush, an overwhelming torrent of memory and sensation and emotion flooding into a body and brain that were raw and new and echoing. Like moving into a new house where your old, familiar furniture no longer quite fit.

The dust was settling in her mind. Her body felt clean and remade. The background prickle and sting of her burns, cuts, and scrapes had vanished.

Dare? she said tentatively. Her mental voice echoed oddly as if the space in her brain had changed somehow. *Are we finished melding, or was that just the first stage?*

There was no answer.

She opened her eyes. A pale blur resolved into Zenobia's face bent over her, her eyes and mouth lined with fatigue and strain, her dark hair threaded with silver, yet still she was a beautiful sight to Jasper's eyes. Beautiful and wondrous as if her eyes were brand new. As if she'd never really seen Zenobia before.

"Zenobia," she said, or tried to. What came out was more like "Zz . . ." and a grunt.

"Sh, sweetie, I've got you." Zenobia propped her up in her arms like a floppy doll. Jasper tried to move and her muscles spasmed and locked like a newborn foal's.

"What happened?" she tried to say. Her mutinous tongue allowed "Wha . . ." to emerge.

"I don't know. You were screaming and screaming. And then your heart stopped. I thought you were . . ." Zenobia pressed her lips together so tightly, they turned white. Crow's feet spread from the corners of her eyes as if the crows of her nightmares were about to burst out of the darkness of her eyes, their wings already spreading through the arch of her eyebrows.

"I didn't . . . Shatter?" Jasper said, forcing her tongue to obey.

"No." But Zenobia's voice held tension, not relief.

She struggled to sit up, and Zenobia helped her. Jasper forced her neck to rotate, the movements coming easier, and let her eyes refocus to take in the room beyond Zenobia's worried face.

Dawn had arrived. So had Nico and the Damaskers.

Torches chased back the newborn morning light that turned everyone into shades of grey. Nico stood in front of the glass doors that led directly into that spear point of up-gee gravity. Grammar, his wrists bound, stood beside him. The half dozen Damasker gangers looked sweaty and exhausted, but they were armed with guns and crossbows. Their scarred young faces were set with the fatalistic determination of those who know they've reached the end of the line.

Two of them held Tom on his knees while a third methodically beat him. Those were the sounds that Jasper's ears had refused to identify, let alone categorize. Now her eyes dispelled denial. The thud and smack of fists on a nose and jaw, the thump of a boot meeting a belly, the grunt of the beater and groan of the beaten, the bubbly, watery sound of breath drawn through a bloody, broken nose and bloody, broken mouth.

All her neurons fired to move all her muscles at once, and she spasmed, arms and legs uncoordinated and jerking. *"Stop!"*

"Oh, you're awake, Jasper," Nico said. "Welcome to the end game."

His arm was slung around Grammar's shoulders. The boy looked as fatigued as the others from the long climb, but his skinny shoulders were rigid and his eyebrows spiky with fear and pain and fury.

The Damasker performing the beating straightened and wiped her bloody fist on her pants. She turned and bared her teeth at Jasper in an ugly grin. It was Vic. She'd once challenged Jasper to a fight, and only Ryan's fast talking had saved Jasper from killing her. "Hey, Pinegirl," Vic said. "Maybe you and me will be getten our fight after all."

Tom, barely conscious, slumped over in the grip of the two Damaskers. His eyes were swollen shut and blood dribbled from his mouth.

Jasper struggled to her feet, grabbing the reins of her

stampeding muscles and forcing them to obey. Zenobia tried to help, but she had no cane and was herself so weak that by the time they were both standing, she was leaning on Jasper for support.

"Just in time," Nico said. "We're about to get to the good stuff."

"This zone is surrounded by ReGeneration warriors," Jasper said. "You won't leave here alive unless you surrender immediately without hurting anyone else."

"Oh, you didn't think I just left one measly sentry below, did you?" Nico said. "I figured the ReGeneration might have an extra way into this zone, based on the stories the kid was telling me about the tunnels, so I left a team."

Only now did her brand new ears identify the sharp, faraway cracks as gunshots. A battle was underway around the base of the Tower. Her heart chilled. Charlie was a member of the ReGeneration raiding party. Ben and Merlot and Ryan had planned to cross the foam too. They could be down there right now getting shot at.

"The ReGeneration will win," she said.

"Crossbows and bows against guns?" He snorted. "Well, maybe if there are enough of them and my guys run out of ammunition first, but they'll still have to climb those stairs, so we've got time, which is all I want."

"And at the end of that time, they'll arrive and you'll die."

His self-inflicted scars traced pathways across his face, the footsteps of his demons running amok on his skin. "I always figured you'd understand that some things are worth dying for, Jasper. Those same things are usually also worth killing for."

Dare, she called in her mind. *Dare, answer me. Are you there?*

No answer.

The dislocating sense that she didn't entirely belong in this body was growing. She was rattling around in a space too large, too strange, and it was starting to reject her. Or she was rejecting it. How could she start the second stage of melding without Dare?

Zenobia pushed herself free of Jasper and stepped forward. She tottered but regained her balance. She trembled but limped toward Nico without hesitation. Every gun and crossbow in the room was trained on her, but no one shot. Nico didn't want Zenobia dead. Not yet.

"Looking a little poorly there, Zenobia," Nico remarked. He gripped Grammar's neck, fingers digging into the boy's throat.

"Would you like me to beg, Nico?" Zenobia stumbled and fell to her knees in front of him. "I'll do anything you ask if you let the rest of them go."

"You'll do it anyway," Nico said with contempt.

"The boy, I barely know him. I've had no contact with him since he was a baby. Just let him go. Hurting Tom, who has been my loyal friend for years, hurts me far more."

Nico shook his head in amazement. "You think your act is fooling anyone?"

"It's true," Grammar said in a raw voice. "She's not wanten me. She's wishen I was dead, like my papa."

Jasper couldn't see Zenobia's face, but Zenobia held very still and said nothing to refute Grammar's words.

"Is that so?" said Nico, studying Zenobia. He shrugged. "It's complicated being a parent. Doesn't mean you're going to enjoy watching what I'll do to him."

Zenobia moved. Quick as lightning she pulled a knife from under her shirt—she'd pickpocketed Jasper's—and struck. But even weary, Nico had better reflexes than a crippled woman who'd been in a coma until a day ago. He jerked away, half turning so the blade, instead of burying itself in his groin, carved a furrow across his thigh. He grunted and backhanded Zenobia hard enough to send her sprawling.

Vic darted over and kicked Zenobia in the belly.

"Stop!" Jasper screamed, running forward. Another Damasker interposed himself between her and Zenobia and pointed a gun at her face.

"Enough, Vic. I don't want her dead yet," Nico said, clearly annoyed that the target of his elaborate revenge was so fragile, she couldn't even endure a minor beating. He shoved Grammar into the grip of a nearby ganger and strode over to Zenobia, who was curled up in a fetal position, dribbling blood from a cut lip.

"Too bad you couldn't have pulled that move on any of the many occasions when you kneeled in front of Darius," Nico said to Zenobia. "Things might have fallen out very differently."

He gestured to two Damaskers. They seized Jasper's arms and dragged her forward and forced her to her knees in front of Nico.

"I saw your face when you thought Jasper had died," Nico continued. "Should've known your weak spot was in front of me all along. Problem is, I had a weak spot for her too." He shook his head. "Stories should always end after the hero kills the bad guy. Otherwise you have to watch the hero slip, slide, and decay into some pathetic crybaby version of the villain they killed. Pinegirl, your story would have been improved by an early death."

A shove between her shoulders sent Jasper sprawling. Instantly, someone pressed a knee to her back, trapping her on her belly. Vic grabbed her right arm and stretched it out in front of her. Jasper twisted her head and saw Nico taking an axe from one of his men.

Horror crept in slowly and then exploded in a nuclear bomb flash. She screamed and writhed and fought. Another body piled on top of her and then another as the Damaskers held her down. She couldn't breathe under their weight. Vic kneeled on top of Jasper's outstretched arm, pinning it to the ground. Nico hefted the axe and widened his stance.

"It's only fair, wouldn't you say, Jasper? Everyone—even your brother and Harmony—lost something to Darius, but you escaped unscathed, a hero. Ever wonder why you survived? I ask myself that all the time."

"No, Nico," Zenobia said, struggling to sit. "I'm the one who shouldn't have escaped unscathed. Take my hand. Take both of them."

"I will," said Nico. "Have patience." But he tossed the axe from hand to hand as if thinking. "You know what? I have a better idea. Let's make the boy choose." He gestured to a ganger, who dragged Zenobia to her knees and held her there. Nico turned to Grammar. "Here's the game, boy. One of them loses a hand. You choose which."

Grammar stared at him. Comprehension dawned slowly in his eyes.

Jasper had lived that moment, and that moment still lived inside her. She'd never forget what it tasted like, the sensation of something fragile and irreplaceable crumbling to ash inside her.

Her stomach bubbled with horror. "Don't make him do this, Nico. Please!"

"It's an easy choice, Grammar," Zenobia said. "He's going to kill me anyway. You have to choose me."

"Maybe it is an easy choice," Nico said. "Especially if, as you say, you and your son have no relationship to speak of. So let's up the stakes, shall we?" He pointed his axe at Jasper. "First option. Jasper loses a hand. Can't be much of a grav-walker with one hand. No more gravving for her ever again."

Jasper moaned involuntarily at the thought.

Nico pointed to Zenobia. "Your mother's right. This was always going to end with her death, but I had planned to make it last a long time. So the second option is your mother dies. But cleanly, right now. So you can cripple your heroic Pinegirl, or you can offer your mother the mercy of a quick death. What'll it be, boy?"

Grammar stood still as stone, blank eyed and grey faced.

"Grammar," Zenobia said quietly. "Whatever happens here, *this is not your fault.*"

"This is a Dalca game," Jasper gasped out from under Vic's weight. "You've become what you hated most, Nico. You're doing exactly what Darius did to me, what he did to *Crane.*"

"For the choices I made and the lives I took, I've earned my fate," Zenobia said to Grammar. "I'm the reason you're involved in this, and for that alone I deserve to die."

Jasper twisted helplessly but couldn't move. "Nico! Don't you want to know what made Crane hate you? The moment that everything changed?"

Nico's grip tightened on the axe, but he hesitated.

"Darius made her choose—she had to kill her pet dog . . . *or her father.* That was the choice she was given. Did anyone ever tell you that? And she did it. She saved your life. But the choice *broke* her."

Nico's voice grated like gravel. "And isn't it appropriate that Zenobia should witness the same happen to her son. The same thing she let happen to my daughter."

"It's okay, Grammar," Zenobia said, her eyes never leaving his face. "I promise it's okay."

"It's not okay!" Jasper screamed. Because no matter if it was a mercy, no matter if it was deserved, if Grammar chose Zenobia, the responsibility for her death would sear its mark into his soul for the rest of his life.

No one knew that better than Jasper.

Grammar shook his head. "No," he said, barely audible.

"That's not one of the choices," Nico said.

Grammar shook his head harder. "I won't."

"Fine. They both lose a hand and we start the game again." Nico lifted the axe above his head.

Grammar twisted and kicked in his captor's arms and shrieked.

Shouldn't she have control over gravity now? Or had it all been a lie? She strained, clawed for something that couldn't be grasped. Nothing.

In her mind Jasper screamed, *Dare!* The cry filled her head and splintered into a thousand echoes, but nothing answered her call. He'd abandoned her.

The axe descended in a shining arc toward her arm.

Zenobia bit the hand of the ganger who held her and jerked free when he yelled.

Grammar head-butted his captor in the face, squirmed loose, and hurled himself at Nico.

Zenobia threw her slight weight against Vic, who lost her balance, loosening her grip on Jasper's arm. Jasper jerked her arm back, out of the axe's path . . .

All too late.

The axe clunked, burying itself in the concrete under the carpet.

Searing, shattering pain consumed her. Jasper screamed until her throat felt like it was tearing in half.

Her hand . . . oh God, her hand burned as if coated in lava. But was it still attached?

The weight on her lifted as the Damaskers got to their feet. Furious, Vic whirled to kick Zenobia in the side.

Nico grappled with a berserk Grammar. Despite his incandescent fury, the boy was outweighed and outmatched and his hands still bound. Two Damaskers had to drag him away from Nico.

Jasper found herself sitting alone on the floor surrounded by a pool of blood, cradling her arm to her chest. The sound of an axe snapping through flesh and bone dug a rusty spoon into her thoughts and stirred them.

Where did her arm end?

She could barely look. Her mind refused to identify the inert shape lying in the blood in front of her.

Her hand throbbed as if it were being eaten by dragons. Ben often talked about phantom pains, how he'd wake up in the mornings convinced his leg had grown back or that it had all been a nightmare. She could feel her hand burning like a thousand suns, but was it still there? Hot liquid soaked her shirt. Light sparkled in front of her eyes.

Dare. But what could he do to help her now? It was too late. She'd had this new body for all of five minutes, and it was already irreversibly damaged.

Her eyes finally dropped, drawn irresistibly to the hot, pooling blood.

Three shapes, not one. Small like carrot nubbins.

Fingers. Not her whole hand. Three fingers severed at the first knuckle.

Jasper retched. There wasn't much to bring up, but her body was powerfully set on ejecting something. It could eject Dare for all she cared—useless goddamn parasitic alien bastard.

"Hold your hand above your heart." Zenobia kneeled beside her, ripping the bottom of her blouse with shaking hands. No one stopped her. She wrapped the fabric around Jasper's hand. It soaked through immediately, and Zenobia tore another piece from her blouse and another.

Numbly, Jasper held her throbbing, swaddled hand to her chest like a half-eaten gingerbread cookie.

"I'm sorry," Zenobia whispered. "I should never have loved you."

Zenobia stood, so frail and trembling and grey with horror and fatigue that no one moved to stop her or restrain her. No one even seemed to notice she was holding a knife again. Under the guise of helping Jasper, she'd picked up the blade she'd cut Nico with.

"Let's skip straight to the ending, Nico," she said, her voice thin but strong. "Grammar, my son, close your eyes."

Grammar stared, uncomprehending, and Tom screamed in denial and anguish. Nico made a sound, lurched forward.

Zenobia set the knife point against her heart and pushed.

The blade sank in softly.

The first rays of the sun pierced the darkness in the east, as sharp and bright as pain and as unrelenting as grief. Silence reigned as Zenobia fell.

28

ONLY GRAMMAR

*Being absolutely essential to someone who is absolutely
essential to you*

~ Veronica Park (*Things I Will Miss/Reasons to Live*)

J asper could never remember how it had come about,
whether it was a bet or a punishment for some trivial
transgression. When she did remember, the memory was
never the same, but always Darius's voice followed her like a
cricket's squeak in a silent house, impossible to locate or root
out or make sense of.

"Your brother's leg. The whole thing."

Your brother's leg, your brother's leg, your brother's leg.

Darius's voice emerged from the shadows above her head, a
god decreeing plague and pestilence to his faithful followers.
Ben stood like a marionette who hadn't quite realized yet that
his strings had been cut. He had two legs and a blank space

where his face should be. Tom and Socrates and Martha wavered, uncertain smears seen through a rain-glazed window.

But Zenobia's face was gravity, the only still, clear point Jasper could focus on in this writhing rag of a memory. The human face had forty-three muscles; Martha taught her that. Jasper watched the movement and arrangement of those muscles in Zenobia's face, the tightening of lines around her eyes, the enigmatic dip of her brows, the flex and release of her lips as she spoke to Darius. What did she say? Her voice was a buzz in Jasper's ears, the low hum of bees in clover promising honey, promising sting.

"Fine," Darius said. "Below the knee then. But she has to watch."

She has to watch.

Reality slipped. Its hold loosened, but Darius's didn't. His hands rested on her shoulders with the weight of damnation.

Martha and Tom moved like rust-jointed automatons, and Ben was a doll stuffed with straw, floppy, two-dimensional in their hands. Tom muttered something to Ben over and over, singsong, nonsense syllables as he folded himself around Ben's upper body to hold him still. Martha looked at Tom as if she was drowning, and Tom looked back and held on.

But Jasper saw nothing, only Zenobia's black-clad belly, for somehow Zenobia had come to stand in front of her and Darius. She was speaking, laughing even; Jasper could hear her voice reverberate through her belly. Zenobia was kissing Darius, teasing him, distracting him. Ben's screams were faint, far away, for Zenobia's arm was somehow wrapped around Jasper's head, covering her ears. She was smothered between Darius's body and Zenobia's, face tucked into Zenobia's ribs, numb, blind, and deaf.

A heart was beating, but it wasn't hers, it wasn't hers.

She heard the thump of Ben's foot falling to the floor.

The thump of Ben's foot . . .

A knife entering soft human flesh was quiet. Blood flowing out of a torn heart was silent.

She heard it anyway. Some sounds reverberated beyond time and memory and the laws of physics.

Now Jasper stumbled forward. She landed on her knees beside Zenobia. Zenobia's eyes were wide open, the irises so dark, they blended with her pupils, holes punched into the void. Inside this small, frail, indomitable body was the womb that had sheltered Grammar at his tiniest and most vulnerable. Inside that punctured chest was a heart that had survived Darius.

Zenobia's chest heaved, fighting for one more breath, one more moment of life even after she'd chosen to die. Jasper pressed her unmaimed hand to the wound, around the knife that still pierced Zenobia's heart.

Blood speckled Zenobia's mouth. Her lips shaped inaudible words.

"I'll save him," Jasper said in a voice she didn't recognize. Crows tore at her insides, bloody beaks and funeral dirge voices.

Zenobia's eyelids fluttered. Her words were so faint, a dragonfly's wings could have drowned them out. "I'd be proud . . . for him . . . to be a Pine."

Under Jasper's hand Zenobia's chest stopped moving. Her eyes stilled, empty windows to a house no longer occupied. The crows tearing at Jasper's heart flew away. What they'd eaten left gaps and chunks and holes and silence.

"No," Nico whispered. *"No."*

Jasper sat and wished for numbness, wished for her hand to hurt more so she wouldn't feel the pain in her chest. Wished for Dare to transform her all over again with fewer nerve endings in her heart this time.

The goblins ate all her wishes.

She gently drew the knife out of Zenobia's chest. Zenobia had torn off so much of her blouse to wrap up Jasper's hand that the remains barely covered her. It was a struggle with only one hand, but Jasper dragged off her T-shirt, her favourite, the one that said GRAV-MASTER on the front. It left her naked to the waist but for her bra. She placed the T-shirt, sweat stained and blood drenched, over Zenobia's torso.

Jasper got up to face Nico, pressing her other hand, truncated and muffled in cloth and throbbing fiercely, to her chest. She didn't know what her face showed, but even Vic took a step back as she approached Nico.

"Let Tom and Grammar go."

Nico's eyes were hollow with shock, caving in to emptiness. "This wasn't how it was supposed to go."

"You really thought revenge was going to give you satisfaction? That you were going to hurt less? That somehow the loss of Martha and Crane would become more bearable? How the fuck did you *think* this was going to go?"

She was distracted by a gasp from Vic. The yellow-haired alpha was staring at Jasper's abdomen. "Pinegirl's scar!"

Jasper looked down. The pine tree Darius had carved, over and over into her abdomen above her hip until ridged scars formed, was gone. The skin was clean and smooth and unmarked. She knew without looking that the bumpy map of scars on her inner thigh that Nico had helped her carve would be gone also. Dare really had rewritten her.

It gave her a twinge to see the scars gone. They were a cruel reminder of an ugly past, but they were also the story of everything she'd overcome.

She looked Vic in the eye. "That's because I'm not the Pinegirl anymore. The Pinegirl's dead. I'm something else."

Vic tried to meet her gaze and twitched. She dropped the crossbow she was holding and backed away, face paling as she clutched at her amulets. Jasper glared around at the rest of the Damaskers.

When Dare transformed her face and eyes, perhaps he had gotten something not quite right. Because when the Damaskers looked her in the eye, they all shrank back, faces turning white and sick. Hands clutched at amulets and lifted, palm out, in warding signs. Weapons wavered and were lowered. The two gangers holding Tom stepped back when he got to his feet, his face swollen and bloody and streaked in tears.

What did they see in her eyes?

Time was unstable. She was coming undone. The Tower tilted around her. Gravity slipped and slid against her skin, intangible as air but with far more heft.

It wasn't only her eyes.

Blood dripped from her shoes to the floor.

Her shoes weren't touching the floor.

She was hovering several inches above the ground.

Gravity curled against her like a cat winding between her legs—uncatchable, unknowable, impossible.

She dropped. Her shoes clacked onto the floor, sticky with blood. The Damaskers jerked and took another step back. One fell to his knees and covered his face.

She grabbed at that sensation of gravity on her body, looking for some hint of control, but it melted through her fingers like water. She was unravelling like a cheap scarf teased by the claws of a cat.

Nico didn't flinch. There was no fear left in him. "Will you kill me now, Jasper?"

She uncurled her fingers from the knife and let it fall. "There's already been one death too many today."

Coming to life, Grammar growled his disagreement. He shoved his bound hands down his pants, pulled out a small blade—the kind Crane always had hidden on her—turned sideways, and plunged the blade into Nico's ribs.

Nico staggered back against the glass door, clutching at the protruding knife. The blade was only a few inches long and couldn't have penetrated far, but it had stunned him.

As if he'd planned the move, Grammar neatly lifted Nico's gun out of its holster.

"Grammar," Jasper said, *"don't."*

He pointed the gun at Nico's face. His every movement had been relaxed, economical, as if he were moving in a dream.

Yes, that was how it had felt, the knife in her hand, her heartbeat throbbing in her fingertips.

But he'd heard Jasper.

"He's da bad man now." Grammar's voice was stretched as thin as telephone wires. His chin was set at a cold, implacable tilt that she recognized. "He's needen to be killed."

"Maybe, maybe not," Jasper said. "But that's not for you to decide."

"Pinegirl been doen it," he said without looking at her.

She stepped forward cautiously, with the sensation of a tilting floor and shifting time. She had stood once where he was standing, but no one had tried to stop her. No one had taken the burden from her hands.

"Murder stains your bones red," she said. "It bends you crooked and dark till you think you'll never breathe straight and clean again. And once you've planted that little seed of ugliness, you'll spend your whole life fighting not to let it grow."

Nico coughed a laugh. "Oh, go on, boy," he said. "You've never looked so much like your father. Go on. Do it. You're a Dalca. You were made for murder. It's in your blood."

Grammar's hand trembled. Jasper wanted to throw herself between him and Nico to protect him from those words, but they'd already been said, already been heard. They'd stay lodged inside him like shrapnel for the rest of his life.

She was beside him now, close enough to see the aching rigidity of his jaw, the jagged furrow in his brow, his mouth tucked in at the corners. She didn't dare touch him. He was an explosion shaped like a boy.

"Yes, you're a Dalca, Grammar. You are Darius's son. But," she added fiercely, "you're also Zenobia's and Martha's, and they wanted you to be good. Nobody can tell you what you are. Only you can decide that. So what'll it be?"

In answer, Grammar pressed the muzzle of the gun against Nico's chest. "I'm not a Dalca," he said ferociously. "Never, never." He straightened and looked at Jasper with his heartbreakingly blue eyes and the wide clear arc of his mother's eyebrows. "I'm only me. Only Grammar."

And he tossed away the gun.

Jasper didn't remember picking up the knife and cutting his arms free. She only knew his skinny arms were wrapped around her with desperate strength, his forehead against her collarbone, and he was shaking or she was shaking or they both were, but as long as they held on, they wouldn't fall apart.

Shouting filled the air—familiar voices.

The ReGeneration warriors surged over the edge of the railing, having scaled the ropes the way Tom had. Never even noticing the ropes, the Damaskers had set no guard on the walkway. Amid the commotion came the sound of dropped guns and crossbows as the Damaskers raised their hands in surrender. One of them babbled hysterically about witches.

"I won't surrender. I'm not going back to prison and I'm not hanging," Nico said quite calmly.

She looked up to see Nico pick up the gun Grammar had

discarded and point it at her and Grammar. She whirled to shield the boy with her body.

"Don't do it, man." Ryan's voice. He stepped up beside her, his gun aimed at Nico. "Don't make me do this."

"I'd take it as a kindness," Nico said.

Ryan lifted his hands, the gun in his right hand pointed harmlessly at the ceiling. "I'm not helping you commit suicide, Nico." He bent slowly and placed his gun on the floor.

"Pick it up, soldier," Nico said. "I said *pick it up*, damn it. I'll shoot her, I swear I will."

"Is this how you'll honour your daughter?" Ryan asked. "That wild, weird, brave, broken girl of yours, she's messed up as hell . . . but she's *finding her way back*. She's glued together a few pieces, untwisted a few knots, made a few unexpected choices. She's figuring out maybe, just maybe, a way to heal and grow. She did all that, and then *your man* shot her and that's . . . that's . . ." Ryan's voice cracked and he spread his arms in a gesture of helplessness, a despairing, grieving rage that words couldn't express. "But she's not dead yet, Nico. She was alive when we left. There's a chance she'll pull through. It's not too late—"

"But it is," Nico said. "If it wasn't already before. She was ready to kill me." He gestured at Zenobia's body. "You think she'll forgive me for that? You think she should?"

"You need to make things right, Nico. How dare you make any less of an effort than your daughter did. You *owe* it to her to live."

Nico's breath came heavy, hitching unevenly in his chest. "That's a nice speech, son. Martha would've said the exact same thing. And you'd both be right." His voice calmed and he sighed. "But I'm tired. And I'm done."

"Nico—"

Ryan's body partially blocked Jasper's view, but she saw Nico lift the gun. The shot was deafening.

She saw Ryan's shoulders slump, saw his head droop, his empty hands drop to his sides. Saw him sway.

Heads he wins, tails you lose.

The gun fell from Nico's hand with a loud clatter. A spatter of blood trickled over the rows of scars on his face, every little mound marking a buried fragment of a shattered life. He fell against the glass door and slowly slid to the floor, leaving a streak of blood behind him. He tipped over and was still.

The devil in blood is paid his dues.

Ryan pressed a hand to his eyes and stood motionless. Then he took a long, ragged breath and released it.

He turned and looked at Jasper. His expression was threadbare, nearly worn through, his cheeks wet. But his eyes were clear. He'd done everything he could. There would be no additional blue dot for the row of ghosts on his arms. No additional death to add to his overburdened conscience.

Nico had made his choice. Had made many choices, all leading him here.

As the Damaskers had, she half expected Ryan to flinch when he met her eyes, but he strode over without hesitation and wrapped his arms around both her and Grammar, his hair sweeping over her head like a benediction. She felt him sigh, his breath stirring her hair. She tucked her face between his throat and collarbone and felt the flutter of his pulse. A butterfly's wing tickled her insides in answer. Grammar was wedged between them, but she wasn't inclined to move from this position. Not ever.

"Jasper!" Ben was there and Merlot and Charlie. Alive and uninjured. They added their arms to the hug until she was sandwiched in layers of love. Trapped in the middle, Grammar made a small sound of complaint but stayed where he was.

This was the real gravity, the energy without a name that was holding her together, holding all of them together. If they held her tightly enough, maybe she wouldn't collapse like a kindergarten craft project made without enough glue.

"Not to start drama," Ryan said after a while, his voice almost normal, "but someone's hand is on my ass and it isn't Jasper's."

"Charlie!" Ben and Merlot said at the same time, and someone jabbed an elbow into his ribs.

"Oh, I thought that was Ben," Charlie said innocently when Merlot had signed Ryan's remark.

"Your left hand, yes," Ben said dryly, freeing his arms from the hug to sign. "What about your right?"

"My bad," Charlie said, not sounding sorry at all.

There was a pause.

"Charlie, that's *my* ass now!" Merlot exclaimed. He backed out of the group hug to sign an emphatically rude comment at Charlie.

"Just returning the favour," Charlie said, "for that one time you grabbed my—"

"That was an *accident!*" Merlot said and signed, "There's enough room on Ben's ass for both your hands. Leave the rest of us alone, damn it!"

Ryan nudged Jasper's head with his chin so that she looked up at him. There was strain in his smile but relief too, a break in the clouds. "Are they always like this?" he asked.

"I think you know the answer to that," she said.

Merlot overheard and interpreted for Charlie.

"Yeah, consider that your welcome to the family, Ryan," Charlie said cheerfully.

Ryan glanced at Ben. So did everyone else.

"Too late to back out," Ben said, giving Ryan a steady look. "You're part of the pack now."

It sounded like a warning, but Ryan only grinned, wide and sunny.

Still wedged between Ryan and Jasper, Grammar muttered sourly, "You're all dumb."

Jasper could feel herself coming apart again, molecules ready to dissolve at the first strong breeze. Dare had said she —they would be the most unstable during the interval between stages. If she didn't progress to the second stage soon, she'd Shatter. She could feel it. Where was he?

"I'm farten," Grammar announced.

The group hug dissolved with remarkable rapidity while Grammar beamed in satisfaction.

Jasper said, "Next group hug must contain at least a two-to-one girl-to-boy ratio. For olfactory reasons if nothing else."

"I nominate Esther," Charlie said after Ben had signed Jasper's comment.

"Yeah, she smells nice," Ben said. "Right, Merlot?"

Merlot's expression slammed into neutral. "Hadn't noticed."

"Oh, you didn't notice on that long ride from the ReGeneration's village to Yorky?" Ryan asked, eyebrows raised. "The one where you were riding double with Esther most of the way? You know, squeezed together on one horse?" He turned to Ben. "How do you make the sign for *liar*?"

"Like this," Ben said. "And this is how you say *liar, liar, pants on fire*." He interpreted Ryan's comment for Charlie, who laughed and high-fived Ryan.

"And this, my dearly despised assholes, is how you say *fuck off*," Merlot said, demonstrating.

Then Ben's gaze landed on Jasper's swaddled hand, which she still cradled to her chest. The strips of Zenobia's blouse were black and had hidden the blood that soaked them, but smears of blood now covered her chest and stained her bra. Ben paled, all laughter disappearing. "Jas, your hand!"

"It doesn't even hurt anymore," she said. The light-headed

feeling, the prickle along her nerve endings, the slither in her spine came from blood loss and shock.

Not her new body coming apart at the seams.

Not her cells coming undone.

Ryan's hands on her shoulders coaxed her to sit on the floor. Merlot draped his Batman sweatshirt over her shoulders, warm from his body heat, but it couldn't warm the expanding void inside, the echoing, empty spaces.

Dare, why didn't it work? What else do I have to do?

She reached out, desperate, clumsy, as if gravity was something to touch, but it dissolved like smoke, wild and ungovernable. Her entire body itched and yearned to be sloughed off like the skin of a snake.

Dare had said they needed to meld completely and unreservedly. Was one of them holding back and preventing the second stage from starting? Was it her fault? Deep down she just hadn't been ready to let go of all the people she loved.

I'm still going to Shatter, aren't I?

Ben spotted Jasper's fingertips lying in the pool of blood and made a choked sound. He lurched away, his limp suddenly pronounced. Charlie moved instantly to his side, but Ben pushed him away and bent over and retched violently.

Merlot and Ryan hurried over to Winnie to discuss the best way to transport Jasper down the rope now that she didn't have the use of her hand. Everyone seemed to have forgotten there was a functional elevator, but Jasper wasn't going to remind them. Tom kneeled, motionless beside Zenobia's body, holding her hand between both of his.

Only Grammar watched Jasper, his eyes too knowing. Still searching for a glimpse of the curse that had taken Martha and Vron and now his mother. She climbed back to her feet and squeezed his shoulder with her good hand. "Ask Ryan to tell you how Crane is."

He blinked suspiciously at her, but the distraction worked. He moved toward Ryan.

Nico's body blocked the glass doors. Jasper kneeled to brush her hand over the raised scars on his face. He'd helped her carve scars into her own skin, a ritual to burn away unwanted memories. His methods for dealing with pain had been neither effective nor healthy, but he'd tried to help her in the only way he knew how.

"I hope you find peace, Nico," she told him and stepped past his body.

She opened the glass doors and wind gusted in. The tingle of a zone border swept over her skin, adding to the sensation that her molecules were vibrating with an alarming intensity.

One step would drop her into up-gee. One step and she'd fall for eternity. She'd fall away from the earth, through the sky and into the airless void far beyond the grasp of a planet and its tiny precious inhabitants.

There she'd Shatter, as she died, amid the cold, enduring stars.

By some miracle no one was looking her way. She had a moment to fill her lungs with all the sky she could breathe. She had a moment to look at her brother, at her friends, and hold them in her heart like a constellation of tiny warm suns.

I did try, Vron.

So did I, Vron whispered back. *It's all we can do.*

The eastern horizon bowed before the sun as its rays caressed her face.

"No, Jasper!"

Grammar's scream shot like an arrow through her heart. It arrested her step forward and made her stumble and reach out for the door frame.

He was running for her, his face a mask of rage and loss and betrayal.

"Grammar, wait!"

He wasn't going to listen. Everyone was looking at her now.

She had to go. "I'm sorry," she said, words he wouldn't hear.

Grammar lunged for her, reaching—and she stepped backwards into up-gee.

She fell up.

And Grammar leaped after her.

29

FALLING

Science fiction, for its inherent hope that humanity will endure, for good or ill, long past our own lifetimes

~ Veronica Park (*Things I Will Miss/Reasons to Live*)

J asper had been falling her whole life. She'd always known this was how she'd die.

An unplanned jump into the void.

The whole world spread out above her head, curving away to infinity. Drowning in an ocean of deep blue dawn. Falling into an eternity of black beyond.

Even the planet knew I didn't belong.

Adrenalin surged through her veins in hot, lightning streaks. Nerves sizzled with every precious sensation—the biting cold, the slicing wind, the lurching drop in her stomach. Every cell sang with the intense, overwhelming conviction: *there will be no surviving this.*

Grammar tumbled in free fall after her, like a waterdrop falling from the icicle tip of the Tower, suspended from the earth's surface above their heads.

No. This wasn't supposed to happen. No one else was supposed to die.

She'd promised Zenobia she'd save him. She'd promised Neverwhen she'd bring him home.

Jasper spread her arms and legs to slow down her fall. After a few long seconds, he caught up with her. He was in wide-eyed, white-faced shock, his limbs rigid.

"Grammar!" she called to him, but the wind tore away her voice.

She reached and finally caught hold of his arm and dragged him close. She wrapped both arms around him so they were falling together. Grammar shivered violently. In her arms he was a fragile collection of bones and sinew and narrow cords of muscle, brittle as an armful of dry twigs.

"We're gonna die." Grammar's voice came in fits and starts in her ear.

"No, we're not," she said with more confidence than anyone could reasonably feel while falling at two hundred kilometres an hour. "We're going to survive this."

Dare? Please tell me we're going to survive this.

If Dare was answering, she couldn't hear him above the whistle of the wind and the thundering adrenalin in her veins. Her fingers were numb, and Grammar's skin felt like ice. She could feel his violent shivers.

Dare!

Gravity was a whisper of silk sliding *through* her, a distinct sensation from the raw assault of the air. She grabbed at it and it faded, almost teasing, just out of reach, a murmur she couldn't quite hear.

She gathered herself in her impatience, her desperation, her determination that Grammar would *not die*, and she trailed mental fingers, gentle, coaxing, through gravity. It was like blowing a bubble in a hurricane wind, breathing life into an unspeakably fragile little orb and gathering it around her.

The wind stopped. They bobbed in mid-air, drifting below the cloud-pocked cheek of the earth.

"What's happenen?" Grammar craned his neck to look around.

His breath came in staccato puffs, tiny white clouds, as if he were a half-frozen dragon. His lips were turning blue, and he rattled against her like a handful of dice. Could she move the bubble and send him slowly downward? She nudged at the tiny gravity zone she'd created and it danced away from her, threatening to dissolve at the merest brush of her mind. She stopped trying and held herself and Grammar still until the bubble seemed stable again.

She tried to calm her mind again to the point of stillness where gravity would allow itself to be controlled, but her entire body was vibrating with cold and barely restrained kinetic energy, as if every molecule sought escape at once.

Dare, she cried inside, despairing. *I'm coming apart. I'm going to Shatter right here if I stay, but I'm too close to the earth still. But if I fall into vacuum, Grammar will die too.*

I'm here. Dare's voice was suddenly close and loud in her head.

She turned her face to the sun. She was aware of the cold, but distantly. The sun's rays split her flesh like a thousand arrows.

What do I do? she asked.

Let go.

Unlike their physical melding, there was no pain. Light and

heat filled her. She could see nothing but white, blank and pure and complete. Had she gone blind?

She remembered Grammar and clutched him. The tactile sensation of his shivering body in her arms filtered back into her awareness.

Let go, Dare insisted.

I can't, she protested. *Grammar will fall.*

Not him. Your body. Let go of your body. We must both release for a moment.

I don't know what that means. But she could feel the urgency of the light and heat flooding her, the itching, shuddering instability of her body, destructive forces gathering inside her like storm clouds.

She imagined letting go of her body, shucking it off like a sweatshirt, opening the grip of her consciousness and slipping away. It was surprisingly easy. Her body was a bomb; she wanted escape.

Then her body wasn't hers anymore. She was an intruder in someone else's house. Utter darkness surrounded her, and she didn't know where the lights were or the door or any yawning abysses that might lie in wait. She was lost, untethered, unwanted, homeless.

A small powerless god in a broken and abandoned space.

She had been betrayed. They were supposed to meld in balance. She wasn't supposed to become the helpless passenger in her own body.

Give me back my body, she screamed inside, but this had no echo, no substance. She felt nothing, not the cold of the sky or the heat of the sun or Grammar in her arms.

If you think a body is hard to give up, Dare whispered from beside her in the darkness, *imagine giving up the universe.*

He showed her galaxies of azure light and ivory whorls of

stars, and paint spatter spray of nebulae in clouds of amethyst, periwinkle, rose, and crimson. Hungry black holes and stars circled by necklaces of perfect pearl planets. Vivid silver blood of dying stars and radiation auras in electric blues and greens wafting on interstellar winds. Space, space to stretch so wide, so far, as big as a soul can stretch—which, when all is said and done, is as big as the universe itself.

She snapped back to the close, unmoored darkness of her mind. Once again she was a bodiless, agency-less parasite, trapped and alone.

Why would you give all of that up? she asked. *Why would you ever choose this single earthbound body over the freedom of the stars?*

His presence was intense near her, this roommate to her soul, as familiar and as strange as the memory of her mother's laugh from long ago.

For the same reason you would, Dare said. *I don't know if I evolved or if I was designed by another species or by a god, but I believe my ancestors began to merge with hosts for a reason no less than this, the only reason that matters: a body is the truest way that exists to touch the universe, to express ideas and beauty and joy, to birth and love other souls. This body is a host for your soul, your consciousness, and if you're willing, I'd share it with you.*

You could just take it and let me die, she said.

That's a Dalca game—choose one to live and one to die. There's an option where both can live in harmony. There always is.

The darkness lightened and they faced each other, clothed in a simulacrum of flesh, Jasper in her own and Dare . . . His face was an arresting and disconcerting version of Darius Dalca with that familiar laughing, volatile mouth. But his eyes were a luminescent, whimsical golden brown—*Vron's eyes*—and they held a straightforward warmth and kindness Darius had never possessed. And those dimples, they were *hers*. He was the man

Darius could have been—the man Grammar would be one day. He had Vron's eyes with all her far-seeing, dreaming wisdom. And he was Jasper, had been a part of her all along. Someone she'd known nearly her whole life but never met. The voice in her head and her confidant, her conscience and her inner demon.

He held out his hand and smiled his own version of Darius's smile, tinged with danger and dare and filled with improbable, incongruous affection. *Well?* he said. *Do you trust me?*

What a question. You're me.

Exactly.

She smiled despite herself. Hope, that irrepressible little balloon. *Wish a fish and hope this time I'll fly.*

She took his hand.

Light grew between their hands, exploding to the brilliance of a supernova, birthing new worlds and ending old ones, eons rising and falling.

Dare smiled at her across an ocean of stars. *Last chance to see the universe. Last chance to let go.*

Gravity stirred and rippled, tangible as water and as elusive.

No, not gravity. Something else.

Some things are meant to be let go—hate and hurt and fear. But not life. I choose to hold on to life, she told Dare. *I choose gravity.*

Her sense of her body returned softly, the brush of wind on her skin and a warm, heavy weight in her arms. She opened her eyes and felt herself present behind them, inhabiting every molecule of her body, every nerve ending, every muscle fibre, every heartbeat.

She was home. She was whole. She was unshattered.

The earth spread out far below her, a green, brown, and blue quilt of flaws and breathtaking life. What was that fragile bond between her feet and the planet's skin when her body lived in the sky and breathed the sky, when the stars pulled goosebumps out of her skin, pulled at her to jump and fall away? No contract existed between her feet and the earth, no promise and no debt. It was a bond of release and return. The name of that bond was gravity, and it had another name that lived in the latticework of her flesh and echoed in the beat of blood in her veins and connected her to all the other people in her life.

Grammar stirred. Although their altitude hadn't changed, his skin was warm to the touch now. He blinked at her, groggy, as if he'd been asleep.

"Jasper?"

Yes, that was her name. It fit like her body fit. "Hey, kid. How do you feel?"

He glanced around sleepily. His arms tightened as he registered once again the planet far below them.

"Been dreamen," he said, his face turned in profile as he stared downward. The slope of his nose was Zenobia's, the frown between his brows entirely his own. Faint freckles across his cheek formed a constellation shaped like a question. "Dreamen you been swallowen the sun."

"Maybe I did," she said. "At least a little bit."

His throat bobbed as he swallowed. "When you been jumpen into up-gee, I been thinken it was the curse."

I thought so too. "No chance. I eat curses for breakfast."

He studied her with crinkled eyes as if trying not to squint against a sharp shard of light. Still weighing whether she could be trusted, whether he could lean on her without her crumbling.

"Curses can be broken," she told him. "If you hadn't jumped after me, I couldn't have broken mine. You saved me."

"Okay," he said finally. Just that, but it was enough. "What are they tasten like, curses?" he asked curiously.

"Like farts, honestly."

Grammar laughed, an unexpected little hiccup of joy. Glass wind chimes catching the light.

There you are, little daughter, whispered the earth. *I see you. I remember you. You've always been mine.*

Gravity danced against her skin with its tingling song and carried them home.

30

THE GATES

Heaven is an old oak tree.
There you'll find me
With two pines,
A paper crane shrine,
A joke in sign,
And the best of wines
To pass the time.
In an old oak tree
Is where I'll be
Dreaming away eternity.

~ Veronica Park (*Map of Heaven*)

"Still nothing?" the Guardian asked.

"His voice is gone." Jasper hauled herself onto a ten-foot unfinished stone wall, the remains of an old construction site, and swung her feet idly. A maple sapling grew from between the bricks. Its leaves were frosting into scarlet and a corresponding autumn crispness edged the air.

She and Tom had planted a similar sapling over Zenobia's grave.

Jasper found herself rubbing at the sensitive stumps of the three fingers of her right hand and clenched her hand into a fist.

The Guardian kneeled, running her hands through the exposed soil. She had spent the afternoon clearing cobblestones and heaving up weed barrier groundsheets left by long-ago landscapers and carrying plastic rubbish into a nearby building so that the ground was clean and free. She hadn't explained why she'd chosen to clear this land so near to the quarantine gates when usually she and the ReGeneration members worked in the wild zones.

Perhaps she knew how often Jasper wandered here just to look at the gates, to confirm they were still closed.

Next spring this whole swath of freshly exposed earth would turn green with new growth. It still took Jasper's breath away at times, knowing that she was alive to see the leaves change colour, that she'd live to see another spring.

"Your consciousnesses were supposed to merge," the Guardian said. "He's part of you now. Feel any different?"

Jasper shrugged. How could she answer that question? Of course she felt different. But she was still herself. Wasn't she?

Sometimes she imagined she saw a slight hesitation, a stutter in the expressions of Ben or Merlot or Harmony in reaction to something she said or how she moved, as if they sensed she wasn't quite who she'd been. At least they no longer avoided looking her in the eye. Whatever it was that had unsettled them—and they'd never been able to explain it—had either diminished or they'd gotten used to it.

Crane had bluntly told her, "Your face is looken weird," but then added dismissively, "But your face was always weird."

"Maybe it's enough," the Guardian said. She let a stream of soil run through her fingers.

"What is?"

"Merging with a host body allows the graviteria to experience the world on a macro level of emotions and ideas and understanding. Can you have those at a cellular level? Who knows? Perhaps it was evolution after all. Perhaps the graviteria themselves are the intelligent designer."

It was a comforting thought if Jasper could accept it. Dare's voice was gone as if it had never existed. Were her thoughts her own anymore, or did some of them belong to him? *It'll still be you on the other side,* Ryan had said.

But what did he know? He had left.

Jasper took a deep, deliberate breath. She was alive. Her shifts were gone. Her deadline had passed. And if Grammar's graviteria ever activated, she could either coach him through melding or figure out how to contain his Shattering.

As if her thought had summoned him, Grammar wandered over from the fox den he and Okuru had been investigating. Grammar gave himself a running start and launched himself up the wall, needing only two kicks to reach the top. He sat astride the wall beside her, long legs dangling. Fuelled by Harmony's cooking, he'd grown at least an inch over the summer. He stood disconcertingly close to eye level with her now.

Okuru trotted to the base of the wall and looked up at them with disappointment. He sat in the grass, panting gently.

Grammar pulled a sheet of paper from a thigh pouch and folded it with leisurely, practiced movements. The last time Jasper had visited Zenobia's grave it was covered with rain-wilted masses of little paper birds. They'd probably been left by Crane or Tom, though; Grammar had never made any mention of visiting his mother's grave.

Some distance away, Crane and Neverwhen bickered,

Neverwhen with her fists full of wild daisies and Crane with her fists full of knives. Neverwhen's cheeks had grown rounder, her skin soft and shiny over the summer; her aunts Sparrow and Ibtisam spoiled her outrageously. Crane still retained an edge of fragility to her thinness but looked more herself in her favourite red jeans with the yellow patches and the T-shirt that read KNIFE TO MEET YOU.

A hundred metres away the quarantine gates remained silently, implacably closed. The humming of the electrified fence itched in the back of Jasper's head, a different tint and tone than the zones. The gates had opened only once in the three months since she'd melded with Dare, since Zenobia had died in the Tower, and that was to swallow up Ryan back into the outside world where he'd come from.

"I'll come back," he'd said, "to let you know what happened. If I can." Because without Titus's help the gates might not open for him again.

"Don't make promises you can't keep," she responded. The goblins that ate wishes would surely gorge themselves on empty promises.

He drew Grammar aside for a conversation the boy refused to reveal to her no matter how much she wheedled. And then Ryan walked through the gates and disappeared.

Sparrow and Ibtisam had approached the gates hoping to reopen trade with the outside despite Zenobia's death. They were turned away at gunpoint. Zenobia hadn't been lying; her outside contact would only trade with her. Unless a new trade relationship could be established, zoners were once again cut off from downieland. Sparrow expressed hope that Ryan could ask around, but he warned them before he left that he didn't have those kinds of connections. Not without Titus.

He hadn't told Jasper how he planned to confront his brother, and every option she thought of filled her with dread.

"Here," said Grammar, breaking into her thoughts. He tossed her the paper bird.

She caught it reflexively in a bubble of gravity. It bobbed in mid-air between them as if for a moment it had transcended its inorganic composition and taken flight. She released the tiny zone, using a muscle that after all this time was still frustratingly hard to flex, and let the folded crane fall into her hand.

"Getten better," Grammar said. She wasn't sure if he was referring to his origami skills or her manipulation of gravity.

She shook her head, reminding herself of the progress she'd made. She didn't shift unpredictably anymore, and that was a huge relief. With a fine balance of concentration and delicacy, she could control her own gravity for short periods of time. She could create small zones and dissipate them. However, the original zones Zenobia had created with her Shattering Jasper couldn't yet budge. Her own zones felt soft and malleable like clay. Zenobia's zones in contrast felt fossilized, turned to stone, stubbornly resistant to her attempts to manipulate them. She hadn't yet managed to dissipate a single one.

The Guardian caught her eye. She asked Jasper those questions every time they met, offered suggestions to try, but nothing had worked. Time, she told Jasper. Control would come with time.

Jasper kicked her heels harder against the stone wall and sought distraction. "How are the knife-throwing lessons coming along?"

Grammar snorted. "For me, okay." Which was true. Anything Grammar set his mind to learn, he mastered eventually.

They both looked over to where Crane was demonstrating once again to a bored Neverwhen how to correctly hold a blade before throwing it. Crane had propped a sheet of plywood against a wall and it was flecked with cuts and dents. With a quick snap of her arm, she threw the knife. It sank tip first into the board and hung there, quivering, for a moment before it fell. Frowning briefly, Crane rubbed at her shoulder.

"Shouldn't be strainen yourself," Neverwhen said, perking up at the chance of ending the lesson.

"I'm fine," Crane said quickly, unwilling to risk her recent freedom from both the infirmary and Ibtisam and Grace's strict monitoring of her recovery.

"Should I be tellen Grace you're overdoen it?" Neverwhen asked, hands on her hips.

"No, no." Crane meekly sheathed her knives.

"Should be doen something less strenuous." Neverwhen smiled sweetly. "Like finishen my hair."

Crane made a face. During her recovery Sparrow and Neverwhen had taken advantage of Crane's hours of enforced stillness to plait her hair. Instead of its usual large afro, her scalp sported cornrows forming neat, curving lines. On the sides of her head those lines swooped and spiked, echoing the shape of an origami bird.

In contrast, on the side of Neverwhen's head, a few cornrows, half-finished, wobbled and weaved and threatened to come undone. Crane's skill wasn't so much the issue as her patience and ability to sit still.

The Guardian stood with her hands on her hips, her long silver braid dangling over her shoulder. She frowned in the direction of the quarantine gates as if lost in thought. "I'll leave you now," she said to Jasper. "Charlie said he and Ben would be ready to go by the evening."

Ben and Charlie had set up a rotation whereby they spent a week with the ReGeneration together, then a week in Yorky together and then a week apart. So far it seemed to be working.

Neverwhen spotted the Guardian preparing to leave. "We

should be goen, Crane. We been promisen to visit Tom today."
She called to Grammar, "You comen?"

"Not today," he called back. His expression stayed neutral.
Since Tom had been revealed as Neverwhen's father, Grammar
had maintained a cool and wary reserve toward him. He would
keep Tom at arm's length until he proved to Grammar's
satisfaction that he wouldn't cause Neverwhen any pain.

Tom and Socrates had moved into Martha's old hermit
residence, preferring the solitude to the hostility and resentment
that would greet them in Yorky as the last remaining Azuros.
Socrates soon moved into a house of his own a block away, but
they shared a garden. Neverwhen's relationship with her father
remained wary and shy but had progressed enough that she'd
visit him every week to help him in the garden. He'd never fully
heal from the injuries caused by Vic's beating, which made tasks
like gardening or cutting wood difficult.

"Don't wanna be goen yet," Crane said with a pout, though
she was beginning to look drawn and tired.

"Too bad," Neverwhen said innocently. "Grace been sayen
she'd be bringen Tom some medicine, so she'll be there."

Moments later she had to break into a trot to keep up with
Crane's brisk pace back toward Yorky.

"Damn, Nev's good," Jasper said.

Grammar grunted amused agreement.

"I should turn her loose the next time Crane goes on about
having unfinished business in Knowles."

This time Grammar's grunt was more equivocal.

"Okay, granted, Knowles is an overflowing cesspit that does
need to be dealt with," Jasper said. "But at the moment she can't
even walk ten minutes without getting breathless. Knowles can
wait."

Speaking of which, Crane would never be able to maintain
her current pace.

Jasper glanced at the Guardian, who nodded. The Guardian had brought her horse. Between her and Neverwhen they would persuade Crane to climb onto its back for the ride home.

The Guardian lifted a hand in farewell, and Jasper waved back.

Grammar ignored the Guardian. He had no trust for the ReGeneration leader, and Jasper could hardly blame him. There'd never be anything more than basic politeness between her and the Guardian either. Jasper maintained a reluctant connection with her because she was the only person left in the zones who was knowledgeable about the graviteria.

"I was thinking about your mama today," Jasper said.

Grammar stopped swinging his legs and stared down at the scuffed toes of his sneakers, already developing holes from hard use. With his added height over the summer had come increased moodiness and irritability. Despite Zenobia's sacrifice to save him, he refused to acknowledge their familial relationship. To him she was the Up-gee Witch and nothing else. But he hadn't snapped at her use of "mama," so that was something.

"I miss her," Jasper said. "Crane and Tom and I are probably the only people in the zones who loved her. Do you want to talk about it?"

He grunted. Ben had created a classification system for these nonverbal sounds of his. Most popular were "Leave me alone," "I don't care," and "Life in general disgusts me." This particular grunt Jasper interpreted as "Maybe I want to talk but I'll never, ever admit it."

She opened her mouth to press the issue further, but he cut her off. "You thinken Ryan's ever comen back?"

She closed her mouth. Struggled to swallow a stiffness in her throat. Finally offered a grunt of her own, meant to convey the nuances of "I don't want to talk about it" and "What if something's happened to him" and the most privately depressing: "Maybe he doesn't want to come back."

Somehow Grammar heard all of those things, fluent as he was in the language of grunts. He reached over, twisted a strand of her hair around his fingers—longer now that her shifts were gone and she had less reason to cut it. He gave an emphatic tug and released it. "He's wanten," he said with certainty.

"How do you know?"

He gave her a look, sly and amused and distant and angry at the same time. Ryan might yet come back, but there were others who never would. Zenobia, Martha, Vron . . . "Not blind, Auntie. Ryan will be comen back. Unless he's . . ."

Dead.

Held prisoner by his angry foster brother.

Happily shacking up with Allison and the baby.

"I been hearen the coyotes howlen last night." With a flick of his wrist, Grammar made a coin appear between his fingers. "I been maken a wish."

"What did you wish?"

Okuru barked. Grammar looked past her and she followed his gaze.

With a tremulous groan, the gates were opening.

She hit the ground with no memory of having jumped from the wall.

A single figure walked out of the gates. Slowly, ponderously, the gates drew shut behind him.

Jasper stared. Surely her eyes were inventing familiarity where she wanted to see it, in the easy set of his shoulders and the swing of his arms and his long, loose stride, the sway of his locs.

"It's Ryan," Grammar said, disbelieving. Then he laughed out loud and shouted, "Ryan!"

The man stopped as if seeing them for the first time. He lifted a hand to his mouth and then into the air, waving.

Grammar ran, long legs sending him flying through tall grass and nodding daisies. Ryan threw back his head and whooped. Grammar skidded to a halt in front of him and solemnly extended a fist, which Ryan solemnly bumped with his own. Then Ryan grabbed him and hugged him and slapped his back. She could hear their laughter rising into the sky like birds.

The sky doesn't begin at the mountaintop.

Her feet had frozen to the ground. She made herself step forward. Walking felt precarious, like every step was downhill, steeper and steeper. It felt like falling.

Grammar chattered excitedly, more voluble than Jasper had ever seen him, his face loose and alive and unguarded, his gestures wide and expansive. Ryan was grinning in response, but his eyes flicked over Grammar's head to watch Jasper's approach. She stopped a safe metre away with Grammar between them.

"And be looken at what I can do now!" Grammar said, pulling out a coin. Laboriously, he walked the coin over his knuckles and back into his palm.

"Wow! That's the best thing I've seen in months," Ryan said with his warm summer eyes fixed on Jasper.

He looked the same, his hair a little longer, his clothing and backpack definitely newer. He still wore the Zombie Princess amulet she'd made him around his neck, along with his dog tags. Was there new darkness in his eyes, new lines around his mouth? What had happened in the three months he'd been gone?

"I can be doen it with my left hand too," Grammar said. "See?"

"Amazing." Ryan squeezed his shoulder. "Hey, kid, is that a skunk Okuru's barking at over there?"

Grammar whirled. "Okuru, no!" He ran after the dog, shouting.

Jasper squinted after him. "That's not a skunk."

"Nope," said Ryan. "No, it's not. Just a cat, I think." He smiled.

Without Grammar to fill it, the space between them seemed too small and too large at the same time.

It begins here, where my skin stops being skin
And becomes air.

"How's the baby?" she asked quickly.

"Healthy," he said. "And not mine. My suspicion was right. Allison had gone to Titus and claimed it was mine because she thought she could get money from him, and he decided to use the lie against me. But she still has her job, and her current boyfriend seems a decent sort, and she's on speaking terms with her mother again, so I think they'll be okay." He nodded firmly as if slamming shut a book.

"I'm sorry," she said.

He cocked his head. "For what?"

"You were going to be a father. Now you're not."

He stared at her for a second. Then he pressed the back of his hand to his mouth and looked away. She watched him blink against the hazy, sweet sunlight, tracking Grammar as he chased Okuru through the long dry grass, raising clouds of dandelion fluff and white butterflies. "More than one way to be a father, I think," he said at last.

She didn't want to ask, wanted to stretch this moment into eternity. But eternity couldn't start until she knew the answer. "What happened with Titus?"

He looked back at her and his eyes were dark and deep and shaded. And as clear as spring water. "We came to an agreement. He won't be sending anyone else into the zones. You and Grammar are safe from him."

"Just like that?" she said incredulously.

"It turns out he was going behind his boss's back, trying to steal some graviteria samples so he could jump ship to a rival corporation." Ryan shrugged. "So I told his boss about it. His boss decided he liked Titus's ambition and initiative and gave him a promotion. Titus knows he's not fully trusted, but he's got a higher position than he'd even been aiming for, so he's happy. He has no further interest in Allison and her baby or you and Grammar. His boss thanked me for bringing the situation to his attention—it gave him leverage against the rival corp, among other things. So in thanks he assured me he'd keep an eye on Titus and keep him out of the zones."

There was more to that story, much more, but for now this was enough.

"And now you're here," she said.

"Now I'm here," he replied. "That was the final favour I asked of Titus's boss, to get me through the gates."

"By the size of that pack, you must be planning to stay for more than a few days," she said tentatively.

"I guess that depends," he said.

"On what?"

"On how far a backpack full of cinnamon will get me."

She opened her mouth but forgot to speak.

"You think I'm joking," he said. He swung the massive pack off his back with a grunt and rummaged inside it. He pulled out a handful of plastic packets filled with brown powder. "I've also got cinnamon sticks if you prefer those, and I got some cinnamon hearts for good measure. What do you say? Does that buy me a few months? A few years even?"

"I'm an alien." Her voice felt strange in her throat.

"An alien's just somebody from someplace else."

She shook her head. "It's not that simple. Ryan. You have no idea who or *what* I am."

"Maybe not," he said. "But I'd like to find out."

When she said nothing, he pushed the cinnamon packets back into the backpack, his hair falling over his face. The movement pulled at his sleeves, exposing his wrists.

"Ryan, your tattoos." She grabbed his wrists before he could pull away and pushed up his sleeves.

The stark blue dots marching up his forearms had represented lost lives, ghosts he'd taken responsibility for, deaths he'd judged to be his fault. Now those dots were connected with a long line that ran from each wrist to above the elbow, forming a slender elegant tree trunk. Each dot was now the junction of a set of branches, delicate and crisp and as hopeful as spring buds.

"There's no meaning or purpose to holding on to guilt unless you can use it to grow," he said at last when the silence stretched too long. "I learned that from you. You've gone through a lot of darkness in your life. But all it did was make you reach for the sun like a tree."

I draw sky into my lungs and it enters my bloodstream.

She held on to his wrists to examine the tattoos, to keep her eyes down. Because as soon as she looked up at him, words would cease to matter.

"Listen, Zeep, I'm not asking anything from you. This is about more than you and me. Homes are hard to come by, and so are families, and the way I felt here in the zones—well, I don't want to lose that." He inhaled deeply. "I feel like I can breathe out here."

"They're pine trees," she said.

"What?"

"Your tattoos are pine trees."

"Yes, well, they're my favourite tree, it turns out."

Really, I am the sky.

She looked up at him finally. The lines of tension around his eyes eased as he studied her face. "You overstocked," she said. "That much cinnamon buys you forever."

"Then it's exactly enough," he said. He turned his hands in her grip and captured her wrists in turn. He looked at her hands, brushing his thumb over the shortened stubs of her three fingers. The light touch over the sensitive skin made her inhale. He gave a tug on her wrists.

Gravity did the rest.

All the best jumps were unplanned. A leap, a breath of sky, sky, sky, and then always at the end of everything, the earth, gravity, home.

"Tell me what you wished the night of the telephone pole," he said in her ear.

"The same thing you did the night before the Tower."

His breath tickled her cheek. "And what's that?"

"The only thing any of us can hope for." She lifted her face to the sun and let its light fill her to the brim and then flow over. "A chance to see the other side of tomorrow."

THANK YOU!

Thank you so much for reading GRAVITY TOWER. I hope you enjoyed your time in the gravity zones with Jasper and her friends.

Please consider leaving a review of GRAVITY TOWER wherever you find reviews. Your review can help other readers find books they'll enjoy. I love to hear from you and appreciate all feedback. It helps me improve and encourages me to keep writing.

For a FREE copy of the prequel novella RULES OF CRANE and exclusive bonus scenes for each book, sign up for my newsletter at www.vrfriesen.com.

Thank you for reading!

BONUS SCENE EXCERPT

BONUS SCENE EXCERPT
SNEAK PEEK
Get the FULL exclusive bonus scene from Crane's perspective
for FREE when you sign up for my newsletter at
www.vrfriesen.com.

The horse was high and broad and unstable. It seemed to move in every direction at once, wobbling side to side and back and forth. Crane was going to fall off any second and hit her head and die, and it would walk all over her with its horrible huge hooves and then poop on her, probably.

"You're not going to fall off," said Grace. She reached behind her to grab Crane's arm. "Hold on to me properly, not just the back of my shirt, and you'll feel more secure."

A moment later Crane found her arms wrapped around Grace's waist. Her hips were already wedged into the saddle behind Grace, her thighs pressed against Grace's, her face close enough to smell her neck, her hair. They were snugged up together like two spoons in a drawer.

Okay, perhaps horses weren't that bad.

"I never thought I'd see the day Esther and Merlot rode a horse together and didn't bicker about it," Grace whispered, stifling a laugh. "He looks as comfortable on a horse as you do."

Crane couldn't care less about Esther and Merlot. She was feeling pretty comfortable at the moment, wrapped around Grace, the horse be damned.

"Are Charlie and Ben a couple again?" Grace said. "Didn't they break up years ago?"

Crane made a "Who knows?" sound. The only couple she cared about was the two of them on this horse. And the memory of Grace saying, *You asked me if I liked you and I said no . . . I lied.*

Grace's voice grew more serious. "This little girl we're all going after . . ." she said.

"Nev."

"Grammar said he grew up with her. She's his best friend. But you—you never said what your connection to her is." She paused but Crane was silent. "You were really upset when you heard she'd been taken."

A ball of acid, awake and alive, stirred in her stomach. She leaned back so the smell of Grace's skin wouldn't be mixed with the thought of *him.* "Dragon." She turned her head and spat. "I been haven chances to kill him, so many chances."

That made Nev's predicament Crane's fault. There were consequences to every decision, even decisions not to act. Especially those.

Grace started to say something, then stopped. A horse with a single rider carrying a torch had stopped to the side, letting the single file line pass him.

"What're you waiten for, downie?" Crane asked as they approached him.

Ryan surveyed the two of them, and his mouth twitched like he was fighting back a smirk. Crane would've thrown a knife at him, just to make a point, but that would've meant letting go of Grace's waist, and she wasn't prepared to do that.

He peered past them. "Where are Jasper and Grammar?"

Grace did something with the reins and the horse stopped. Witchcraft. "They were supposed to be behind us." She twisted around to look, and so did Crane. The tunnel stretched empty and dark behind them.

"I'll go see what the holdup is." Ryan clicked his tongue and the horse responded like it was a magic spell. He rode back the way they'd come.

Even if Jasper and Grammar had been delayed, they shouldn't be in any danger. The ReGeneration hated the Damaskers. And the Guardian was weird and undoubtedly a witch, but she was an ally of Zenobia's. And Zenobia was there —mysteriously, miraculously, refusing to explain how she had survived, but the important thing was she was safe from the Damaskers. Even if Tom and Socrates were—*No, don't think about that. Don't think about them swinging from a noose.*

The ReGeneration village was the safest place Jasper and Grammar could be. But Crane had already failed to protect Grammar twice—once when the Damaskers had captured him in the underground shopping mall and again when the combined forces of the Damaskers and Knowles gangers had attacked their camp. She had to make sure.

"Be maken the horse turn around," Crane said. "Be followen the downie."

FULL bonus scene is available only to newsletter subscribers.
Sign up today at www.vrfriesen.com!

COMING SOON

Stay tuned for V.R. Friesen's exciting new series, CHILDREN OF GRAVITY!

Grammar is the son of a monstrous warlord and the scientist who caused the Shattering. He's also the last remaining unshattered host of the alien graviteria. Or is he?

Five years have passed since the events of *Gravity Tower*. Grammar struggles to fit in to a community that remembers his parents all too well. To make matters worse, a gang war is brewing and Grammar and his friends are caught in the middle of it.

The isolation of the gravity zones is broken when an unexpected visitor appears at the quarantine gates. The news he brings sends Grammar and Jasper careening into the strange world of downieland and straight into a treacherous web of wealth, politics, secrets, and lies, bringing them face to face with the shocking truth about the graviteria.

They'll have to race against time to stop a plot that could lead to global war...or a shattered planet.

For exclusive updates and sneak peeks of the CHILDREN OF GRAVITY series, sign up to the V.R. Friesen newsletter at www.vrfriesen.com!

ACKNOWLEDGMENTS

As always, I must thank the usual suspects of Jen and Santi for reading all my drafts, Agata for a fantastic cover, Erin, Renee, Tessa, and Caroline for formatting, editing, and advising.

To the folks at Laziza Café, who see me more often than my friends and family do, half this series was written while mainlining your chai lattes. Thanks for not charging me rent!

In a series that celebrates strong sibling bonds, I would be remiss not to mention my epic lineup of siblings who have been so instrumental in the shaping of me: Elvira, Irma, Walter, Annie, Lavina, Reynold, Jennifer, Larry, Gordon, Gerald. And let's not forget everyone who bravely married into our clan, plus all my brilliant, beautiful, charming, delightful nephews and nieces!

Thanks to Mom and Dad for creating a safe harbour from which we could all set sail. A special shoutout to Dad and his office, always full of books from garage sales, yard sales, library giveaways. My reading habit started in that room filled with old, discarded, pre-loved books.

Sam, Sam-ah, soul friend, *anam cara*, I can feel your belief in me from across the ocean! When you asked, I told you this series isn't about Namibia. But in a way it is because everything I felt, learned, and loved there saturates my writing—the intense friendships, the hugs and inside jokes, the shenanigans and heart-to-hearts, and the lasting grief of leaving. Namibia is woven through these books, with all the bittersweetness of happiness that must come to an end. So to you, Sam, and all my dearest *okaume* and everyone who changed my life in Namibia, *ondikuhole unene*. There are too many of you to name and I don't want to leave anyone out, but I remember and love you fiercely and miss you to this day. With you, my friends, I'll always be forever young.

Jenn, James, Liam, Maya, you'll always be my family and home away from home.

Jen, we joke that we were born in two bodies only because there was too much awesome for one of us to contain alone. Glad you're sharing that burden with me. When I wrote Vron's reason to live for chapter 28, I was thinking of you.

ABOUT THE AUTHOR

V.R. Friesen has been writing stories since shortly after she learned the alphabet. She grew up on the beautiful East Coast of Canada and now lives on the equally beautiful (but in a different way) West Coast, in Vancouver, BC, with one of her many siblings and a cat. She can usually be found drinking chai lattes, cheering on her favourite basketball team, or reading voraciously in science fiction, fantasy, young adult and dystopian fiction.

Find her online at www.vrfriesen.com and on social media as @vrfriesen.writer.

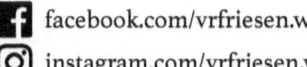

facebook.com/vrfriesen.writer

instagram.com/vrfriesen.writer